BARBARA
NADEL

The **HOUSE** of **FOUR**

HEADLINE

First published in Great Britain in 2017
by HEADLINE PUBLISHING GROUP

First published in paperback in Great Britain in 2017
by HEADLINE PUBLISHING GROUP

1

Cataloguing in Publication Data is available from the British Library

ISBN 978 1 4722 3465 0

Typeset in Times New Roman by Palimpsest Book Production Ltd,
Falkirk, Stirlingshire

Printed and bound by CPI Group (UK) Ltd, Croydon CR0 4YY

Headline's policy is to use papers that are natural, renewable and recyclable
products and made from wood grown in well-managed forests and other
controlled sources. The logging and manufacturing processes are expected to
conform to the environmental regulations of the country of origin.

HEADLINE PUBLISHING GROUP
An Hachette UK Company
Carmelite House
50 Victoria Embankment
London EC4Y 0DZ

www.headline.co.uk
www.hachette.co.uk

Trained as an actress, Barbara Nadel used to work in mental health services. Born in the East End of London, she now writes full time and has been a visitor to Turkey for over twenty years. She received the Crime Writers' Association Silver Dagger for her novel *Deadly Web* and the Swedish Flintax Prize for historical crime fiction for her first Francis Hancock novel *Last Rights*.

Praise for Barbara Nadel:

'Intelligent and captivating'   *The Sunday Times*

'Inspector Çetin İkmen is one of detective fiction's most likeable investigators, despite his grumpy and unsociable character . . . think of him as the Morse of Istanbul'   *Daily Telegraph*

'Impeccable mystery plotting, exotic and atmospheric' *Guardian*

'The delight of Nadel's books is the sense of being taken beneath the surface of an ancient city which most visitors see for a few days at most. We look into the alleyways and curious dark quarters of Istanbul, full of complex characters and louche atmosphere'
                                                              Independent

'Nadel's evocation of the shady underbelly of modern Turkey is one of the perennial joys of crime fiction'   *Mail on Sunday*

'Gripping and unusual detective story, vivid and poignant'
                                                              Literary Review

'Crime fiction can do many things, and here it offers both a well-crafted mystery and a form of armchair tourism, with Nadel as an expert guide'   *Spectator*

'[İkmen . . . . been strikingly estab . . . . locales are a partic . . . . *ood Book Guide*

By *Barbara Nadel*

This book is dedicated to the memory
of Professor Josef Vanek (1818–1889).
Physicist, revolutionary and magician
to Sultan Abdülmecid I of Turkey.

Cast List

Police:

Inspector Çetin İkmen – middle-aged Istanbul detective

Inspector Mehmet Süleyman – Istanbul detective and İkmen's protege

Commissioner Hürrem Teker – İkmen and Süleyman's boss

Sergeant Kerim Gürsel – İkmen's sergeant

Sergeant Ömer Mungun – Süleyman's sergeant

Dr Arto Sarkissian – police pathologist – an ethnic Armenian

Constable Barçın Demirtaş – traffic officer also linguist

Inspector Ahmet Cıngı – organised crime detective

Sergeant Deniz Akgunduz – organised crime officer

Turgut Zana – technical officer

Others:

Fatma İkmen – Çetin's wife

Gonca Şekeroğlu – Süleyman's mistress – a gypsy

Selin İnce – a cleaner at the Devil's House

Bilal İnce – Selin's husband

Ali Baykal – works in the Grand Bazaar
Barış Şekeroğlu – Gonca's cousin
Saira Öymen – tram passenger
Elif Büyük – homeless heroin addict
Ali Erbil – Elif's boyfriend, also a homeless addict
Yiannis Apion – an Istanbul Greek
Father Anatoli Ralli – a Greek priest
Marina Ralli – his wife
Sami Nasi – a stage magician
Rüya – Sami's assistant
Hasan Dum – a gypsy gangster
Dr Aksu – a psychiatrist
Rauf Karadeniz – a retired lawyer
Erdal Bey – practising lawyer
Aslan Gerontas – mentally ill street boy
Gila Saban – witness
Richard Oates – British witness
Fatima, Yücel, Kanat and Kemal Rudolfoğlu – the four residents of the Devil's House

Another day, another torment. The old woman was going mad and had lately taken to following her around the house talking nonsense at her. Cleaning the toilets was bad enough without having her raving on about voices in the walls. But a job was a job, and as Bilal always said, maybe Fatima Hanım would leave her something when she died. She'd told him he was living in a fantasy if he thought that. The old witch was mean as well as wicked.

Selin opened the apartment door and went inside. Most of her employer's possessions made her shudder anyway. Who would want massive faded sofas stuffed with ancient horsehair? She actually hoped they weren't going to come her way when Fatima Hanım died. Although she did like the old woman's dressing table, which was made entirely of gilded glass. She had a notion it was French, although it was more likely German because that was where Fatima Hanım's father had been born.

Mercifully the apartment was quiet, which meant that Fatima Hanım was probably still asleep. Selin went straight to the kitchen and put the kettle on for tea. As usual, every surface was covered with the detritus the old woman left in her wake whenever she tried to cater for herself. Cheese, uncovered by the sink, a half-sliced onion, broken biscuits scattered on the floor and round the waste bin. What she really needed was live-in help, but that wasn't going to happen. No one in their right mind would actually want to sleep in that awful rotting building. It was bad enough visiting almost every day.

1

Waiting for the kettle to boil, Selin had a cigarette. Bilal had forbidden smoking ever since he'd become a member of the AK Party, and so she had to get her cigarettes in where she could. The old woman didn't mind. In fact she sometimes smoked too. It felt good to have a quiet smoke after a whole weekend of abstinence. Bilal had made them all go to a party rally, even the kids, and Selin had been required to be on her best behaviour. Surrounded by pious, covered women, she'd felt completely out of her depth. Bilal reckoned it was because she wasn't covered. She knew he wanted her to cover, but she wasn't going to do it. She hated covering.

There was still no movement from the old woman's room. Selin made the tea, and while she waited for it to brew, she had another cigarette. The smoke helped to keep at bay the smell of old person, which was strong on this occasion. But then it always was when Fatima Hanım had been alone all weekend.

A fucking mosquito! Ali Baykal winced. With a pile of folded kilims on his head, he couldn't very well stop and scratch where the bastard had bitten him. And it hurt! If only he'd worn that awful jacket his mother had tried to get him into, maybe he wouldn't have been bitten. The tiniest vest in the world just didn't do the job when it came to determined insects. But it was as hot as a kettle in the Grand Bazaar in July, and also, girls didn't like boys who wore their fathers' jackets. Especially when their father had been dead for ten years.

People were looking at him now. Was he pulling a face as he tried to deal with the pain? It was getting worse! What kind of mosquito had attacked him? It was agony!

Ali put his bundle down. He'd have to take a look. A man came over to him and said, 'What's happened?'

He put a hand on Ali's shoulder.

'I've been bitten,' he replied.

'Bitten?'

'Yes.'

Ali looked down, and it was then that he saw blood. Pumping out of his side, running down his vest and into his sweat pants. Suddenly he felt very weak . . .

Chapter 1

The cleaner's name was Selin İnce. A plain, uncovered woman in her forties, she kept saying that she hadn't done anything wrong, and Çetin İkmen tended to believe her.

'Bilal is always saying that bad things will happen unless I cover,' she said as she visibly trembled. Only the cigarette between her fingers was holding her up.

Inspector Çetin İkmen of the İstanbul police led her towards a dusty sofa and made her sit down.

'I don't think your employer's death has anything to do with your choice of clothes,' he said.

Away in the largest bedroom of what was a vast nineteenth-century apartment, the department's pathologist, Dr Arto Sarkissian, was already at work on the corpse of a very old woman. But it was only a formality. The blood-soaked hole in her chest left little doubt as to the cause of death of Miss Fatima Rudolfoğlu.

İkmen sat down opposite Selin İnce. From there he could also watch his officers as they began to search for the bladed instrument that had killed the old woman.

'Have you seen anyone hanging around the building in the last few days?'

'No. People don't come here any more. Haven't done for years. Only me and Mr Yücel's man, Osman.'

İkmen frowned. 'Mr Yücel's man? Who's Mr Yücel?'

'He's Fatima Hanım's brother. He lives on the ground floor. Osman does odd jobs for him. Shopping and things.'

İkmen had been having a wonderful breakfast of heavily sweetened Turkish coffee and three cigarettes at his desk when he'd got the call to an address on the Asian side of the city. All he knew about the district of Moda was that it was fashionable and expensive. Although close to the old disused Moda ferry stage, which he had visited as a child, fifty years ago, the huge Ottoman house that contained Fatima Hanım's apartment was unknown to him.

'So does this brother know . . .'

'Oh no,' she said. 'They don't . . . they didn't speak. None of them do.'

Finding the unnamed alleyway between a coffee shop and a fashion house that led to number 130 Moda Caddesi had been a mission in itself. Unearthing the mansion behind its protective curtain of bindweed, ivy and rotting garden furniture had challenged İkmen and his officers still further. The pathologist, Dr Sarkissian, who had been obliged to park his car down near the ferry stage, had arrived exhausted. And now there was not only a dead woman, but an uncommunicative brother too. And what had the cleaner meant when she'd talked about 'none of them'?

'None of who?'

She put one cigarette out and lit another. İkmen saw little hope for Selin İnce as a modest, covered woman.

'Mr Yücel, Mr Kanat and Mr Kemal,' she said. 'They don't speak, any of them.'

'And Mr Yücel is Fatima Hanım's brother?'

'And Mr Kanat and Mr Kemal,' she said. 'There are four siblings. They all live in this building, in different apartments. But they've not spoken to each other in my lifetime. Probably not in yours either.'

İkmen had been born and brought up on the Asian side of the city, in the working-class district of Üsküdar. Now that he lived in the European part, he, in common with most 'Europe dwellers', rarely ventured to this side of the Bosphorus. It was a whole other world, and this one in particular was clearly out of the ordinary.

Selin İnce began to cry again. 'You won't put me in prison, will you?' she said.

İkmen's sergeant, Kerim Gürsel, waved at him from the kitchen. İkmen stood.

'I doubt it very much, Mrs İnce,' he said. 'I'm sorry, I'm being called . . .'

Kerim Gürsel was a good-looking man in early middle age. He was also, to İkmen's delight, a person of great initiative.

'I bought some cappuccinos from that café on the corner,' he said. He pointed to a box containing cardboard cups on top of the cooker. 'I talked to the owner.'

'He must've seen us fighting to get in,' İkmen said.

'Let's say he was intrigued. Wanted to know why we were here. I told him we'd had a call.'

'Everything and nothing.'

'Yes. But what he told me was interesting,' Kerim said. 'Did you know that this house is called the Teufel Haus?'

'The Devil's House?'

'In German, yes,' Kerim said.

'Mmm.' The dead woman had a part-Turkish, part-Germanic surname. But why call your house the Devil's House? Was it some sort of joke?

'Anyway, there's coffee if you want it, sir.'

İkmen patted him on the shoulder. 'Thank you. Stay with the cleaner, I'm going to talk to Dr Sarkissian.'

'Yes, sir.'

The old woman's bedroom was pure French-inspired Ottoman: ornate, stuffy and, in this case, filthy. Either Selin İnce was forbidden from cleaning it, or the task was too big for her.

7

The pathologist, an overweight, slightly owlish Armenian, looked up. 'Ah, Çetin.'

'Arto.'

Çetin İkmen and Arto Sarkissian had been friends since childhood, and so they very rarely used formal titles even in front of others.

'So, a stabbing,' İkmen said.

'Yes, straight through the heart,' the doctor replied. 'One blow. No sign of a struggle. With any luck the victim was asleep when it happened. She'd certainly taken enough drugs to make that possible.'

İkmen had seen a tray with numerous bottles of pills beside the bed when he'd first looked at the crime scene.

'What sort of drugs?'

'I've not made a full inventory yet,' the doctor said. 'But so far I've spotted warfarin, various blood-pressure medications, sleeping tablets, an antidepressant, tranquillisers . . .'

'The diseases of old age,' İkmen said. 'We have this to come.'

'Speak for yourself,' Arto said. 'Some of us are already there.'

Both men were of a certain age, İkmen coming up for sixty and the doctor one year older.

'Could her meds have killed her before she was stabbed?'

'Oh no, there's far too much blood. No, she was alive when she was attacked, heart pumping away . . .'

İkmen walked over to the old woman's bed and looked at her. Tall and thin, Fatima Rudolfoğlu, even in death, had a strong jawline for a woman the cleaner reckoned had to be in her nineties. She also had a thick head of steel-grey hair.

'Well, I suppose I should go and break the bad news to her brothers,' he said.

'Where do they live?'

'In the three apartments below this one,' İkmen replied. 'Apparently they never spoke.'

Arto frowned.

Only the oldest traders in the İç Bedesten, at the very centre of the Grand Bazaar, were calm about the closure. Mainly antique dealers, they'd seen it all before and knew that to rail against policemen like Sergeant Ömer Mungun was pointless.

'He's only doing his job,' a white-haired Armenian said to the Muslim owner of the shop next to his.

'Ah, young people!' the Muslim said. 'So impatient! Events happen when God wills. There is nothing mortals can do.'

But other traders were not of the same mind.

'When can we reopen?' A young Kurdish man thrust his face into Ömer's. 'Eh?'

'I don't know,' Ömer said.

Ali Baykal's blood was still on the ground, and every gate into the Grand Bazaar was being closed on what should have been one of the busiest days of the summer tourist season. But that wasn't Ömer's problem. What mattered to him was that a twenty-year-old man was fighting for his life after being stabbed in the side of the chest. Also, although surrounded by uniformed officers, Ömer was without the guidance and gravitas of his superior, Inspector Mehmet Süleyman, who was supervising the closure of the gates into one of İstanbul's oldest structures.

'That boy didn't work here,' the elderly Armenian said.

'I know,' Ömer said. The young victim worked at a carpet shop on Sahaflar Caddesi. According to his traumatised employer, Ali didn't have an enemy in the world.

'He was carrying kilims on his head,' the Armenian's neighbour said.

'Yes.'

Ali Baykal had been taking the small flat rugs over to an

antique shop owned by his employer's brother just outside the İç Bedesten. He'd needed them to cover up a patch of damp that had appeared on his floor. This wasn't unusual in a building that had been in continual use since the fifteenth century. Sometimes parts of it just gave out.

Ah, here you are! Ömer said to himself as he watched a tall, elegant man move through the crowds of confused shoppers and traders who were now effectively trapped inside the bazaar.

'Ömer.'

Inspector Mehmet Süleyman's voice was as deep and dark as his fine head of thick black hair. The scion of an old Ottoman family related to the imperial rulers of what was then the Ottoman Empire, Mehmet Süleyman was spectacularly handsome and he knew it. He was also, at forty-five, at the height of both his physical and intellectual strength.

'Sir.'

'Do we have any CCTV of the incident?' Süleyman asked.

'Mr . . .'

'Gevorgyan.' The Armenian antique dealer pushed in front of Ömer and shook Süleyman's hand. 'My cameras may have caught something. Mind you, they are pointed at the front of my shop . . .'

'One of mine is positioned towards the street,' said Mr Gevorgyan's neighbour. He bowed to Süleyman. 'I am Devlet Türkoğlu. I specialise in antique jewellery with a particular interest in art deco . . .'

'Do you.'

Süleyman had a way of putting people down without actually saying anything offensive. It was the tone of voice he used, which was, to say the least, dismissive.

He said to the traders, 'Well let's see your CCTV records.' He looked at Ömer. 'Any news on the victim?'

'No, sir.'

A man pushed his way to the front of a large knot of shoppers. 'When are we going to be allowed out of here?'

His face was red and he was clearly very agitated.

Süleyman turned what Ömer had come to recognise as his coldest gaze upon him. 'When you have been questioned and processed by my officers.'

'Yes, but—'

'Unless you want to spend some time in my cells, then you will shut up and wait,' Süleyman said. 'A young man has been assaulted. I want to know who did that, as I'm sure you do.'

He turned away from the man and followed Mr Türkoğlu into his shop. Ömer looked at the crowd in front of him and then glanced away. They were hot, confined and having a bad time. Things could very easily turn ugly – especially with Süleyman in one of his not infrequent imperious moods.

'They're all out,' Kerim Gürsel said.

'All of them?'

'Yes. Can't get an answer from any of their apartments.'

İkmen turned to the cleaner, Selin İnce. 'Do Fatima Hanım's brothers go out a lot?' he asked.

'No, never,' she said. 'They're all even older than Fatima Hanım. Mr Yücel has a man, Osman, as I told you; I see him on the stairs from time to time. I don't know what Mr Kanat and Mr Kemal do. I've only ever seen them through their windows.'

'Do you know where this Osman lives?' İkmen asked.

'No,' she said.

'Do you know his surname?'

'No.' She thought for a moment. 'But I do know he usually comes on a Monday morning. The old people need help after the weekend.'

'So he may yet arrive?' İkmen said.

'Yes.'

'Any idea what time?'

'No. I think he comes when he can,' she said. 'I've known him to be just arriving as I'm leaving.'

'Which is when, usually?'

'One p.m.'

İkmen looked at his watch. It was 11.30 a.m.

'What about telephones?' he said.

'What, them?' she said. 'No. They never had telephones. Fatima Hanım wrote letters.'

'Letters? To whom?' İkmen said.

'I don't know,' the cleaner replied. 'I just posted them.'

Gonca Şekeroğlu didn't usually leave her large house and family in the old Jewish quarter of Balat. Everything she needed was there – her children and grandchildren, her father, her work, and sometimes her lover.

At one time, gypsies like Gonca had only lived in specific parts of the city, like Sulukule, now demolished, and Hasköy, which was gentrifying at an alarming rate. Now the Roma people could be found almost anywhere, including, in the case of Gonca's cousin Barış, just outside the Grand Bazaar.

A copper-beater by trade, Barış, whose shop was opposite the Beyazıt Gate, was a man who missed little. As soon as he'd seen Inspector Mehmet Süleyman supervising the sealing of the bazaar's gates, he'd called his cousin.

'Mehmet Efendi is closing the bazaar,' he had said, using Süleyman's princely title. 'Such power that man has!'

Gonca had been compelled to see that. Standing in the middle of a huddle of pious black-clad women, she looked like a multi-coloured statue of Venus, with her ankle-length hair and low-cut summer dress in many shades of red, green and orange. The women looked at her with suspicion, especially when Barış, a tiny stick of a man, ran up and kissed her.

'Do you know what's going on?' she asked.

Barış led her away from the women and into his shop.

'Word is that a boy has been stabbed,' he said.

'Where? In the bazaar?'

'Yes.'

'Was there a fight? Was it carpet men?'

'According to my friend Sarkis Bey, the boy works in a carpet shop, yes,' Barış said. 'But there was no fight. The stabbing happened right outside Sarkis Bey's shop. So far, the boy lives.'

'Do the police have the person who did this?'

'Not as far as I know. It's why they've shut the bazaar.'

After taking tea with her cousin, Gonca went outside and once again found herself in amongst the covered women. They talked about how unsafe the city was becoming and complained about the police.

'They just swagger about looking down their noses at people,' one woman said.

Another shook her head. 'My husband works in the bazaar. Who knows what this will do to his business? Who was that man closing all the gates? Was he a policeman?'

Gonca smiled. She wanted to say, *Yes, he is a policeman and he's all mine!* but she didn't. The covered women wouldn't be impressed – or rather they wouldn't show that they were impressed. Had they seen her Mehmet, even they, surely, would feel some sort of sexual stirring. Gonca knew that she did. She sent her lover a text to let him know that when his day finished, she would be waiting for him.

And because she was beautiful, and because she had bewitched him, Gonca knew that Mehmet Süleyman would already be hot with desire for her.

Chapter 2

Some of the younger constables were itching to use the battering ram. İkmen let them.

'Oh, to be young and full of machismo,' he said as the team waited for the order to break down the door.

Osman Babacan, Yücel Rudolfoğlu's casual carer, had turned up at 1 p.m. and opened the door to the old man's apartment. İkmen had found Yücel in the same position as his sister, face upwards on his bed with a stab wound to his chest. Stone dead.

Now they were preparing to break into Kanat Rudolfoğlu's second-floor apartment.

Commissioner Hürrem Teker, who had arrived after the discovery of the second body, said, 'Break it down.'

The door was a fine example of Ottoman hardwood carpentry, but it didn't stand a chance against four young lads with the kind of muscles a skinny middle-aged man like İkmen could only dream about.

Once the team had broken through, İkmen turned to Arto Sarkissian. 'A tiny wager on cause of death,' he said. 'How about it?'

The doctor shared his friend's graveyard sense of humour. 'If he's been stabbed through the heart, you owe me a bottle of rakı.'

İkmen scowled. 'I was going to say that.'

They walked towards the shattered door.

'Ah, but I got in first,' the doctor said. 'Are you on?'

The two men shook hands.

Teker was first into the apartment. What had started out as a single suspicious death was developing into something far more sinister.

Kanat Rudolfoğlu's apartment was ghastly. Filthy and unkempt, it smelt of urine and damp, and there were faeces on the floor of what had once been an elegant entrance hall. Commissioner Teker said, 'This is an outrage. How can anyone live like this?'

'From what we can gather locally, this family has been all but forgotten,' İkmen said. 'The old woman's cleaner told us that no one has visited for years.'

'And yet Fatima Rudolfoğlu had a pile of prescription drugs by her bed, so she must have seen a doctor at some point.'

'Maybe they were just repeat prescriptions,' the doctor said. 'Didn't the cleaner say she used to pick them up for the old woman?'

'Yes,' İkmen said.

The door into Kanat Rudolfoğlu's bedroom was open; as expected, he was lying on his back. Arto Sarkissian approached the bed first and declared that the old man had, on the face of it, died in exactly the same way as his siblings.

As İkmen left to go and organise the breaking-down of Kemal Rudolfoğlu's front door, the doctor said to him, 'You owe me.'

'I know.'

Once they'd found the body of the final Rudolfoğlu sibling, Commissioner Teker said to İkmen, 'And so what began as a simple murder turns into something even darker.'

'Oh yes,' İkmen said as he walked around one of the most extraordinary bedrooms he had ever seen. 'And I think that Mr Kemal, at least, had some very unusual interests.'

A cross between a laboratory – complete with retorts, bell

jars, titration tubes – and a museum of curiosities, Kemal Rudolfoğlu's bedroom was an unnerving place.

'What was he?' Teker asked. 'Some sort of scientist?'

İkmen looked into the empty eye sockets of a human skull and said, 'Not exactly.'

The beautiful, chaotic, treasure-filled Grand Bazaar of İstanbul is over five hundred years old and contains five thousand shops. In the summer months it can attract upwards of two hundred and fifty thousand visitors a day. Add to that the number of traders and artisans who work in the bazaar, and one gets what is in effect a small city. It was a small city that Mehmet Süleyman had closed off from the world.

An owlish technician called Turgut Zana had come out from police headquarters to look at CCTV footage of Ali Baykal's progress through the bazaar that morning. A jeweller called Moris Taranto had been the first person to realise that the victim was bleeding, but he hadn't witnessed how that might have happened. No one had, and so far, narrowing down the masses trapped inside the bazaar to a few possible suspects was proving difficult. Footage from outside Sarkis Gevorgyan's shop, where the boy had collapsed, was unilluminating.

'Turgut Bey . . .'

'Sssh! Go away!'

Zana was looking at footage from the camera outside a shop specialising in Christian Orthodox ikons. The owner, a perfectly round Turkish woman in her sixties, was shocked at the way the man who had stomped into her shop like a storm-trooper took this rebuttal.

Süleyman noticed the look on her face. 'My fault,' he said. 'I disturbed him.'

Officer Zana had never been an easy man. A Kurd, originally from Diyarbakır, he'd come to policing via a range of technical jobs, including film-making and Internet security. His work-ing-class parents had noticed when he was very small that their boy was 'different', and had spent every penny they had on his education. It was said that Turgut Zana had never dropped a grade. He was also one of the few people who could tell Mehmet Süleyman to shut up.

Ömer Mungun arrived. 'How's it going?' he whispered to Süleyman.

'I've no idea.'

Ömer looked over at the Kurd. 'Mmm.'

'What's happening outside?'

'A lot of unhappy people,' Ömer said.

'Reinforcements?'

'On their way, but the commissioner's left for a situation over in Moda. Serious, I'm told.'

'As serious as a random stabbing in the Grand Bazaar?'

Ömer Mungun took Süleyman's arm and led him away from the Kurd and the woman. 'Four suspicious deaths, all the same family,' he said. 'Inspector İkmen—'

'A person in a black tracksuit.'

They both walked across to where the Kurd was hunched over a monitor.

'Passes on the right side of the victim.' Turgut Zana pointed at the screen. 'Raises one arm, slightly . . . there.'

He pointed at the screen.

Süleyman, peering over Zana's shoulder, could feel the Kurd's discomfort – he didn't do proximity.

'Can you make the image any clearer?' he said.

'If I could, I would have done so before I showed you,' Zana said.

Süleyman would have bawled anyone else out for speaking to him in such a manner, but he knew it was pointless. Turgut Zana wouldn't understand.

'Is it a man or a woman?' Ömer asked.

'Impossible to tell,' the Kurd said. 'A man or a very slim woman.'

'Probably a man . . .'

'You can't make that assumption. We don't know. Accept it.'

Süleyman saw Ömer's face redden, so he moved him to one side.

'Turgut Bey,' he said. 'Describe this figure factually to me in your own words, please.'

The owner of the shop whispered to Ömer, 'He's not right, is he?'

Ömer said, 'No, hanım, but he is very clever.'

'He's very rude . . .'

Turgut Zana said, 'Medium height, very slim. Wearing a black tracksuit – I'd say Ralph Lauren or maybe Lacoste. There's a small logo on the left breast but it's not possible to make it out. Shoes are trainers, but shabby. I'd say he or she was fashionable, that he or she had money, if it wasn't for the trainers. People who care about labels have to assemble the entire look. This is either someone poor who has stolen or borrowed an expensive tracksuit, or a wealthy person in disguise.'

'Just using shoes?'

'Why not?' He peered at the screen again. 'Anything is possible in an infinite universe.'

'Yes, but—'

'Do you want my professional opinion or don't you, Inspector Süleyman?'

'Of course, I—'

'Then listen,' he said. 'I'd estimate the age at anywhere between sixteen and thirty. If we say this is a man, then I should add that middle-aged men do wear tracksuits, as we know, but they move differently. This person moves with the fluidity of

18

youth. He's carrying nothing, so he either lives in the city, where he can get access to his possessions easily, or he is too poor to actually have anything. Sadly, apart from his footwear, he is really rather nondescript.'

'Colouring?'

'He's wearing a hood that is shading his face. But given where we are and the fact that he apparently has no possessions, he's probably not a tourist. Statistically he will be a Turk or a Kurd, so in all probability dark. And he is with someone.'

The figure on the screen looked as if he was entirely alone. The nearest person to him, apart from Ali Baykal, was a very short, fat woman wearing a headscarf.

'And I don't mean the woman,' the Kurd said. 'She's irrelevant. But you see that figure behind the man in the tracksuit . . .'

Süleyman saw a very out-of-focus figure, almost a ghost. 'Yes.'

'Well if you look at the footage from outside the shop where the victim fell, you can see that this figure here and our track-suited person are walking together, talking. I'd say that this, er . . .'

'Accomplice.'

'Accomplice is taller, probably male, but again I can't be sure. He or she is wearing a grey hooded top and blue jeans.'

'So two men?' Süleyman said.

'Or two women, or one of each,' said the Kurd. 'I really can't definitively gender either of them.'

'Alchemy?' Commissioner Hürrem Teker folded her arms across her chest. 'Seriously?'

'When I was a child, we had an alchemist in Üsküdar,' İkmen said. 'I know that was back in the 1950s, but when you think that alchemy is probably two-thousand-plus years old, it's quite reasonable to assume that it wouldn't die out quickly.

I know of at least one man who still practises the dark arts in this city.'

'Yes, but . . . alchemy?'

'I remember the alchemist in Üsküdar,' Arto Sarkissian said. 'He was Greek. My father used to visit him.'

Hürrem Teker, unlike her predecessor, Commissioner Ardıç, wasn't yet fully accustomed to the occult layers of İstanbul with which Çetin İkmen and Arto Sarkissian were so easily familiar. 'Wasn't your father a doctor?'

'Yes,' Arto said. 'But he sometimes consulted the alchemist when he didn't know what to do.'

'About how to treat his patients?'

'Oh no,' he said. 'About life. My father was a very sad man, you know, madam. I suppose these days one would call him a depressive. The alchemist was a very wise person; my father learned a lot from him.'

'And so this . . . paraphernalia . . .'

'I don't know what it all means,' İkmen said. 'But I can see that he was trying to synthesise something in these flasks. He clearly used the fireplace because it contains burnt wood, and there's a scorched retort stand in the middle of the detritus, probably used to hold a flask with something or other inside. Then there's the skull, what looks like a wand . . .' He picked up a book from a shelf. 'Pentagram on the cover, written in Latin . . .'

Arto held out his hand. 'Let me see.'

İkmen gave him the book.

The doctor read, '*Theatrum Chemicum – The Chemical Theatre* – by Lazarus Zetzner.' He opened the book. 'Ah. Yes. Astrological signifiers, the Kabbalah . . .'

'Isn't that witchcraft?' Teker asked.

'Sort of. But a more accurate description would be magic,' İkmen explained. 'Alchemy wasn't just about creating gold from base metals, it was also about transmutation of the soul.'

'What does that mean?'

'I'm not entirely sure,' İkmen said. 'Becoming an enlightened being – something like that. Or rather, in some cases. Other alchemists professed to use magic to give themselves power. Some interpreted this as consorting with the Devil.'

'God! Is this relevant, Çetin Bey?' Teker said. Clearly tired of such arcane talk, she shook her head again.

'It could be,' he said.

'How?'

'Well, madam, we have four dead bodies in a building where an alchemist once lived, a building that we have been told by local people is known as the Devil's House.'

Just circulating the Kurd's description of Ali Baykal's attacker and his or her accomplice to the officers on duty at the bazaar's eighteen gates stretched Mehmet Süleyman's patience. Separating out those who didn't approximate these descriptions, and checking those who did, was interminable. But the bazaar had already been closed for almost one whole day; it couldn't be shut for a second. The traders would riot.

At 5 p.m., Mehmet Süleyman called his mistress, Gonca Şekeroğlu.

'I got your text,' he said. 'I'm not going to be able to see you tonight. I'm sorry.'

'Ah.' She sighed. 'You know I came to see you this morning. Cousin Barış called me to tell me there'd been an incident in the bazaar. He saw you. Sadly, I didn't.'

He lowered his voice. 'I miss you.'

'That's good,' she said.

He laughed. 'You are a terrible woman, Gonca!'

'Which is why you adore me.'

She ended the call.

Ömer Mungun, who had been waiting patiently to speak to

his superior, said, 'Sir, we've found a boy in a black tracksuit hiding in one of the workshops.'

The five thousand shops in the Grand Bazaar didn't reflect the overall size of the complex. Behind modern glass shop windows lurked cavities in stone once used by the Byzantines, where carpets were repaired and fake designer handbags created. Even the roof concealed silversmiths' workshops, corridors full of clothing alteration specialists and men making leather belts.

Süleyman said, 'Where?'

'In the roof above the Bodrum Han, behind a load of junk in the back of a leather workshop. The owner says he doesn't know him.'

'Has he spoken?'

'No,' Ömer said. 'I'm not sure whether he can. He looks spaced out to me.'

'Where is he now?'

'I left him under guard in the owner's office,' he said.

The two men walked south-westwards from the İç Bedesten to one of the bazaar's many ancient caravanserais. The Bodrum Han was famous for its leather goods.

When they arrived, they found a tiny, chaotic office space filled with smoke, leather offcuts, two enormous uniformed officers and a small, frightened-eyed boy.

Ömer Mungun said, 'Has he spoken?'

'No, Sergeant.'

A chair was found for Süleyman, who sat opposite the boy.

'My name,' he said, 'is Inspector Süleyman. Tell me your name.'

The boy just shook. He had the sort of face that could have been sixteen or thirty. He was young, but it was impossible to tell how young. Süleyman looked at his feet. His trainers were shabby.

'Are you Turkish?'

Still the boy remained silent. Süleyman looked up at Ömer Mungun. 'Did you find any ID on him?'

'No, sir.'

He was very dark. Could he be perhaps a Syrian refugee?

'Are you from Syria?' Süleyman asked. But the boy didn't respond.

'A young man who works in this bazaar has been stabbed,' Süleyman continued. 'We need to find out who did it.'

'I told him he looked like the offender, sir,' the bigger of the constables said.

Süleyman looked at him furiously. 'Why did you do that? Are you stupid? Then again, I know the answer to that question . . .'

'Sir . . .'

'If he does speak Turkish, you've just sent his brain into meltdown.'

'Sir!'

'Oh don't give me any ridiculous excuses!' He looked at Ömer. 'Where do we get these morons, eh, Sergeant?'

But before Ömer Mungun could answer, the boy let out a sound that reminded Süleyman of the noise a cat makes when it's calling for its mate. The smaller of the two constables pinned him to his chair with one, brutal arm.

'What is it? What—'

'Satan has started his work,' the boy said. His voice was soft and gravelly and it made Mehmet Süleyman's flesh turn cold. 'The Lord of Hell is here. Right here.' He looked into Süleyman's eyes. 'At your left elbow.'

'Hasn't that place been empty for years?'

Alican Ablak was a man of indeterminate age. A fashion designer by trade, he had the groomed beard and smooth skin

23

of what Kerim Gürsel would call a 'hipster'. He also had a very nice apartment with views of the Sea of Marmara on one side and the back of the Devil's House on the other.

'No, sir,' İkmen said. 'Four elderly siblings lived there.'

Ablak shook his head. 'Don't know anything about it.'

'How long have you lived here, Mr Ablak?' İkmen asked.

'Me? Five years.'

The apartment building had probably been built in the 1960s, but the decor was most definitely modern. Matt black and dulled chrome was everywhere.

'Five years?' another, far deeper male voice said.

İkmen turned in time to see an old man with a stick walking slowly into what the younger man had called 'the drawing room'.

'You were born here, Alican,' the old man said.

'Papa . . .'

'From the police, yes?' the old man said to İkmen as he sat down on an enormous black sofa.

'Yes, sir. Inspector İkmen.'

'Ah.' The old man grunted as he settled himself. 'I am Bülent Ablak, this silly boy's father. With the exception of the two years he was married, my son has lived in this apartment all his life.'

Alican's face reddened. 'Papa . . .'

'And that's fifty years ago.' He laughed. 'Contrary to appearances – I let my son decorate the place; well, why not? – this is my apartment, Inspector. Please, do sit.'

İkmen sat on a large leather chair opposite the old man. 'You have to forgive Alican,' Bülent Ablak said. 'In his line of work, they all lie about their age.'

'Papa, you know that's the way it is!' his son said. 'Fashion is just like that. It's a youth thing.'

'Well, then fashion is a fool,' Bülent said. 'Fifty years old and going out to clubs with women young enough to be his daughter, Inspector! Can you believe that?'

He could, but İkmen didn't say so.

'Mr Ablak, as I told your son, I'm here about the house next door,' he said.

'Ah, yes. I saw your vehicles outside the Devil's House.'

'You call it the Devil's House?'

'Oh, that's not its real name,' the old man said. 'Don't know what that is. I don't think I ever have. Why do you want to know?'

'There have been some . . . incidents inside the house,' İkmen said. Together with Commissioner Teker, he was due to give a statement to the press in two hours' time. If he hadn't seen Alican Ablak standing on his balcony looking at the old building, he wouldn't even have thought about joining in the house-to-house enquiries himself.

'Do you see much movement in and out of the Devil's House?' he asked.

'I occasionally see a middle-aged woman,' the old man said. 'But if you want to know whether I ever see the Rudolfoğlus, the answer is no. Not for years. But then how would I know them after all this time? They are my parents' generation. To be honest with you, I never think about them.'

'Any reason?'

'What, apart from the fact that they entombed themselves when I was an infant in a house that can now hardly be seen through the weeds in its garden?'

'Have you never been curious about them?'

'If I ever thought about them, I imagined they must be dead. Are they dead?'

'Yes,' İkmen said.

'What? All of them?'

'Yes.'

Alican Ablak sat down next to his father. 'You always told me that place was derelict,' he said.

25

'Well it is.'

'Not if people lived there. Why—'

'I didn't want it to intrigue you when you were a child,' he said. 'You might have gone in there. Wouldn't have looked good, would it? Son of a lawyer breaks into house? Also, to go into it all would have made me sound ridiculous.' He looked at İkmen. 'I don't know how you stand on such things, Inspector, but I was brought up at a time when superstition of all sorts was frowned upon. Atatürk's republic didn't believe in ghosts or saints or any of the other supernatural rubbish our forefathers subscribed to. Pity they still don't . . .'

The old man looked miserable for a moment, then he continued, 'But anyway, that place was thought to be cursed. That's why it's called the Devil's House: because its original owner was believed by some to be the Devil.'

Alican laughed. But İkmen didn't.

'Why did they think that?' he said.

'He beat his servants, but who didn't in those days? He was a paşa, so he could do what he liked. I don't really know,' the old man said. 'My mother disliked him just because he was a foreigner.'

'What kind of foreigner?'

'German,' Bülent said. 'He was seconded to the Ottoman army in the Great War by our ally the Kaiser. Got that house and a wife out of it too. Rudolf Paşa, Ottoman soldier and father of the four old fossils who rotted in that house.'

'I've been told that none of the siblings spoke to one another,' İkmen said. 'They lived in separate apartments.'

'Yes, that's true.' Bülent nodded. 'Why, I don't know. There used to be stories.'

'Like what?'

'I can't remember, but I do know that my mother thought the four of them were bewitched.'

26

'By whom?'

'Their father,' he said. 'According to my mother, Rudolf Paşa didn't want anyone to be happy, and that included his own children. But then the Devil wouldn't, would he?'

Chapter 3

Lolling his head out of his office window probably made him look mad, but Mehmet Süleyman didn't care. He'd spent much of the previous night trying to make sense of the ramblings of a boy whose name he still didn't know. The black-tracksuited youth was sometimes the Sufi poet Rumi, sometimes a fairy, sometimes a demon called Emre. By the time he called for a psychiatric assessment, Süleyman was beginning to think that maybe the boy really was some kind of mystical being. Not that it mattered. Forensic analysis of his clothes would reveal whether or not he was carrying any blood droplets from Ali Baykal.

Süleyman lit a cigarette. At four o'clock that morning, what had been a case of violent assault had become a murder. Surrounded by his family, Ali Baykal had slipped out of the coma that had followed on from the surgery he had been given, and plunged into death.

'Whatever the question, suicide is never the answer,' he heard Çetin İkmen say.

He looked back into his office. 'Did I forget to lock the door?'

'Yes.'

'Oh God.'

İkmen closed the door and locked it.

'Well, in terms of who caused the most chaos in this city yesterday, I'd say that you win.' He sat down. 'I just got to shut a few roads in Moda, while you closed the Grand Bazaar.'

'Never again.' Süleyman offered İkmen a cigarette. 'In the

last twenty-four hours I've been shouted at by shopkeepers, watched more CCTV footage in the company of Turgut Zana than is good for anyone . . .'

İkmen lit up and laughed. 'Poor Turgut, he can't help the way he is.'

'Maybe not, but . . . Then we had to take statements from some very bizarre witnesses, which culminated in what I can only describe as an audience with a boy who, by turns, believes he is a fairy, a poet and a demon. I had to call the psychiatrist. And all this against a background of a bazaar full of people, all of whom had to be processed before they could leave. If you were to include statements, the contact details the officers took down yesterday would reach to the moon. I'd put money on it.'

'Oh don't make bets,' İkmen said. 'I made one with Dr Sarkissian yesterday and ended up owing him a very expensive bottle of rakı. My gambling days are over. Where's Ömer?'

'I sent him home.'

'Which is where you should be.'

'Can't. I've got to see Teker at ten.'

'I've just seen her,' İkmen said. 'She's a little, well, stressed . . .'

'You know our victim died?'

'Yes,' İkmen said. 'Any idea about motive?'

'None so far. He came from a nice, ordinary working-class family. Father was a railwayman until he died ten years ago. Mother lives off his pension and does some cleaning for a couple of pansiyons in Sultanahmet. One older sister, married with a baby. The kid was a normal twenty-year-old. Worked for a carpet dealer, into girls, computer games and music. No hint of radicalisation. Everybody liked him.

'And you? What has happened in Moda?'

'Four elderly siblings stabbed in their beds,' İkmen said.

'Wow.'

'Mehmet, have you ever heard of an Ottoman commander called Rudolf Paşa?'

'No. My father may have done, but . . .' He shrugged.

Muhammed Süleyman Efendi, Ottoman prince and Mehmet's father, had been dementing for years. Once a valuable fount of imperial knowledge, he was cared for by his wife and Mehmet's older brother Murad. He didn't even know his own name.

'Rudolf was German,' İkmen said. 'Lent to the empire by the Kaiser during the Great War. He stayed on, married a princess and lived out his life after the war in the house he'd moved into when he first arrived in İstanbul. Our four dead bodies are his children.'

'They must be ancient!'

'Indeed. The youngest, Fatima Hanım, was ninety-six. Their house is an enormous late Ottoman pile hidden behind what I can only describe as a madness of foliage, hemmed in by 1960s apartment blocks. However, it isn't one house any more. At some point the siblings took up residence on different floors, which were converted into apartments. It's said they had some sort of falling-out – I don't yet know why – and hadn't spoken for decades. Strange, eh?'

'Strange that you didn't know about this before,' Süleyman said. 'I've always thought you knew every weird corner of this city.'

'Oh, it gets weirder,' İkmen said. 'I eventually found out that the house was originally called the Tulip Kiosk. But no one who knows anything about the place calls it that. It is said that Rudolf Paşa was a bit of a bastard, who may have dabbled in black magic, and because of that, it's known as the Devil's House.'

'Oh, the Devil again,' Süleyman said wearily as he lit another cigarette.

'Again?'

'The boy I called the psychiatrist out to told me that the Devil was standing at my left elbow. He said, "The Lord of Hell is here.'"

'Did he?' İkmen said.

'Yes.' Süleyman yawned. 'Clearly mad.'

'Mmm.' Çetin İkmen looked out of the window and up into the brightening morning sky. Another hot day in the golden city on the Bosphorus, and yet again, he thought, they were pondering on the nature of evil.

Kerim Gürsel had never been in charge of such a large crime scene before. Çetin İkmen was usually in control, but he'd had to return to police headquarters in order to brief Commissioner Teker. And so for a short period of time, Kerim was the boss.

All the bodies had been removed the previous day. Now the forensic searches had begun. The scene-of-crime officers had started with Fatima Rudolfoğlu's apartment, and a lot of the old woman's possessions had already been taken away.

Kerim walked back into the bedroom. Only the frame of the bed remained, the mattress and bedclothes having gone to the forensic institute for analysis. A number of small items had also been removed. As well as a lot of dried-out cosmetics and battered hairbrushes, the strange glass dressing table was home to many small boxes. They came in all shapes and sizes; some made from wood, others glass, and some of tarnished metal that might have been silver. He opened a couple and found sad little collections of used lipsticks, hair grips and even a couple of teeth.

What had this woman done with her life? Locked away in a house with three brothers she never spoke to? The cleaner reckoned that Fatima Hanım had become demented over the past few months. Why had it taken so long? Kerim knew that he himself would have gone mad under such circumstances. If none of the old people had spoken to each other within living memory, then something terrible must have happened between them. Did that thing have anything to do with their deaths?

He opened a big metal box in front of the dressing table mirror. Very thin writing paper sprang out. It was like the stuff people used to write on to send letters by air mail. Thin and so therefore cheaper to post. He picked up a sheet. It was covered in a shaky, pallid scrawl that he found he couldn't make out. Then he realised it was written in Arabic script.

Saira let another tram go. It was already hot, and being rammed in with a load of other heavily sweating people was not an attractive prospect. Then there was the way she looked. She had decided to wear the burqa the previous year. Her mother had been horrified, but after Saira had been on the Haj, it had just seemed right. And it had pleased Adnan. Not that her husband had forced her to cover. He hadn't. But he'd been unable to hide his pleasure when she decided for herself.

It was almost eleven o'clock. She was due at her in-laws' apartment in Aksaray. She was going to be late. Even if she phoned them, she knew they'd be suspicious. Tophane to Aksaray wasn't far and didn't take that long, but she still wouldn't get there on time. If only she hadn't missed the bus from Beşiktaş to Tophane! Her mother-in-law particularly would think she'd been up to no good.

The tram stopped and several people struggled to get out. Saira pushed her way in.

'It isn't Arabic, it's Ottoman.'

'Ottoman?'

'Before Atatürk formulated the new alphabet in 1928, we—'

'Yes, I know what Ottoman script is,' Kerim Gürsel said. 'But why is it here?'

He held up one of the old woman's letters.

Constable Kahraman said, 'Her father was an Ottoman commander.'

'Even the children of the Ottoman elite had to learn the new alphabet, Constable,' Kerim said.

Kahraman shrugged. 'Maybe she didn't. Locked away in this house . . .'

'And anyway, how do you know Ottoman?' Kerim sounded surprised; most people considered Kahraman to be a bit 'lacking'.

'I don't,' Kahraman said. 'I can't really read it. I just know it when I see it.'

'How?'

'My dad knew it,' he said. 'My grandfather never learned the new alphabet. He was an imam back home in our village, and all his books were in Ottoman. Dad taught me the alphabet one winter. But I can't actually translate.'

İkmen, who had been watching the exchange, took the letter from Kerim's hand.

'How many of these are there?' he asked.

'I don't know, sir,' Kerim said. 'The box on the dressing table was full of them.'

İkmen handed the letter to Kahraman. 'Can you make out the signature on this? At least I think it's a signature.'

The constable carefully traced some script at the bottom of the page with his finger. Then he said, 'It's Kemal Rudolfoğlu.'

'Her brother,' Kerim said.

'With whom she did not speak,' İkmen said. 'I wonder whether she replied to him by letter?'

'Scene of crime have only just started work on the other apartments,' Kerim said. 'Do you want any letters like this kept to one side?'

'Yes,' İkmen said. 'They may signify nothing of any importance, but if Fatima and Kemal were communicating by letter, I want to know what they were communicating about.'

'You'll have to get someone who can read Ottoman properly,' Constable Kahraman said.

'Yes.' İkmen shook his head. 'You know, the only time I have ever seen anyone write using the Ottoman script was when I once saw Dr Sarkissian's father write a note to his ancient gardener. Sadly that was fifty years ago and Vahan Sarkissian is long dead.'

'What shall we do, sir?' Kerim asked.

'Well, I understand that the government wants to put the learning of Ottoman back on the educational curriculum, but we can't wait for that,' İkmen said. 'I imagine we'll have to call upon an academic. Let's see how many of these letters turn up, and then I'll decide what to do next. If you find any letters in modern Turkish, keep those separate.'

He walked out of the old woman's bedroom. Kerim sent Constable Kahraman back to his duties in Fatima Rudolfoğlu's bathroom.

The boy was a living caricature. Raving, foaming at the mouth and occasionally laughing, he was a typical madman. Commissioner Hürrem Teker was deeply suspicious.

'If ever I saw someone playing at being mad, that is it,' she said as she closed the viewing hatch in the cell door.

Mehmet Süleyman, whose ex-wife Zelfa had been a psychiatrist, had thought that way too – at first. But so far there was no forensic evidence that connected the boy to Ali Baykal's killer. And Süleyman was now inclined to believe in the young man's madness.

'I have to say that he looks genuine to me, madam,' he said.

'And apparently to Dr Güven.' Teker shook her head. 'Psychiatrists are, I have to admit, a mystery to me. Why do *you* think this boy in genuine, Mehmet Bey?'

'Apart from the lack of forensic evidence?'

'So far.'

'So far,' he agreed. 'It's the way he looks at these entities he claims to see. All I can say is that I feel he really does see them. He follows them with his eyes. There's a communication. I'm no expert, but I've seen enough of this behaviour in the past to get a notion of what is genuine and what isn't.'

He was alluding to his ex-wife, but Teker didn't refer to Dr Zelfa Halman. One didn't.

'You think the boy sees the Devil?' she said.

'I wouldn't go that far,' Süleyman replied.

'You don't believe in the Devil?'

Teker was well known for her lack of religious conviction, but in spite of that, Süleyman knew that his answer needed to be politic.

'I don't know,' he said. 'I believe that evil exists. In this job it's impossible not to believe that. But whether it is personified, I can't say. I have no evidence for it.'

'Except this boy.'

'No. He sees something you and I don't see. What I'm saying is that it's real to him. He's not faking. That's what Dr Güven has observed.'

'Mmm. I presume you know that the house I attended with Çetin Bey yesterday is called the Devil's House?'

'Çetin Bey mentioned it, yes,' Süleyman said.

'Yes, he's very comfortable with the occult,' she said. 'Rather in his element.'

She began to walk away, but then she stopped.

'Maybe have Inspector İkmen take a look at your boy, Mehmet Bey,' she said. 'Given his close relationship with things not of this world, I would be interested to see what he thinks.'

Süleyman bowed. 'Madam.'

* * *

35

The covered woman had fallen out of the tram when a great crowd of people got off at Zeytinburnu. At first no one dared touch her, and so she lay on the platform surrounded by confused onlookers. Her face was completely covered and so no man even attempted to go to her. It was only when an equally heavily veiled woman whispered to the uncovered woman beside her, 'I don't think she's breathing,' that anyone dared investigate.

This woman, a tired middle-aged seamstress, got down on her hands and knees and located the woman's face without compromising her modesty. She put her hand against what she had to assume was an open mouth. Then she said, 'No, she's not breathing. Get an ambulance.'

A man took his phone out of his pocket while a woman from the back of the crowd pushed her way forward.

'I'm a nurse.'

She knelt down on the ground beside the woman and began to remove her burqa. Some people gasped, but she ignored them. Once she'd uncovered the woman's arms, she felt for a pulse. There was nothing. She ripped the cloth away from the woman's face, then she tilted her head back and lifted her chin in order to clear her airways. She placed her cheek beside the woman's mouth, but there was no sign of breath. Onlookers began to move in to see what she was doing.

'Keep out of the way!' she yelled. 'Has someone called an ambulance?'

A man's voice said, 'Yes.'

The nurse began chest compressions, but in the almost certain belief that this was too little, too late. She'd seen bodies like this woman's before. Sudden Adult Death Syndrome was more common than people thought. She looked at the face that had been behind the burqa, and was horrified by how young it looked.

Chapter 4

'I didn't like Dr Tanis,' Arto Sarkissian said.

Çetin İkmen drained his gin and tonic and said, 'Another?'

Arto threw the last of his rakı down his neck. 'Why not?'

The Mosaik Bar was only a minute from İkmen's apartment in Sultanahmet and had been his favourite watering hole for years. Even his cat, Marlboro, frequented the Mosaik, sitting on a stool beside his master and eating small pieces of fish donated by the staff. İkmen called one of the waiters over and ordered more drinks.

'If he'd owned up and said that he hadn't seen Fatima Rudolfoğlu for decades, I could have had some respect for him,' Arto continued. 'But he lied. Said he'd seen her to review her medication in April.'

'How do you know he didn't?'

'Because Fatima Hanım was diabetic and he didn't know,' Arto said. 'And I spoke to the prescribing pharmacist, who told me that none of her prescriptions have changed in over a decade.'

'Sure the pharmacist doesn't have personal stuff with the doctor?'

Their drinks arrived, together with a small plate of anchovies for Marlboro, which İkmen put on the table so that the cat could eat alongside him.

'I can't be sure, no,' Arto said. 'But that still doesn't account for missing Fatima Hanım's diabetes. She could have had it for years. The man's a disgrace!'

37

İkmen shook his head. 'That four extremely elderly people should be murdered in their own homes is a disgrace too,' he said. He lit a cigarette. 'Arto, can you read Ottoman? I know your father could . . .'

'My father *was* an Ottoman,' Arto said. 'But I'm not, and so, no. My brother and I were brought up to be modern boys. You know that! Is this about those letters you found?'

'According to the one officer we have who can just about make out the Ottoman alphabet, it seems that the Rudolfoğlu siblings wrote to each other a lot.'

'How would you define "a lot"?'

Marlboro hissed at a smaller, dirtier cat underneath the table and then very extravagantly ate a piece of fish. İkmen smiled. 'We're still collecting the letters,' he said. 'I've no idea whether having some of them translated will shed any light upon the Rudolfoğlus' deaths. But if we can find out why they were at odds with each other, maybe that will provide us with some clues.'

'Forensics will take some time,' the doctor said. 'There's a huge amount of material.'

'Including the accoutrements of alchemy,' İkmen said.

'Yes, I saw your face light up. Do you think Kemal Rudolfoğlu actually practised it, or did he just like said accoutrements?'

'I saw traces of what could have been chemical substances in some of the jars,' İkmen said. 'But whatever it was had desiccated, and so who knows when that equipment was last used?'

Arto shook his head. 'I remembered the name of the alchemist back in Üsküdar today. It was Manolis. Can't recall any surname. My father just used to call him Manolis Bey.'

'Do you know what he and your father used to talk about?'

'Not really, although I have realised as I've got older that Father suffered far more from depression than we knew. I think he didn't understand his place.'

'But by your own admission, Çetin, the world had largely forgotten the Devil's House and its occupants.'

İkmen stroked Marlboro's head again. 'Largely, but not completely,' he said. 'Someone knew them. Someone knew or thought they knew something very alarming about them.'

The dead woman was called Saira Öymen, and according to her husband, she had suffered from a heart murmur. It was unusual for a young person to die from such a condition, but not unknown. She had been in a very stressful and confined environment when she died. But the police, who had brought her to the hospital from the Zeytinburnu tram stop, where she had been discovered, did not suspect foul play. Saira Hanım had been a good, pious, quiet woman who had simply been going to visit her in-laws.

But neither her virtue nor her known heart condition meant that Saira Hanım's body could avoid an autopsy. Even though he was, in line with Islamic tradition, desperate to bury his wife, Adnan Öymen told Dr Şahin Uslu the truth. She hadn't seen a doctor for months. There had to be an investigation.

Dr Uslu had been a pathologist all his working life, so he knew that an external examination of a corpse was often just as informative as any internal observation. For instance, it was often possible to see whether a person had liver damage just by looking at the colour and condition of their skin. Dr Uslu removed Saira Öymen's clothing, which he handed to his assistant.

She'd been an attractive young woman. Slim, red-haired, and fair-skinned underneath the bruising that marked her torso and her left thigh. Dr Uslu wondered, as he often did when he was looking at a heavily bruised female corpse, whether her husband had hit her where it wouldn't show. Not that it would show anywhere if a woman was covered. Unless he discovered that the bruising had played a part in the woman's death, he wouldn't mention it to the husband. There wasn't much point. If Adnan

41

Öymen was the sort of man who hit women, he wouldn't change just because a doctor told him off. Wife-beating was all too common, which was sad and awful, and Dr Uslu shook his head at the thought of it.

'Everything all right, Doctor?' his assistant asked.

'Yes, yes.'

Şahin Uslu's father had hit his mother. A so-called modern man, pro-Western, anti-religion, Kemalist, he had beaten her into brain damage. It wasn't something easily forgotten, even though Şahin had tried.

Saira Öymen had been punched in the stomach, but the bruises just above her pelvis were not new. In fact her entire torso was discoloured by bruising that all looked slightly faded. Not so the top of her left leg, which was marked by one large, heavy dark purple bruise. He lowered his head to look at this more closely, which was when he saw the puncture wound.

There was a flap in the cell door through which, every so often, pairs of eyes would appear. He didn't know who they belonged to, but they weren't the Devil. *He* was out in the city, causing chaos.

He'd known for months that the Devil would come. He'd appeared in his room a couple of times, which was why in the end he'd had to buy tinfoil and black paint to put over his windows. But then Belkis Hanım had thrown him out. She'd taken his rent first, though, the old hag. Then she'd taken down the tinfoil and let the Devil in. She'd learn. She had learned. Only two days later, when she was out shopping, the Devil had burned her house to the ground. Then he'd skipped away to better things. Killing.

Even though he hadn't seen the attack in the Grand Bazaar, he knew it had to have been the work of the Devil. Now that he was in the city, anything was possible. But who had called him? Someone had to summon the Devil. He only came if he was invited. Who had been so reckless as to think that such an act would end well?

'I'm not saying I don't believe the boy. I actually do,' Mehmet Süleyman said. 'What I am saying is that I've seen offenders try to convince us they are mad when they're not. I have to be careful.'

'You think this boy is mad because he tells you that the Devil has come to town?'

Gonca was brushing her hair in front of her dressing table mirror, looking at his reflection, naked on her bed.

'If I say yes, you will accuse me of being small-minded.'

'You can be,' she said. 'When it comes to belief, magic . . . Çetin İkmen—'

'I am not Çetin İkmen,' he said. 'Teker wants him to see the boy. But I don't know what good that will do.'

She smiled. 'You're much better-looking than Çetin Bey.'

She saw him rake his fingers through his hair.

'Come to bed,' he said. His tone was desperate, almost whining. It annoyed her.

She put her hairbrush down and turned. 'Don't order me around, Mehmet Bey.'

She saw him lower his gaze, but he said nothing.

'It's not my fault that your only suspect is a boy you think is either mad or playing at madness. Much of your confusion comes from the fact that you can't accept that evil may be personified,' she said. 'But the Devil is real, Mehmet. Trust me.'

'Why?'

She discarded her dressing gown and climbed naked on to the bed.

'Because I love you,' she said. 'And because I have seen the Devil.'

43

'Where?'

'Everywhere.'

He kissed her breasts. She could have stopped the conversation there. Men were such single-minded idiots when it came to sex. But he'd started it and she was determined to give him her opinion.

She held him away from her with one hand while she massaged his penis with the other – to reassure his ego.

'I've seen the Devil in the faces of politicians many times,' she said. 'I see him in the eyes of the property developers who demolish people's homes, and outside the windows of jewellers' shops in all his lurid glory.'

'Gonca—'

'He exists, Mehmet,' she said. 'He uses the souls of the greedy, the power-crazed and the vengeful. If that boy you have in your cells really has seen the Devil, then he is just the same as me, and am I, your lover, a madwoman?'

'I don't know,' he said as he straddled her. 'All I do know is that I need you.'

She laughed. 'Well come on then, my prince. We can't have you coming too soon like a frustrated teenager.'

Had he really heard what she had said before he gave himself over to making love to her? Gonca hoped so. But what she hadn't told him was what she had heard from her father and some of the other old gypsies that she knew. The pulse of evil in the city had quickened of late, so they said. Only the Devil himself could make that happen. The old people interpreted this as the Prince of Darkness coming to claim his own.

Chapter 5

'Letters? Only very rarely saw her write any.'

Selin İnce was a pleasant enough woman, but Çetin İkmen seriously doubted her abilities as a domestic. Fatima Rudolfoğlu's apartment, though cleaner than those of her brothers, had been far from spotless.

'So you were unaware of the fact that Fatima Hanım and her brothers wrote to each other?' he asked.

'News to me,' she said. 'As far as I knew, they never spoke and so they didn't communicate.'

'You went to the bank for your employer, and the post office?'

'Which is why I know she only ever sent a few letters,' Selin said. 'Through the post, that is. She must've slipped any letters she wrote to the old men under their doors. But I never saw her do it. To be honest, Inspector, I never saw her leave her apartment at all. I did her shopping, such as it was, and no one else visited, not for ten years at the very least. That Osman who did for Mr Yücel might know something.'

'He claims he doesn't.'

'Oh, well then . . .'

'Mr Osman Babacan, like you, knew nothing of any letters between the siblings, and yet there were a considerable number. All four of them wrote to each other on a regular basis. We've found drawers full of them in all the apartments. Are you sure you've never seen anyone apart from Mr Babacan come to the house?'

'Certain,' she said. 'Why would they? That house is a terrible place these days, full of mould and rot and rats. And it's not as if Fatima Hanım, at least, had anything of value. A few bits of jewellery was all.'

'How did you come to work for Fatima Hanım, Selin Hanım? If the Devil's House is so forgotten, how did you know about it?'

'Oh, I'm Moda born and bred,' she said. 'My grandmother worked in the house for Perihan Hanım – that's Fatima Hanım's mother. She was only a girl when she started there, my grandmother, but she loved Perihan Hanım, and so when my mother was old enough, she had her work in the house too. But by that time Perihan Hanım was dead and so Mum only worked for Fatima Hanım. She rarely saw the gentlemen. I took over ten years ago.'

'Did your mother or your grandmother ever say why the house was divided up into apartments?' İkmen said.

'No. Fatima Hanım and her brothers no longer spoke, but Mum and Granny never told me why. Don't know if they knew. But even if they had, they wouldn't have said. Very private about their employers, they were.' She shook her head. 'As for me, I never spoke to anyone about what I did, except to my husband. It was sad. I don't know what was going on with the old men, but in the last few weeks of her life, Fatima Hanım began to go demented. I told her to call Dr Tanis, but she wouldn't. Said he was a crook.'

'In what way was Dr Tanis a crook?'

She shrugged. 'Don't know. He always did her pills up for her correctly.'

'You say she was beginning to dement,' İkmen said. 'Why did you think that?'

'Because of the ghosts,' she said.

'Ghosts?'

46

'Yes. She said she could hear them in the walls. Of course, I couldn't. There's no such thing as ghosts, although my husband would disagree. Said she heard them talking.'

'About what?'

'She never said. But it upset her. One time she took to her bed and pulled the covers over her head. That wasn't like her. In spite of her age, she was always fearless. Sometimes when I used to leave her to go home, I'd ask her whether she was frightened to stay in that great big apartment all on her own. But she wasn't. She always said she wasn't frightened of anyone. In fact she used to say that people should be frightened of her.'

At first she thought they were men. Then, as they got closer, she noticed that the shorter of the two figures moved more like a girl. They were mucking about, pushing each other and laughing. They looked a bit scruffy, and as Gila passed them, she clutched her bag a little closer to her side. The city was full of pickpockets and all sorts of undesirables, especially now there were so many refugees from Syria on the streets. Just briefly she saw a pair of very pale eyes underneath a dark hood, but then she looked away.

The Galata Bridge was always busy, day and night, especially in the summer, when the city was full of tourists. Then there were the fishermen who hung their lines into the waters of the Bosphorus on one side and the Golden Horn on the other, all hoping to catch something tasty for their lunch or supper. Gila lived in trendy Cihangir, amid the ornate nineteenth-century buildings of the late Ottoman period, but she worked across the bridge in the Old City for a small publishing house whose office windows looked out over the Grand Bazaar. Usually she took the tram to work, from Karaköy to Beyazıt. But this morning she hadn't been able to face it. Every tram had arrived packed and so she'd decided to walk. It was a beautiful day, so why not?

She had almost reached the end of the bridge when she heard a commotion behind her. Some people were shouting, and someone was on the ground. She walked back, and as she got closer, she realised that the people were speaking English. A woman was screaming for help, and one of the fishermen was trying to get the person on the ground, a man with grey hair, up on his feet. Another man was shouting at the fisherman to leave him where he was.

'Can I help?' Gila said.

The man who had pushed the fisherman away looked up. Gila saw that he had blood on his shirt.

'He's been stabbed,' he said.

'Your friend?'

'Yes. Get an ambulance or something, will you!'

Gila took her phone out of her handbag and dialled 112.

Selin İnce's husband Bilal had the look of a man who had prob-ably been a bit of a villain in his youth. Short and powerfully muscled, he reminded İkmen of a bouncer outside a low-rent brothel where the punters were all drunk. Mr İnce, however, was a born-again Muslim, a fact that he was very keen to impress upon Çetin İkmen. Not that İkmen was about to discount him as a suspect in the deaths of the Rudolfoğlu siblings just because of that. The policeman would reserve judgement until forensic reports were in and he'd managed to check out Mr İnce's account of his movements over the previous weekend.

Once the interview was over, İkmen went outside to the car park for a smoke, where he was approached by that very unnerving technical officer, Sergeant Turgut Zana. İkmen was only really on nodding acquaintance with Zana, and so he was surprised when the Kurd walked up to him and said, 'You need someone who can read Ottoman script. I know such a person.'

48

İkmen hadn't exactly broadcast the existence of the Ottoman letters to the whole department, but somehow Zana had found out. Maybe it was because people often had conversations around him without actually noticing he was in the room.

İkmen lit his cigarette. 'And who is that, Sergeant?'

'She's in the traffic department.'

'A woman.'

'Constable Demirtaş,' Zana said.

'Do you know how well Constable Demirtaş can read Ottoman script? She'd need to be fluent.'

'She studied it at university.'

If she did, she was wasted in the traffic division. But İkmen knew it had to be true. Sergeant Zana wouldn't make it up, because he couldn't. Lies were not precise, and he didn't do anything that wasn't a hundred per cent accurate.

'Well then, with the permission of her superiors, she'd better come and see me,' İkmen said.

'She's already had that conversation,' Zana said.

'Really?'

Again, he wouldn't lie, but how had Zana managed to tell this constable about İkmen's case and persuade her to speak to her superiors in such a short space of time? If İkmen hadn't known that wasting words on pointless details like that would only irritate the Kurd, he would have asked him. Instead, he said, 'I'd better meet her.'

'She finishes her shift at six p.m. May I instruct her to come and see you then?'

İkmen had planned, barring accidents and emergencies, to be ensconced in the Mosaik Bar with a glass of cognac at 6 p.m. He scowled. Then he had a thought. Everyone knew how he led his life, even, probably, this Constable Demirtaş.

'You may,' he said. 'Tell her to meet me at the Mosaik Bar in Sultanahmet at six.'

Unlike some of İkmen's colleagues, Turgut Zana didn't look at all surprised.

'Very well,' he said, then turned and walked away.

The local woman who had accompanied the British couple, their two sons and a friend to the hospital was called Gila Saban. She was clearly very shaken up, but not nearly as traumatised as the family of Mr Simon Oates. He had been dead by the time the ambulance arrived at the Cerrahpaşa Hospital. While the family mourned, Süleyman interviewed Miss Saban.

A pale single woman in her early forties, Gila Saban was well-spoken and, in spite of the ordeal she had just been through, keen to help in any way she could.

'Mrs Oates told me that her husband just dropped to the ground,' she said. Süleyman had bought her a coffee from a stall outside the hospital, which she clung on to with white knuckles. 'I saw the blood. I called the ambulance.'

Süleyman had learned of the attack when the ambulance service called police headquarters to request an escort for their vehicle. Could another sudden stabbing mean that the incarcerated boy in the black tracksuit was innocent? Or was this maybe a copycat offence?

'Did you see anyone near the family?' he asked.

'I had been in front of them, so no,' she said.

'I imagine you know that the Galata Bridge has a reputation these days.'

'For pickpockets, yes,' she said. 'I always make sure the clasp of my handbag is facing inwards when I walk across. But I don't think Mr Oates was robbed. My understanding is that they were all looking at the views when he was just, well, stabbed.'

'Did you see anyone running away from the scene, towards Eminönü or Karaköy?'

'Not that I remember, no,' she said. 'One of the fishermen on the bridge came over to help, but he was doing all the wrong things. Then some other fishermen came and tried to keep Mr Oates warm with their jackets. He was still speaking then.'

'Did you hear what he said?'

'Not really,' she said. 'My English is good, but in a situation like that it was as much as I could do to call the ambulance and try to comfort Mrs Oates.' She frowned. 'What I did see, although this probably reflects my own prejudices more than reality, was a couple of young people clowning around.'

'Where?'

'They were coming towards me, from Eminönü. They were laughing and jumping around. They made me feel a bit . . . uncomfortable for some reason. But they didn't say anything to me, and once they'd gone—'

'Towards the Oates family.'

'I guess. Once they'd gone, I thought no more about them.'

'Can you describe these young people?'

'A bit. One was wearing jeans. The other was dressed in a black tracksuit or one of those all-in-one things, I think. With a hood.'

'With a hood? Are you sure?'

'Oh yes. They both wore hoods. Until they got closer, I thought that both of them were male. Then I saw that the shorter of the two, the one in the tracksuit, moved like a woman. Oh, and as they passed me, I saw that one's eyes.'

'The woman?'

'The one I believe is a woman, yes,' she said. 'They were very strange. So pale. Grey, I imagine. But in the sunlight they looked almost silver. Like two drops of mercury.'

Physically Fatima Rudolfoğlu hadn't been in bad shape for such an old lady. There was some evidence of arthritis, her liver was

51

fatty and her kidneys were not in a good condition. But in spite of her untreated diabetes, there was nothing immediately life-threatening. According to her cleaner, the old woman had started to dement, but then at her age that was to be expected. Had she not been stabbed through the chest, Arto Sarkissian was convinced she would still be alive. Ditto, amazingly, her brother Yücel, who had been one hundred years old.

However, even before he began to work on them, the pathologist knew that the bodies of Kanat and Kemal Rudolfoğlu were going to be different. Kanat, who had lived in an apartment so filthy it stank, presented with multiple pressure sores and a jaundiced complexion that indicated liver failure. The corpse was emaciated, and Arto wondered when he had last eaten, and what. His brother Kemal was also stick thin, but his corpse was free of sores and only a very pale shade of yellow. He, however, had a large mass sticking out of his right thigh. A tumour, although whether it was malignant or not was yet to be deduced.

Toxicology on all four bodies had come back from the laboratory. All except Kemal had taken various medications for things like arthritis and constipation. But there had been no substances in excess in any of their systems – and that included alcohol. They had all died in exactly the same way, which was via a single stab wound to the heart. Given their advanced age, whoever had killed them had not had to be physically strong. Mental strength was another matter. Stabbing one person through the heart required a high degree of resolve. Doing it four times indicated a determination and conviction that was unusual and frightening.

The thought made Arto Sarkissian shudder.

Whoever this offender was had killed four times, almost certainly while his victims slept. What else was he capable of?

*   *   *

'Inspector Süleyman?'

He looked up from his phone. He was standing outside the hospital, trying to get a signal and smoking a cigarette.

'Yes?'

'I've been trying to reach your department, then I was told that you were here.'

The man was wearing a white coat, so he was probably a member of the hospital staff.

'You are?'

'Şahin Uslu,' he said. 'I'm lead pathologist here.'

'Ah.'

The two men shook hands, rather awkwardly on Süleyman's part as he attempted to juggle both his cigarette and his phone.

'I know you are busy,' Dr Uslu said. 'I've heard about that unfortunate incident on the Galata Bridge . . .'

'The victim will not come into your hands but will be sent to our own pathologist, as we believe this is part of an ongoing series of attacks.'

'Yes, well I may have more work for you, Inspector,' Şahin said.

Süleyman frowned. 'How so?'

'Yesterday evening, the body of a young woman was brought in. She'd died aboard a packed tram that had originated at Kabataş. She was discovered at Zeytinburnu. I should say here that this woman is not the first person whose body has been delivered to me from a packed tram. People with conditions like angina and asthma do succumb in such ghastly conditions from time to time. And this woman had a heart murmur.'

'What has that to do with us?' Süleyman said.

'Everything, I'm afraid,' Dr Uslu said. 'Because it wasn't the heart murmur that killed this woman, but an overdose of heroin. And before you say anything, she was no user.'

'How do you know?'

'Because the drug was, I believe, administered to her by force. I found heavy bruising on her left thigh, at the centre of which was a puncture wound.'

'She was spiked?'

'Through her clothing, I checked. That was where the drug was administered, and there was a lot of it.'

'You're certain it was heroin?'

'Absolutely.'

Could this be a third murder perpetrated in public? Süleyman put his cigarette out and then immediately lit another. Heroin? Not the drug of choice on the streets for a long time; that was a cheap synthetic cannabinoid called bonzai. Heroin was expensive.

'You should also know, Inspector,' the doctor said, 'that the woman's torso is covered with old bruises, possibly inflicted by her husband. Her name was Saira Öymen; she was twenty-four, covered, and had been travelling on that tram alone. The husband is keen to bury her body, but I have not released it. Perhaps your own pathologist would like to confirm my findings?'

Chapter 6

Although moth-eaten and cockroach-infested, the Devil's House was not yielding very much in the way of useful forensic evidence. So far, no identifiable fingerprints belonging to anyone apart from the Rudolfoğlus and their retainers had been discovered. Or footprints. Strange that rooms so mired in filth should result in so little evidence.

İkmen was at his usual table outside the Mosaik Bar. As ever, his cat sat in the chair directly to his right, eating small pieces of fish donated by the waiters, while İkmen drank cognac and smoked. Unusually, he was without human company, although not for long, he hoped. He was waiting for the Ottoman language graduate who worked in Traffic to turn up.

Had this Demirtaş woman been recommended by anyone except Turgut Zana, he would have been tempted to believe the whole thing was a joke. But Zana didn't make jokes. What was a woman who had studied something so complex and unusual doing looking at CCTV screens in the traffic division?

'Inspector İkmen?'

He'd been looking down at a kitten that Marlboro had been hissing at underneath his table, so the first thing he saw was a pair of black boots. Then he saw the biking leathers, then the face. She was very dark, but if she was a friend of Turgut Zana's, she was likely to be. She was also very statuesque, and extremely handsome.

'Constable Demirtaş, I presume.'

He held out his hand, which she took with a smile. Her grip was firm and dry, like a man's.

'Sit down,' he said.

'Thank you.'

She took off her heavy leather jacket and placed it under the table with her helmet. The kitten was long gone.

'What would you like to drink?' İkmen asked.

'Just Coke,' she said. 'I'm driving.'

'Quite right. Where's your bike?'

'I've a friend who works at the Ambassador Hotel,' she said. 'He lets me park in front of the entrance. The boys on the desk keep an eye on it for me.'

İkmen caught the attention of one of the waiters and ordered their drinks.

'What kind of bike have you got?' he asked.

She smiled. 'A Ducati Streetfighter 848. It's my baby.'

'Sounds powerful.'

'It is.'

'I may be wrong, but I don't see your friend Sergeant Zana riding fast bikes,' İkmen said.

She laughed. 'Turgut? No. He's done the statistics and decided it's far too dangerous.'

'How do you know each other?' İkmen offered her a cigarette, which she took.

'We grew up on the same street, in Diyarbakır,' she said. 'He was always the go-to kid if you had trouble with mathematics, and I did. Turgut used to do my homework – and almost everyone else's. He was easily the brightest boy in our district, and when he got into İstanbul University, well, that confirmed it.'

Their drinks arrived.

'What about you?' İkmen asked.

'Languages were always my thing,' she said. 'At home, like most people in Sur district, we spoke Kurmanji. But of course we all learned Turkish too, and because my mother's native tongue is Zaza, I learned that as well. I can get by in Arabic, but when I went to high school, I fell in love with English.'

'Why on earth are you wasting your life in Traffic?' İkmen asked. 'I have enormous respect for my colleagues in that department, but your language skills, surely, must have prepared you for a career in academia or—'

'It's a job,' she said. 'It means I'm able to live here in İstanbul and have my bike.'

İkmen shook his head. So much talent, just thrown away. Young people deserved better. The reality, however, was that there just weren't enough jobs.

'Turgut told me that you need someone to translate some documents written in Ottoman Turkish,' she said.

She obviously didn't want to talk about her employment status, and İkmen knew that he should get to the point.

'Yes. Another of your talents, I believe.' He took a sip of cognac and then continued, 'Why Ottoman, may I ask? Like Sergeant Zana, you're—'

'Kurdish,' she said. 'Why not? Our history is inescapably linked to the Turks. Whatever we may think of each other, we share a past. Also, isn't there a saying about knowing as much as you can about your enemy?' She smiled.

İkmen smiled too. 'Point taken. Well, Constable Demirtaş, do I have a puzzle for you. As I'm sure Sergeant Zana has told you, I am currently working on a case involving the murder of four people, all members of the same family.'

'In Moda.'

'Correct. These people, three in their nineties, one over a hundred, were siblings who didn't speak to each other: three men and a woman. They all lived in the house where they had been raised, which at some point they had converted into four

57

separate apartments. All four were stabbed through their hearts by an unknown killer for reasons we do not understand.'

Demirtaş shook her head. 'That is macabre. I heard about the deaths on the news, but of course we don't get details.'

'So far we have no witnesses, no incriminating forensics, a couple of unlikely suspects and a lot of questions,' İkmen said. 'What may provide some answers are letters written by the siblings, one to another. Sadly for us, they are in Ottoman. Luckily for you, given your interests, they may provide an insight into the language as written by some of the last people to employ it in the country.'

'That is interesting.'

'I was hoping you'd say that,' he said. 'So if I can arrange with your superiors for your secondment to my department, will you do it? I won't lie, I will put you under pressure. We need this information yesterday. Trust me, these killings were deliberate, ritualistic and freighted with a meaning we can't even guess at the moment. What I can promise you in return is a cool, spacious office all to yourself, as much moral support as you require, tea—'

'I'll do it,' she said. Then she laughed. 'You don't have to beg.' She leaned forward and stroked Marlboro underneath his filthy, whiskery chin. 'I'm the girl who rides a Ducati Streetfighter, Inspector. Nothing makes me sweat.' She looked up at him. 'And I'm a Kurd.'

Moda was the sort of place where Kerim Gürsel could almost be himself. Liberal and arty, heavy on coffee shops and restaurants, it had once been the home of the late great king of Anatolian rock musicians, Barış Manço. It was an easy place for a gay man to be, even if he was a police officer.

Kerim had spent the afternoon getting into the cellar of the Devil's House, which was no mean feat. The only entrance that was visible had been bricked up for decades, and when he and a group of constables had managed to get in, they'd found a filthy, dark, cavern-like space filled to the ceiling with discarded furniture. Had Miss Rudolfoğlu's 'voices' been, in fact, this furniture shifting as the timbers supporting the house expanded in the humid İstanbul summer? Kerim didn't know anything about acoustics, but he did know that old buildings made noises. He'd been to Inspector Süleyman's parental home once. A nine-teenth-century wooden villa in the pretty Bosphorus village of Arnavautköy, the entire structure had creaked like a sailing ship.

Now out of the stifling atmosphere of the Devil's House, Kerim was reluctant to go back to the small apartment in Tarlabaşı that he shared with his fake wife Sinem. His lover, the transsexual Pembe Hanım, would almost certainly be there too, but for once he wanted to be alone.

As a child, Kerim had visited Moda occasionally with his parents. His father had an aunt who had lived in an apartment overlooking the long-disused ferry terminal on the Sea of Marmara. An elegant late Ottoman structure, the terminal had always been one of Kerim's favourite pieces of city architecture. A bright summer evening was the perfect time to take a gentle stroll down to the old building and look at the sea. On his way back, he decided to stop for a coffee in the garden of the Koço restaurant, which was where his great-aunt used to sometimes take the family when they visited.

He wasn't the only loner having a drink beneath the trees and looking at the deep blue waters of the Sea of Marmara. There were plenty of couples, but also a lot of people enjoying drinks, cigarettes and sometimes books on their own. And if Kerim was hard up for company, there were always the many well-fed street cats to entertain.

But he wasn't to be deprived of human company for very long. An elderly man who walked with a stick was finding it difficult to lower himself into a chair, so Kerim went over to help him.

'Oh, thank you,' the old man said as Kerim made sure that he was comfortable. 'This blasted arthritis will render me house-bound!'

'I don't think so, sir,' Kerim said. 'You just need a little help sometimes.'

The old man put a hand on his arm. 'Do let me buy you a drink to show my gratitude . . .'

'It's nothing,' Kerim said.

'But I insist!'

Kerim Gürsel had been brought up to respect elderly people, and so he sat down opposite the old man, Rauf Bey, and accepted a coffee from him. Rauf Bey himself drank whisky, which, he claimed, had a beneficial effect upon his joints. Before he retired, the old man had been a lawyer.

'Property law was my speciality,' he told Kerim. 'Obtaining planning permissions and land permits. Don't think I'd like to do that now.'

Kerim, unwilling to get into yet another conversation about the iniquities of modern property development, said, 'So do you live in Moda, Rauf Bey?'

'Yes,' he said. 'All my life. It's always been a very accepting sort of place. I like that. A man like myself can live alone – with the exception of my fish – with no questions asked. I can barely believe we have a multiple murderer in our midst.'

'Oh, the . . .'

'The Teufel Ev, yes,' he said. 'I had not even realised that the Rudolfoğlus were still alive! Modern people lead such isolated existences.'

Kerim had a choice. He could tell the old man he was a police officer involved in the investigation, or he could keep it to himself. People in smart suburbs like Moda generally disapproved of the police, regarding them as fascists. But Kerim liked Rauf Bey, and so he told him the truth.

Rauf Bey nodded. 'Bringing bad people to justice is a good thing,' he said. 'Whoever killed the Rudolfoğlus must have been an unusual character. I mean, I count myself as old at seventy-five, but they had to be in their nineties at least.'

'Yes.'

'Frightening,' he said. 'Who would murder the frail elderly like that? Not that the Rudolfoğlus were particularly nice people. Locking themselves away with their secrets! And their father was a terrible man.'

'I've heard.'

'My father once told me that Rudolf Paşa used to whip his servants with a strap tipped with silver spikes. Can you imagine such a thing! And that youngest son of his was no better, desecrating a shrine. That house was named for the Devil for a very good reason – if one believes in such things, of course.'

Kemal Rudolfoğlu had been the youngest of the three boys. He had also been the one that Inspector İkmen believed had practised alchemy. But when had he desecrated a shrine, and where?

Rauf Bey was cheerfully forthcoming. 'Oh, years ago,' he said. 'Before I was born. He can't have been much more than thirteen. Not that his age is any excuse.'

'Do you know what he did to this shrine?' Kerim asked.

'The story goes that when he was discovered, he was trying to dig up the floor,' the old man said. 'God knows why. If the old owners of the restaurant were still here, they'd probably be able to tell you. But they went back to Greece.'

Kerim frowned. 'This restaurant?' he said.

'Yes.'

'Why? Did Kemal Rudolfoğlu desecrate their church?'

'No, the ayazma of St Katherine,' said Rauf Bey.

'That's a spring, isn't it?'

'Yes,' he replied. 'It's in a cave where, it is said, a miracle-working ikon of the saint was discovered hundreds of years ago. And it's right underneath this restaurant.'

Had they lost interest in him? No one had come to peer at him through that flap for many hours. He didn't like it when they did that, but it was still better than just him and his head. Because in spite of his best efforts to keep him out, the Devil had got in.

He was going to carry on killing, so he said. He'd only stop when he wanted to, and anyone who tried to make him stop was a traitor. But how could you be a traitor to the Devil? The whole thing was confusing. He'd always been good, so why had the Devil chosen him?

The door opened suddenly, making him jump. Instinctively he shrank into the one blanket they'd given him.

A policeman in a uniform loomed in the doorway.

'Inspector says you can go,' he said. 'On your feet!'

He jumped up. *You can come killing with me if you want*, the Devil said.

'No!' he exclaimed.

'No what, nutter?' the policeman said.

He pulled him through the door and pushed him along the corridor.

'Back on the streets with you!'

The Devil tried but failed to make him respond with *Drop dead, son of a whore!*

There were taps around the walls from which, presumably, the sacred water flowed.

'I've no idea why I never knew this was here,' Kerim said as he looked around the tiny shrine. When the old man had taken him down the steps at the back of the restaurant, he'd realised he'd seen them many times before. What he hadn't noticed was the doorway they led towards.

'I assume your family are Muslim,' Rauf Bey said.

'Yes, but pretty secular,' Kerim replied. 'I've been inside more churches than mosques.'

'Few people come here,' the old man said.

Dark ikons depicting St Katherine, the Virgin and Child and the Crucifixion were displayed in glass-fronted cabinets at the rear of the small chapel. Unlit candles lay in bundles beside a sand-filled trough. One lit candle stood in a second trough, a sign of a prayer offered to the saint for protection, for the dead or just out of habit.

'It's said that fishermen found this spring back in Byzantine times,' Rauf Bey said. 'Then they found an ikon of St Katherine and someone decided that this was her sacred spring. *Voilà!* A shrine dedicated to St Katherine.'

His eyes glittered in the candlelight, and there was a moment when Kerim felt as if the old man might be coming on to him. But then it passed.

'So how do you know that one of the Rudolfoğlu boys tried to dig up the floor?' Kerim asked.

'I don't *know* anything of the sort, young man.'

'No, but you said that it was said . . .'

'By a friend of my late father, yes. He was very upset about it. Konstantinos Bey was Greek, so he felt the violation acutely. Also, so my father said, it was Konstantinos Bey who found the boy.'

Kerim shook his head. 'What happened?'

'Konstantinos Bey stopped him.'

'Is there a police record of the incident, do you know?'

Rauf Bey shrugged. 'I don't know, but I doubt it. Konstantinos Bey used to work for the Rudolfoğlus.'

'In what capacity?'

'He was their gardener. Apparently he was very good at it, too, according to my father. Quite the artist in his time, Konstantinos Apion.'

'I take it he's dead?'

'Oh, long ago,' the old man said. 'But I believe his son still lives in the city.'

'Do you know him?'

'No. Why do you ask?'

'The Rudolfoğlus were recluses,' Kerim said. 'So we're looking for anyone who may have had contact with them, recently or in the past.'

'That house of theirs has to be worth a fortune, or rather the land beneath it is,' Rauf Bey said.

'We are looking for any potential beneficiaries,' Kerim said. 'But as far as we know, the Rudolfoğlus all died without issue.'

'Yes, I imagine they did.' He shook his head. Then he smiled. 'Unless, of course, Fatima Hanım had the Devil's child.'

In spite of being a shithole full of thieves and con men, İstanbul was a good place to be if you were on the streets and needed somewhere to sleep. While half the city was being torn down, the other half was under construction, which meant that the homeless could usually find somewhere to bed down. This time it was an old shop in the upmarket Bosphorus village of Yeniköy.

'I could get used to this,' the girl said as she threw her jacket on the floor and sat down. 'Bosphorus views! Look!'

Her partner, a young man in jeans and a T-shirt, stood and smoked by a shattered window. Huge, thick shards of broken glass littered the floor. 'We've been lucky the last few weeks,' he said. 'Come winter it'll be fucking awful again.'

'Oh, enjoy the fun while it lasts!' the woman said. She took a small tin out of her tracksuit bottoms and laid it on the ground in front of her.

The man shook his head.

'What?' She rolled up the sleeve of her sweatshirt.

'You're being greedy,' he said.

'And you're never ready to get fucked?'

He looked away as she wrapped a filthy handkerchief around her thin arm and took a syringe out of the tin.

'You'll end up in the nuthouse,' he said softly.

She laughed. 'So what's new? You think that one more hit here or there is going to make any difference? Anyway, we're having fun!'

She slapped up a vein in the crook of her elbow and shoved the needle in. As she plunged the contents of the syringe into her body, she sighed with relief. Then she lay back and closed her eyes.

He waited as long as he could, as long as the irritation in his skin would allow, and then he took the syringe from her limp fingers and looked at it. She'd left precious little for him. He sat beside her. 'You're a selfish bitch.'

But she didn't hear him.

He unknotted the handkerchief around her arm and pulled it tight around his own bicep. Then he injected himself with the bloodied needle and lay down. He nuzzled into her shoulder and thought about how much he loved her.

Chapter 7

Nobody really knew how many people lived in İstanbul. Some said twelve million; some fourteen million. Others claimed that if you took the refugees from Syria into account it was more like sixteen million. Ömer Mungun didn't claim to know any more than anyone else, but what he did know was that the population of the city was huge. Every journey by car and especially by public transport confirmed this. As he looked at the CCTV footage from inside the tram where Saira Öymen had died, he wondered how anybody managed to stay sane.

Just identifying the woman was difficult. There were at least five covered women in that part of the carriage at any one time, and every time someone else got on, the whole configuration of the compartment changed. Sometimes the Öymen woman had her back to the sliding doors, sometimes she was in the middle of the carriage, and at one point she appeared to be leaning against someone's suitcase. Those around her shifted. Also, and just to make identifying what might have happened to her even more difficult, Saira Öymen herself was a cipher. Because her face was covered, there was no expression that might give a clue as to when and by whom she had been attacked.

So far ten people had come forward to speak to the police about what had happened, but none of them had seen anything untoward. Süleyman had spoken to the woman's husband, who had admitted that he had hit her but who denied any involvement with her death. Adnan Öymen had proudly declared himself 'no junkie', while claiming, with no sense of irony whatsoever, that his wife needed the odd slap in order to make her aware of her wifely duties.

Ömer played back a piece of footage that showed Saira Öymen looking at someone on her left. Another covered woman, so it seemed. Süleyman was convinced there was a connection between this and the attacks on the Englishman crossing the Galata Bridge and the boy in the Grand Bazaar. True, they were all random, but this one had included a narcotic substance while the others had been straightforward stabbings. Were they connected?

Tired, Ömer paused the CCTV and leaned against the back of his chair. The small office opposite Süleyman's was being prepared for someone who was coming to help Inspector İkmen interpret some old letters from his crime scene in Moda. Apparently these letters had been written by his victims in the old pre-republican Ottoman script. It was like Arabic, which Ömer knew, but obviously there were references and idioms he would be unable to interpret. He wondered why anyone had bothered to learn Ottoman. The president had said that he wanted people to learn it, but that was only very recently. Like his own language, Ottoman had, for many, many decades, been consigned to history.

But then, as Ömer knew only too well, some things came back.

Çetin İkmen's late father had always said that the Beyoğlu district of Çukurcuma contained more spies, con men and those with shifting identities than anywhere else in the whole of the city. Forty years ago, he'd had a point. But now Çukurcuma, though still in places shabby, was also very chic. Attracted by its many antique shops and cafés, the elite had moved in some years ago and created an artistic quarter that included the author Orhan

Pamuk's famous 'Museum of Innocence'. All this change did not mean, however, that the old Çukurcuma of the spy, the career criminal and the relentlessly eccentric had entirely disappeared.

İkmen hadn't climbed the many stairs up to the tiny apartment at the top of the old Mirzoyan Building on Faık Paşa Caddesi in over ten years. But with no obvious heirs to the Rudolfoğlu estate on the horizon, and because the alchemist of Üsküdar was long dead, he didn't feel as if he had a choice.

When he knocked on the scarred door, he wasn't sure that he'd find anyone in. He had to wait. But when the door opened, he saw a familiar face and figure.

The man frowned. 'Çetin İkmen?' he asked.

'Do I look so different?'

'Yes, you've got old,' the man said.

'Well you haven't, which means, I imagine, that you are still practising the dark arts. Which is excellent.'

The man shrugged. 'Come in,' he said. Then he called out, 'Rüya, dear, we have company.'

The Ottoman language expert was a cop! And a woman! Who was hot!

Ömer Mungun could hardly believe his eyes when he saw Kerim Gürsel escort what looked like a leather-clad escapee from one of his fantasies into the small office opposite the one he shared with Süleyman. Against all his own moral standards, Ömer pressed his ear to the door so that he could hear what they were saying.

He'd heard Kerim call the woman 'Constable' when she arrived; now he was saying, '. . . the office I share with Inspector İkmen, or across the corridor, which is Inspector Süleyman's office. The inspector or his sergeant, Ömer Bey, will always be able to answer your queries if we are out.'

'Thank you,' she said.

'Pleasure.'

Kerim could be so charming. But he was married, and so he was completely out of the running. Ömer felt his head spin. God, he'd only just seen this woman! What was he thinking?

'Now, can I get you some tea?' Kerim asked.

'I don't suppose you have coffee, do you?' she said. 'I know it's really impertinent of me, but . . .'

'Not at all! What would you like, latte, cappuccino . . .?'

'Well . . .' He heard her laugh a little. It was pleasantly husky. 'You know I come from the east, so I like my coffee strong.'

'Ah, Turkish coffee.'

'Perfect,' she said. 'But really strong, if that's OK, and no sugar. For reasons I won't bore you with, I was brought up on mirra coffee.'

Ömer felt his heart jump in his chest.

'What's that?' Kerim asked.

'It's a very condensed coffee,' she said. 'Brewed many times for many hours. People in Mardin district love it.'

'But you said you're from Diyarbakır.'

'I also said that for reasons I won't bore you with, I was brought up on mirra.'

They both laughed. Ömer ran away from the door before he heard any more. For a native of the eastern city of Mardin like himself, just hearing the word 'mirra' was enough to set the heart racing. He wondered what the constable's name was, and whether she always wore motorbike leathers.

He hoped so.

Even though he looked barely fifty, Sami Nasi was actually almost seventy. He'd been one of İkmen's father's students when he'd taught English at İstanbul University. Çetin remembered him as a good-looking and enthusiastic student. He could still see that person even in the gloom of the apartment.

'Come and meet Rüya,' Sami said. 'I think you'll approve.'

İkmen took his shoes off at the door and followed his host through into a room filled with books, cabinets and a large copper alembic still, which crouched on the floor amid a forest of test tubes held upright in retort stands.

'Still looking for that tiny gap then, Sami?' he said as he lit a cigarette.

Sami Nasi looked over his half-moon glasses and frowned. 'Your mother wouldn't have mocked me, Çetin.'

'And I am not mocking you either,' the policeman said. 'I don't entirely understand you, but I'm not mocking you. My mother was a witch so she didn't need proof of the unseen. Ditto the occultists I've met over the years. I don't know why you do. That's all.'

'Your mother, with respect,' said Nasi, 'was not a skilled stage magician. Anyway, what do you want?'

But before he could answer, İkmen saw the face of a woman looking at him. She smiled and said, 'Hello.'

He didn't answer immediately. Even by İkmen's somewhat outré standards, responding to a disembodied head, albeit a cheerful one on a silver platter, was unusual.

'That's Rüya,' Sami said. 'My assistant.'

'Hello . . .'

She smiled again.

'I repeat, İkmen, what do you want?' Sami said. 'I know anyway, but . . .'

'I want to know if you know anything about a family in Moda.'

'The Rudolfoğlus.'

İkmen sighed and sat down in the nearest free chair.

'I read the newspapers as well as people,' Sami said. 'My grandfather was acquainted with Rudolf Paşa. I'm sure you've worked out that had to be a possibility, so I know it's why you're here.'

'It's not the only reason,' İkmen said. 'But you have me on the first count. So Josef Paşa knew Rudolf Paşa.'

'Yes, but not for long,' Sami said.

A voice from the other side of the room interjected. 'Sami, do you want me to make tea?'

He looked at the disembodied head and smiled. 'Rüya, darling, you just stay where you are and look beautiful.'

'OK.'

'You don't mind about the lack of tea, do you, İkmen?' Sami asked.

'No, I'm just glad you didn't stop me smoking. Now, to get back to your grandfather . . .'

'Rudolf Paşa sought him out,' Sami said. 'He wasn't difficult to find. He performed all over the city and used his father's name.'

'His alleged father,' İkmen said.

Sami threw his hands in the air. 'Have it your way,' he said. 'He used the name of the great Hungarian magician Josef Vanek, originator of the only motile disembodied head illusion and lover of my great-grandmother Vanna. Happy?'

'Sami, I have no doubt you are, one way or another, a magician's progeny, but you are also an extremely confusing man who cannot be taken at face value,' İkmen said. 'Now, please continue.'

'Rudolf Paşa shared my grandfather's interest in the gap,' Sami said. 'The space between reality and illusion where real magic resides – if it does. This led him inevitably to the occult and the Kabbalah. He became fascinated by the connections Kabbalists believe exist between base matter and the divine.'

'Only a step away from alchemy,' İkmen said.

'Which Rudolf Paşa is well known to have practised. And yes, my grandfather did guide him in his early investigations. But then he stopped.'

'Why?'

Sami produced a bottle and two glasses out of nowhere and sat down. 'Cognac? It is French.'

'How delightful,' İkmen said. 'Yes. Small one. But doesn't the lady . . .'

He looked at where the head of Rüya had been, but she'd gone. Just an empty silver platter remained.

'Probably wanted to take a shower,' Sami said. 'We've been practising all morning.'

'Does this mean that you plan to perform again?'

'No point in having an assistant if I wasn't. Three years ago it occurred to me that, while disembodied head tricks are common, no one was doing my great-grandfather's act. Allowing the audience to interact with and actually hold the platter with the head bleeding on to it is something few can do. And that, if nothing else, Çetin, proves beyond doubt that my great-grandfather was indeed Josef Vanek. He taught my grandfather that trick when he returned to İstanbul in the late 1870s.'

'Maybe he just thought your grandfather would be interested,' İkmen said.

Sami glared at him. He knew that İkmen was aware that his great-grandmother had been a Syrian prostitute, and that his grandfather could have been the result of a liaison with almost anyone. But Vanek had undoubtedly taken an interest in the family, and Sami had inherited the head illusion unchanged from the nineteenth century.

'Can we please get back to Rudolf Paşa?' İkmen said.

Sami sighed. 'I never spoke to my grandfather about this, and so I got it second hand from my father.'

'What?'

'Alchemy is an art,' he said. 'I have been practising it all my adult life. My aim is to find the truth, the gap between reality and the unseen. Rudolf Paşa, according to my grandfather, had another aim.'

'Don't tell me: he wanted to make gold.'

'And power. But he didn't want to put the work in. Any work.' He sipped his cognac. 'He did what the lazy always do and made a pact with the Devil.'

'Ah, now . . .'

'I don't know whether he did that literally or not. Who am I to say? But according to my grandfather, someone died so that Rudolf Paşa could try and create gold. Someone was sacrificed. And yes, I do mean sacrificed to the Devil.'

İkmen lit another cigarette. 'Who?'

'I've no idea,' Sami said. 'I imagine it was probably someone who wouldn't be missed. A homeless person, perhaps. We'll probably never know. This happened at the beginning of the twentieth century, when my grandfather was already well into middle age and had other things on his mind: my father must have just been born.'

'So he ceased his association with Rudolf Paşa.'

'Yes, although he did perform for him once more, just before the First World War. Rudolf Paşa was a member of the Oriental Club.'

'That club for the Ottoman elite and foreign diplomats,' İkmen said.

'A lot of them were German,' Sami said. 'They had, maybe still have, a place out in Moda, near Rudolf Paşa's palace, where they used to meet in the summer months. My grandfather put on a show for them. But that was the end of it. My father used to say that my grandfather told him Rudolf Paşa looked thin and haunted.'

'The strain of living with guilt?'

'Maybe. But then anyone who takes a short cut to knowledge will pay the price,' Sami said. 'In this world or the next. And you know something, Çetin, they always realise this far too late.'

'I was looking over at Seraglio Point, the Topkapı Palace,' he said. 'None of us have ever been here before, Inspector.'

Richard Oates was the elder son of the dead man, Simon Oates. He'd just recently left university. He was the only member of the Oates party capable of talking to Süleyman without breaking down. However, the policeman was well aware that it was a terrible strain for such a young man to bear.

'You saw no one approach your father?'

'No.' He shook his head. 'Not only was I looking away, but I was also talking to my brother.'

'Paul.'

'Yes. The first time either of us knew anything was wrong was when we heard my dad grunt.'

'What did you do?'

'Nothing until Mum said, "Simon!" like Dad had done something stupid or something. Then I looked and saw that he was on the ground. Uncle Ben was trying to help him. Then some of the guys who had been fishing came over. I remember seeing blood, but for some reason I didn't think it was Dad's. Probably because there was a lot of it. Dad was screaming by this time, which was when that woman came to help. She called the ambulance.'

'Miss Gila Saban.'

'If that's her name,' he said. 'Can't thank her enough. She told the fishermen to go away because they weren't helping. Dad was just bleeding out by that time . . .' He put a shaky hand up to his head. 'Uncle Ben . . . er, Mr Benjamin Clarke, he was trying to staunch the bleeding, but he couldn't. The stomach's not like an arm. I . . .' He shrugged. 'I don't know what to tell you.'

Süleyman looked down at his notes. 'Well, let me ask you about Mr Clarke. Is he the brother of your mother, maybe?'

Richard Oates smiled briefly. 'No, he's my godfather,' he said. 'No relation, just a friend of Mum and Dad's from university. He's always been there for us.'

'I see.'

Richard Oates's face reddened.

Süleyman wondered whether his tone of voice had been unconsciously suspicious. Or was it his phrasing?

'No, I don't think you do,' Richard said. 'Uncle Ben isn't involved with my parents. Not in the way you think.'

'I do not—'

'I saw it on your face,' the young man said. 'People make assumptions because we all hang about together. But Uncle Ben is gay, OK? And before you start thinking God knows what about that, he's never touched me or my brother. I hope that's clear?'

His aggression had just erupted. Not violently or loudly, but it was clear that something very subtle in Süleyman's demeanour had made him bridle. Maybe the family and their friend had a lot of experience of suspicion. Or maybe Richard was just hypersensitive after his father's death.

'Yes,' Süleyman said. 'I apologise. I meant no offence.'

The young man said nothing.

'Did any of your family see anyone who might have attacked your father?' Süleyman asked.

Richard paused. Then he said, 'To be honest with you, Inspector, I've not even asked my mother. At first she just screamed and cried, and now all she does is sleep.'

Mrs Oates had needed to be sedated after her husband's death.

'Uncle Ben was walking alongside my dad when he was stabbed. But he says he didn't see it happen.'

'Did he notice anyone walk close to your father?'

'I don't know.' He shook his head. Then he frowned. 'Mind you, there was a kid . . .'

Gila Saban had said there had been two.

'He was sort of skipping along the pavement. Coming towards us. I didn't think anything of it at the time, because he was just a kid. He must have passed us . . .'

'At the same time as your father was stabbed?'

He shook his head. 'Around then,' he said. 'Sort of . . . I didn't take much notice, because I was looking at Seraglio Point. The only reason I think I remember him at all is because of his eyes. Really, really pale, you know, quite . . . well, off-putting.'

Chapter 8

Dear sister,

This is my annual Bayram letter. Again I ask with hope in my heart that you might finally comply with my request that can only be to the benefit of your soul. If it is the will of Allah that I outlive you, I will tell the entire tale, leaving no detail unexposed. I will not be mindful of the wishes of our brothers, Kanat and Kemal, as I have always been mindful of yours. I do not know whether they are aware that, on occasion, I can hear them both. These aural observations have left me in little doubt that Kanat lives in a hell of grief, while Kemal is become the kind of madman you and I both know only too well.

Fatima Hanım, I beg you to end this. Free our brothers, me and yourself before it is too late. You know what it is you must do. Did I not say this on that very first day? In spite of everything I remain your most affectionate brother,
Yücel Paşa

Barçın Demirtaş rubbed her temples. Deciphering official documents in Ottoman script was hard enough, but the spidery handwriting of a very old man made it doubly difficult. Then there was the content, which was disturbing.

Prior to this, she'd transcribed a letter from Fatima Hanım to Yücel Paşa, which seemed to tell a very different story, full of cheerful and seemingly heartfelt allusions to her affection for her brother. But Fatima's letter had also been a plea. She wanted to see her 'soul' Yücel and look upon his handsome face once again before she died. If only he would just open the door to his apartment and let her inside, then all would be well and they would be happy again. From the dates on the letters it seemed she'd written hers about a week before his request that she do something to free them all.

A knock on her office door temporarily interrupted her thoughts.

'Come in.'

She heard the door open and then close. Turning around, she saw two men, both smartly dressed. The younger and darker of the two had the kind of slanted eyes she was accustomed to seeing in the east. The older, taller man was a type of person rarely seen outside western Turkey. Slim and muscular, he too had black hair, dappled with flecks of grey, but his features, though large, were sensual, his eyes a little sleepy. Barçın had a good idea who he was because Turgut had told her that one of the homicide inspectors was 'thought to be handsome'. As usual, Turgut hadn't a clue. Barçın felt herself blush for the first time in years. Her attraction to him was instant.

'Constable Demirtaş?' the taller man said.

'Yes . . .'

'Sorry to disturb you, but I thought that since we are neighbours, we should introduce ourselves. I am Inspector Mehmet Süleyman, and this is my sergeant, Ömer Mungun.'

She stood up and shook their hands.

'I believe that Sergeant Gürsel has told you that if you have any problems while he and Inspector İkmen are out, you are welcome to come to either Sergeant Mungun or myself.' He smiled.

'Yes. Thank you, Mehmet Bey,' she said.

'No problem.' He walked over to her desk.

'These are the letters?'

'Yes, sir.'

He looked at Sergeant Mungun. 'Ömer?'

Mungun picked up one of the letters and frowned. 'Difficult handwriting,' he said.

She laughed. 'Nightmare.'

He smiled. 'I could probably transliterate,' he said. 'But Ottoman is not Arabic . . .'

'I know,' Süleyman said, a little high-handedly, she thought. 'Sergeant Mungun is from Mardin, so he can speak, read and write many languages.'

'Oh,' she said. 'I come from Diyarbakır.'

Sergeant Mungun's sallow complexion turned bright red. What did *that* mean? Was he embarrassed that they were both from the east?

'I, er, must confess that I knew you came from Diyarbakır. Sergeant Gürsel told me,' Ömer Mungun said. 'Um, he also told me that you like mirra.'

'Yes, I do,' she said.

'We, um, that is my sister and I, we make it at home. I can bring you some.'

'That's really kind,' she said. 'I'd like that.'

'But in the meantime, we have work to do, Sergeant Mungun,' Süleyman said. He bowed slightly. 'Constable Demirtaş.'

'Oh, er, thank you for your time, Mehmet Bey,' she said.

'My pleasure.'

When the men had left, Barçın sat down at her desk again. Her heart was beating fit to burst, and she was hot and exhausted. She'd never felt such a severe rush of lust in her life. And he was so meticulously polite! She breathed slowly to calm her nerves. What he had also been, however, was entirely disengaged. He'd agreed to look after her for Inspector İkmen, which he would do in an honourable manner. No more, no less. Sergeant

Mungun, on the other hand, had looked at her the way she had looked at Süleyman.

Barçın allowed herself a moment to steady her nerves, then she went back to the letters.

'İkmen.'

He took the call as he was walking towards Kabataş ferry terminal. He was on his way to meet Kerim Gürsel at the old Koço restaurant in Moda.

'Çetin Bey, this is Murad Peker from Ziraat Bank,' the caller said. 'You requested information about the financial status of the Rudolfoğlu siblings.'

'Ah yes,' İkmen said. 'Thank you.'

'I have emailed you full details, but I thought you'd like to know that, in short, the three brothers were effectively destitute.'

'Destitute?'

'For decades,' he said. 'Only Fatima Hanım had an income. She made monthly allowances to each of her brothers.'

'But they never spoke!' İkmen said.

'Maybe not, but money was transferred from her account to each of her brothers on the twenty-seventh of every month,' Mr Peker said.

'And where did she get money from?' İkmen said.

'From her father, or rather her father's investments. Rudolf Paşa bought shares in the 1890s in a German auto company called Daimler, which later became Mercedes Benz.'

'Fortunate. And he left all of those shares just to his daughter?'

'Yes.'

'How strange.'

'I thought you'd find that interesting,' Mr Peker said. 'You might also like to know that she was sole owner of the house, too. You may wish to pursue that through the family lawyer.'

'I will,' İkmen said. 'Thank you.'

He boarded the Kadıköy ferry deep in thought. If Fatima Rudolfoğlu had been the only beneficiary of her father's legacy, why had she even allowed her brothers to live in the house? Maybe the letters Constable Demirtaş was transcribing would shed some light on the matter. He was also very keen to speak to the family's lawyer, although Erdal Bey of the high-end firm of Kenter and Kenter was, apparently, still on his way back from his holiday in Hawaii.

İkmen sat down next to a sad-looking man of about his own age whose clothes smelt of stale cigarettes and rakı. They looked at each other briefly, acknowledged a fellow weary attitude to life with a nod and then looked out of the ferry window.

There were two basic ways in which what Rudolf Paşa had done could be viewed. Either his daughter was his favourite to the exclusion of all others, or for some reason he hated his sons. And what of his Turkish wife? As far as İkmen knew, the children had all been minors when their father died; why hadn't he left his worldly goods to her? Or had he? All he knew about Rudolf Paşa's wife was that she had been an Ottoman princess called Perihan. He didn't know when she had died, or how. In fact, he realised, he didn't know how the Paşa had met his end either.

Bilal was anxious, and so he was smoking again. He hated himself for it, but his wife was relieved. He had been unable to go out and look for work that morning. Now he was sitting on the sofa, curled up in front of the TV set.

'I don't know how you can be so calm,' he said to his wife when she sat down beside him. 'You've seen *CSI*. They'll know I've been in there.'

Selin İnce had always known she was much more intelligent than her husband.

'That's a television programme,' she said. 'It's not real.'

'The tests and all that are,' Bilal said. 'That's what the police do now. They'll know I've been in Fatima Hanım's apartment, I tell you!'

'Months ago, yes,' Selin said. 'I've cleaned since then; time has passed.'

'They still might find a hair or something. Selin, they made me give a sample for DNA. DNA! If that matches to a hair they find in the old woman's apartment . . .'

'It means what? That you've been to the workplace of your wife. What's wrong with that?'

'Well, yes, I—'

'You came with me one day because Fatima Hanım wanted her bedroom window frame nailed shut,' she said. 'What's wrong with that?'

'Nothing!'

'So . . .'

'Oh, I just hate having dealings with the police,' he said. 'That İkmen character made me nervous.'

'Well, I have to prepare mantı for tonight's dinner,' Selin said. 'Not all of us can just sit about. Pull yourself together. The old witch was nothing to you. Forget her.'

She went into the kitchen and shut the door.

Bilal curled into a ball and wondered whether it would have been better to tell İkmen about how he'd repaired Fatima Hanım's window. But he already knew the answer to that question.

The hospital's test results were identical to his own. The victim, twenty-four-year-old Saira Öymen, had died from a dosage of heroin of about 100 milligrams. Not enough to kill a seasoned addict, but plenty to put an end to a non-user. In addition, the drug had been cut with caffeine. In a person with mild heart arrhythmia, like Saira, could that too be significant? A concentrated dose of caffeine could lead to uncomfortable palpitations, but it was unlikely that would have killed her. Combined with heroin, however, it had proved lethal.

Arto Sarkissian was surprised that Saira hadn't vomited, especially when she became unconscious. But then there had been little in her stomach to bring up. It was also quite possible that the unaccustomed heroin had depressed her system so severely she had rapidly lost consciousness and stopped breathing at the same time. Even then she could still have been sick, but . . .

Mehmet Süleyman finally answered the call and Arto gave him his results and opinions. When he'd finished, he asked, 'Have you questioned her husband yet?'

'Yes. He's a somewhat stiff-necked individual, but there's no evidence he was on that tram – he has an alibi – and I can also say that he is almost certainly not a user. What I cannot understand,' Süleyman continued, 'is why anyone would kill someone using heroin. If the killer is a user himself, then why would he waste his own drug? And if he isn't an addict, why go to the bother of getting hold of heroin in order to kill? We've so far had two other seemingly random killings in the city, neither of which has employed heroin as a weapon.'

'I'm afraid I don't know,' Arto said. 'All I can tell you is that a heroin overdose can take hours to kill a user, but this, at most, took half an hour because she wasn't an addict.'

'So when do you think she died?'

'I've looked at the CCTV footage from the tram, but unfortunately, like Sergeant Mungun, I can't see her demeanour change because she is covered. Also, her body is held up by all the other passengers. But we know she got on the tram alive and we know it takes roughly forty-five minutes to get from Kabataş to Zeytinburnu. She was dead on arrival, so assuming the drug took half an hour to kill her, we're looking at the attack happening ten to fifteen minutes after she boarded. Do you have no witnesses, Inspector?'

'Only the woman who attempted to give her CPR, a nurse,' he said. 'You know how reluctant people are to come forward these days.'

'Sadly, I do.' Arto shook his head. Was İstanbul really becoming emotionally colder as it grew in size? He didn't know. 'I'll email you my report,' he said.

'Thank you, Doctor.'

Arto put the phone down. What was happening in his city? Why were apparently innocent people being killed for no clear reason?

'Well,' İkmen said, 'I must say that this case is revealing my appalling ignorance of İstanbul heritage. I almost feel as if I should hang my head in shame.'

Kerim Gürsel had met him at the Koço restaurant and then taken him to the ayazma of St Katherine. It was his first visit to the shrine.

'The ayazma is a Greek Orthodox shrine,' Kerim said. 'The people at Koço care for it on a day-to-day basis, but it is administered from the Aya Triada church on Bahariye Caddesi. I wanted you to see it so that you would understand my confusion over a story I've been told about this place.'

'Concerning the Rudolfoğlus?'

'Yes. A long-time local resident I met last night told me that when Kemal Rudolfoğlu was a boy, he reckoned about thirteen, he was caught desecrating this shrine by trying to dig up the floor.'

'Did he know when, exactly?'

'No. The reason I've brought you here, sir, is so you can see how solid this floor is.'

İkmen looked down at the stone slabs beneath his feet.

'So I'm here to disprove this person's story?'

'No,' Kerim said. 'Not necessarily. Kemal was young and the floor is very hard, but that doesn't mean he didn't try to pull the slabs up. What I . . . what we don't know is why.'

'And Kemal is dead,' İkmen said. 'Although we think he practised alchemy and we have been told that his father pursued a dark path. I've actually had that confirmed this morning. It's possible he followed in his father's footsteps, I suppose.'

'Yes, and we may also have some further corroboration,' Kerim said. 'I've arranged to meet with a priest at the Aya Triada at two o'clock. First thing this morning, I performed a search for someone with the surname Apion, but nothing came up. If the man I spoke to last night can be believed, Kemal Rudolfoğlu was prevented from damaging this place by someone called Konstantinos Apion, who was the Rudolfoğlus' gardener.'

'Long dead.'

'Yes, but my source told me that he believes his son still lives in the city.'

'And yet it seems not . . .'

'On the face of it, yes,' Kerim said. 'But you and I both know that a lot of Greek and Armenian families changed their surnames to ones that were more, well, Turkish.'

They had. Especially in the wake of attacks on Greek property in 1955.

İkmen nodded.

'I hope this priest, Father Anatoli, might be able to help. He does know the Devil's House.'

It was dark and damp inside the little shrine. İkmen could hardly make out the faces on the ikons in their glass cabinets. Although it provided some cool relief from the heat of the day outside, it was a melancholy place and he wanted to leave.

'We'll return to the crime scene and then go to see your priest at two,' he said. 'Who was your informant, by the way?'

'An old man called Rauf Karadeniz. He used to be a lawyer. Not criminal. A little odd.'

'Odd?'

'Told me he lives with a fish he calls Zenobia. I don't know what kind of fish. I didn't dare ask, to be honest.'

'This city has always been a hotbed of eccentricity,' İkmen said. 'I once had to go to a house in Sultanahmet where the resident, a young and rather pretty woman, had dug out a swimming pool in her basement for her twenty Van cats. She had entirely undermined the foundations of her neighbour's property.'

Kerim shook his head.

'I don't know the name Karadeniz,' İkmen said. He began to walk towards the exit. 'Come along, let's get out of here. We need to talk about the Rudolfoğlus' finances.'

Commissioner Teker didn't look up from her computer screen. But she knew that Süleyman had arrived, because she told him to sit down.

He sat. Then she looked at him.

'Three people have been murdered in public and you have let your only suspect go,' she said.

'With your approval, madam. The boy couldn't possibly have killed victims two and three because he was in custody at the time.'

'And yet he could have killed the boy in the Grand Bazaar,' she said.

'There was no evidence to connect him to that victim – except his very florid insanity. I couldn't hold him just for that.'

'And so what do we do now, Mehmet Bey?' She sat back in her chair and crossed her arms over her chest. 'People – and I include myself in that category – are beginning to wonder whether we have even the faintest idea about who we are looking for. Do we?'

A man and what could have been either another man or a woman could just be made out from CCTV in the bazaar, and the one witness to the attack on the Englishman on the Galata Bridge had talked about seeing a boy and a girl messing around in the vicinity. The attack on the tram had no useful CCTV footage and no witnesses.

'It could be two men, or a man and a woman,' Süleyman said. 'The only relative certainty is that they're young. According to the Galata Bridge witness, one of them has very pale blue or grey eyes. As to hair colour, they were both wearing hoods.'

'In the bazaar *and* on the bridge.'

'Yes.'

'Then circulate that description,' she said. 'I'm surprised you haven't done so already.'

'I was waiting . . .'

'For what? For someone else to die?'

'No . . .'

'Circulate it,' she said.

'Yes, madam.'

He was just about to leave her office when she said, 'Have you seen Inspector İkmen today?'

'No, madam. I imagine he's out.'

'And so is his sergeant,' she said. 'On the Ottoman script translator's first day. Poor organisation. I hope you are looking after Constable Demirtaş, Mehmet Bey.'

'Yes, I am,' he said. 'Although I have to say that Constable Demirtaş appears very comfortable, madam. Çetin Bey set everything up for her.'

'If you say so,' she said.

As he walked back to his office, Süleyman wondered why Teker had been so hostile, especially on the subject of Çetin İkmen. Was it perhaps because of what her predecessor Commissioner Ardıç had called 'İkmen going esoteric'? But then rumour was that İkmen had spent much of the morning with a man who called himself an alchemist.

Chapter 9

Her ribs hurt. Until she realised she'd been kicked, she thought maybe she had bronchitis again.

A man shouted, 'Get up!'

She opened her eyes. Ali was already standing up. He looked shaky. He was coming down. She wondered what time it was, what day.

The man who had shouted at her was fat and sweaty. He stood beside another man who looked as if he wrestled bulls for a living.

'Fucking junkies!' the fat man said. 'You think you can just break in anywhere and make yourselves at home!'

Elif got to her feet. She felt cold even though she knew that outside it was blisteringly hot. The sun shone harshly through the broken windows of the old shop.

'Who are you?' she said.

'Who are we?' the fat man said. 'Who are *you*?'

'We needed a place to sleep, Bey Efendi,' Ali said in his best creepy, craven arsehole voice.

'So why'd you think you could come and use my place?'

'We thought it was empty, Bey Efendi. We—'

The bull-wrestler kicked him in the groin and Ali sank to the floor. Elif felt an overwhelming urge to spit at the fat man. But she didn't. She didn't have to prove anything to anyone, and that included herself. But that didn't mean he didn't have it coming. He did.

'We'll go,' she said, picking up her rucksack as she moved towards Ali.

'You'll clear up the shit you've left all over my place,' the fat man said.

'What shit? We went to sleep.'

The fat man grabbed her around the back of the head and pulled her towards the middle of the room. He pointed to a pile of what was clearly dog faeces on the floor.

'That shit!' he said.

'That? That's dog shit,' she said. 'Any fucking moron can see that!'

It was then that he hit her and all hell broke loose.

Like most of the Greek Orthodox churches in İstanbul, the Aya Triada in Moda had once hosted a large congregation. But ever since the population exchanges between Greece and the newly formed Republic of Turkey in 1923, the Greek community had been dwindling. Some academics had calculated that it was now as low as just over two thousand souls in the whole country. Father Anatoli Ralli's disgruntled face seemed to Çetin İkmen to mirror all those years of decline, line by deep line.

'He changed his name to Mustafa Kaiserli,' the priest said.

'Did his family come from Kayseri originally?' İkmen asked.

'No. His real name, Apion, is Byzantine. Yiannis is a Byzantine Greek, like most of us here in our ancestral city.'

The subtext here was that İkmen and Gürsel, as Turks, were newcomers to İstanbul.

'But I imagine, like many of our people now, he wanted to just get on with his life and not have to answer any awkward questions. So he changed his name. Last I heard, he lived in Beşiktaş.'

'Does he come to Moda to attend church?' İkmen asked.

'No. Why would he?'

'I don't know . . .'

'Yiannis has made a new life. His father was almost a hundred years old when he died; he drove him mad.'

That had to be Konstantinos Apion, the Rudolfoğlus' gardener.

'Is Yiannis an old man?' Kerim asked.

'Not compared to me,' the priest said. 'Fifty something.'

'His father had him late . . .'

'His father did a lot of things wrong,' the priest said. 'When he stopped working for the Rudolfoğlus, he just did nothing. Kept by his own mother, whose house he eventually inherited. Some people said he had been cursed by that family.'

'What do you think?'

'I think that the children of Rudolf Paşa who told poor Konstantinos to go were as evil as their father. I don't remember them, but my parents did. Horrible, unnatural children.' He shook his head. 'No wonder their poor mother died young, after living with that German for all those years, and then with those children.'

'What was the matter with the children?'

'My mother said that they were just like statues. Always silent, staring, looking down their noses at people.'

'They were the children of a paşa,' İkmen said.

'They kicked my father's dog to death,' the priest said. 'Apparently they laughed. Said it didn't matter because it was a Greek dog. Do paşas' children normally behave like that, Inspector?'

İkmen sighed. 'No. No, I'll give you that.'

'My mother always believed that one or all of those children of the Devil's House killed Perihan Hanım.'

'Their own mother? Why?'

'Why not?'

The priest looked at him with stern, stony eyes.

İkmen waved a hand. 'Well, anyway,' he said, 'do you know

anything about the desecration of the ayazma of St Katherine by Kemal Rudolfoğlu?'

'Of course. That was why Konstantinos Apion was dismissed by the Rudolfoğlus,' he said.

'Because he caught the young Kemal digging up the floor?'

'If you already know the story, why ask me?'

'Because you might know why a thirteen-year-old boy was trying to raise a stone floor,' İkmen said.

'Well, I don't.'

'Anything underneath the ayazma?'

'Not as far as I know.'

'So why would Kemal dig it up?'

'I don't know. He was a little vandal.'

'I don't suppose you can be any clearer about this Mustafa Kaiserli's whereabouts than just Beşiktaş?' İkmen said.

The priest thought for a moment, then he said, 'No.'

Sergeant Mungun was sweet. First thing in the morning he'd walked into her office with a cezve and a tiny handleless cup and poured her the first cup of mirra coffee she'd ever had in İstanbul. Bitter and powerful, it was the genuine article made by a genuine son of Mardin. Barçın was bewitched. Whenever she filled her cup from the cezve, she smiled. Not so when she looked down at the Rudolfoğlus' letters.

A letter from Kanat to his younger brother Kemal dated, in the Muslim calendar, 14 Shaban 1369 barely made sense. Barçın had calculated that the year 1369 corresponded to 1950, so the Rudolfoğlus had all been under forty. The letter started abruptly, then it rambled.

Kemal,

Hamlet wrestled with mortality. I wrestle with consciousness. Why is it? Why can't you do something about it? You who create life (I've heard you). And if I hear you, so will she. You have been warned. Yücel is silent. Do you think he might be dead? Have you done anything to him? The lavatory is broken and I don't know what to do.

Your brother,

Kanat

Sergeant Gürsel had told her something about the Rudolfoğlus and their apartments. Kanat's had been the dirtiest. When he'd gone into the bathroom, Gürsel had found that neither the lavatory nor the shower worked. Could the lavatory have been broken since 1950? Only the bath had been operational. Had he used that as a toilet?

'Constable Demirtaş . . .'

The sound of a voice shocked her a little, and she gasped.

'I'm sorry I startled you,' Çetin İkmen said.

She looked up at him. 'Don't worry.'

'I realise that what you're doing must take a very high level of concentration.' He sat down opposite her. 'That said, I wondered whether we could have a discussion about what you've discovered so far.'

'Of course.'

'Are you yet gaining any impressions of the Rudolfoğlu siblings? Character traits? Habits?'

'The way they write falls into two groups,' Barçın said. 'One group is the three men, and the second group is Fatima Hanım.'

'The way they write?'

'There's paranoia in the men's letters,' she said. 'They all talk about concepts like consciousness, redemption, freedom, interspersed with banal stuff about broken lavatories and power cuts. Between the three of them there is a lot of discussion of "her", which I take it is Fatima Hanım.'

'How do they talk about her?'

'Yücel seems to tread carefully when he writes to her or mentions her to his brothers. The other two are angry. In fact they're all angry at her for something, but Yücel doesn't seem to be afraid. In this letter I've just read from Kanat to Kemal, it looks as if the latter may have had a woman with him in the house. That was back in 1950. Kanat talks about Kemal creating life, which I assume alludes to sex. He tells his brother that he can hear him, and warns him that "she" might be able to as well.'

İkmen leaned back in his chair. 'The old woman's cleaner said that in the last weeks of her life, Fatima Hanım heard voices in the walls.'

'But this was 1950.'

'Mmm. How does Fatima Hanım communicate with her brothers?'

'With great affection,' she said. 'From her perspective, if her letters are to be believed, there is no issue between herself and her siblings. She asks after their health, and towards the end of her life, she begs her brother Yücel to let her into his apartment so she might see him. This was in response to a letter from him begging her to allow him to tell about something. He says that Kemal is a madman because of this thing, and Kanat is consumed with grief. As yet I've no idea what it might be. Yücel won't tell while Fatima is still alive, so he says. But he will if and when his two brothers die.'

'Long ago Rudolf Paşa and his wife engaged a Greek gardener,' İkmen said. 'We've been trying to trace his son, who apparently still lives in the city. I've just come from an interview with a Greek priest over in Moda who very powerfully underlined the conviction some people had that the children had somehow taken on the supposed evil from their father. He even expressed a belief that maybe the children killed their mother.'

'Well that would cause chaos in a family, to say the least,'

94

Barçın said. 'But if that happened, how would they be able to get away with it, sir? They were children. When did their mother die?'

'Nineteen thirty-one,' he said. 'Her husband had died three years earlier. I suppose I need to know *how* she died. Not just the myth, the real story.'

'Do you think the gardener's son might know?'

'He might. I also have to speak to the family lawyer, who, hopefully, returns to the city tonight. Then we will find out who, if anyone, is now the proud owner of the Devil's House. Have you found any communication about money in the letters?'

'No, sir,' she said. 'Could that be significant?'

'Yes. The family banker told me that Rudolf Paşa left all his assets to his daughter when he died. She was nine at the time. Everything her brothers had, she gave them.'

'That is extraordinary!'

'Yes,' he agreed.

'It could account for their strange relationship,' Barçın said. 'But then again, would someone go mad or suffer from grief over something financial?'

İkmen smiled. 'Oh yes,' he said. 'Most definitely. Although I do think there is more to this than just money. A gut feeling only, but then as you will discover through working for me, Constable Demirtaş, I have come to trust those over the years.'

He rose to go.

'Oh, sir,' she said. 'There are a few letters written in modern Turkish mixed in with the Ottoman. Do you want me to look at those?'

'Yes, when you can,' he said. 'Especially if, although it is unlikely, they are between the siblings.'

'Are you going out?'

He put his phone back in his pocket before Ceyda could see it.

'Maybe. Why?'

'I heard you talking on the phone,' she said. 'Don't worry, I couldn't understand anything you were saying.'

'Ceyda . . .'

'And I don't care,' she said. 'Go, stay, do what you like.'

He put a hand on her shoulder. 'Don't be like this,' he said. 'Don't you want me to get a job?'

'Yes,' she said, 'of course I do.'

'To get a job I have to leave the house.'

'Yes. And yet much as you leave the house, you never get even close to a job, do you? Don't speak to me.'

She walked into the kitchen and shut the door. Once again his wife wasn't talking to him. It didn't make him happy, or sad either, if he were honest.

Mustafa Kaiserli left his small apartment in Beşiktaş and made his way to the ferry stage.

Ömer had made a pot of that awful mırra coffee for İkmen's linguist. He'd brought it in with an almost feverish look on his face. Süleyman hadn't seen his deputy present his gift to Constable Demirtaş, but he could imagine the scene. The garbled speech, the blushing. He'd done that himself when he was young. What he'd rarely done in his youth, however, was fail to pick up on signs women gave out about whether they found him sexually attractive. Constable Demirtaş liked Ömer Mungun, but that was all – mainly because she only had eyes for his boss.

Süleyman had seen it so many times before, he knew he wasn't mistaken. And she was a very attractive, intelligent and sexy young woman. Her body, voluptuous but firm, actively aroused him. But his days of cheating on Gonca Şekeroğlu were over. He'd decided some years ago that what he didn't need in his life was a feud with a tribe of gypsies. He just hoped that Ömer didn't get hurt.

He was on the point of closing his eyes after a hard day's work when Gonca arrived home surrounded by grandchildren.

'There's a rumour that the Corpse Eater is dead,' she said as she shooed the kids into the garden and unpacked her bag on the floor. When she finally found what she was looking for – her cigarettes – she lit up.

Süleyman swung his legs down from the couch and sat up. 'I don't really know what you're talking about. Is this some sort of criminal?'

'Of course!' she said. 'You know him! The yalı gypsy. His family live in Tarlabaşı. Owns property in all the posh places on the Bosphorus.'

'Do you mean Hasan Dum?' he said.

'That's him. He owns not just one yalı, but every other yalı on the Bosphorus. They say he put his own brother's eyes out. My father hid me from him when I was a girl because he knew that if he saw me he would want to marry me. And although the Corpse Eater was rich even back then, my father didn't want me to go to him because he was so ugly.'

'Not because he kills people?'

'He doesn't really eat corpses,' Gonca said. 'But he comes from Zonguldak, where the stupid Turks believe we eat our dead.'

Süleyman had never heard of that before, but he could believe it. In the past, the fact that the gypsies didn't bury their dead immediately had confused some people.

'So what have you been told about Dum?' he asked.

She sat down next to him on the sofa and moulded herself into his side. 'He and his Hungarian bodyguard, Gabor, were found dead in one of his properties in Yeniköy.'

'He had properties in Yeniköy?' Süleyman had known that Dum owned a lot of the waterside villas known as yalıs, but he hadn't realised that the gypsy had climbed to the heights of the very poshest Bosphorus villages.

'Only recently,' she said. 'The rumour is that he and Gabor were found cut to pieces. I don't know how. Hasan was the only proper gypsy crime lord in the city. All the others are just kids buying up shit land and defending it with illegal guns. The Corpse Eater and his man were always heavily armed. How did that happen?'

If the rumour was true, then Süleyman too wondered about that. Hasan Dum, his men and his family had no limits. Whoever had killed him would pay in ways Süleyman didn't want to think about.

'Let's find out. I'll call headquarters,' he said.

Gonca shrugged. The rumour had been enough for her. Now that it was out of her system, she was no longer interested.

Süleyman made the call in their bedroom, away from the many Şekeroğlu kids, Gonca and her numerous daughters. He'd known Deniz Akgunduz for years. Younger than he looked, grizzled, addicted to a range of substances, he'd worked for the organised crime unit for most of his career. Much of that had been spent undercover inside some of İstanbul's most violent gangs.

'I've heard that Hasan Dum is dead,' Süleyman said.

'Fucking right.'

Sergeant Akgunduz had been obliged many years ago to adopt the casual cussing that characterised so many gang members. Now it was just part of who he was.

'How? Didn't he have his bodyguard with him?'

'Gabor Karpathy. Yes. Equally dead. Fantastic fucking day for this city, Mehmet Bey. Two psychopathic cunts finished off in one day.'

'Yes, but . . . how? Weren't they both armed?'

'Imagine so,' Akgunduz said. 'Had nothing on them when they were found, though. Never seen anything quite like it. The whole place, what used to be a shop, just dripping with blood. Like something out of a splatter movie. It was like Dum had been unzipped.'

'Unzipped?'

'Cut from his chin to his groin. The Hungarian's got no face and also no dick. If it's a gang hit, that usually ends up in the victim's mouth. Not this time.'

'So where is it?' Süleyman asked.

'Gone,' he said. 'Taken as a souvenir, proof of death, who the fuck knows.'

'But you think it was a gang hit?'

'Best explanation so far, man,' Akgunduz said. 'Although there's been no word on Dum being in blood to anyone lately. Locals said they saw a couple of junkies lurking about the place last night. But then you know Yeniköy people. Probably just some kids from religious families looking for a place to fuck.'

Süleyman frowned. 'A couple as in a man and a woman?'

'So the aunties of Yeniköy say.'

'Well then you and I maybe need to talk,' Süleyman said.

'Much as I don't approve of the police, and in spite of the fact that you haven't bothered to come and see me for years, I do like you,' Sami Nasi said. 'And in that spirit I have been looking at anything relating to the Rudolfoğlus.'

Çetin İkmen smiled. Sami was a genuinely unknowable probable charlatan. But he did sometimes know things that others didn't, and his heart was usually in the right place.

'One of Grandfather Josef's many hobbies was recording unusual deaths,' he said. 'My father said he always wanted to replicate some of the more lurid examples in an illusion. But he never did, and so I think he was simply just morbidly curious.'

'Magicians have always been in the business of showing us life and death,' İkmen said.

'Yes. But to the point,' Sami said. 'In 1931, Josef made notes upon the death of Perihan Rudolfoğlu, minor Ottoman princess and wife of the late Rudolf Paşa.'

'Interesting. Did this information come from press sources?'

'No. Josef knew her doctor.'

'The family doctor?'

'No, her own doctor. One of those who had worked at the imperial court. I'll come back to that. Anyway, Perihan Hanım died of kidney failure brought on by septicaemia.'

'Not uncommon in the days before antibiotics,' İkmen said.

'No, but the doctor's description of how she died is not for those with a weak stomach. Edited highlights include her abdomen swelling to twice its normal size, turning purple and then necrotising, the overwhelming smell of urine in the room where she died, the black pus she vomited, the fact that she became delirious and started screaming about being bewitched. Also she wouldn't see her own children. Whenever the doctor suggested she might want to say goodbye to them, she went berserk, dragging her fingernails across her face and growling like an animal. The doctor, who was called Kevork Sarkissian – same name as your friend Arto – recorded that it took Perihan a week to die. Josef noted that Kevork told him he wanted to put her out of her misery, but Perihan wouldn't take anything. All the way through her ordeal she kept repeating that her suffering was deserved.'

Being sick before the discovery of antibiotics had been gruelling and frequently agonising. İkmen's father had told him all about it. But Perihan Hanım's death had been particularly gruesome. Kevork Sarkissian, Arto's grandfather, had been a court doctor and so he must have had access to the best pain control available at the time. But if his patient wouldn't comply, what was he to do?

Arto obviously had no knowledge of this connection between his grandfather and the Rudolfoğlus or he would have told İkmen.

'Do you know how Perihan got septicaemia?' he asked.

'No. There's just the account of her illness and then her death, which apparently happened when she had her head down the toilet.'

İkmen only vaguely remembered Arto's grandfather. But he had known Arto's father, Vahan, who he recalled had not been the sort of man to throw things away. Both his sons had taken after him. Were Perihan Rudolfoğlu's medical notes still somewhere in Arto's vast Bosphorus-side house?

Later, when he couldn't get hold of Arto, he told his wife about it. She said, 'You know sometimes, in the old days, when women had abortions, they succumbed to septicaemia. My mother knew women that happened to.'

İkmen thought as he went to sleep that night about how Perihan had been widowed for three years when she died.

Chapter 10

Everything about the scene indicated frenzy. As Süleyman placed each photograph on Teker's desk, they just got worse.

'My informants tell me they know nothing,' said the other man sitting in the commissioner's office with Süleyman. This was Inspector Ahmet Cıngı, the public face of the organised crime team. 'They're lying.'

'They're career criminals, of course they lie,' the commissioner said. 'The gypsies have recently moved into Yeniköy real estate?'

'Dum bought a yalı off some desperate paşa's grandson,' Cıngı said. 'The old shop where he was found used to be owned by Armenians. The story is that Dum's boys just walked in.'

'Did they secure the property?'

'They don't need to. Word gets around in the criminal world. Firms try not to tread on each other's toes. Usually.'

'Even in Yeniköy?' she said. 'I know it's not exactly a hotbed of organised crime, Inspector Cıngı, but what about squatters?'

Cıngı shook his head. 'Commissioner, you know as well as I do that there's no part of this city that is unaffected by organised crime. And I include what some may regard as legitimate businesses here. İstanbul is for sale and the competition is intense. Only the strong will survive, and there are people who have robust views about gypsies getting any kind of cut.'

'Given your experience, who would you put in the frame?' Teker asked.

Cıngı leaned back in his chair. 'Dum started his criminal career working a car-parking scam with a load of other kids for an old Kurd in Tarlabaşı. Because a Kurd gave him his first break, he always had a soft spot for them. He'd had problems with the nationalist right-wing families; he was a gypsy, so to them he was scum. For his part, he saw them as a bunch of crazy fascists. Problem is that some of them work in the legitimate world now. They have expensive lawyers, and the protection of those who have influence.'

'Yes, well, it was ever so,' Teker said. 'Are you saying that those you suspect are untouchable?'

'I'm saying it may be problematic. And if none of these people are involved . . .'

'Disturbing a nest of hornets is always a fearsome prospect,' she said. 'And so Inspector Süleyman, over to you . . .'

He looked up from the disturbing photograph.

'When I spoke to Sergeant Akgunduz last night, he said that local people had reported seeing a man and a woman near the old shop in the last few days,' he said.

'Yeah. Auntie talk, you know,' Cıngı said. 'They described them as junkies. But I'm not sure they'd know a junkie if they fell over one.'

'I accept that,' Süleyman said. His parents lived in the genteel Bosphorus village of Arnavautköy, which was very like Yeniköy inasmuch as it had a large, if dwindling, population of nosy and fearful elderly people. 'But as you know, Ahmet Bey, I am currently looking for a couple who we suspect may have attacked two individuals on the street. A third killing, which happened on a tram, may have been perpetrated by the same people, but we can't as yet place such a couple on that vehicle. I'm not saying that Dum's killing is part of this pattern, if indeed such a pattern exists, but looking at this picture I am struck by the disorganised nature of what happened in Yeniköy. Or rather that is how I'm reading it.'

103

'You know that gang members can create a disorganised scene to give that impression, right?'

'Of course. But I don't think we can afford to overlook my investigation,' Süleyman said. 'I am desperate to find this couple, and if they did kill Dum and now have firearms that once belonged to him, that doesn't bear thinking about.'

'Got any idea about motivation?' Cıngı said.

'None. No connection between the victims as far as we can tell. It appears random. Do you know why Dum went to that property yesterday?'

'His wife says he was doing a check on all his recent acquisitions.'

'So maybe he found our couple trespassing on his property.'

'Maybe.'

Commissioner Teker drummed her fingers on her desktop. It was clear she wanted this meeting to end. She said, 'I think it would be of benefit to both investigations for you to share information. This would be particularly useful with regard to forensics. Inspector Süleyman, I'd like you to attend the scene of Hasan Dum's demise. It may be that you can identify something of interest to your investigation while you are there.'

The children wouldn't leave him alone. He'd tried to hide behind the dustbins in front of the Syriani church, but they'd found him. They'd had help.

Now they were throwing rotten fruit and other stuff that may have been dog shit at him. He put his hands over his head. All he wanted to do was sleep. But they wouldn't let him. Or rather, the Devil wouldn't. He could see him standing behind the children, egging them on to torment him.

'Oh God, but you do set me some tasks,' Arto Sarkissian said as he embraced his old friend Çetin İkmen. 'My father's patients are one thing, but my grandfather's . . .'

İkmen looked up at the Devil's House. 'I spoke to Dr Kötil at the Forensic Institute yesterday. There's still much to go through, but what he did say was that none of the doors to the apartments appear to have been forced. There's no sign of a break-in. So whoever got in was let in.'

'Possibly,' Arto said. 'Çetin, even if by some miracle I manage to find my grandfather's patient notes, what on earth is the significance of how Perihan Rudolfoğlu died? That happened in 1931!'

İkmen shrugged. 'The siblings were all killed very deliberately,' he said. 'Also the killer was apparently let in. So he or she was known, probably. This, to me, all points to intent. They were killed for a reason, and unless they became drug dealers in their dotage or indulged in online gambling, I can't see how they can have made too many enemies since the 1930s.'

'Do you know yet who will inherit the house?' Arto said.

'Yes. I finally managed to speak to the family lawyer this morning.'

'And?'

'Fatima Hanım left it to her brothers,' he said. 'In the event of their deaths, everything has been left to the Oriental Club.'

Arto raised his eyebrows. 'She wasn't a member, surely?'

'No, but her father was,' İkmen said. 'And he had a lot of power over his children.'

'You don't think the club . . .'

'Not really,' İkmen said. 'But of course I can't absolutely rule it out, since it is a beneficiary. I will have the pleasure of the club later. Just came to show Constable Demirtaş the house. She's inside with Sergeant Gürsel. What brings you here?'

'Oh, I'm off duty today,' the doctor said. 'I was passing.'

'Passing? You live on the other side of the Bosphorus.'

'Passing, in the area, what does it matter?' Arto said.

A large apartment block was being built next door to Arto's

dignified Ottoman house. He hated being there, especially, as now, when his wife Maryam was staying with her sister in Chicago.

'I don't like to ask you to spend time digging through your grandfather's things, but he did live in your house . . .'

'I know.'

'I'll come and help you.'

'And have two of us deafened by pneumatic drills, concrete mixers and the banal chatter of men who believe that rich people are better than they are because God has rewarded them with money?'

'These are the workmen on the site?'

'Mainly from the Black Sea coast, I am told,' Arto said.

İkmen shook his head.

'I will do my best to find what I can,' Arto said. 'I don't ever remember my father talking about any of my grandfather's patients, except those from his days at Yıldız Palace.'

'Who did he treat? Not the sultan?'

'No,' he said. 'His doctor was a Byzantine Greek. Grandfather Kevork attended to some of the young princes. Then during the First World War he worked as a field doctor treating our troops in Arabia. When the republic came in, my understanding is that he found work wherever he could. But I never heard him mention Perihan Rudolfoğlu.'

'She was a princess,' İkmen said. 'Minor, admittedly. Don't know how she was related to the sultan.'

'I'll do what I can,' Arto said. 'But for now I'm going to try a new coffee shop I've heard about over here.'

'Oh?'

'Yes,' he said. 'Apparently it's full of anarchists.'

İkmen smiled.

* * *

106

They'd finally found a place in İstinye. Home to a vast new shopping mall, this Bosphorus village still had the odd unexplored corner. They'd walked in silence from Yeniköy once they'd changed into the clothes in the rucksack. She'd wanted to just leave what they had been wearing, but Ali had found a plastic bag and shoved it all inside, then strapped it into the rucksack.

They found a gate first, which led to a pile of rubble and a few archways that had once been some sort of public building. They slept in the long dry grass for many hours. When Ali did finally speak, he realised that his voice was hoarse.

'We'll need to burn everything.'

She looked up at him from underneath a crumbling arch. 'Why?'

'Why do you think? It's all covered in blood. We killed people.'

'That's the idea,' she said.

He didn't reply. She was mad. But it wasn't as if he'd come into it blind, except of course that love was blind and he loved her.

'We'll burn everything and then move on,' he said. He looked away from her. 'And I mean everything.'

'Can you read?' she said.

The sudden change of subject brought him up short.

'Yes.'

'Have you seen anything about us in the newspapers?'

'I haven't been looking at newspapers.'

He emptied the bloodied plastic bag out on the ground, then added some pieces of wood that were lying around.

'Unless you look, we won't know if we're famous,' she said.

It had never occurred to Ali that Elif couldn't read. But then when they'd first met, all he'd needed to know about her was that she was beautiful and she was in trouble. A pale-eyed, black-haired Kurdish girl was lucrative for the city pimps, who'd made her service fat businessmen from Russia. He'd freed her. What

107

he hadn't been able to do, however, was cure her addiction. How could he? Ali Erbil had been a heroin addict himself for ten years. They'd used together. They'd stolen from the designer shops his mother frequented in Nişantaşı to feed their habits. Now they were killing and she was loving it. He was helpless.

He put a match to the pile of wood and clothes and watched as it burned away the blood of those men who had terrified him. How had it happened? Ali wasn't sure. One minute the men were shouting at them; the next, they were dead. Elif had launched herself at them like an animal, screaming, pushing that piece of glass in her hands up through the main man's stomach, slashing at the other man's throat as he piled in to help his fellow. They'd both been armed; why hadn't they shot her? All he could think was that they had been as shocked as he had when it happened. Only when it was over did Ali realise that Elif was laughing. Now she had their guns. And the penis she had cut from the dead body of the younger, taller man.

'You must throw that on the fire too,' he said when she took it out of her pocket. She didn't want to, but he grabbed it from her and did it himself.

Then he said, 'We'll need to move on soon.'

'Where?'

'Somewhere we'll fit in. I've had enough of those posh places.'

She smiled. 'Tarlabaşı,' she said.

The sight of those apartments in Moda would haunt Barçın. Even stripped of most of their contents, they had been dark and filthy. Some of the strangest stuff had been taken to a room just down the corridor where, so Sergeant Gürsel had told her, İkmen intended to spend time looking at it. What a strange little man he was. People whispered that he was secular, and yet he used terms like 'magic' and 'alchemy' and visited, so it was said, some very odd people.

Barçın looked at her desk. The Devil's House letters had come to her in no particular order, and so every time she picked one up, she had to first search for the date, transcribe it into the Roman calendar, and then find out who was writing to whom. As far as she could tell, none of the letters had been delivered by post. She imagined the four old people slipping letters underneath each other's doors like naughty children.

She began to read.

My dear Kanat,

I have taken your last, spiteful missive hard, as I imagine I was meant so to do. You accuse me of becoming our 'foul' father without for a second wondering why I may do some of the things that Rudolf Paşa did. How you and I could live in the same house and you have no knowledge of Father's pursuits is beyond me. Those arts that you condemn may be used for ill or for good. My study is of the latter. You know why. Please leave me alone to put right that which you tear yourself apart over every day.

I remain your loving brother,
Kemal

This was dated 12 October 1945. What arts did Kemal mean, if not the art of alchemy? According to İkmen, his apartment had been full of alchemical paraphernalia. But what business was it of Kanat's if he did that? What was it to him if his brother wanted to try to make ordinary metal into gold? And why should anyone tear themselves apart over it? It seemed that their father Rudolf Paşa had attempted the same thing, possibly through ill means or for a bad purpose. But what did that mean?

She entered her translation on to her laptop and then looked at the next letter. From Fatima Hanım to Kanat on 1 June 1953.

My dear Kanat,

Because of the heat, I must open a window at night, as I know you do too. I hear your tears and they break my heart. Dear brother, if you would only come and see me, I know that I could allay your fears and soothe your pain in an instant. Please come to me, my soul Kanat. I miss you as I would miss water in the desert.

Your loving sister,
Fatima

Barçın was about to transcribe the letter when she noticed one single word written at the bottom of the page—

'Mirra?'

Oh God, it was Sergeant Mungun with yet more coffee. It was very kind of him, and she did like mirra very much. But every day, almost every hour, was a little excessive.

She looked up and smiled. 'Oh. Thank you,' she said.

He put the coffee down on her desk. 'No problem.'

He clearly wanted to talk, but she really didn't. He obviously had an interest in her, which he had made more than plain, and she thought he was nice, but that was all.

'Constable—'

'I'm sorry, Sergeant Mungun,' she said. 'But I really don't have time to talk at the moment.'

'OK.'

She saw the reflection of his slightly disappointed smile in her computer screen. It made her feel unkind, and she cringed. When he'd left, she breathed a sigh of relief. She'd only known him a few days, but already he was oppressing her. Why were so many men from the east so needy?

She dutifully took a sip of mirra and then looked back at the letter. The word in pencil at the bottom was *Die*.

* * *

110

Çetin İkmen had never been a great swimmer. He knew enough about the sport to be able to save his own life, but that was it. Swimming for pleasure, like football, was something he didn't understand. Usually.

But the late-afternoon heat was frying his brains and the Oriental Club's deep blue swimming pool looked incredibly inviting. However, he also felt totally out of place among the fashion-model wives wearing golden bikinis the size of small handkerchiefs and looking down their carefully sculpted noses at him. Unlike him, they were not drinking Fanta but gin and tonic; like him, they were almost certainly secular. It was in places like this that İkmen just about managed to appreciate why so many people continued to vote for a political party that was religious in origin. Ordinary people could relate to religion, but this club was alien, even to him.

'Inspector İkmen?'

A very smart man wearing a light summer suit offered his hand. İkmen made to rise, but the man pressed him back into his seat.

'Don't get up,' he said. 'I'm Adnan Selçuk. I'm one of the club's lawyers.' He sat. 'Can I get you another drink? Something to eat?'

'Another Fanta would be good. And an ashtray, if of course you allow smoking . . .'

'I smoke myself,' Mr Selçuk said. He called over to one of the many waiters walking around the pool: 'Ashtray here. And a Fanta.'

'Thank you, sir,' İkmen said.

The ashtray arrived as soon as he'd spoken, and Adnan Selçuk offered him a cigarette. They were very fancy, black with a gold collar round the filter.

'Black Sobranie,' the lawyer explained. 'Always stock up when I go through the airport. Now, Inspector, I understand from Erdal Bey at Kenter and Kenter that the club is named as beneficiary in the will of a murder victim.'

'Yes,' İkmen said. 'Fatima Rudolfoğlu.'

Mr Selçuk leaned back in his chair and smoked for a moment before speaking. 'I saw something about your investigation when the bodies were discovered. Tragic. I didn't know there was any connection between the club and that family until our membership secretary Burak Bey told me.'

'Rudolf Paşa was one of the original members,' İkmen said.

The club had been founded, in part, by foreigners. Diplomats from England, Germany and Russia, members of old Levantine families, and Ottoman soldiers and intellectuals. It was said that the first revolution against the Ottoman Empire had been plotted inside the walls of the old club when it was on İstiklal Caddesi over in Beyoğlu.

'Yes,' Mr Selçuk said.

'You know that Rudolf Paşa had a certain reputation?'

'Ah, I believe so. The story of the final days of the Ottoman Empire is crammed with outré and very strange people.'

'Rudolf Paşa practised magic,' İkmen said. 'Not, we believe, for benign purposes either, hence his reputation as a friend of the Devil.'

'Mmm. Unfortunate.'

'Indeed. However, that is no reflection on your organisation.'

'No.'

'But given the fact that Miss Rudolfoğlu and her brothers have all died in suspicious circumstances, we have to look at anyone who might benefit from a bequest. The house is in a terrible condition, but even a casual glance at local property prices in the area leads me to believe it has to be worth in excess of five million euros. It's a historic house in a very convenient and affluent neighbourhood.'

'Absolutely. We are both grateful and thrilled, if a little apprehensive about our good fortune,' Mr Selçuk said. 'To inherit a place called the Devil's House is somewhat odd. But . . . I suppose you want to know how much we knew about this bequest, don't you, Inspector?'

'I'll need to see any relevant legal documentation, yes.'

'That won't be a problem. We've already located the file, although I have to say that all of this was unknown to most people here until today.'

'Most people?'

'A couple of our older members claim to have known about some sort of arrangement with the Rudolfoğlus' lawyers, although they never knew any specifics.'

'Well according to Erdal Bey, the documentation is clear. Basically the club inherits provided Fatima Hanım and all her brothers are dead. And as you must know, the entire family died at the same time.'

'Yes.'

'This is not normal or natural, and so we must investigate. Sadly for you, this will mean that you won't get your inheritance for quite some time.'

Mr Selçuk smiled. 'I'm sure we'll manage.'

'I'm sure you will too,' İkmen said. 'In the meantime, I'll need to speak to these older members who have some memory of the bequest.'

'Of course. Let me see if I can find them for you.'

Chapter 11

If he just walked into police headquarters and told them who he was, they'd ask him how he'd known they wanted to find him. He'd seen nothing in the press or online, but obviously they were looking because they'd been to see Father Anatoli. The priest had admitted he knew him, and even told them that he lived in Beşiktaş. What he hadn't said was that Mustafa Kaiserli still did go to church in Moda. There he could, just briefly, be Yiannis Apion, just like when Ceyda occasionally went to the Ahrida Synagogue in Balat and played at being Rebekah for a while.

Father Anatoli hadn't made any sort of effort to hide him.

'Why should I?' he'd told him on the phone. 'You haven't done anything wrong, have you?'

'No, Father,' he'd said.

So should he now tell the police that the priest had called him after their visit, or should he just wait for them to turn up at his door? Because they would, and that was fine. And so he decided to leave things as they were. Father Anatoli had denied the police his contact details, which could annoy them. It was best just to keep quiet.

Mustafa Kaiserli crossed himself at the threshold to the ayazma of St Katherine and felt himself relax into Yiannis Apion.

His grandfather Kevork Paşa had been the first member of the Sarkissian family to live in the Peacock Yalı. The construction had been ordered by Kevork's father, Garbis Paşa, who had died just before its completion. The peacock-tail motif that decorated both the inside and outside of the building had been a nod to the far south-eastern origins of the Sarkissian family. In the Armenian quarter of the largely Christian town of Midyat, white peacocks were still common.

Arto Sarkissian climbed wearily to the top of his house and unlocked a door. From the window on the landing of the fifth floor he could easily see the construction work that was proceeding at such an insane pace on the land next to his property. Another metal-and-glass monstrosity. He pushed the infrequently unlocked door open and walked into a room stacked with furniture and crates.

Like his father Vahan, his grandfather Kevork hadn't lived very long. He'd died when Arto had been a small child, and so all he knew of him came from distant memories of tales told by his father, and a few photographs.

He'd been a court doctor, then a military doctor, then, when the Armenian elite lost its place at the top of society, he'd worked for just about anyone for a price. Arto knew he shouldn't be surprised that Kevork Paşa had worked for the Rudolfoğlus. Maybe Perihan Rudolfoğlu had remembered him from his days at Yıldız Palace?

The room wasn't big, but it was full, not just of his grandfather's possessions but his father's stuff too. From on top of a battered suitcase a portrait of Arto's mother Mimi looked sternly down. Were she still alive, she'd know exactly where to look. Mimi had known everything. Arto avoided her gaze and opened the top drawer of a large oak chest. He looked inside and shook his head. Black-and-white photographs. Hundreds, maybe even thousands of them, all flung in in no order whatsoever. Unable to resist, he picked up a handful and looked at himself aged twelve with his father in the garden. Even then he'd been fat.

The next photograph was of himself and Çetin İkmen on the beach at Ataköy, out near the airport. Again he looked as if he'd just swallowed a football, while Çetin was so thin he could have been a famine victim. He threw the photographs back in the drawer and closed it. It was going to be a long night.

Three women had offered to fuck him for money before he'd even arrived at the end of the street where the older members of the Dum clan lived. That was Tarlabaşı. What was slightly more unusual was to see an elderly man sitting in a large chair in the middle of the road. Luckily Gonca had warned him this might happen. Hasan Dum's father, Irfan, was receiving condolences and gifts of food and drink from the people of Tarlabaşı. Normally the body of the dead person would be in the house ready to be viewed by friends and relatives. But Hasan Dum's body had still to go through a full post-mortem investigation, and so the main protagonist was absent.

Inspector Cıngı had already interviewed the dead man's relatives, who said that they knew of no one who had anything against their wonderful father, son and husband. Dead gangsters were always perfect, in Süleyman's experience. Of course his car had already been noticed by people in the area, which was why he was keeping his distance. The Dums knew him even if he didn't know them. But he wanted to see who came to pay their respects. He'd already noticed a Kurdish fence of his acquaintance.

He lit a cigarette and wondered how people got from the sight of a body lying, effectively, in state to the notion of that person's relatives eating him. Even someone like him, a casual Muslim at best, found the idea of an unburied body unpleasant, but he knew that Christians and gypsies liked to view their dead. It was strange, but it had never occurred to him that they might be consuming them. Were people in Zonguldak really so ignorant?

116

There were a lot of women lining up to kiss the old man's hands. Many of them carried trays of food, probably helva, which was a traditional mourning gift. The men brought bottles of rakı. Gonca had told him that the actual funeral would be a noisy affair. There'd be lots of weeping, and men would fire rounds from pistols and rifles into the air – if they were lucky. If they weren't lucky, at least one person would get shot by mistake, and then the whole party would decamp to a local hospital, where the victim would probably die. Then there'd be another funeral.

What he hadn't been expecting was gun play before the funeral. But he heard two distinct shots, and then he heard screaming. Mehmet Süleyman got out of his car and took his own gun out of its holster.

'There.' Barçın Demirtaş pointed to a very faint scrawl on the bottom of the page. 'It says "Die",' she said.

'How unpleasant,' Çetin İkmen mused. 'And you think this letter from Miss Fatima to her brother Kanat was given back to her with that word written on it?'

'I do. It was found in her effects,' she said. 'The animosity between these people is enormous. A letter from Kemal to Kanat is all about how hurt he is that his brother thinks he's like his father. Kemal claims that he is trying to put things right between them.'

'How?'

'It seems via sorcery,' she said. 'That's what people believed about their father, wasn't it?'

'Yes. That he was in league with the Devil.' İkmen shook his head. 'If I remember correctly, Miss Fatima was conciliatory.'

'Yes. But only Yücel is in any way sympathetic to this. I get the feeling he wants to . . . not make up with her, but find a way to bring them all together again somehow. But Kemal and Kanat are absolutely set against their sister and I don't know why.

Whatever it was had to be serious. There's real hatred in these letters, and I've not done much more than scratch the surface. Also, sir,' she said, 'I get the distinct impression that we're never going to find out from the letters what this issue is. Every time I read one and think I may be close, the narrative disappears into obscurity or elaborate Ottoman modes of expression.'

'Mmm.' İkmen opened his office window and lit a cigarette. He offered one to Barçın, but she declined. 'In my career I've investigated a few crimes that have their roots in the distant past,' he said. 'They're not impossible to solve, as I have proved, but they are problematic. Fatima Rudolfoğlu bequeathed all her money and property to the Oriental Club in the event of the deaths of herself and her brothers. Only men so old they can barely articulate their own names remember this now. I know; I met them this afternoon at the club's stunning place over in Kadıköy. Rudolf Paşa was a member, but none of his children joined. Why would Fatima leave such a considerable sum of money to an institution she is not connected with?'

'I've no idea. The club hasn't been referred to so far.'

'I'd say that maybe she was a daddy's girl. She did what she did for her father, but we have no evidence of this, do we?'

'Not so far,' Barçın said. 'Kemal is horrified to be compared by Kanat to his father. I've not found anything about her parents in Fatima's writing. What was their father supposed to have actually done, sir?'

'Ah, now there's a thing,' İkmen said. 'I've not been able to track down anything you'd call concrete proof. There are rumours about consorting with the Devil, about violence. I even have it from one particularly strange source that Rudolf Paşa practised alchemy for the purpose of creating gold from base metal, and further, that he used human sacrifice to achieve this.'

'So where's all the gold?'

'You may well ask,' İkmen said. 'But what it seems to all boil down to is that he was a bit of a bastard to those who worked for him. And who wasn't in those days? That said, however, I did discover while I was at the club that my unreliable contact's grandfather did indeed put on a magic show for the members, including Rudolf Paşa, just like he said.'

'Your source is a stage magician?'

'Yes. Sami Nasi. Calls himself Professor Vanek for reasons I won't bother you with. But I know for a fact that his grandfather was a magician, that he knew Rudolfoğlu and that he played the club. Whether, as Sami told me, Rudolfoğlu actually asked his grandfather to help him with his alchemical work, I don't know. Sami also claims to know how Perihan Hanım died, but until I get some verification on that, I'm not going to go there, for the time being.'

'Rudolf Paşa doesn't sound like a nice man,' Barçın said.

'Oh, there's no doubt about that. But did he, as Sami claims, actually sacrifice someone to the Devil, and if so, how does that have any bearing on the deaths of his children? Because if it doesn't, then all this research is useless to us.'

'You mean if the house was just broken into?'

'I don't think that's likely.'

'No.' She paused. 'But what if the past is irrelevant anyway? What if they were killed by someone who was in dispute with them recently? Like Yücel and Fatima's carers?'

'Not impossible,' İkmen said, 'but they both have alibis, and I don't mean their own partners or children.'

Barçın sighed. 'I'll just have to carry on then, won't I, sir?'

'You will,' he said. 'I wish I could help you, truly, but I am far too ignorant.'

'Oh you're not ignorant, sir,' she said. 'God, you treat me so well here! And to work with my actual brain for once . . . I just can't believe my luck.'

* * *

In spite of being a nominal Christian, Arto Sarkissian was not a great believer in miracles. Every year on the night of 14 September, one person was always 'cured' of something up at the Armenian Church of the Holy Archangels in Balat. But were they? Really? Arto would never venture an opinion. So it came as some surprise to him that just beyond midnight, he began praying to a deity he barely acknowledged to help him find Perihan Rudolfoglu's medical records.

He wanted to help Çetin İkmen, but the chances of finding anything about his grandfather's patients in all that clutter were slight. Also, he'd realised that even if he did find anything written down, it was likely to be in Ottoman, which he couldn't read. It meant he couldn't even identify anything relevant.

If he was going to get any sleep at all before the pneumatic drills and earth-movers started up again in the morning, he'd have to go to bed. Not that he felt he'd be able to actually sleep. But to his surprise, he did. And it was in that sleep that he remembered something, or rather, someone.

'Put the gun down.'

Did the black-tracksuited boy recognise him?

'Remember me? I'm Inspector Süleyman,' he said.

The boy withdrew still further into the shadow of the dustbin he was squatting beside. But the gun was still trained on Süleyman. It was a big, flash Beretta. He'd seen similar weapons in the hands and on the hips of gangsters more times than he cared to remember.

When he'd been in custody, they'd never managed to identify the boy in the black tracksuit, and so they'd just referred to him as 'Mehmet'. Any man whose name was unknown was always Mehmet.

'I know that gun isn't yours,' Süleyman said. 'Where did you get it?'

As far as he knew, the boy hadn't shot anyone. The only witness to the two shots that had been heard, a young prostitute, said she'd seen the kid point the thing at a rat. When the gun had discharged the first time, the recoil had taken him by surprise and he'd fallen back behind the dustbins. The second shot had been an accident.

A gypsy man Süleyman recognised as one of Gonca's relatives started to move towards him.

'Stay back!'

'Ah, Inspector Süleyman . . .'

'Stay back!'

The magnetism of guns never ceased to amaze him. A shot would go off, and rather than heading in the opposite direction, a large section of the population would actually run towards the report. It was madness.

'Keep back and keep everyone else as far away as possible,' he said to the gypsy. 'Understand?'

'Yes, sir.'

But although he did keep others away, the idiot himself didn't move very far. Süleyman had called for back-up, and was praying that it arrived soon. Being alone in Tarlabaşı with an armed man and hundreds of spectators was not good.

He looked the young man in the eyes. 'I don't for a moment believe that is your gun. I also don't believe that you mean anyone any harm.'

'There was a rat.' His voice was tremulous. Was he still fearful of the Devil, or had some other fixation taken hold of him since he'd been in custody?

'I know, you tried to kill it.'

'He sends them to bite us, to spread disease.'

'Who does?'

'The Devil.'

Süleyman heard a car draw up. Gonca's relative said, 'They've arrived, Mehmet Bey.'

He'd spoken to Ömer, and so he hoped that it was the sergeant who had come. Out of the corner of his eye he saw police uniforms and, mercifully, Ömer Mungun. He called to him: 'Sergeant Mungun.'

'Sir.'

'I know him,' the boy in the black tracksuit said. 'I've seen him before.'

'Ömer Bey is my sergeant,' Süleyman said. 'You can give the gun either to me or to him. It's up to you.'

For a moment it looked as if the boy hadn't understood. But then he said, 'Why would I do that?'

Ömer Mungun approached, slowly and alone. The uniformed officers at his back trained their weapons on the boy.

'Because you can't have a gun on the street,' Süleyman said. 'It's dangerous.'

'Other people have guns.'

'I know. Bad people.'

'You have a gun.'

'Yes. I'm a police officer. I'm allowed to have a gun.'

'To fight bad people.'

'In part,' he said. 'To protect—'

'I'm protecting everyone,' the boy said. 'He means to destroy us all.'

'Who?' He knew who the boy meant, but he had to ask.

'The Devil. I've told you before, he is at your back. He means to put an end to you! To us all!' He began to cry.

Ömer was now level with his superior. 'Sir,' he murmured.

'Where did you get the gun?' Süleyman asked the boy.

He continued to cry.

'If you give me the gun, we can talk,' Süleyman said. 'I promise I won't let the Devil harm you.'

'You can't do that!' He was laughing though his tears. 'He's unstoppable. Don't you understand? Those people understood, why can't you?'

'What people?' Ömer asked.

The boy looked at him and frowned. Had he already forgotten who Ömer was?

'What people?' Süleyman reiterated.

He shook his head. 'They understood. They believed.' He raised the gun and pointed it at Süleyman. 'They gave me this to kill the Devil.'

'How am I expected to remember anything? I'm practically fucking dead!'

Mesrob was Arto Sarkissian's only surviving uncle. Now eighty-five, he'd lived in New York for the past forty years. In attitude, language and accent he was entirely American. And yet he had once lived in the Peacock Yalı and had been the favourite youngest son of Arto's grandfather Kevork.

'It must be the middle of the fucking night in Turkey,' the old man shouted down the phone line at him. 'What are you doing up?'

Arto explained in as succinct a way as he could to an ill-tempered old man several thousand miles away.

'Oh, Papa was full of stories about pashas and princesses,' Mesrob said. 'I didn't take any notice of their names. I knew he had worked at the palace as a young man. He saw the sultan, Abdül Hamid, a few times. He didn't treat him, but he did treat his astrologer. Mad. The sultan, not the astrologer. *He* was just manipulative.'

'The man I'm trying to find out about was a German,' Arto said. 'Rudolf Paşa.'

'There were lots of German pashas in the First World War. Some of them stayed on when it was all over.'

'Yes, Uncle, like this one, Rudolf Paşa.'

'And all this is because of that Turkish friend of yours?' the old man said.

'Çetin İkmen, yes. He's a policeman.'

'Mmm. Turkish police. Always complete bastards . . .'

'Uncle Mesrob, if you don't know Rudolf Paşa, then do you remember Grandfather talking about his wife? She was called Perihan Hanım and she was a princess. This was in 1931.'

'I'd only just been born then.'

'Yes, I know.'

'Perihan is a name I don't know. How do you still manage to live in Turkey? It would drive me nuts. All that army shit they go in for, the toilets . . .'

'What about the Devil's House? Did you ever hear Grandfather talk about that? Something happened in that house in 1931, something bad. Çetin thinks that whatever it was may have caused the deaths of the four children of Rudolf Paşa and his wife Perihan.'

There was a long silence, and then the old man said, 'No. No. Devil's House? No.'

Arto felt deflated. Talking to his uncle made him feel about ten again. A helpless child in amongst a sea of loud, bitter Armenian relatives, trying to be heard.

'Did I ever tell you about how my son, your cousin Levon, escaped from the World Trade Center on 9/11? Boy, now that is a story!' the old man said.

Arto hadn't heard the story, but he did know it from the duplicated letter Uncle Mesrob had sent him at Christmas 2001.

'Twenty-eight flights of stairs he ran down! Twenty-eight!'

'Uncle, what about the name Teufel Ev?' Arto said. 'Does that mean anything to you?'

There was only a short pause this time. 'Ah, you mean that confinement he had such trouble with?'

'So you do remember it? That name?'

Although what did he mean by 'confinement'?

'Sure. But I never heard it from my father. He was dead by the time that came up.'

'By the time what came up?'

Arto heard his uncle sigh. 'Your grandmother was talking. She was pissed at the way the Turks just seemed to forget her husband. How he'd saved the lives of this prince, that princess, some court dwarf . . . I said, as gently as I could, that no one cared about the Ottoman royal family any more. She said he'd saved Turkish soldiers in the war. On and on, and I just listened, or made like I was listening, and then she finally told me about my father's one and only admission of failure. She said it never left him.'

'What was it?'

'Like I say, a confinement in some place over on the Asian side called the Teufel Ev. Weird name. A woman was having a baby, a rich woman who paid him to attend. He was good at that stuff. He'd delivered babies before. But on that occasion he must've screwed up, because he lost first the child and then the mother. My mother said he told her he could have done more to save them. He blamed himself. But then that was typical of him. Maybe it's an Armenian thing? I don't know.'

Chapter 12

The boy in the black tracksuit was back in a police cell. The gun he'd waved at Mehmet Süleyman was at the ballistics laboratory. In the end he'd given it up quickly and easily. The rat he'd tried and failed to kill was no doubt celebrating being alive by nibbling on rubbish in the gutters of Tarlabaşı.

'Going to be another boiling day,' Ömer Mungun said as he looked out of Süleyman's office window at the rising sun.

Processing and questioning the young man had taken a long time. Then they'd had to circulate his description of the couple who had given him the gun. It hadn't been exactly comprehensive, but the boy had mentioned the woman's light, almost luminous eyes. Both officers had been up all night, and in a few minutes they'd be on the move again – back out to Tarlabaşı.

'If they've got any sense they'll have left the area,' Ömer said as he watched Süleyman light up yet another cigarette.

'I don't know that sense comes into it,' Süleyman said. 'According to the boy, the woman just walked up to him and gave him the gun.'

'In order to protect the city from the Devil.'

Süleyman shook his head. 'It can't really have happened like that. The boy's clearly suffering from some sort of psychosis.'

'And yet his description of the woman's eyes conforms to what we've been told about our hit-and-run female killer,' Ömer said.

'Maybe he read it somewhere . . .'

'And maybe he didn't. Maybe he saw that woman. What we don't know is whether she really did give him the gun.'

'A Beretta Centennial is a limited edition,' Süleyman said. 'It's hand-carved. It's the sort of thing far-right American politicians like – and gangsters. Something big and powerful to wave around.'

'Perhaps if this couple are the same ones who killed Hasan Dum and his henchman in Yeniköy, it's the gypsy's gun.'

'If that's the case, why give something so hard-won and valuable to a mad vagrant on the streets of Tarlabaşı?' Süleyman said.

Ömer shrugged. Then he frowned. 'Sir, wouldn't the henchman also have been carrying?'

'Yes. Of course. But he was clean when Forensics examined the body.'

'Which means there is potentially another gun still on the street.'

'Yes.' Süleyman checked his own weapon in the holster underneath his armpit. 'If we're lucky, we'll find it. If we're really fortunate, we'll also find this couple.' He stood up. 'Come on. Inspector Cıngı and his officers are waiting to give Tarlabaşı a rude awakening.'

Barçın Demirtaş hadn't been able to sleep. Maybe it had been the conversation she'd had the previous evening with İkmen about magic and the Devil that had kept her awake. Or perhaps she'd come to the station before dawn to make absolutely certain that she saw Inspector Mehmet Süleyman before he left to go about his business.

In the short time she had managed to sleep, she'd dreamed about him. It was just lust. She thought how disdainful her friend Turgut Zana would be if he knew. It made her laugh. Turgut's struggles with the foreign land of emotion sometimes made her look at herself in ways that could be useful. Pining over a man who was with someone else was a hiding to nothing. Turgut had described Süleyman's lover, Gonca Şekeroğlu, as a 'massive gypsy'. Barçın laughed again. How massive was 'massive'? Was the woman obese? Was the inspector one of those who liked to fuck fat women?

When she'd arrived at her office, the entire corridor had been dark. But now she noticed light coming in through her window. Outside in the station yard, cars and vans were being started up and their lights switched on. There were voices, and groups of officers wearing riot helmets and bulletproof vests stood about in groups, talking and smoking. Something was going on. But she wasn't part of it. She was a simple traffic officer, temporarily employed as some sort of expert. Soon enough it would be back to speeding fines and parking violations for her.

She picked a document off the top of the pile of letters nearest to her. It was dated 1 July 1955.

My dear brother Kanat,

I know you won't believe me, but I need you to be acquainted with the notion that I have had some success. A mere glimmer only, it is a presence of sorts. I even believe it has voice. If this is no false dawn, then maybe we can all soon begin our lives again. With newly clean souls, who knows what we may yet achieve? Please do reply, dear Kanat. You are my brother and I love you.

Ever yours,
Kemal

The noise outside the window increased. Barçın looked out and saw Inspector Mehmet Süleyman putting on a bulletproof vest. She wondered what was happening. Sergeant Mungun by his side, Süleyman climbed into a van full of uniforms in riot gear.

128

She'd only have to say the word and Ömer Mungun would take her out and treat her like a queen. He was young, attractive and intelligent. He was clearly into her. But . . .

Another man from the east? Barçın cringed. She hadn't been with a man for two years because of her last boyfriend. Şeymus had come from just outside Mardin and he too had been handsome, intelligent and really into her. In fact he'd been so into her he'd threatened to kill her when she'd refused his proposal of marriage because she wanted to work for a while longer before she became a wife. He'd also told her the bike had to go. That had been non-negotiable. Disentangling herself from Şeymus had taken almost a year and had involved a move to İstanbul. She didn't want to go there again.

She went back to the letters. What did Kemal mean? What was the success he spoke about? And how could it have a voice? What was 'it'? And was knowing that Kemal was apparently a sort of magician making her think he had created a being of some description?

She wondered whether Kanat had ever replied, and if so, what he'd said. She'd loosely arranged the letters into piles according to who had written them. Kanat had been the least enthusiastic writer and so that pile was small. She began to sort through it, looking for anything in 1955.

Ali was crying.

'We don't have time for this shit!' he said. 'We have to move!'

Elif didn't respond. If her eyes hadn't been open, he would have thought that maybe she was asleep. There was also the issue of the gun she had pointed at his head.

She'd given the other gun to some mad boy she'd got into conversation with. The boy was convinced the Devil was after him and so she'd given him the gun so he could protect himself. Had she believed him? Or had she done it for a laugh? Or to increase her own notoriety? If he was any sort of man he would kill her. But he couldn't.

'The police will be back,' he said. 'They took the boy away and he will have told them about us. You know what they are like. They can get blood out of stones. We have to get out of here!'

When the police had come to arrest the boy, Ali had pulled her into a derelict building, where they'd hidden underneath rubble for what had seemed like an eternity. Only when the streets had become calm again had he dared to look around. What he'd seen had made him shudder. Uniformed officers still wandered Tarlabaşı, and he had been certain they would be found at any moment. Then, about an hour ago, they had suddenly all disappeared.

'We have to go before the cops come back!'

'Why?' she said.

Why?

'Because they'll fucking arrest us,' Ali said. 'Because you gave a gun to a nutter!'

'He needed to protect himself . . .'

'You don't believe that!'

But he knew that was very possibly untrue. Elif believed all sorts of strange things. She swore she'd seen a monstrous beast swimming in the Bosphorus one day. He'd not seen anything. But then he knew all too well that smack talked to its addicts in unpredictable ways. That was what he'd always liked about it: the way it took you away from reality.

When he'd found her, she'd been working selling bonzai in Edirnekapı. She was addicted to the stuff, and her skin had already started to crack and bleed. The gross Syriani gangster who ran the operation made her have sex with him when she wasn't out peddling the synthetic cannabis half the city seemed to be dependent on. Ali had been stealing heroin from his father's surgery for years. It hadn't taken much effort to get a bit more for Elif. She'd liked it, and had quickly switched from bonzai to smack. And then his father had caught him.

'People have to know who I am!' she said. 'I told you that, and why!'

She'd never said who her parents were, or where she'd come from. The Syriani had been father, mother and husband to her since before she could remember, by turns brutalising and loving her. When she wasn't either working or sucking him off, her mind was fixated on trash television. Reality shows, inane chat, talent contests and soap operas coloured her desperate world; when Ali met her, she was addicted to high drama and the notion that anyone could be famous and rich provided they wanted it enough. Once, he'd taken her to an audition for *That Voice is Turkey*, a singing competition based on some European show. She'd sounded like a scalded cat and had been laughed off the stage. It was the cruellest thing Ali had ever seen. She'd self-harmed for months.

He pulled her to her feet.

'We don't have time for this!' he said. 'You might want to get yourself arrested, but I don't.'

'So fuck off then!' she said.

'I mean I don't want either of us to get arrested!' he said.

She didn't answer immediately. In that time he heard vehicles move through the district and then stop. Lots of them.

Fatma İkmen placed a glass of tea and a plate of fresh bread, cheese, butter and honey in front of Arto Sarkissian. 'Breakfast sets a man up for the day. Eat.' Then, with a withering look at her husband, she left the kitchen. İkmen never ate breakfast.

Once she was out of earshot, he said, 'If you don't want it, I'll give it to the cat.'

But Arto was already eating. 'Wouldn't dream of it,' he said. 'But I assume your breakfast . . .'

131

'In the cat,' İkmen said as he lit up his third cigarette of the morning. 'Vast ragged males like Marlboro need all the calories they can get round here. Sultanahmet's female cats are only impressed by size and possibly scars. God, you're early, Arto!'

'I wanted to see you before either of us became embroiled in our work,' the Armenian said. 'I spent much of last night looking for my grandfather's records, but to no avail.'

İkmen shrugged. 'It was a long shot.'

'But I did get to speak to my Uncle Mesrob in America.'

'Your father's younger brother, right?'

'Yes.'

He told his friend what his uncle had said about the Teufel Ev.

İkmen frowned. 'I knew Perihan Hanım died from septicaemia,' he said.

'How?'

'Sami Nasi told me.'

'Well, septicaemia may arise from numerous scenarios, including childbirth and abortion,' the doctor said.

'Rudolf Paşa had been dead for three years at the time of his wife's death. But given what she died from, I am unsurprised.'

'So not his child.'

'No. Remarriage? Do you know?'

'Uncle Mesrob made no reference to any husband,' Arto said. 'Just the woman and the baby and how sad my grandfather was that they both died.'

'And yet,' İkmen said, 'back in the 1930s, having a bastard child would have brought shame on any family. Even more so on the family of a paşa. The death of the child, surely, was the best outcome.'

'Unless she wanted it? Perhaps she really loved its father.'

'Male or female?'

'Mesrob didn't know,' Arto said. 'Maybe it's recorded somewhere in my grandfather's effects, but . . .' He shrugged. 'All he said was that the child died, and then its mother. My grandfather felt guilty about it for ever afterwards. News to me, but I can't see why Mesrob would lie.'

İkmen put his cigarette out, lit another and finished his tea. 'If Perihan Hanım did want that child, how was she going to explain it?' he said. 'Ignoring the wider world for a moment here, what was she going to tell her children?'

'Perhaps they knew. This happened in the early years of the republic, remember. Atatürk was pulling the country kicking and screaming away from the Ottoman Empire and the strictures of religion.'

'Yes, but as we know, those pre-republican attitudes persist; some would say they just get stronger to this day. I repeat, what was she going to do? Hide in that house for the rest of her life?'

'Maybe she thought she could brazen it out?'

İkmen shook his head. 'According to your uncle, your grandfather cared that he'd lost mother and baby. Just professional pride, do you think?'

'I can't be sure, but I doubt it,' Arto said. 'You remember my father and how deeply he cared about his patients. One of the reasons why I work with the dead is because I know I couldn't find enough inside myself to care as thoroughly as I should for living patients. My father inherited his clinical mores from my grandfather. I believe old Kevork cared.'

'Mmm.' İkmen heard Fatma's footsteps in the hall. 'She's coming back,' he said. 'You'd better finish your food or she'll shout.'

Arto quickly buttered a piece of bread and threw it into his mouth.

Fatma walked into the kitchen and eyed him suspiciously.

The Armenian chewed and smiled.

* * *

133

Only one letter had been written by Kanat Rudolfoğlu during 1955. It was addressed to his brother Kemal. But was it a reply to the letter from Kemal that she'd read earlier? Barçın leaned back in her chair and studied it again.

Kemal,
You are insane. There is nothing to be done. Bear your pain like a man. I hate what you do and why. I hate you. Not as much as I hate that woman, but almost. I'd like to die soon so that I don't have to hear your madness through my walls any more. You are dead to me. Kindly stay so.
Kanat

'That woman' had to be Fatima Hanım. Why so much hatred for her? But then why such vitriol towards Kemal? What had they done?

Tarlabaşı was sealed off from the world. Houses, shops, apartments, derelict sites – people ran into the streets carrying children and valuables, while addicts dropped bags of bonzai out of windows or flushed them down toilets. Half-dressed transsexuals kicked sleeping men in vests out of their beds. On one street officers led four handcuffed men out of a derelict house, followed by the three Kalashnikov rifles they'd stashed behind an old fireplace.

Mehmet Süleyman had no great confidence in the operation, which in his opinion should have been carried out as soon as the boy in the black tracksuit had been arrested. Even if he had been given the gun by this couple he'd told them about, they had to have moved on by this time. But then a small group of uniforms had stayed in the area for most of the night, so perhaps they had been scared enough to stay put?

Inspector Cıngı of the organised crime unit wasn't the easiest man to work alongside. The grieving Dum family knew him well, and a huge amount of police time and energy was being used on them and their properties. Admittedly a few hand weapons had been recovered from the Dum patriarch's house, but unless the boy had stolen one of their guns, the Dums were irrelevant. He couldn't help thinking that Organised Crime were using large numbers of officers usually assigned elsewhere to make sure the family didn't get any expansionist ideas in the wake of Hasan's death.

Ömer Mungun had gone to talk to a couple of men who only spoke Aramaic. Like him, they came from the district of Mardin and were probably of Syriani origin, which meant that they were Christians. When Ömer had finished taking their details, he walked over to Süleyman.

'Anything?'

'No, sir,' the sergeant said. 'Although the younger of the two, Luko, suggests we go and see old Sugar Barışık.'

Süleyman smiled. Was she really still alive?

Sugar Barışık was a fat, elderly prostitute who knew everyone and everything in Tarlabaşı. She ran a sex shop in a basement near the Syriani church. Süleyman hadn't seen her for at least two years, but once inside her hovel, it was as if no time at all had passed.

Still sitting in her broken chair, surrounded by dildos, handcuffs and countless stray cats, Sugar looked at Süleyman and said, 'Hello, gorgeous.'

'Sugar Hanım.'

She smiled at Ömer. 'And your young friend.' She laughed. 'Oh, if I were forty years younger, I'd fuck you both just for fun. We could have a threesome! You'd have liked me when I was young, you know.'

'I'm sure,' Süleyman said.

'I had a figure like Venus back then, and a mouth that was the gateway to heaven, if you know what I mean.'

He did.

'Mind you,' she said, 'I don't know why you brought all your ugly friends along with you. Pushing people around, taking their drugs off them . . .'

'We found a very sick young boy with a powerful gun here last night,' Süleyman said.

'What? The one who shot at a rat? You arrested him? He's out of his mind.'

'Yes, but some people gave him a gun, Sugar Hanım,' Ömer said. 'We need to find them because we think they've got another one.'

'Mmm.' She looked down at the floor. The dead eyes of a disembowelled mouse stared back at her. Süleyman remembered that Sugar didn't often formally feed her cats. Or clean. 'You know we get all sorts coming through here these days,' she said. 'Now that everyone's on that bonzai shit, they come here to score. Posh, some of them. Doesn't appeal to me, though. Can't see the pleasure in being out of your head. And it gives some of them heart attacks. I could get one of them just walking up the steps into the street . . .'

'Sir . . .'

Süleyman looked at Ömer Mungun.

'Yes?'

'Sir, don't look. At the window,' the sergeant said.

'What?'

'It's a young woman with very pale eyes.'

As the two men came out of the shop, Ali took hold of Elif's arm and said, 'Run.'

'Er, excuse me . . .' a voice called out.

'Run!'

He pulled her along behind him. But she was off her face.

'Come on!' he said.

136

She was laughing now. Her arm felt like a piece of waterlogged vinyl, and the toes of her trainers caught on every stone in the road so that he had to hold her up.

'Stop! Police!'

'I've got a fucking gun!' she yelled.

Ali saw her try to put her hand in her jacket pocket, but she was so fucked, she couldn't get anywhere near the weapon.

A very dark young man was almost catching them up, while an older, taller man brought up the rear. And there were other coppers: on the street corner in front of them, coming out of a shabby grocer's shop, cuffing some kid with his head in his hands. They'd either be caught or shot. No other scenario was realistic. Ali stopped.

Elif laughed. 'I'll shoot the lot of you! Bastards.'

But as she moved her hand, Ali got in first and took the gun. Suddenly the noise on the street stopped completely. Then the sound of multiple weapons being primed and raised and aimed made him wet his pants.

Chapter 13

Mustafa Kaiserli was married but had no children. His apartment in Beşiktaş was, İkmen reckoned, worth about a quarter of a million euros. He owned it and so he had money. But other than that, his life seemed to be quite sparse and dull.

'Ceyda works,' he said in answer to Kerim Gürsel's question about his employment status.

'Your wife.'

'Yes. She's a tour guide. You know there's not much I can tell you about the Devil's House.'

İkmen had told him on the doorstep what he wanted to talk to him about.

'Your father worked there.'

'Yes. But way before I was born,' he said. 'He left when Rudolf Paşa's wife died.'

'Do you know why?'

'No. All he ever told me was that shortly after the woman died, he was asked to leave.'

'By the children?'

'I imagine so,' he said.

'Mr Kaiserli, did you know that your father caught one of the Rudolfoğlu children, a boy called Kemal, desecrating the ayazma of St Katherine in Moda?' İkmen asked.

'Yes, although I don't know anything about it.'

'What do you mean? You don't know why the boy was damaging the shrine, or why your father was there?'

'Neither,' he said. 'My father never spoke about it.'

'So how do you know about it?' İkmen said.

'I'm Greek,' he said. 'We're a small community. When something happens to one of us or to one of our historic places, we know about it.'

'Do any of your fellow Greeks have any theories about it, do you know?'

He sighed. 'Only about when it happened,' he said. 'We weren't popular at the beginning of the republic. We were seen as traitors, a fifth column invading from Greece. That boy was very young, he'd recently lost his father, the Ottoman Empire had disintegrated, his country was ruined and even his place in society as a member of the aristocracy had gone.'

'I've worked out, if indeed Kemal Rudolfoğlu was thirteen at the time, that the attempted desecration happened in 1931,' İkmen said. 'Quite a long time after the republic was declared in 1923, but the same year as Perihan Rudolfoğlu's death and the same year your father was let go from the Devil's House. Do you think he was dismissed because of his intervention at the shrine?'

'I don't know.'

'He didn't ever say?'

'No.'

Mustafa Kaiserli, aka Yiannis Apion, clearly didn't want to talk. A small, grey man in his fifties, he had the look of someone for whom life was a spectator sport.

'Do you know what your father did after he left the Devil's House?' İkmen said.

'I wasn't born until the fifties,' Kaiserli said. 'My father was in his forties by then, and disabled.'

'How did he become disabled?'

'He was hit by a tram and lost a leg. Before I was born. I don't know what he did for work after he left the Devil's House. I don't ever remember him working. My mother worked.'

'Is your mother still alive, Mr Kaiserli?'

'No, she died back in the 1960s,' he said.

'And your father?'

'Four years ago. I nursed him myself. He was ninety-eight years old.'

'Incredible,' İkmen said. 'You know that the four Rudolfoğlu siblings were all over ninety when they were murdered.'

He shrugged.

'Did you ever see the Rudolfoğlu siblings?' İkmen asked.

'No. Why would I?'

'You were born and brought up in Moda.'

'Yes, but my father never spoke about his past,' Kaiserli said. 'All I knew as a child was that he'd worked as a gardener for an Ottoman family. I didn't know where until I was much older. I'm sorry the old people are dead, but I don't think I can help you.'

'Maybe not.' İkmen smiled. 'Although I do have to ask whether your father was maybe bitter about losing his job at the Devil's House.'

'What, all those years ago?' He laughed. 'If you're looking for a reason why the Rudolfoğlus were murdered, then you've come to the wrong place. My father didn't care about them, and I never knew them.'

Later, back in his car with Kerim Gürsel, İkmen said, 'There are so few Greeks in the city these days. I wonder what they think. I mean, imagine if you felt you had to change your name just to fit in.' Then he remembered that he knew something about Kerim that most certainly set him apart. 'But of course you do know,' he added.

'I've never had to change my name, sir.'

'No, but . . .'

'And I am married – to a woman.'

'Yes, but both of you . . . Well, you know what I mean.'

'Yes, sir.'

Kerim and his wife Sinem's sexuality was a closely guarded secret, known only to a select few.

İkmen started the car. 'Logically the Rudolfoğlus got rid of the gardener Konstantinos Apion when their mother died to save money. But as we know, the house belonged in law to Fatima Hanım, and she was only twelve.'

'Her brothers must have had a hand in it too,' Kerim said.

'Normally I'd agree,' İkmen said. 'But in this case, I do wonder. When Perihan Hanım died, the siblings parted. I wonder how quickly after his employer's death Konstantinos Apion was let go from the Devil's House.'

His phone rang.

'Shit.' He took the call, which was from the Forensic Institute.

Hanging out of his office window, a cigarette between his lips, Mehmet Süleyman was trying to make himself feel normal. With his heart smashing against his ribs, this wasn't easy.

The man had just given himself and the gun up without a murmur. But the woman . . . Ömer had borne the brunt of her. Kicking, scratching, biting. Once they'd brought her under control, Süleyman had sent his sergeant to hospital. Like the man, the woman was a junkie, which meant that she could be carrying all sorts of bacteria.

The man, Ali Erbil, was being booked in by the custody team, who would sort out whether he wanted a lawyer or not. Süleyman knew he'd have to interview both of them, but he also knew he'd start with Mr Erbil. The woman, who was called Elif, was currently screaming in a cell awaiting the arrival of a psychiatrist, who would, hopefully, sedate her.

Unlike the gun they'd recovered from the black-tracksuited boy, the weapon Erbil had given up was a very ordinary Glock. He wondered whether the man would continue to be compliant.

A knock on the door almost made him scream. But frayed as his nerves were, he knew he hadn't locked his office door. And he didn't care.

'Come in, it's open.'

It was the Kurdish traffic cop.

'Oh, er, sorry to disturb you, sir,' she said. 'Do you know when Inspector İkmen is getting back?'

'No, I'm afraid I don't,' he said.

She was looking at him strangely, with her head on one side, her brow furrowed.

'Is anything the matter?' he asked.

'No. I just need to show him something. His phone is off, and . . . Inspector Süleyman, are you all right?'

'Why?'

'You're very pale, sir,' she said. 'And you have some blood on your collar. I saw you leave early this morning . . .'

'We may have arrested the people responsible for the killing in the bazaar and the murder on the Galata Bridge,' he said. 'I've yet to interview the suspects. One of them put up a fight.'

'And injured you!'

'No,' he said. 'I'm fine. A little shocked, that's all. The blood, I'm sorry to say, is Sergeant Mungun's.'

'Is he all right?'

He motioned for her to sit down and offered her a cigarette.

'Bitten and scratched. I sent him to hospital,' he said. 'Our suspects are both, from the state of their arms, heroin users, and so one can't be too careful.'

'No.'

'Is there anything I can help you with, Constable?'

'Perhaps,' she said. 'As you know, sir, I'm transliterating letters found at the crime scene in Moda.' She shook her head. 'The victims had such strange relationships with each other. At times it almost seems as if they were living in a fantasy. Not a pleasant one.'

'Perhaps they were. Living in a fantasy.'

'Maybe, but I'm becoming concerned that everything I'm doing might be irrelevant. They can't have killed each other, and yet so much of what I'm reading exhibits murderous intent. Do you know whether there has been any word from the forensic investigation?'

'No, I don't,' he said. 'All I do know is that Inspector İkmen is out with Sergeant Gürsel. Ah, now that's a thought. Have you tried his number?'

'Sergeant Gürsel?'

'Yes. Çetin Bey is, as I'm sure you know, not a lover of technology. He switches his phone off whenever he feels he can. But Sergeant Gürsel is a true son of the twenty-first century and so his mobile is always on. Try it.'

She smiled. 'That's a good idea. I will.'

She rose to leave. He caught a glimpse of the tops of her breasts. He wondered how they would feel – and taste.

He stopped her. 'Oh, Constable, we left at dawn this morning,' he said. 'If you saw us go, you must have been here very early.'

'Yes.' She felt her face colour. 'I couldn't sleep,' she said. 'There's so much material to go through.'

Was that the truth? From the blush on her cheeks, he wondered. But then what else could she have been doing?

'Don't work too hard,' he said. 'I understand completely that you want to do a good job. But don't wear yourself out. Çetin Bey is an individual who attracts intense loyalty – I know; I used to work for him – but he wouldn't want you to make yourself ill.'

'No, sir.'

* * *

143

Every section of her viscera itched. Her skin was entirely calm and her eyes were shut, but inside everything was churning, irritating, howling. She knew she looked at peace because she'd seen how the coppers had reacted when that doctor had spiked her. She knew what it was. The stuff they gave the loonies so they could throw them into hospitals where they'd be tortured and raped. She'd grown up listening to stories told by roaming prophets on the streets about the poison that made a person calm outside while killing him inside. Somehow she'd get round it. It had to stop sometime, and when it did, she'd strike. She'd sunk her teeth into that copper and she hadn't seen him since. Had she killed him? That would be a coup. An unlooked-for bonus.

Her Syriani father/lover had killed, and he'd thrown a million euros on his bed and had sex with her on it while she watched the singing contests on the television. She loved the girls with the big hair and high voices who cried. Their tears fell on to the diamonds stitched on the silk dresses they wore. Sometimes they wiped their eyes with their long painted nails, and just occasionally, you'd see their handsome boyfriends in the audience. Lucky girls. Lucky famous girls who didn't itch inside and who didn't want to kill the world.

If they kept her like this forever, Elif still wouldn't believe she was being punished for what she'd done. Murder was never punished. Murderers got rich. Girls who had sex with men were punished, and she'd done that all her life. Only Ali hadn't made her do that. If they needed money, he did it. But Ali was unusual. He was a saint.

'Sometimes, if my wife wasn't feeling well, I'd help her. She's got women's trouble now. It's her age.'

İkmen looked at the overweight, slightly rumpled figure of Bilal İnce and knew that the guilt on his face was not in his imagination.

'Really,' he said. 'Your wife didn't mention taking you to her place of work.'

'She must have forgotten.'

'I find that hard to believe. But if you say so . . . How many times did you go to the Teufel Ev?'

'Two or three,' he said.

İkmen took note of the photograph of the Kaa'ba in Mecca on the wall, the little light-bulb flag of the AK Party on top of the television. 'You're a good Muslim, Mr İnce.'

'Yes, of course,' he said, as if that was in some way a given.

'Well then you will know about the value of telling the truth,' İkmen said.

Bilal İnce nodded.

İkmen leaned across the coffee table towards him. 'If you don't care about lying to the police, then I imagine you do care that Allah is watching and listening. And before you think about justifying your actions by asserting that Fatima Hanım was some sort of infidel, then remember that, through her mother, she was also a member of the Ottoman royal family. My understanding is that the political party you claim to support holds the Osmanoğlu family in high regard. Also, if it's any help to you, I can tell that you're lying. I've been doing this job for forty years, and trust me, it's written all over you. Oh, and there's forensic evidence too.'

Bilal İnce picked up the remote control. For a moment, İkmen thought he might be about to turn the TV up to drown out his words. But instead he muted it. Then he stood up and walked into the one small bedroom in the apartment.

Kerim shrugged. But İkmen stayed where he was and waited. Bilal İnce was too fat to climb out of a window, especially one that was three floors up. And in the course of time, he duly returned.

He placed a thin twist of paper on the coffee table. 'I took it.'

İkmen put on a pair of latex gloves and opened the parcel. It contained a large boncuk, or evil eye talisman, encased in thick yellow gold. The blue eye stone looked as if it might be a sapphire.

'My brother's daughter is having a baby any day now,' İnce said. 'My brother is a builder; he gets contracts all over the country. He makes a fortune. My sisters too have money. One is married to an IT specialist and the other to an official in the Fatih mayoral office.'

'And you're a . . .'

'I'm sick,' he said. 'A back problem. Selin works, but she earns nothing. It's true that sometimes I have walked with her to work, for the company. But this day . . .' He sighed and rubbed his hands over his face.

'Which was when?'

'A month ago. Three weeks . . . I'm not entirely sure.'

'You took this boncuk.'

'I couldn't face it, not again,' he said. 'Everyone bringing expensive presents for yet another family baby, and Selin and myself turning up with some bit of trash. My own children looking at me as if I'm a piece of dirt. I saw it on the old woman's dressing table and I took it. A moment of weakness. But I didn't kill her, I swear.'

İkmen looked at the jewel. 'Did you find it in this paper?' he asked.

'No,' İnce said. 'That was lying on the dressing table. I wrapped the boncuk up in it so that it wouldn't make a noise in my pocket. I didn't want Selin to know.'

'So theft with forethought,' İkmen said.

'Yes.' He bowed his head.

The paper was covered in weird, shaky-looking Ottoman script. Had Fatima Hanım been looking at one of her letters and left it on her dressing table?

146

İkmen looked up at Kerim Gürsel. 'Charge him with theft, Sergeant.'

'Yes, sir.'

Ali Erbil wasn't just another junkie.

'Your father is an oncologist,' Mehmet Süleyman said.

He'd chosen to interview the man because, according to the custody staff, he wanted to talk. The woman was another matter. She, he felt, even under sedation, would have to be approached with caution.

'Yes,' Ali answered.

'Oncologists have access to very powerful pain medications,' Süleyman said.

'If you want to know whether I stole my stuff from my dad, then the answer is sometimes,' Ali said. 'But he didn't throw me out because of that. My dad's a really nice man. I left. Does my dad know I'm here?'

'Yes. He would like you to have a lawyer.'

'I don't want one,' he said. 'God, Dad must be so upset!'

Dr Erbil had been upset when the police had arrived at the door of his smart Nişantaşı apartment, but he had also been relieved that his son had finally been found alive.

'At the moment,' Süleyman said, 'you are being held for possession of an illegal firearm plus a quantity of heroin. You are also implicated in the supply of another illegal firearm to a third party. In addition I have reason to believe that you and the woman we understand is called Elif Büyük may have been involved in crimes of violence in this city. I should point out to you now that we possess forensic material from three sites where people have been murdered in the course of the last seven days. Those sites are the Grand Bazaar, Zeytinburnu tram station and the Galata Bridge.'

'I see.'

147

'Would you like to consult a lawyer?'

'No.'

'Very well. Then will you tell me what—'

'I did it all,' he said. 'I killed those people. I killed all of them. I did it on my own.'

Barçın Demirtaş knocked on İkmen's office door and then went in. She held the thin piece of paper that Bilal İnce had given to the detective.

İkmen offered her a seat. 'Well?'

'Well,' she said, 'it's a letter from a very young Fatima Hanım to her father.'

She sat down.

'Interesting. What does it say?'

'It's a promise,' she said. 'In short, Fatima Hanım is promising to make sure that her mother behaves properly when her father dies.'

'When was this?'

'It's dated 1928.'

'The year Rudolf Paşa died.'

'Yes. So Fatima would have been nine. Not that the letter is what you'd call childish,' she said. 'The handwriting is immature but the content is . . . well, I think it's remarkable.'

'In what way?'

'This was a girl who was all over her father,' Barçın said. 'On one level it's a love note, and I do mean that. The passion this child expresses is bordering on something that makes me very suspicious. But it's the way she talks about her mother that really makes me shudder. Again, passion, but this time hatred. A little girl, telling her father that she'll make sure that her mother behaves in a proper way once he has died; that she won't let her be alone with a man and that she'll ensure that she covers in public. If Rudolf Paşa really wanted Perihan to behave in this way, then he must have become completely Ottomanised.'

'Some of them did,' İkmen said. 'A number of the German troops converted to Islam. But then again, that might just have been his character. Lock my door, will you, please, Constable.'

'Yes, sir.'

İkmen lit a cigarette. 'Now,' he said. 'According to our pathologist, Dr Sarkissian, his grandfather, Dr Kevork Sarkissian, attended Perihan Hanım when she gave birth to a child in 1931. His source, an elderly relative, did not mention any husband. Also we don't know whether, at birth, the child was alive or dead. What we do know is that Perihan must have had sex with a man in spite of her daughter's promise. The story goes that the princess died of septicaemia, but we don't know how soon that happened after she gave birth. What we have to ask ourselves is: did her children know? And if they did, what does that mean?'

'You think they killed their own mother?'

'I think it's possible, though maybe it wasn't all of them.'

'Fatima was only twelve,' Barçın said.

He shrugged. 'Never heard of child murderers, Constable?'

'Yes, but . . .' She shook her head. 'Sir, I've not been able to talk to you about the letters until now. I've been really conflicted about them.'

'In what way?'

'I can't work out whether all this hatred between the siblings is just an illusion. Today I've read a series of letters about Kemal from the other three. Fatima to Kanat, Yücel to Fatima, et cetera. What he is doing – sorcery, I guess – bothers them. Kanat calls him insane. He exhorts him to take his punishment, whatever that is, like a man, and says he hates him and wishes he were dead. Kanat also openly hates "that woman", who I assume is Fatima.'

'Well if she killed their mother, what can you expect?' İkmen said. 'Plus we know that their father left that house and all his worldly goods to Fatima.'

'This is just so strange. Kanat even wants to meet with Fatima and Yücel to talk about Kemal. I don't yet know whether that ever happened.'

'Mmm.' İkmen leaned back in his chair. 'These were people who came from a much-maligned background at a time of fear for the old elites. The Ottomans were perceived by many as being responsible for the First World War and for the ruination of the empire. Many of them were still afraid for their lives. And they were superstitious. We know that Kemal practised alchemy, which his siblings would have believed was a real force for evil.'

'But how does that relate to their deaths?' she said. 'If at all?'

'Maybe it doesn't. We know that nothing was stolen – bar the boncuk taken by the husband of Fatima's carer – and sometimes people kill for kicks, though that's rare. All I can say, Constable, is keep on looking. I've had an email from Forensics, who have discovered some unidentified DNA material, so someone we don't know about yet must have been in that house. Normally we'd have at least some CCTV footage. But the Teufel Ev has no cameras, and over the years the house has all but disappeared. Nobody thinks about it. It has become a tangle of weeds and trees behind some shops.'

'What about Yücel Rudolfoğlu's carer?' she asked.

'Background checks have revealed nothing of any importance,' İkmen said. 'He has no connection to the family, no criminal record. He's a genuinely philanthropic man who chooses to care for elderly people by day while working as a dancer in a gay bar at night. Forensically he's clean.'

Chapter 14

He saw her when they moved him to another cell. The woman who had given him the gun, slung between two policemen, her head down, a thin thread of drool hanging from her mouth. He asked them why she was there, but they just told him to shut the fuck up.

The woman herself didn't say a word, didn't even look in his direction. As they disappeared down a corridor with her, he shouted, 'Be careful, sister! They're not who you think they are!'

Then he got a slap and so he became silent. But at least he'd warned her. He could see those coppers' horns through their caps, their tails sticking out of their trousers . . .

'I hate confessions,' Çetin İkmen said.

'I only like them when they're genuine,' Mehmet Süleyman replied. 'And this one isn't.'

It wasn't often that the two men had time to meet, talk and drink on their own. Usually İkmen's sorties to the Mosaik Bar were large gatherings, but this evening it was just the two of them. Even İkmen's cat Marlboro was elsewhere.

'He's covering for the woman,' he continued.

'Ah, the magnetism of the female . . .'

'She's a junkie,' Süleyman said.

'So is the man, according to you.'

'Yes, but at least he can read,' Süleyman said. 'Actually Ali

Erbil has been extremely well educated, partly abroad. Father's an oncologist. He was brought up in a well-appointed apartment in Nişantaşı.'

'Ah, but as we know, the delights of smack transcend all classes,' İkmen said. 'I take it this woman is not someone of whom the man's father would approve?'

'Her soliciting career goes way back into her childhood,' Süleyman said. 'Elif Büyük is a street addict. Can't read or write and was probably born into prostitution. She's also, I am sure, mentally ill.'

'Not a winning combination.'

'No, but Ali loves her.'

İkmen shook his head. 'Who knows where the heart will lead, eh? Does Mr Erbil's confession stand up?'

Süleyman frowned. 'I'll come to that.' He took a sip from his whisky glass and lit a cigarette. The fierce heat of the day had finally abated and been replaced by a tolerably warm evening. Both men were enjoying being outside.

'So, apart from the fact that he's in love with this woman and comes from a rich family, what else do you know about Ali Erbil?' İkmen said.

'He has a degree in Natural Sciences from Cambridge University. He was going to do a PhD, but then his sister died, so he came home. That's when the addiction began. He stole from his father, drugs and money, wouldn't look for work, and then three years ago, he left Nişantaşı for life on the street.'

'Which can't have been comfortable.'

'No. But reading between the lines, it would seem that his relationship with Elif Büyük made it bearable. Love among the syringes. Ali's father wants him to have a lawyer, even though he has refused representation. He turned up with one this afternoon.'

'Who you sent away.'

'What else could I do? Ali's an adult. Although I think that in his way, he is as mentally ill as his girlfriend.'

'Not many addicts escape mental scars,' İkmen said.

'The problem is,' Süleyman said, 'that in part his story does stack up. I've no doubt he's involved, but as a sole perpetrator . . .'

'What has he admitted to?' İkmen asked.

'The lot, and more.'

'Which is?'

'The killing of Ali Baykal in the Grand Bazaar, of the Englishman Simon Oates on the Galata Bridge, and of the gangster Hasan Dum and his Hungarian henchman Gabor Karpathy. He has also held his hands up to the murder of Saira Öymen in the tram car. Mrs Öymen was killed by a large dose of heroin, but initially, at least, I was rather erring on the side of her husband being the perpetrator, even though I had no evidence to that effect.'

'Why?'

'He beat his wife. And when I say beat, I mean there was damage to her internal organs.'

İkmen wrinkled his nose. 'Vile!'

'The few witnesses we have had to these killings have described the assailants as a couple,' Süleyman said. 'In addition, I was told this afternoon that the gun the woman gave to the boy in Tarlabaşı used to belong to Hasan Dum. These are probably the people we've been looking for, but Ali wants Elif to go free and I don't.'

'You think she stuck the odd syringe in?'

'I think she was the prime mover. Ali Erbil, in spite of the smack, is just too, well, mild.'

'See how he shapes up when he can't get his fix,' İkmen suggested.

'Yes, well, I may be wrong,' Süleyman said. 'I accept that.

153

But you know what happened to Ömer when he tackled that woman. Her fingers nearly caught one of his eyes, and that bite on his neck is no joke. I've ordered psychiatric appraisals on both of them, but I think she's the one who actually committed the acts of violence.'

'Do you know why?'

'No. Ali Erbil isn't big on explanations. He just wants to confess with no questions asked.'

İkmen lit a cigarette.

'Sadly for him, the relatives of these victims won't be satisfied with a confession,' Süleyman continued. 'When someone you love dies, you need to know why.'

'Even when you don't love them,' İkmen said. 'If I don't find out why the Rudolfoğlu siblings died, even if I know who killed them, I will consider my investigation a failure. Not that it looks as if I'm going to come up with a perpetrator any time soon.'

Turgut Zana wasn't the most exciting person to spend time with, but at least he was familiar. And he had promised to take her to Balyan Patisserie in Kadıköy and buy her the most heavenly ice cream dessert in the world. Ever since she'd arrived in İstanbul, Barçın Demirtaş had been devoted to Balyan's signature confection, Kup Kurmanji. Made from caramel sauce, Chantilly cream, nuts and, of course, ice cream, it was something that would always make her happy and never let her down.

There was no way she was going to ride her bike over the Bosphorus Bridge to get to Kadıköy, so she'd decided to leave it in police headquarters car park. She was bending down checking that it was secure when she heard a familiar voice.

'Constable Demirtaş, is that your bike?'

She turned and looked up. It wasn't easy not to appear

154

shocked. His face was covered in deep iodine-soaked scratches, and a huge lint pad on his neck stuck out over his shirt collar.

'Yes, Sergeant Mungun,' she said. 'I thought you were in hospital.' She stood up.

'They patched me up, gave me a few shots and then I was free to go,' he said.

'Not to work?' she said. 'Surely?'

'No.' He smiled. 'I know the boss has left. I came by to pick up my laptop. I thought I'd be coming back here after the operation in Tarlabaşı this morning, but of course I didn't, and I need it.'

'Success this morning,' she said. 'Except for your, er, your . . .'

He shook his head. 'You know it was a woman?'

'Yes, Inspector Süleyman told me.'

'I'm on antibiotics, and I've had a tetanus shot, a rabies shot and an HIV test.'

'You must be exhausted,' she said. 'How did you get here? You didn't drive, did you?'

'No.' He smiled. 'You know, or maybe you don't, that people often get Inspector Süleyman wrong. He really looks after people who work for him. He sent one of his friends to get me.'

'That's nice,' she said.

'Yes. I'll have to grab my computer and go or I'll hold her up. I like your bike.'

'Oh yes,' she said. 'Although I'm leaving it here tonight. I'm meeting a friend in Kadıköy.'

'And you don't want to have to battle across the bridge.'

'Who does?'

'Ömer! Come on!'

The voice was deep and husky.

He looked across the car park and waved at a tall, curvaceous woman leaning on the boot of a very old Mercedes.

'One minute, Gonca Hanım,' he called back. 'Sorry!' He turned back to Barçın. 'I have to go.'

'Of course.'

He ran towards the building Barçın had just left. When he'd gone, she took a moment to look at the woman she knew was Mehmet Süleyman's mistress. So this was Gonca the gypsy. Not exactly beautiful and not exactly young, she nevertheless had a distinct glamour about her that was emphasised by her vivid eye make-up and dramatic clothes. A tightly fitted black lace jacket above a long black fishtailed skirt gave her a gothic look. Hardly 'massive', as Turgut had described her, though she did have a very large, half-exposed bust, and the bun she'd created with her hair was so big it could have been a hat. Significantly, she was sensual. Even when she picked dirt from underneath her long bright red nails, she did it in such a way that it looked like a sex act.

Barçın wondered how this woman would feel if she knew that her lover had been staring at another woman's breasts. She'd seen him.

Father Anatoli knew that one was supposed to sip rather than gulp the sacred water from the St Katherine ayazma. But it had been so hot all day long, and he had been out and about since dawn. Just because his congregation was tiny didn't mean that his responsibilities were small. He had two significant buildings to look after – the shrine and the church. And the latter was vast. Built for many thousands of Byzantine Greeks, it now played host to a congregation of barely a hundred, and that included, in the winter, Syrian refugees just trying to get in out of the cold. Lately, some Kurds had come to Moda with tales of trouble brewing again in the east. He'd let them sleep in the church. Father Anatoli remembered the 1990s, when the so-called 'white Toros' murders had plagued the Kurdish population in places like Diyarbakır and Mardin. White Toros cars, it was said, had roamed the streets of Kurdish towns, their occupants kidnapping and then killing local people. The Kurds said the murders were orchestrated by the government of the time, but no one really knew. The crimes were still unsolved.

Not for the first time, Father Anatoli prayed for the souls of the Rudolfoğlu siblings. None were omitted. He also, though it pained him to do so, prayed for the souls of the parents of those children. He had never known any of them, so who was he to judge things they had done so many years ago? All he had to go on were stories told to him by those who were far from perfect themselves. He just hoped that eventually the police would give up on the case and forget about it. Those who had done wrong would be punished by God and their own consciences in the fullness of time. To bring such horror into the light after so many years was, he felt, the work of the Devil. It would only bring with it more pain and distress than he knew he could bear. But then he was a weak man and he recognised it.

It was that bloody Çetin İkmen's fault! Meddling with things he shouldn't. Sami cursed himself for giving the policeman information. He was at least partly to blame. İkmen hadn't exactly twisted his arm, had he? Why had he done it?

Rüya was sleeping now, poor little thing. He'd probably traumatised her for life. She'd almost certainly leave, and then his heart and the act would lie dormant again for who knew how many decades. He'd be dementing by the time he managed to recruit anyone else, and if word ever got out, that would be impossible.

He fixed the sword back on the wall and sat in front of his open window. Down on the street, people were enjoying the warm evening, blissfully unaware of the havoc that was being wreaked by forces unleashed by the overly bold and unwary. Things had started to go wrong just after the elections. The country had begun to drift in directions that suggested bad entities were on the move. Then the Rudolfoğlus had been murdered and suddenly it was as if their father was back again, ably assisted by his evil adjutant Dimitri Bey, sending his Turkish troops to die in the deserts of Arabia and dancing with the Devil in the basement of his palace. It was said that he could make grass die just by looking at it, that he had sex with prepubescent children and that his daughter was a witch.

Sami hadn't told İkmen everything. Maybe he shouldn't have told him anything if this was going to happen.

Rüya walked in from the bedroom and sat beside him. Sami Nasi didn't know whether to reach over and take her hand. He couldn't look at her.

'Rüya . . .'

'These things happen,' she said. 'I knew the risks. You've never hidden them from me.'

She was twenty-seven years old, and yet how much more mature was she than he? Now he looked at her, at the sweetness of her face and the enormous bruise on her neck. Only at the last minute had he realised that if he didn't flatten the blade of his great-grandfather's sword, he would take her head. She'd got away with a black, swollen bruise the size of a fist, but she was still alive.

'I could have killed you,' he said. He put a hand up to her face. She kissed it.

'But you didn't,' she said. 'Sami, darling, if I had wanted to have a life of security, I would have married my cousin Necmettin and stayed in my village. But then I met you and fell in love, and this whole new world of risk, magic and glamour opened up. As I said, these things happen.'

'Yes, but—'

She put a finger on his lips, then kissed him. 'Tomorrow we'll do the trick again,' she said. 'And it will be fine.'

He was glad that she was so confident. He wasn't. But then Rüya just thought that what had happened had been an accident. Sami wasn't going to tell her any different. He didn't want to do the trick again until he could put things right.

Realisation had come to Ali Erbil late. Even with his confession, the police weren't going to let Elif go. She'd assaulted one of their own. They didn't take kindly to that. Also, that Inspector Süleyman hadn't believed him. He'd kept on asking him for details he couldn't remember. He'd invented some things completely. But then it had all ended up in a sort of fog.

Before the incident in Yeniköy, he'd been able to convince himself that what they were doing was some sort of anarchical statement. He knew that if the oppressed didn't rise up against their corrupt masters and take ruthless action, nothing would ever change. And Elif was the most oppressed person he had ever met. He had known that poor, illiterate and abused people existed, but he'd never encountered one before. She'd told him terrible stories in their early days together. About being so hungry her belly swelled; about having sex with one old man after another; about the miscarriages she'd had in the street like a feral cat. But what he hadn't really understood, until Yeniköy, was the extent of her rage.

Both those men had been armed. All Elif had was a shard of glass. But she'd gone at the older man in a frenzy so intense it had temporarily paralysed the other character. She'd wounded them both so badly that she'd had to do very little to finish them off. But she'd done more than a little. He'd watched her, mesmerised by her need to spill more, more and then yet more blood.

When she'd finished, her victims had been barely recognisable and she'd been red all over.

She'd thought she could leave looking like that! He'd had to almost rip her clothes off her back. Eventually he'd got her to change by talking about those things she wanted to talk about. Fame and glamour. She wanted to be someone. She wanted to be what he had been when he'd been at home with his parents: a person who had things. He'd tried to explain to her that things meant nothing, that diamonds didn't make you happy and that the only way to true happiness was freedom. But she'd had so little in her life, she couldn't understand.

He'd let her do what she wanted, pandered to her, and this was where they had ended up. Where he'd known they always would. He could try and convince himself that what they'd done was anarchy, but it wasn't. It was envy, spite and a bloodlust he couldn't understand. Elif was insane. He'd fallen for a madwoman.

He'd have to tell the truth. If he did, maybe she'd get treatment. But that would mean locking her away forever. Unless he too went mad. He began to kick his cell door. Just gently at first, and then more and more violently as his anxiety increased. Some bastard in the custody detail yelled, 'Shut the fuck up!' But he carried on. Eventually he heard a key being inserted in his door and he backed away. A cop almost frothing at the mouth with fury rushed in and grabbed him by the throat.

'You never heard of bedtime, posh boy?' he said.

Ali swallowed. 'I need to speak to Inspector Süleyman.'

His phone had rung, for once, after they'd finished making love. Usually when he was required in the middle of the night, it rang just as he'd entered her or when she was going down on him. Then she'd bitch and moan, quite rightly, as they disengaged and he got dressed. It put Mehmet Süleyman in a bad mood. But this time was different. Full of the afterglow that followed good sex, he strode into the interview room prepared to listen.

Ali Erbil had a cut above his right eye that hadn't been there the last time he'd seen him. Süleyman sat. 'Well?' he said. 'It's the middle of the night. What do you want to say to me?'

'I didn't kill anyone,' Ali said.

'Didn't you?'

'No,' he said. 'It was Elif. She's crazy. I've tried to protect her. I love her, but . . . Look, I know you won't believe me . . .'

'On the contrary, Mr Erbil, I have absolutely no problem believing that Elif Büyük is a murderer. You saw what she did to my sergeant. What I have been struggling with is why. I know you took the blame for her because you love her. That I do understand.'

'Before I tell you anything, you must promise me that you'll get Elif some help,' he said.

Ali Erbil was sweating. Süleyman didn't know when he'd last had a fix, but it had to be many hours ago. Was he going to try and cut a deal in exchange for heroin?

'I have already ordered psychiatric reports on both of you,' Süleyman said.

'On me?'

'You are, by your own admission, addicted to heroin. That's a psychiatric issue. It means I can't rely upon what you say to me.'

'But I'm telling you the truth now!' Ali said.

'You said you were telling me the truth when you signed your confession.'

'Yes, but that was . . .'

He was sweating hard now, and his face was grey. 'Look,' he said, 'I'm not asking for a fix, all right? I feel like my guts are fucking dissolving and my head's in a shit-storm, but—'

'Just tell me,' Süleyman said.

161

He wasn't usually this calm, but he still had the vision in his mind of Gonca kneeling down in front of him, breathless and naked.

'I met Elif in Tarlabaşı,' Ali said. 'She was working for this fat Syriani, selling bonzai. She was addicted to it. She also sold herself. She was the most beautiful girl I had ever met. I said I'd take care of her. I said I'd make her somebody.'

He'd got her off bonzai by getting her into heroin. An expensive proposition that, once Ali had left home, the two of them had funded mainly by shoplifting and pickpocketing. They'd lived on the street, occasionally breaking into derelict properties and sleeping in them for one or two nights, until they'd found somewhere more permanent, or so they thought, back in March.

'It was a cellar,' Ali said. 'Some great old house. No one disturbed us – at first. We could dream. Elif's were about being on television and having a kitchen studded with diamonds. I just wanted to burn the world.' He swallowed. 'Then it ended.'

'What did?'

'We thought the place was empty, but then I heard noises. Someone else was there.'

'In the cellar? Who?'

'It was a man. I saw him once, but I don't think he saw me. I didn't like it. We'd become unsafe again and I told Elif that we had to go. She was destroyed.'

'In what way?'

'She wanted to hurt someone, something,' he said. 'I truly think that if we'd been able to stay there, she would have got over her obsession about being somebody. I think she would have settled down. She was content with me. But then it was as if she was on a mission or something. Yet another thing taken away from her. It was too much.'

'Couldn't you and this other man have shared the basement?'

'No,' he said. 'We didn't know who he was. He looked old and as if he was some kind of landlord. He wasn't one of us.'

'When was this?' Süleyman asked.

'When we left? Two weeks ago, maybe a bit less.'

'And where was this house?'

'Over on the Asian side,' Ali said. 'In Moda.'

Chapter 15

Were she to die, then we could return to how we were . . .

Had the brothers killed Fatima and then killed themselves?
Dr Sarkissian had ruled out suicide, but had he been right to do
so?

That communication had gone from Kemal to Yücel in 1963.
Clearly if they had killed Fatima they had waited a long time to
do so. Barçın didn't find a reply. That didn't mean there wasn't
one; some letters might have been lost. Kanat particularly had
lived in filth and chaos, and a lot of the pages that had been
found in his apartment were too badly defaced to read.

She'd spoken about this job to Turgut, after he'd railed for a
good hour about how the security situation was deteriorating in
the east. His father had been arrested for something and held for
two days at his local police station before being released without
charge. Turgut had declared that he was going back to Diyarbakır
as soon as he could. What he'd do there, he hadn't said. But
Barçın had noticed how he kept on talking about 'us', and what
'we' must do to rectify the situation. He was far more Kurdish
than she was and he knew it. He'd said, 'Of course you'll stay
here,' as if he'd had a bad smell under his nose. It had made
her feel like an outcast. She'd changed the subject to the
Rudolfoğlus.

Going into the complexities of the relationships between the
siblings and their parents had taken almost an hour. Turgut, as
was his way, had listened in silence.

She'd said, 'It's as if an avenging angel came down and did away with them.'

Surprisingly for him, Turgut had said, 'Maybe that is what happened.'

Barçın had been staggered. Turgut didn't believe in anything supernatural.

Then he'd said, 'You have referenced several people who knew about the animosity between these siblings. The house may have been hidden by undergrowth but it was and still is there. People know. They know about the father who courted the Devil, about the daughter who was abused by that father . . .'

'We don't know he actually had sex with her.'

'Seems likely,' Turgut had said. 'The way he got her to love him so obsessively is part of how paedophiles operate. She was a child. When her daddy did things to her, even if she didn't like them, it made him happy, and the happier he became, the more he claimed to love his little girl. When he died, she got everything. Putting all the ridiculous Devil stuff to one side, Rudolf Paşa was a control freak. Alive or dead. And although İkmen may trust those privileged arseholes at the Oriental Club, I don't. Rudolf was a member, and I'd put money on the notion that at least one of the other members knew what he was really like.'

'But why kill them now?' Barçın had said. 'If someone knows all this, why now? The Club doesn't need the money.'

'How do you know? A lot of those old secular organisations are struggling these days.'

Barçın left her room and went to visit Çetin İkmen. When she walked into his office, she found Inspector Süleyman with him.

'Oh, I'm sorry . . .'

'Come in, come in,' İkmen said and offered her a chair. 'This concerns you, Constable Demirtaş.'

She sat. 'Sir?'

'It seems we have a development,' İkmen said. 'Inspector Süleyman arrested two people yesterday in Tarlabaşı who, it would appear, are responsible for this spate of killings we've been experiencing on our streets. However, one of those people is also claiming that he and his partner stayed at a property that may be the Teufel Ev, as recently as two weeks ago.'

'Oh.' She looked at Süleyman. 'One of these people bit Sergeant Mungun? Heroin addicts?'

'Yes,' he said. He turned to İkmen. 'Constable Demirtaş and I had a conversation when I returned to my office.'

'He actually named the Teufel Ev?' she said.

'No. He says he doesn't know the name of the place,' Süleyman said. 'But the description he's given means that it could be. We're taking him over to Moda and I'm going to let him show me where he thinks he stayed.'

'Where he thinks he stayed?'

'You know how vague the memory of an addict can be, Constable.'

'Ah, yes.' She frowned. 'Do you think these addicts may have killed the Rudolfoğlus?'

'We don't know,' Süleyman said. 'It seems the woman killed the boy in the Grand Bazaar, the tourist on the Galata Bridge, a woman on a tram, and the gangster Hasan Dum and his bodyguard in Yeniköy.'

'One woman killed all those people?'

Barçın began to feel cold. That woman was down in the cells, just below her feet . . .

'We think so, yes.'

'So all this research I've been doing . . .'

'Has shone a light on a chapter of this city's history that had been lost,' İkmen said. 'And, of course, we cannot assume that these people killed the Rudolfoğlus. They had no motive that we can see at this time.'

166

'They had no motive for killing anyone except Dum and the Hungarian,' Süleyman said.

'True. But they were simply getting off the streets in the basement of this house,' İkmen said. 'That's right, isn't it?'

'Yes,' Süleyman replied. 'Personally, Çetin Bey, if the house in question is the Teufel Ev, I don't think this couple killed your victims. They liked it there. They could shoot up in peace and dream the days away in relative comfort. The only reason they left, according to the man, was because they saw someone else in the basement.'

'Who?'

'We don't know. Another man, apparently. I spent most of last night trying to prise the truth out of this man we have in custody, and I'm still not sure he has a real grasp of the facts. And now he's going into heroin withdrawal, that isn't going to get any better.'

'Shouldn't he be put on to a heroin substitute?'

'The psychiatrist has only just arrived,' Süleyman said.

Barçın felt as if the guns Turgut had primed had been spiked by this latest development. Until this man was taken over to Moda, there was nothing else to be said. She went back to her office and wondered how Gonca Hanım had reacted when her man had been called away from her bed.

'Do you hear voices?'

Elif had spoken to a psychiatrist only once before. The Syriani had found some washed-up alcoholic who said he was a psychiatrist to come and talk to her. He'd wanted to know why she kept on cutting herself. Of course it had been simple. She'd cut herself because she didn't want smelly old men to desire her. Blood was a turn-off. They never wanted her when she was menstruating. So if she cut, they wouldn't want her at other times either. But she hadn't told the Syriani's alcoholic psychiatrist that. She'd just said she didn't know why she did it. Then he'd asked her whether she heard voices, and she'd said no. After that, the Syriani had let the psychiatrist have sex with her in lieu of payment. He had reeked of bourbon.

This man smelt of cigarettes.

'No,' she said. It was vile the way her words slurred. It made her sound stupid.

'What about visions? Do you see things that aren't real?'

He should talk to that boy she'd given the gun to! He saw the Devil everywhere.

'No.'

She'd sympathised with that boy. Just because she couldn't see the Devil didn't mean he wasn't there. People wrote off kids like that too easily. Evil was real, and anyway, giving him the gun had been an adventure.

'Do you remember attacking the police officer?' the psychiatrist asked.

'No.'

Of course she did, but she wasn't going to tell him that. The police took attacks on their officers personally, so if she could hide behind being mad at the time, maybe they'd let her out of this hellhole. What she knew for a fact was that Ali was not telling them a thing about her. He'd own up to everything and then she'd be this poor manipulated woman who the public would take to their hearts and make into a star. Or if he was tortured into telling on her, she'd become the city's only female serial killer. That would be cool.

'Do you remember attacking anyone?'

'No.'

The woman on the tram was the one that stuck in her mind. She hadn't meant to do anything that day. But those judgemental eyes peeking over that niqab had been too blatant to ignore. The bitch was labelling her a whore because she wasn't covered. She

168

could see it. She always had her 'works' tin in her pocket – with her syringe loaded with gear and ready to go, her tourniquet, and a pipe the Syriani had given her many years ago. She'd shoved the needle into the cow's leg when she got off at Beyazıt. Ali hadn't even noticed. She'd only told him when they'd left the tram stop. The woman had sagged as she passed her but she hadn't looked at her. Maybe she thought she'd been bitten by an insect.

'Elif, I don't think you're telling me the truth,' the psychiatrist said.

She wasn't, but how did he know? She wanted to say 'fuck you', but she didn't. If she got agitated again they'd give her more of that medication that had turned her insides to rat-infested irritated gloop. Unable even to speak, she'd screamed in her head for what had seemed like days.

'I am,' she said.

'I don't think so,' he repeated. 'Elif, you should know that your partner has told us about the killings.'

Of course he had. He'd confessed as she'd known he would.

'He says that you committed these murders, and by that, I mean you alone. Ali's involvement was as an accessory to your crimes only.'

But no, that wasn't right! Ali would never, ever have said anything like that.

'He is co-operating fully with the police,' the psychiatrist continued. 'I should also tell you that it is Ali's opinion that you are unwell and so not responsible for your actions. He wants you to get help. So do I. But I can only do that if you tell me the truth.'

The Syriani had always said that: 'If you tell me the truth, I'll take care of you.' But he'd lied. She'd told him the truth, given him the tiny bit of money she'd taken for herself from whatever the punters gave her, and the lying bastard had beaten her until her eyes closed up. The truth was just another trap, and she wasn't going to fall into one of those.

'Fuck you,' she said. 'You're lying!'

'Elif, I don't think that's very helpful . . .'

She saw the two uniforms who had come into her cell with the doctor move closer. They thought she was going to attack the old prick.

'I know what you're doing,' she said. 'Fucking with my head. Ali would never tell lies. He doesn't. I know he's confessed and you're just trying to get your claws into me too. Well it won't work. Fuck you.'

'Elif . . .'

'This shit you've given me is killing me! You fucking bastard!'

She was on him before she even knew. Nails tearing at his face, trying to get a mouthful of his flesh. A baton smashed into the side of her head, but still she tore away at anything and anyone she could grab.

Then she felt a stabbing pain in her thigh, and after a few seconds her viscera was being gnawed by rats again, while inside her head she screamed for death.

As he walked out of the cell, nursing a cut to his forehead, she heard the psychiatrist say, 'Whether she's mad or not, I don't know. But she is dangerous. I have no doubt at all that she could kill if she wanted to.'

And for once, he was right.

'You are a fool!' Selin shouted.

Finally the kids were out of the house and she could berate her husband in peace.

'I was fed up with being the poor relation!' Bilal said. 'The old woman didn't need that boncuk! She didn't need anything except a merciful death!'

'Don't say that!' Selin replied. 'Fatima Hanım wasn't the best employer in the world, but she paid me. Now I'm out of a job.'

'Her father was a foreigner and a devil.'

170

'Oh not that again!' She threw her hands in the air in exasperation. 'Ever since you got religion, you've been more downright pathetic than ever before. If you think I'm ever going to join you in that now, then you've another think coming.'

'Apostates—'

'I am not an apostate,' she said. 'I believe in God and I love our Prophet, blessings and peace be upon him. What I don't believe in is this nasty religious one-upmanship that goes on these days. I don't believe in judging people. Only God has the right to judge. So if Fatima Hanım was a child of the Devil, then let's allow God to sort that out, shall we? And anyway, you were the one who committed the sin of theft, not me!'

Bilal threw himself down into a chair. 'My honour is at stake,' he said. 'Your family are all poor; you don't understand.'

'Oh, I think I do!'

'Every time someone gets married or has a baby, it's always me who gives the cheapest present,' he said. 'I'm sick of it!'

'So get a job!'

He began to stand, one fist raised.

Selin pushed him back down again. 'Raise a hand to me and your honour will be the least of your problems,' she said.

Bilal slumped, and for a moment neither of them spoke. At the very least he was going to have a criminal record for theft, so getting a job was going to be harder than ever. He was also still under suspicion for the possible murder of Fatima Hanım and her siblings, and had been forbidden to leave the city.

When he did speak, he sounded like a petulant child. 'Anyway, why isn't that queer under suspicion? That one who used to suck Mr Yücel's cock.'

Selin flinched at the crudeness of his speech. 'Osman Babacan?' she said. 'Yes, he's gay, but why do you think he had sex with Mr Yücel? Proof?'

'Those people always—'

'Of yes, of course,' she said, one hand on her hip, the other flailing a tea towel in the air. 'I forgot. Gays always have sex with any man within a twelve-kilometre radius. Must have had sex with you then!'

Infuriated, he stood up and slapped her across the face. 'I am no queer!' he roared.

Selin held her burning cheek. 'And Mr Babacan is no murderer! If they'd found any evidence against him, the cops would have dragged him in by this time. You are such a stupid bastard.'

He raised his hand again. 'Don't speak to your husband like that, woman!'

But Selin got in first. She punched him so hard that he staggered backwards into his chair, twisting his ankle as he fell.

She loomed over him. 'And don't you dare touch me ever again, or I will besmirch your precious honour by killing you!' she said.

It wasn't cold; in fact once again the weather was hot. But Ali Erbil shivered as he walked around Moda handcuffed to Mehmet Süleyman. He'd never had methadone before. The psychiatrist had said that it would ease his withdrawal symptoms from heroin, but it hadn't. He felt like shit. Two other cops in plain clothes accompanied them, looking, they probably thought, natural. Ali's time on the streets had taught him a lot. One of those things was that you could always pick out an undercover policeman. People were staring at them. He was sure of it.

But that wasn't his concern. What was exercising his mind was something that psychiatrist had told him back in his cell. Not in relation to himself, but to Elif. It had boiled down to the notion that if a person was found to be insane, then she or he would receive treatment in a hospital. Under these circumstances, Elif might well spend the rest of her life in hospital, but at least she wouldn't have to live in some prison cell with a load of gangster women who would torment her, or with guards who would rape her. And the same applied to him. If he carried on being sane, he would be found guilty of assisting a murderer, and would go to prison however many strings his father might try to pull.

Realisation had come during the long journey across the city and the Bosphorus Bridge to Moda. The psychiatrist had talked very easily to him. Did that mean he thought he was normal, whatever that was? If he did, then Ali would go to prison, which meant he'd never see Elif again. As far as he knew, men and women were held in the same building in a psychiatric hospital. Had he been too quick to tell Süleyman that Elif had killed those people? He hadn't thought it through. He'd needed a fix and his brain had been all over the place.

They stopped at that restaurant near the old pier head, the Koço. He'd been there once, as a child, with his parents. The inspector ordered tea and they all sat outside so that he could smoke.

If Ali remembered correctly, there was some sort of Christian shrine nearby. But what was also nearby was that house. Hidden away behind tangled plants and trees like a lost castle from a fairy tale. They'd been happy there for a while, himself and Elif. How could he ever forget it?

Gossip was a dangerous thing, especially in a small community. Rumours ran around the tiny Byzantine Greek population like rabid rats. It was insular and unhealthy, and it proved yet again to Father Anatoli that they were probably a society in terminal decline – at least in their pure form. Most of the young married out. Many to other Christians, some to local Muslims or Jews. It was sad, but it was also inevitable, and at the very least, a more inclusive community would hopefully

173

put an end to some of the hysteria that plagued so many of his parishioners.

He'd put a closed sign on the door of the ayazma so that he could be alone. An almost forgotten subsidiary to his church, the sacred spring of St Katherine had been the subject of some mad speculation over the years. In 1955, during the anti-Greek riots, people had said that the Turks had destroyed it. They hadn't. In the 1990s, a story had gone around that the Turks who had taken over the Koço restaurant from its original Greek owners were going to brick up the shrine. Then at the beginning of the year someone had started a rumour that the local youth wing of the ruling AK Party were planning to have the ayazma closed.

Father Anatoli had made an appointment with the local AK branch, who had assured him that the shrine was in no way under threat. But the rumour had persisted. Several congregants had insisted upon guarding it at night whenever they were able, and Father Anatoli was under constant pressure to pray for its safety. Some people had put forward the idea of dismantling it and rebuilding it in the church. But that was unrealistic. The shrine was basically a cave. How did one even begin to rebuild a cave? It was ridiculous. But that idea, too, was persisting.

He knelt in prayer until someone knocked at the door. Normally he would have told whoever was outside to go away. But he knew who it was and so he said, 'Enter.'

They almost went past the narrow alleyway that Çetin İkmen had told him led to the Teufel Ev. If you didn't know where it was, it was unlikely, Süleyman thought, that anyone could ever find the place unaided. The alleyway led to a tangled garden barely contained by a low wall topped by metal railings. Even close up, the house was only just visible. According to İkmen, access to what had once been the driveway was around the other side.

174

Overshadowed and hemmed in by 1960s apartment blocks, the type of building the Teufel Ev conformed to was familiar to the Ottoman Mehmet Süleyman. Classed as a 'small palace', it had been built at the beginning of the twentieth century in what was known as the new baroque style. That meant it was fussy and ornate. Mehmet Süleyman had been born in just such a building before his family had to sell in order to pay their creditors. The Ottoman elite had never been very good with money.

The man cuffed to his wrist said nothing. The place he had described where he and Elif Büyük had hidden themselves away had sounded very like this house. But Ali Erbil wasn't saying anything. Eventually Süleyman said, 'Is this the place?'

He just shrugged.

'What does that mean?' Süleyman said. 'Is it familiar or isn't it?'

For a good minute Ali didn't say anything. Had he even heard the question? He'd been extremely quiet on the journey across the Bosphorus. Had he maybe thought that he might not recognise the place? Or had the whole notion of an empty house in Moda been some sort of smack-fuelled fantasy?

'No,' he said at last. 'I don't recognise it.'

'Are you sure?' Süleyman said.

He paused again, but this time only for a second. Then he said, 'Yes. I'm sure.'

Nobody understood. The Devil didn't parade around swishing a tail, showing off horns or doing any of that crazy medieval stuff priests talked about in church. He was everywhere. That was the point! He was in the air that everyone breathed, behind the shoulders of the businessmen who worshipped at the altar of money and in the eyes of the people who sought to cheat the poor. Every day he was getting stronger. But there was no one who could oppose him because he'd taken over everyone's thoughts. Even when he'd worn metal on his head to keep the Devil out, he'd still been able to hear him in the distance.

Even when that kind girl had given him a gun, he hadn't been safe. There could be no defence against the Devil. But her kindness had touched him. She'd been an unusual light in his dark world even if the man with her had been saturated with evil.

The boy sat in a corner of his cell and watched something skitter across the cold stone floor. Now the Devil was tormenting him. He shouted, 'Stop the tricks!'

For a moment, when his cell door opened, he thought that was one of his little temptations too. But when he saw who was in the doorway, he wondered . . .

'I really do think that the Lord of the Flies should consider getting himself a publicist,' Çetin İkmen said. 'He seems to be everywhere these days.'

Sami Nasi didn't smile, but İkmen ignored him. Sami had always been in a strange psychological place with regard to the supernatural. Not unlike Çetin İkmen himself.

'We've a boy down in our cells who's been going around the city, as far as we can tell, in pursuit of the Devil,' İkmen continued. 'Not that his philosophy is easy to get a handle on. We didn't even know who he was until this morning, when his mother came to find out if she could see him. She found his picture online. Apparently we sometimes put photographs of unknown people online these days. I didn't know. I don't do online unless I can help it.' He paused and looked Sami in the eyes. 'What is it? Why are you here? Do you have any—'

'I lied to you, Çetin Bey,' Sami interrupted. 'I didn't tell you something and I've been punished.' He put his head down. 'Now I must confess.'

İkmen said nothing. He'd known Sami a long time and knew

that whatever it was he had to tell him needed to come out in its own time. Silently he offered Sami a cigarette, which he took. İkmen knew he hadn't smoked for years, but somehow it seemed appropriate. Also he wanted a smoke himself. He locked his office door and opened the window. Dust from the car park floated in and made him cough. He lit Sami's cigarette and then his own.

'Last night I almost killed Rüya,' Sami said.

'Almost?'

'We were practising the head trick,' he said. 'It went wrong.'

'How?'

Sami just looked at him.

'I see,' İkmen said. 'If you told me, you'd have to kill me.'

'Something like that.' Sami breathed in deeply. 'All you have to know is that Rüya is fine. In fact she's much better than I am. If I let her, she'd try the trick again today. But I'm not up to it.'

'So you've come to me for . . . what do the Catholics call it? Absolution?'

'I've come to give you information,' he said. 'Listen, Çetin Bey, my grandfather knew Rudolf Paşa well. The German pursued him. Knowing that his father had been Josef Vanek, Rudolf wanted to know how he performed his magic.'

'Did he tell him?'

'Of course not! Rudolf Paşa was obsessed with the occult. He was convinced that my grandfather performed his tricks with the aid of the Devil. He saw him as some sort of Faust. He offered him money, a position at court, sex . . .'

'Sex?'

'Rudolf Paşa was a paedophile,' he said. 'There were even rumours about his daughter.'

'So I gather,' İkmen said.

'You know?'

'Some intelligence has reached me to that effect. Is that what you came to tell me, Sami?'

Sami coughed, but carried on smoking. 'Only in part. Rudolf Paşa's interest in the occult went back a long way, back to Germany. But it really took root in the First World War. This came from my grandfather to my father to me, so it may not all be correct.'

'Go on.'

'Rudolf was with General Fakhri Paşa's troops in 1916 guarding the Hejaz railway and the city of Medina in Arabia,' he said. 'Those troops really suffered. Subjected to constant raids by the British and the Arabs, driven mad by thirst, and those under the direct command of Rudolf Paşa also had to contend with his cruelty. With the help of his İstanbul Greek adjutant, he'd peg men out in the sand to make examples of them. They didn't even have to do anything wrong. He was brutal and he delighted in his brutality. His men called him the Devil; Dimitri Bey the Devil's Disciple. It was even said by some that they sacrificed young soldiers in weird black magic ceremonies.'

'My understanding of the campaign in the desert is that things did happen that some attributed to the supernatural,' İkmen said. 'I believe General Fakhri Paşa himself experienced visions. Knowing what we know about deserts and mirages, I think that maybe these things have been overstated.'

'When Rudolf Paşa arrived back in İstanbul, he went to see my grandfather and threatened him. His secrets or his life. My grandfather said he looked like a madman. He raved about how he had forced his wife to carry the child of the Devil. My grandfather was very frightened and so he agreed to go to the paşa's mansion with all his magical paraphernalia and show him. But he didn't. The city was under occupation by the British by then, so my grandfather moved his family to another part of town. The empire had been defeated and a lot of people were on the move. But he did discover later on that year, when he saw Rudolf Paşa at the club, that he had become a father again. He already had three boys, but now he had a girl.'

'Fatima.'

'The child of the Devil. I should add here that it was my father who was superstitious and he was the one who told me this story. Like my great-grandfather, who started life as a physicist back in his native Hungary, my grandfather was a rationalist. He thought Rudolf Paşa was mad. But he kept away from him and my father told me to keep away from his children. There were stories. Kemal desecrated a shrine. And the death of Rudolf's wife.'

'Ah.'

'I expect you have discovered that it was in childbirth,' he said.

'Yes. Do you know who the father was?'

'No. As I've already told you, Rudolf Paşa practised alchemy. A blood sacrifice was rumoured to have been involved, although as far as we know, the paşa never managed to produce gold. What my father always reckoned was that that sacrifice allowed him access to what he called the dark arts. Some would describe it as raising the Devil. A very Christian notion, but then Rudolf came from a Christian country. Now whether you believe in such things or not is irrelevant. Rudolf believed in them, and he probably passed that belief on to his children. I don't for a moment think that Perihan Hanım's doctor, Kevork Sarkissian, deliberately killed the child she had by another man, but I wonder if he was persuaded by those children not to save its life.'

'That's possible,' İkmen said. 'The doctor was an Armenian in a city that didn't like Armenians.'

'Exactly.'

İkmen leaned on his desk. 'Sami,' he said, 'do you know anything about Kemal's desecration of the shrine of St Katherine?'

'Only that one of the Rudolfoğlus' servants caught him.'

'After which he was dismissed. By the children.'

'Probably saw any intervention to stop them doing what they wanted as some sort of insult,' he said. 'Especially a servant.' He finished his cigarette. 'You know, Çetin Bey, it was my father's belief that Perihan Hanım herself killed her baby. That she just couldn't bear the thought of it having to live in that house with that girl.'

'Fatima.'

'Yes.'

Fatima, who had promised the father she loved too much that she would make sure her mother behaved. How had the twelve-year-old felt when she discovered that her mother was pregnant and therefore she'd failed? Had Fatima killed the baby? Was that why her brothers had hated her? But that couldn't be right, because they would have been dishonoured by their mother too. Would they not have applauded their sister's actions?

But if they had, why had they all lived separately and only communicated by letter for ever after? And what, if anything, did that incident many decades ago have to do with their murders?

There was an axiom he'd read somewhere to the effect that murder got easier with every killing one performed. Ali didn't know; he'd never killed anyone. But he'd seen it done.

When had Elif decided that she was going to kill? He didn't know. They'd left that house in Moda when he'd seen the man, and then she'd become depressed. Dark, as she called it, until the light took over, as it did, and she decided she was going to be famous. She'd skipped about like a gazelle.

Ali had tried to remember whether he'd even known that the killing in the Grand Bazaar was happening. But he couldn't. Everything else was clear, but not that one. He'd asked her afterwards who it was she had stabbed, and she'd said, 'Just a boy!' Then she'd laughed and Ali had laughed with her. He liked it when she was happy. He'd do anything to keep her that way. She'd be far happier in hospital than she would be in prison. And so would he, because he'd be near her. He'd have to be mad.

He'd looked at that house and he knew he'd registered no recognition whatsoever. Madmen didn't. The only thing that worried him was the man who had, albeit unconsciously, driven them out of the house. They'd been back at the Koço when he'd seen him, and Ali was sure it hadn't showed on his face. Süleyman hadn't been looking at him, but had he maybe noticed something different about him later? The man himself had been oblivious, or so Ali felt. He had always been sure that he hadn't seen either of them in the house, but could he be certain?

One thing he was sure about was that it was best to keep quiet about the house, the man and everything else. If he was going to be with Elif in hospital, he'd have to do something quite dramatic. Remaining silent and possibly unmoving was a good place to start.

Chapter 16

The boy's mother was Armenian. Her husband, who was deceased, had been Greek.

'We shouldn't have taken our son to church,' she said to Mehmet Süleyman. 'I never wanted Aslan to be religious. I am not myself. I rejected my faith a long time ago. But my husband was different. Orthodoxy is in the bones of the İstanbul Greeks. Whatever was going on, Petros would take Aslan to Divine Liturgy every Sunday. Sometimes I'd go, sometimes not.'

'You think the boy's faith was bad for him?' Süleyman asked.

'Not in itself,' she said. 'I'm assuming you're a Muslim, so what you must understand is that our churches are full of pictures.'

'Ikons.'

'Exactly. They represent sacred figures like Christ, the Virgin Mary and the saints. I'm sure you know these images well.'

He smiled. His brother's late wife had been an İstanbul Greek.

'What you may not know,' she said, 'is that some of these ikons also represent images of the Devil. He's usually tempting a saint or hiding in an olive grove. He's always up to no good and he almost inevitably has horns, red skin, a tail and hooves. The Orthodox are not as bad as the Catholics; the stone devils on the roofs of their churches are truly terrifying. But for a sensitive child like Aslan, even the pictures were too much. He has been afraid of the Devil since he was a small child. I think I fooled myself he would grow out of it, whatever that means.'

Süleyman liked Mrs Gerontas. About his own age, she was

an attractive, intelligent woman who worked as a researcher for the national television station, TRT. By her own admission, her job was her life, particularly since her husband's death.

'I neglected my son,' she said without emotion. 'I am multilingual and so my employers often sent me on assignment abroad. I left Aslan with my husband's mother, who filled his head with superstitious rubbish. I should have put a stop to it, but I didn't. I wanted to work, and when Petros died, I had no choice.'

'We think your son has been living on the street for some months,' Süleyman said. 'And yet I can't find any record of a missing person called Aslan Gerontas.'

She shook her head. 'Again that is my fault, Inspector,' she said. 'I knew Aslan was only taking his medication sporadically and was becoming bizarre. I knew I needed to take him back to his psychiatrist. But when he told me that he was going to visit an old school friend in Alanya, I was relieved, I admit it. The friend, Barbaros, had always been a good companion for Aslan. He seemed to understand him, he could calm him down, and he is a doctor.'

'Did he get to Alanya?'

'No,' she said. 'Although I didn't know that until yesterday, when I saw his photograph online. I know it's useless and pathetic to say that I'm consumed with guilt – I mean, who cares? – but I am. I went to France to do some research into the life of the Empress Josephine, then on to Spain to set up meetings with the local gypsies in Seville. It was fascinating.' She sighed. 'I didn't give a thought to Aslan. I'd like to say it's because I've been driven to distraction by his illness over the years, but that isn't true. Not entirely. I am a selfish bitch.'

'No,' said Süleyman. 'From what I understand about mental illness, it is very difficult to live around. One receives very little in the way of, well, reward.'

'He's my son, he doesn't need to reward me,' she said.

He noticed that her eyes were wet. But he didn't allude to it. This was a proud woman who had, if not deliberately, let her own son down.

'I came back last month,' she said. 'No word from Aslan, so I fooled myself he was having a wonderful time by the seaside. Petros's mother died last year, which meant I didn't even have her to spur me into action. I gather Aslan hasn't hurt anyone.'

'No,' he said. 'I arrested him for being in possession of a gun, which we later discovered had been given to him by another person living on the street.'

'God!'

'He attempted to shoot a rat, which is how we became aware of his presence in Tarlabaşı, but he missed.'

'He doesn't know how to use a gun,' she said.

'Clearly.' He frowned. 'Your son needs hospital treatment,' he said. 'I'm sure you know, but I am simply passing on what I have been told by our psychiatrist. Aslan is clearly mentally ill and so the prosecutor will not be seeking a conviction.'

'I appreciate that,' she said. She shook her head. 'You know, I don't just blame the images in the church. Aslan did fixate upon them, but the priest didn't help.'

'In what way?'

'I've no idea why – I'm not Greek, so how can I – but he was always on about the Devil,' she said. 'Apparently he is everywhere, there's no escape, and where we lived when Aslan was a child was a particularly bad place for sin.'

'Where was that?' Süleyman asked.

'Moda,' she said. 'Liberal and lots of fun. I loved it.'

İkmen stood in what had once been Fatima Hanım's drawing room. Now empty, it had been an elegant room that must have had beautiful views of the Sea of Marmara before the surrounding apartment blocks were built. When Rudolf Paşa lived here, it had probably been a bedroom. He wondered whether it had been Perihan Hanım's room. Had she and her baby died here?

One set of unknown DNA had become three. It didn't help. In his more fanciful moments he wondered whether the spirit of the dead baby had come back to avenge itself on the family. But he knew that was nonsense. The dead were always the least of anyone's worries; it was the living who caused trouble. It was the living who had raised the spectre of the Devil – whatever that was – in the city, and the living also who had killed four old people in their beds.

'You know, sir,' Kerim Gürsel said, 'that old man I met at the Koço, who first took me to the ayazma, said that some people believed that it was Fatima rather than Perihan who gave birth to the Devil's child. Do we know whether Fatima ever had a child?'

'No. That's a good point,' İkmen said. 'I don't yet have Dr Sarkissian's full report on the body. I'll ask him. God, her own father's child! Makes you shudder. She was nine when Rudolf Paşa died. If she did give birth, it must have torn her apart.' He shook his head. 'Can such a young child even become pregnant?'

'I don't know.'

His phone rang.

'İkmen.'

'Çetin Bey.'

It was Süleyman.

'Mehmet Bey,' said İkmen, 'what can I do for you?'

'It's what I may be able to do for you, actually,' he said. 'Do you know a Greek Orthodox priest called Father Anatoli Ralli? His church is the Aya Triada in Moda.'

'Yes,' İkmen said. 'A pugnacious sort of man. But he gave me enough information to track down the son of the Rudolfoğlus' gardener. Why?'

'It transpires that he may have had a heavy influence upon

185

Aslan Gerontas, our black-tracksuited boy. According to Gerontas's mother, Father Anatoli was apt to give sermons about the wiles and ways of the Devil.'

'Was he now?'

'Mrs Gerontas believes that these homilies had a profound and negative effect upon her son, who as I'm sure you know has severe mental health problems.'

'Ah, Moda,' İkmen said, 'the very entrance to Hell.'

'So it would seem. But seriously, I thought you'd like to know, given your Devil's House and its attendant legends. Hopefully Aslan is going to be taken to Bakırköy tomorrow morning.'

'Hospital's the best place for him.'

'I agree. But in the meantime, I wonder if you'd like to help me try and get something out of him about, amongst other things, Father Anatoli. Aslan is a native of Moda, so you may find him interesting. Also the male partner in my random street-crime duo seems to have clammed up, while the woman is, well, heavily sedated. He didn't identify your Teufel Ev, I should also tell you.'

'Disappointing,' İkmen said.

'Maybe.'

'What do you mean?' İkmen asked.

'Well I don't think he was telling the truth.'

'Why?'

'Because I saw recognition in his eyes,' Süleyman said. 'And also his demeanour has changed completely since we visited Moda. As I said before, he's gone silent on me. Silent and motionless, to be exact. I fear he may be trying to convince me that his psychiatric assessment was incorrect.'

'He's attempting to pull a mad one,' İkmen said.

'Exactly.'

İkmen shook his head. 'So common,' he said. 'They finally realise that prison with all its attendant horror may be in the offing and decide that going mad is probably the best way out of it.'

'And in this case the psychiatrist has declared Ali Erbil's girlfriend and partner in crime really mad,' Süleyman said.

'So even more incentive.'

'Absolutely,' he said.

The mortuary refrigerator made a very low-level humming noise. It wasn't supposed to, but it was old and needed to be replaced. A chest of drawers of the dead. Arto Sarkissian found himself staring at it after Çetin İkmen's call. Fatima Rudolfoğlu's body was in number four.

He'd still been wrestling with the horror of what he'd found when İkmen rang. When he'd written his preliminary report on the woman, he hadn't been sure. Now he was; in fact he'd known for some days. He simply hadn't been able to write it down. Putting it on paper, baldly, in black and white, diminished it.

Fatima Rudolfoğlu had been a mother. The child had been delivered by Caesarean section, which made sense given the age Çetin İkmen had said was most likely, assuming that her father had impregnated her. Nine. Not that he could be entirely sure she'd been that young.

Arto wondered who had performed the section. His grand-father? If he had, surely that would have traumatised him much more than the deaths of Perihan Hanım and her baby? Maybe he hadn't attended Fatima? But if he hadn't, then who had? And why hadn't that doctor also attended Perihan Hanım's pregnancy?

Kevork Sarkissian had been a quiet old man. Arto remembered him as a presence in his father's drawing room rather than an active member of the household. He'd been kind and affectionate to Arto and his brother Krikor. It was difficult to imagine him doing anything that would cause harm. Perhaps he had and perhaps he hadn't. Çetin İkmen had asked Arto to speculate about whether his grandfather might have killed Perihan Hanım's baby, but he couldn't. It was too painful. Only concrete evidence could convince him that Kevork Sarkissian had been capable of that. He'd told İkmen, who had suggested that maybe Constable Demirtaş might come to the Peacock Yalı and help him search for his grandfather's papers. Her Ottoman transliteration skills were becoming stretched.

However, it was what İkmen hadn't said that had really struck home. A well-off Armenian doctor at the end of the First World War would have been a person at risk. Most Turks would have assumed that such a person would have welcomed the British, French and Greek occupying powers. Some had. But Arto's father always said that the Sarkissian family had kept its collective head down. When work came along, his father did it, and when it didn't, the family suffered.

Various scenarios came to mind, up to and including the idea that maybe Perihan Hanım had paid Kevork Sarkissian a very large sum of money to destroy her child and keep his mouth shut. From the little he knew about his grandfather, Arto couldn't see it. But then he hadn't been there. His father had never pretended that their family had suffered as much as some after the First World War. Many of the poorest had starved. But he had occasionally talked about how cold they had all been in the winter, about the servants who had been let go due to lack of money, and of the sight of the Sarkissian women scouring the streets for wood to burn, dressed in little more than rags. Had his grandfather committed the ultimate sin for money? Or had the Rudolfoğlus simply threatened to point the finger at the Sarkissians as traitors and then wait for those maddened by war wounds and hunger to destroy them?

Arto had never hated his job before. This was a new experience for him.

The caretaker had told him that Father Anatoli was at home. İkmen tried ringing his mobile one more time from outside the

188

church, and then told Kerim to drive to Yusuf Kamil Paşa Sokak. He'd imagined that a priest had to live next door to his church, but apparently Father Anatoli and his wife lived in an apartment.

Yusuf Kamil Paşa Sokak was famous for the Barış Manço Museum. One of the few Ottoman houses left in the area, it was where the originator of Anatolian rock music and national treasure Barış Manço had lived until his death in 1999.

'I used to love his TV show in the nineties,' Kerim said. '*From 7 to 77* on TRT 1.'

İkmen smiled. Although entirely disapproving of Manço's long hippy hair, his wife had been a big fan, and had watched his music and chat show religiously for its entire eight-year run.

However, it wasn't Barış Manço's elegant house that captured İkmen's attention as they drove down Yusuf Kamil Paşa Sokak, but the police car outside the apartment block opposite.

İkmen and Kerim Gürsel showed their badges to a uniformed officer standing beside the car.

'We're going to apartment number five,' İkmen said.

'You were called too?' the constable said.

An ambulance pulled up behind İkmen's car.

'What's going on, Constable?' İkmen said.

'Suicide,' the young man replied.

The marble-tiled bathroom was very apt for the scene that greeted Çetin İkmen. A naked man with a long grey beard slumped in a bath filled with his own blood. Father Anatoli Ralli looked like a Roman general, forced by a jealous emperor to take his own life. In a room at the other end of the apartment a woman cried and screamed her misery in rapid Greek.

A young man with a strawberry birthmark on his neck was in charge of the scene. Sergeant Düzen had come from the Kadıköy police station. It was the first time he'd ever attended a suicide investigation, and not only did he have the deceased man's howling wife to contend with; he also had to deal with one of İstanbul's most recognisable police officers.

'Do you think Father Anatoli might have been murdered?' he asked İkmen when he came out of the bathroom.

'I'm sure the post-mortem examination will reveal that,' İkmen said. 'What do you think?'

'I think it looks like suicide, Çetin Bey,' he said.

'Me too. He slit his wrists. Just how the ancient Romans used to kill themselves,' İkmen said.

'But he was Greek.'

'Strictly he was a Byzantine,' İkmen said. 'An heir to both the Greek and the Roman empires. He was also a priest in a religion that prohibits suicide. Did you find any sort of letter? Maybe to his wife . . .'

'I don't know,' Düzen said. 'This was on the bathroom floor.'

He held up a piece of paper. İkmen took it from him and said, 'Greek.'

'Yes. None of us can read it.'

'My sergeant isn't fluent, but he's good enough,' İkmen said. He told Kerim Gürsel to come out of the bathroom and translate.

While Kerim looked at what might have been the last communication from Father Anatoli, Sergeant Düzen said, 'Inspector, Çetin Bey . . . er, may I ask how you came to be here? When I was assigned to this job . . .'

'Coincidence,' İkmen said. 'If you believe in such things. I came to speak to Father Anatoli, but it seems I am too late.'

'Oh, what . . .'

'As I'm sure you know, I am working on the Rudolfoğlu murders,' İkmen said.

'Ah.'

Kerim Gürsel cleared his throat.

'Kerim Bey.'

'I think it might be a quote from something,' Kerim said. 'It sounds like it ought to be. "At his best, man is the best of creatures, but separated from law and justice, he is the worst."'

'Very true,' İkmen said. 'Although I've no idea who said it. Might have simply been Father Anatoli in a moment of insight.' He turned to Sergeant Düzen. 'I'm assuming the woman crying is his wife.'

'Yes.'

'Is there anyone with her?'

'No. She can't speak Turkish.'

'How do you know that?' İkmen asked.

'Because she just yells away in Greek,' he said.

'Doesn't mean she doesn't speak Turkish,' İkmen said. 'When people are in shock, they do strange things. Was it her who called the death in?'

'I don't know,' Düzen said.

'Well someone must have done, and unless there's someone else in this apartment . . .'

'No.'

'Then it must have been Mrs Ralli, and she had to have spoken Turkish in order to make herself understood,' İkmen said. 'You see? Simple.'

Marina Ralli had been born in İstanbul in 1949. But after the anti-Greek riots of 1955, her family went to live in Greece. She didn't return to her birthplace until she met and married her husband Anatoli in 1970.

'I found him when I came back from shopping,' she told İkmen.

'Did you have any idea that he might do this?' İkmen said.

She paused for a moment before saying, 'Not this.'

'But he was unhappy?'

'Always,' she said. 'People thought that because of his tough

191

exterior he was a man without any feelings. But he was always fragile.'

İkmen put the piece of paper that had been found in the bathroom in front of her.

'Can you tell me what this is?' he said.

She read it, then looked up. 'It's Anatoli's writing.'

'We found it in the bathroom,' he said. 'On the floor. I believe it's something to do with how a man is no better than an animal without justice.'

'It's Aristotle,' she said.

'Do you know why your husband might have written that and left it on the floor?'

The Rallis had never had any children. All Marina's family were in Greece. She was hollowed out by grief. Only İkmen had been able to get anywhere near her, and that was because he was the only person in the mayhem of a crime scene who had exhibited patience. While she screamed and tore at her clothes, he had just sat and waited for the winds of misery and pain inside her to subside. Turkish women behaved in much the same way when they were bereaved. He had known that an end would come sometime. And it had.

She said, 'My husband was a sad man and a sensitive soul. All that aggression he showed to the world wasn't him. It was self-protection. He also struggled.'

'With his faith?'

'Yes. Many priests do. The modern world is not an easy place in which to bring people to God. Anatoli's real problems were more down-to-earth. Being spiritual father to a congregation like ours can be a terrible thing.'

'Why?'

She looked at the window, then down at her lap.

'Hanım?'

She shook her head. 'You're a Turk,' she said, 'but I am

192

going to say what I must and you can hate me or not, I no longer care.'

'I won't . . .'

'We are an old community here in Moda,' she said. 'Most of my husband's parishioners remember 1955. I know you people don't want to talk about it, but that's too bad.'

'A terrible thing was done in 1955,' İkmen said. His father had locked him and his brother in their old house in Üsküdar while he went out and looked for his Greek students. He'd only found two. But he'd brought them back and had later arranged transport to take them to Greece. He'd been one of many Turks who had tried to stop the slaughter.

'Living with the memory of people wanting to kill you is hard,' she said. 'Anatoli had to listen to the stories often. Sometimes he would come home and lock himself away for hours.'

'Did he ever tell you anything?'

'No. What passes between a priest and his parishioner is private,' she said. 'But I know it wasn't easy for him, and I don't just mean the stories. There are so few of us in the city now, we are almost invisible. There is fear, resentment, there are things people do that they shouldn't. And no, I won't give you examples.'

She was hostile and he accepted that. The anti-Greek riots of 1955 had been the final bloody death knell for the Byzantine Greeks. Most had left the country. Those who remained, İkmen always felt, did so not out of defiance but with an air of inward-looking fatalism. Someone had to be the last Byzantine in order to finally put out the light.

'When you are the repository of people's stories of horror, of guilt, of anger and grief, unless you are very strong, you will break,' she said. 'Although . . .'

She shook her head.

'Although what?'

'I didn't expect this,' she said. 'Not suicide.'

'No one does. Marina Hanım, can you tell me whether your husband was particularly agitated lately? I will be honest with you. I consulted him a few days ago about a man of Greek origin.'

'He never told me that,' she said. 'He wouldn't. He was a good priest; he shared his confidences only with God. To me he was always sad. Loving, but broken. What he didn't do was break the rule of either God's law or the law of this land.'

'Which would make the quotation from Aristotle confusing,' İkmen said.

'It would if my husband hadn't always believed himself to be bad.'

'Are we not all sinners?'

'Yes, but not like that,' she said. 'All through his life he's . . . he believed that he had something bad inside him. He would never explain. I tried to reassure him that it wasn't true. But he wouldn't have it. He always said I knew nothing. When he was like that, he cried.'

'Did he cry often?'

'No.'

'Do you know when he last cried?'

'I comforted him one afternoon last week,' she said. 'We held each other, as we always did at such times, until his tears had dried. But I think he may have cried last night.'

'You don't know?'

'That time he hid it from me. Just a few tears, but I could tell. I could also tell that he didn't want to be comforted,' she said. 'Then he went to bed.'

'Did your husband go out yesterday, hanım?'

'To the ayazma of St Katherine, yes,' she said.

'To perform a service?'

194

'No, for solitary prayer. He went when he could. I do know there were rumours some time ago that the shrine was going to close. I think some people believe it is unused. My husband made a point of going there to pray whenever he was able. It was a place that was very close to his heart. There were a few members of the congregation who used to go regularly too. I think Anatoli had some letters about it somewhere.'

Bad news spreads like blood. A tiny wound emits a drip that becomes a streak that turns into a pool. News of Father Anatoli's death spread across the city along the thin tendrils of the Byzantine Greek community, oozing into the smallest outposts, like Tarlabaşı and Beşiktaş.

The man whose name had been Yiannis Apion, Mustafa Kaiserli, learned of it from his wife Ceyda. Although Jewish, she knew the Greeks through her husband. She'd met Father Bacchus, the priest of the Aya Triada in Beyoğlu, on the ferry. As soon as she finished with her tour group, she went home and told her husband.

Mustafa was not a demonstrative man, but the fact that he greeted her news with silence made Ceyda feel cold. Her husband had always liked Father Anatoli. His predecessor, Father Kostas, had been a significant influence on Mustafa when he was a child. When the old man died and Mustafa moved to Beşiktaş, he'd kept in touch with Father Kostas. Father Anatoli had continued this. Both his Greek past and his old home were important to him. When his father died, Mustafa had his body taken across the Bosphorus to Moda for burial. Father Anatoli had performed the funeral service. It had been incomprehensible to Ceyda. But all the Greeks had cried, all except her emotionally stunted husband.

Chapter 17

Ouija boards, astrology, Tarot cards and the gypsy women who practised witchcraft in the dark basements of Tarlabaşı were all gateways to the Devil. Çetin İkmen, as the son of a witch, wondered whether he too qualified as a demonic tempter.

'Father Anatoli told you this?' Süleyman asked the boy.

It was the first time that Çetin İkmen had seen the black-track-suited boy, Aslan Gerontas. Thin and dark, he had several teeth missing, but otherwise, he was a handsome lad. It was a shame he was the epitome of most people's conception of a madman. It was difficult to get past those staring eyes and nervous tics to the person underneath.

'Priests know everything,' the boy said, which İkmen took as a 'yes'.

İkmen and Süleyman had decided not to tell Aslan about Father Anatoli's death. Neither of them knew what effect it would have on him.

'Priests and the lady I met,' he said.

'What lady?'

'With the gun,' he said.

Elif Büyük.

'She knew I needed to protect myself.'

İkmen leaned forward. 'Aslan,' he said, 'when did you know that the Devil was after you?'

For a moment the boy looked as if he hadn't understood. But then he said, 'He's after all of us. He's everywhere.'

'Did Father Anatoli tell you that?'

'I've known it all my life,' he said. 'A boy fell to the ground one day in the Grand Bazaar and the Devil took him. I saw him.'

'How do you know that?' İkmen said.

'Because that lady who gave me the gun tried to save him.'

'Tried to save him?' Süleyman said. 'The woman who gave you the gun?'

Elif Büyük had stabbed Ali Baykal in the side. At least that was what her lover Ali Erbil was saying.

'Yes,' Aslan said. 'She let the Devil out of him. I saw her.'

'The Devil?'

'Yes,' he said. 'He's at his strongest when there's blood. Father Anatoli told me that.'

'Mirra?'

Barçın turned around. Ömer Mungun was standing behind her. He carried a tiny cup and saucer.

As far as she was concerned, he was on sick leave. 'What are you doing here?' she said.

She'd been completely wrapped up in her reading.

'I'm fine,' he said. Then he smiled. 'I was bored.'

'You're supposed to be bored, you're sick,' she said.

He put the cup and saucer on her desk.

What she'd just read had given Barçın Demirtaş a lot to think about. She'd grown accustomed to feeling not exactly sorry for Fatima Rudolfoğlu, but to having some sympathy for her. More so since she'd received an email from İkmen. Fatima Hanım, he'd stated, had given birth to a baby when she was very young. It seemed most likely it was her father's. Was that why her brothers had hated her so much? Barçın had assumed it was because Fatima alone had inherited her father's property, but maybe it had more to do with her pregnancy. Even now a lot of men assumed that a girl who 'got into trouble' had brought her condition on herself

197

whatever the circumstances. Back in the 1920s, that view would have been even more prevalent. And now this, from Fatima to Yücel in February 2015:

If you and our brothers wish to do this, I will stop you. You will not taint my father's house any further. Do you really think that you can invoke God's mercy with such a pathetic gesture? You are all snakes! I curse you.

What did she mean? What did the brothers want to do that would taint the house?

She heard Ömer Mungun clear his throat. She had been a little tetchy with him, but he had interrupted her train of thought. And the mirra thing, sweet though it was, had begun to get on her nerves. It was obvious that he wanted to have some sort of relationship with her. Why didn't he just ask her out? That way she could say no and the whole thing would be over and done with. Of course he was afraid that might happen, which was why he was saying nothing.

Eventually she said, 'I'm in the middle of something. Inspector İkmen needs me to focus.' Then the guilt kicked in and she added, 'If you're back tomorrow . . .'

'I am.'

'Then maybe we can have lunch.'

He smiled.

'Talk about Mardin and—'

'Great. But I'm also free tonight.'

'Oh. Oh, OK then,' she said.

'About six?'

'Fine.'

She was already regretting her invitation as he left. Taken at face value, Ömer Mungun was a kind, intelligent, handsome young man. But he was from the east and so he had the capacity to turn into a monster of tradition, jealousy and sexism. Barçın cursed her own weakness.

'I see it now. I see it. Ali gives me all the credit and so I become famous and he doesn't. He loves me so much, you know.'

The psychiatrist had given Elif a different drug, one that didn't turn her into a zombie. It just agitated her so she couldn't keep still. And she drooled. Every time she spoke, a line of saliva would drip down on to her chest, soaking her T-shirt.

After interviewing Ali and Elif for a second time that afternoon, the psychiatrist had given his opinion of their crimes as a case of *folie à deux*. This condition, where the dominant partner in a couple – in this case Elif – transmitted their psychotic beliefs to the other in order to create an incident or perpetrate a crime, was very rare. Originally the psychiatrist had pronounced Ali Erbil sane. Then he'd pulled his silent act and that had changed. But neither policeman was convinced.

'He didn't betray me! I understand what he was doing!'

Two big constables were in the cell with them; one by the door, the other behind İkmen and Süleyman.

'Elif, are you saying that you killed five people without help from Ali Erbil?' Süleyman said.

'Yes!'

She threw her arms in the air and did a little dance.

'Did you tell Ali that you were going to do that?'

She danced and laughed but said nothing.

Süleyman rephrased the question. 'Elif, when you left the house in Moda, did you tell Ali that you intended to kill people?'

This time she stopped. A large gobbet of saliva hung from her lip like a teardrop. 'The house?' she said.

'Yes, the house in Moda,' he repeated. 'You stayed there, in the cellar. Remember?'

'Cellar . . .' It was just as if someone had flicked a switch in her head. 'Oh yes,' she said. 'I was happy there.' She sat on the floor.

'But then Ali saw a man and he feared you'd be discovered.'

'I didn't see a man,' she said.

'But Ali did.'

She shook her head. 'We went. I hated it. I wanted to go back. But we kept on moving.'

'You stabbed a man called Ali Baykal in the chest,' Süleyman said. 'In the Grand Bazaar.'

She smiled. 'A carpet boy,' she said.

'Why?'

'Why not?'

İkmen said, 'You must have had a reason. Did the carpet boy maybe abuse you in some way?'

'No.'

'No?'

'Killers are famous,' she said. 'If you kill, you can have any house you like. I know people who kill, they always have nice houses.'

İkmen approached her slowly and sat down beside her. 'What people?' he asked.

'People on the street.' She looked up at him. 'Don't tell me it's a lie, because I know it isn't. People get what they want if they kill people.'

She stood, suddenly. Her face became red and the uniformed officers began to move towards her. İkmen held up a hand to stop them, just as his phone began to ring.

'People who kill go to prison,' Süleyman said.

Elif spat at him. One of the uniforms grabbed her by the shoulders and pushed her to the floor.

'Everything evil is famous and beautiful!' she screamed. 'I've seen it! I know!'

İkmen answered his phone.

Her grandmother, who had been called Muazzaz, had been a very unpleasant woman. One of the reasons why Selin İnce had never wanted to cover was because Muazzaz always had.

It had been Muazzaz who had cared so passionately about Perihan Hanım. Her princess had been more dear to her than her own family. Selin's mother Nazlı, Muazzaz's only child, had been nothing more than an inconvenience. Completely cowed by Muazzaz, she'd looked after Fatima Hanım because her mother had told her to. When Nazlı had become too old to carry on cleaning at the Teufel Ev and Selin had taken over, she'd told her mother that she wasn't going to take any crap from the old woman.

'You've been treated like rubbish by the old witch all your life,' she'd said. But then Nazlı had told her why she'd had to bend the knee to Fatima Hanım, and Selin hadn't slept for a week.

She wasn't a religious woman, but she was superstitious, and although every rational bone in her body screamed that Fatima Hanım could no longer do her any tangible harm, she still feared her. That policeman, İkmen, could try as hard as he liked, but he'd never get anything more than what she'd already told him. Like that stupid lump, her thieving husband, he was going to be kept in the dark. After all, whether he existed or not, Selin didn't want any trouble with the Devil.

'He met someone, at the ayazma,' Marina Ralli said.

Now outside Elif Büyük's cell, İkmen could still hear her raving inside. He looked across at Süleyman, who nodded and went back in. The constable he'd left holding her down was a massive character, not above sitting on those he wished to subdue. If he did that to Elif, he'd kill her.

201

'Marina Hanım,' İkmen said. 'I'm sorry, we're having a few problems here. What can I do for you?'

'Anatoli met someone at the ayazma of St Katherine,' she said. 'The day before his death. I got around to looking at his diary. There is so much to do, I should have done it before . . .'

'It's no problem,' İkmen said. 'I understand. That you have done anything given the circumstances is . . . well, it's amazing.'

'The problem for me is that I know this person,' she said. 'And I'm sure that whatever made Anatoli kill himself, well, it can't have had anything to do with him.'

If she knew the man her husband had met at the ayazma, then he was almost certainly Greek. And as the wife of a Greek priest, she didn't want to make trouble for one of Father Anatoli's parishioners.

'Hanım,' İkmen said, 'you told me that your husband cried the night before he died, after he'd been to meet this person. Can you remember whether he was particularly upset when he returned from the ayazma?'

She paused for a moment. 'He was quiet. Thoughtful. But then he often was. I really thought nothing of it until I heard him crying. If I'd imagined for a second that he was going to kill himself, I would never have gone out shopping in the morning. Çetin Bey, the man he met is a good man. He does no harm. I don't want to cause trouble for him.'

'And yet you've called me,' İkmen said.

'Because I must find out why Anatoli died.'

'Precisely. In all probability this man had no influence on your husband's decision. I expect they met, maybe prayed together and then parted without anything sinister passing between them.'

'I think that too!'

'So tell me his name so that I can eliminate him from my investigation,' İkmen said. 'I will speak to him. It will be an

202

hour out of his life and nothing more. He may even know something about your husband that we don't that might explain why he took his own life.'

He heard her sob, just the once. For a moment he thought she might put the phone down on him. But then she said, 'All right. His name is Mustafa Kaiserli, and he lives in Beşiktaş.'

The massive constable had bruised her but not broken anything. Süleyman had sent him away and was now alone with Elif Büyük except for Constable Yıldız. The constable wasn't a bad man, even if he was slightly dense. Once, long ago, he had been Gonca's lover. But she'd tossed him aside, tossed everyone aside for Süleyman.

'Elif, you must tell me the truth,' Süleyman said. 'No one is saying that you didn't commit these murders, and I am not for a moment suggesting that Ali should take any of the credit for them. But he won't talk now and so I need you to speak for him.'

She said nothing. Süleyman briefly closed his eyes. Had the oafish Constable Alphan silenced her?

He took the photographs İkmen had given him out of his jacket. There were four: views of the Teufel Ev from each side.

'Do you know this place?' he asked.

He was sure that Ali Erbil had recognised it. Why he was not admitting to it was a mystery. But there had been a flicker in his eyes when he'd first seen it. Also, how many other places were there in Moda that fitted the description he had given during his first interview?

'It's called the Teufel Haus, the Devil's House,' he said.

That caught her attention, and she looked up.

'It's said it was once owned by a German who was a magician,' he said. 'But it's been lived in by four siblings for years. Until someone murdered them. Was it you?'

Fixated on the images in front of her, Elif touched the pictures with almost reverential gentleness.

'Elif, you have confessed to the murder of the carpet boy in the bazaar, the Englishman on the bridge, the lady on the tram and the two men in the shop in Yeniköy. Believe me when I say that there is no way the world will not know your name. Now I want you to tell me the truth about these four siblings. Three men and a woman, all over ninety years old . . .'

He stopped because she was crying. Touching the photographs as if they were sacred relics, stroking them, kissing them and crying.

'You were happy here?' he asked.

She didn't answer, but he knew. Ali Erbil had said she'd been happy in that cellar. Now he knew where it had been. Probably the only place she had ever experienced stability. A pause for breath in a life hurtling towards the edge of a cliff.

'You could sleep without worrying about being attacked,' he said. 'You could rest, take your smack in peace.'

'Went shopping,' she whispered. 'Me. I went to the shops.'

'This was your place?'

'Yes.'

A knock at the door almost broke the spell that had taken hold of that cell. Süleyman told Yıldız to attend to it.

'Elif,' he said, 'did you kill the four old people who lived in this house?'

She wiped her eyes with her sleeve. 'No,' she said.

'Because it would have jeopardised what you had come to see as your home?'

'Because I didn't know they were there,' she said. 'And even if I had, I wouldn't have done anything. Not then.'

Out of the corner of his eye, Süleyman saw İkmen enter the cell. He held the girl's gaze.

'Elif,' he said, 'would you have killed all those people on the streets if you'd been able to stay in this house?'

She frowned as if she had a pain in her head. 'I don't know.'

'What I'm trying to get at is whether you killed just because you wanted to be famous, or—'

'Only unhappy people want to be famous!' she said. 'Didn't you know that? If we'd stayed at the lovely house, I wouldn't have needed fame.'

Süleyman felt a hand on his shoulder and looked up into İkmen's face.

'I need you to come with me,' the older man whispered.

Elif Büyük looked down at the photographs of the Devil's House. 'Can I keep these?' she said.

Chapter 18

He took her to his favourite restaurant. It specialised in south-eastern Turkish food. It was also on the same street as İkmen's favourite bar, the Mosaik. Ömer knew that as well as Barçın, but she suspected there was probably an element of showing off in her date's choice of venue. Not that she disliked him. Ömer Mungun was quite a catch. If only Barçın could get where he came from out of her head. And Mehmet Süleyman.

They sat down at a table outside on the street. They decided between them to order a half-bottle of rakı, ice and a jug of water. Alcohol would, Barçın felt, make her feel more relaxed.

When the drinks arrived, Ömer poured out large measures of the thick, clear rakı into tall glasses and then topped them up with water and ice. As the liquid turned cloudy, a strong smell of aniseed was released and Barçın took a long, luxurious drink.

'I don't come here as often as I'd like,' Ömer said. 'But they have some Arab specialities. I grew up with that food.'

'Of course.'

The fact that his eyes slanted upwards wasn't helping. They reminded her of Şeymus.

'I don't know what you want to eat,' he said. 'But I like their Aleppo kebab. Do you know it?'

She did. A hot, spicy lamb dish that came with a salad.

'Yes,' she said. 'I'll have that too.'

They talked and drank. Ömer was easy company, and after a while she forgot that maybe İkmen would walk along and spot them. He didn't. Then Ömer asked her what she thought of his boss.

'A lot of women fall for him,' he said. 'I get it. He's like a movie star. Then there's the whole Ottoman thing.'

She smiled. She rather liked that too.

'Other men are intimidated,' he said.

'Are you?'

'I used to be. But actually, when you get to know him, you realise that's just him. He can't help the way he looks or who his parents are any more than the rest of us. He's not an easy man, but he's been very kind to me. He struggles with himself.'

She lit a cigarette. 'Struggles with himself?'

'He wants to be like Çetin Bey,' he said. 'A truly good man. A man who doesn't carry a gun because he feels that if he can't get out of a situation using his wits, then he's not fit to be a police officer.'

Barçın was shocked. 'İkmen doesn't carry a gun?' she said.

'Not unless he's forced to,' Ömer said. 'On a day-to-day basis, no. He hates them, just as he hates violence of any sort. I've even heard it said that once, years ago, when the boss lost it, physically, with a prisoner, İkmen almost had him dismissed.'

'God.'

'Süleyman can have a terrible temper.'

Barçın shook her head. That wasn't good. But it didn't make him any less attractive.

'Would you rather I called you Yiannis or Mustafa?' İkmen asked.

'You can call me Mustafa. That will be easier for you.'

He looked terrible. His skin was grey and his eyes blank. Sitting in a chair on the balcony of his apartment, Mustafa Kaiserli, aka Yiannis Apion, looked as if he'd just seen his own death.

İkmen sat down opposite the man, while Süleyman stood. In the depths of the apartment, Ceyda Kaiserli cooked in silence.

'I'll call you Yiannis,' İkmen said.

'Are we going to police headquarters?'

'And why would we do that, Yiannis?' İkmen asked.

He looked up for the first time. 'I've been expecting you,' he said. 'Did Father Anatoli record our meeting in his diary?'

'The one the day before he died? Yes,' İkmen said.

The food was great, the rakı even better. Ömer ordered a second half-bottle and they both began to get giggly.

'My parents didn't want me to become a police officer,' Ömer said.

'What did they want you to do?' Barçın asked.

'Well, my father and his father and his father and . . . you know how it goes, back to the beginning of time . . . they all herded goats down on the plain. So he wanted better for me, as you can imagine, and anyway, I'm allergic to goats.'

She laughed.

'So I went to university, in Mardin, where he could keep an eye on me, and then he bought me this shop, selling souvenirs to the tourists. It was all cheap rubbish, and whenever there was any trouble . . .'

'PKK . . .'

'And the rest,' he said. 'The city was locked down. I was bored out of my mind.'

'And so you joined the police.'

'With about a million caveats from my father about not becoming one of the enemy. My sister had already left to go and train as a nurse.' He suddenly looked serious. 'Poor Dad.'

Barçın drained her glass and poured herself another drink. 'My mother took to her bed for a week when I got the bike,' she said. 'She was convinced I'd be working in prostitution within the year.'

'Kurdish parents, eh?'

They both toasted Kurdish parents, and Barçın wondered what it would be like to go to bed with Ömer. Şeymus, for all his athleticism, had been a very unadventurous lover. Later, when their relationship was over, she suspected that he went to working girls to indulge his more unconventional urges. He'd wanted to marry her, and so anything beyond straight sex had been out of the question. Did Ömer think that way? she wondered.

Barçın went to the bathroom to refresh her make-up. Was it just the booze or did she really now find Ömer Mungun impossibly sexy? She'd not had sex since Şeymus and she wanted it. It was a hot evening and she was drunk, and the only image in her mind was of the two of them lying naked on her bed.

Ömer wasn't Şeymus, she told herself. But he was into her. Then again, where would be the harm if they just had casual sex?

Ceyda Kaiserli put a jug of lemonade and three glasses on the balcony table and then went back inside the apartment. Mehmet Süleyman pulled a chair up to the table and sat down beside Çetin İkmen.

Yiannis poured them each a drink.

'My father, Konstantinos Apion, began working for Rudolf Paşa when he was a child,' he said. 'His father, Serafim, had worked as a gardener for various paşas over the years. Rudolf Paşa allowed him to design the garden of his house from scratch. It was a great opportunity. And it came with accommodation.'

'Where?'

'Before those apartments were built around it in the 1960s, there was a small row of stables that belonged to the Rudolfoğlus,' he said. 'There was also accommodation for grooms and other servants. My father was born there.'

'So the Rudolfoğlus must have sold the land,' İkmen said.

'I guess. I don't know,' Yiannis said. 'Growing up, I knew my father had worked for Rudolf Paşa and I knew that he'd been dismissed after Perihan Hanım's death, but I didn't know much else. Dad only told me the full story when he was dying. I'll be honest: for a long time I thought it was the morphine talking. He had chordoma, which is a type of bone cancer that affects the skull and spinal cord. He had radiotherapy and painkillers, which became progressively stronger as time went on. By the time we got to the diamorphine stage, he was off his head, and so for a while I didn't take any notice of his stories about the Rudolfoğlus. I hardly listened. But then his words began to seep into me, and what I'd been doing for years began to make sense.'

Süleyman lit a cigarette. 'What do you mean?'

'Dad and Father Kostas, our priest when I was a kid – and later, Father Anatoli – always encouraged me to spend time at the ayazma of St Katherine. I knew that other people went there to pray for various reasons, but I just found it gloomy.'

'And yet you did as you were asked?'

'Until I met Rebekah.' He shook his head. 'Ceyda.'

'Your wife.'

'Yes. She didn't want to leave Beşiktaş, and so I moved here with my dad. He died here. I knew that Rudolf Paşa was supposed to have been bad,' Yiannis said. 'He and Dimitri Bey did unspeakable things to the troops under their command in the desert.'

'Do you know if this Dimitri Bey's family are still in the city?' İkmen asked.

'Maybe, maybe not, When people started changing their names in the fifties, nobody knew who anyone was any more. Father Anatoli would have known.'

'How?'

'Father Kostas told him everything when he came to Moda.'

'Everything about . . .'

'About who the Rudolfoğlu siblings murdered, and why,' he said.

'And who was that, Yiannis?' İkmen asked.

'That, Inspector,' he said, 'was my sister.'

Ömer took her home to her apartment. The kapıcı of the block saw them arrive, and Barçın said, 'That's Serkan Bey.'

Ömer raised an eyebrow. Typical of his kind, the kapıcı was narrowing his eyes at the couple even before they entered his building.

'Does he know what you do?' Ömer asked.

'Yes,' she said.

'Then I'd better show him my badge,' he said. 'I mean, what could be wrong with a fellow officer escorting a colleague home?'

They'd kissed in an alleyway to the side of the restaurant where they'd eaten. She'd felt him go hard against her belly and she'd wanted him to fuck her then and there. But then he'd hailed a cab driven by a pious man and they'd had to keep their hands to themselves.

Once past the kapıcı, though, all that changed. Loosened by drink, they stumbled up the staircase to her first-floor apartment, where he pinned her up against a wall. They fumbled with their clothing, laughing, until he lifted her up on to his penis and fucked her.

'My dad and Perihan Hanım became lovers,' Yiannis said. 'They really were in love. She was still a young woman and beautiful. She'd been widowed for three years from a husband she had grown to hate.'

'Why had she grown to hate him?' Süleyman asked.

'I don't know for sure. Maybe the rumours about him consorting with the Devil were true. Dad said he ignored his wife. The only person he cared about was his daughter, Fatima. And all the girl cared about was him. There were dark rumours about that.'

'True?'

'Again, I don't know. But Dad would say that Fatima Hanım was known as the Devil's child with good reason.'

'Our pathologist is of the opinion that Fatima Hanım gave birth to a child,' Süleyman said. 'Do you know anything about that?'

'No,' he said. 'Once my father had been dismissed by the Rudolfoğlus, he had no further contact. Perihan Hanım was dead, and those bastards hated him and he hated them.'

'We have been considering the possibility that Fatima Hanım had her father's child,' İkmen said.

'She was nine when he died.'

He shrugged. 'Sadly, it happens.'

Yiannis shook his head. 'Dad never said anything like that. And neither did Father Anatoli.'

'You're sure Father Anatoli knew about this?'

He looked away. 'His predecessor told him,' he said. 'He and I talked about it.'

'His predecessor told him what, exactly?'

'That my dad was the father of Perihan Hanım's little girl.'

The third time they had sex, Barçın went on top. As she raised and lowered herself on his cock, Ömer squeezed her breasts. Even drunk, he was a better lover than Şeymus had ever been. When he finally came, he pulled her down on his chest and put his arms around her. Covered in sweat, Barçın knew that she was permeated by a heavy sexiness that just wouldn't stop.

How had she ever found this man irritating?

She licked his stomach, his hips and his balls. She took his cock in her mouth. She heard him grunt and moan, then, all too soon for both of them, it was over.

Later, as they lay in each other's arms, she heard him say, 'I

212

thought at first that you didn't like me. I thought that maybe I annoyed you.'

'You did,' she said. 'A bit.'

'Why? Was it the mirra? Was it too much?'

'A little.' She smiled. 'But you've made up for it now, Sergeant.'

Laughing, he rolled on top of her and parted her legs. She grabbed his cock and guided it inside her. But as she closed her eyes, it was Süleyman's face she saw in her mind.

İkmen felt genuinely sad for Konstantinos Apion. Perihan Hanım, who according to his son had been the love of his life, had died, and so had his daughter.

'We had found out that Perihan Hanım died not long after her confinement,' İkmen said. 'Septicaemia.'

'Yes,' Yiannis said.

Süleyman leaned forward. 'Why didn't you come to us with this before?'

'May I have a cigarette, please?'

'Of course.'

İkmen gave him one.

'I gave up two years ago,' Yiannis said. 'But . . .'

He smoked. Then he took a deep breath. 'The child my father called Sofia was delivered by the doctor Kevork Sarkissian Paşa,' he said. 'Everything was normal and the child was healthy. Perihan Hanım was exhausted, but the doctor felt able to leave her in the care of a female servant. My father briefly saw the baby and he told Perihan Hanım that somehow they would bring her up and be together. But he was only sixteen. He knew nothing. I sometimes wonder what Perihan made of that. She was so much older and she must have realised it wouldn't be possible.

'That night she started to have pain. She was sick many times and so the servant took Sofia away. I think she was going to

213

look after the child herself, but then her mistress started fitting. The servant sent a message to the doctor, but she didn't dare leave Perihan Hanım, and so the child was alone in her cot in the bedroom next door. At some point between the time that the servant took the baby away and when the doctor went in to see her, Sofia died.'

'How?'

'She was murdered,' Yiannis said. 'When my father saw the body, he thought that only she had done it. But it wasn't just her, it was all of them.'

'All?'

'Fatima Hanım and her brothers,' he said. 'They took turns. Each one of them knifing her through her tiny heart.' He sobbed.

İkmen looked at Süleyman. His face was grey.

'You are sure?'

'She admitted it!' Yiannis said. 'To her mother, to my father, to the doctor! She said she'd done it to regain her family's honour. They couldn't have a Greek bastard in their midst!'

'You are talking about Fatima Hanım?' Süleyman said. 'She was twelve.'

Yiannis looked up, his face red with fury. 'What does age matter when a person is truly evil? She was! Her brothers, behind her, cried! They begged forgiveness from their mother, but she told the doctor to take them from her bedroom and never bring them back. She said they were dead to her.'

The boys had cried. Separation from their mother had been more than they could bear. But not Fatima. If this story were true, then she hadn't cried. And so as a baby died, a great hatred was born. A hatred so intense it had governed all four of the Rudolfoğlu siblings' lives right up until the moment someone else had killed them.

'So do you understand why I didn't tell you before?' Yiannis asked.

'I imagine you're going to tell me that you didn't kill the Rudolfoğlus,' İkmen said.

'No, I didn't,' he said. 'And if Father Anatoli was still alive, he would support me.'

'Tell me what Father Anatoli knew about this,' İkmen said.

'More than I did.'

It was late, and dark, and İkmen was exhausted from a day of hard work and by the awful details he'd just heard about a child's death. If Fatima Rudolfoğlu had really orchestrated the killing of that baby, then no wonder some called her the Devil's child. But had she? And what about the child she herself had once carried? Had she killed that too?

'As I told you before, Father Kostas told Father Anatoli and—'

'If Father Anatoli knew more about all this than you did, do you think he knew about a child born to Fatima Hanım?'

'I don't know. He never said. I've never heard that before. Inspector, as soon as I found out how the Rudolfoğlus had died, I knew that if you found out about Sofia you'd think I had killed them. But I swear I didn't.'

Süleyman said, 'Did you confide your fears to Father Anatoli?'

'Yes. He said that if I tried to hide from the police, it would go badly for me. So when you turned up, he gave you just enough information to find me, hoping you'd track down the real murderer in the meantime. But that didn't happen. What puzzled him was how you knew of my existence.'

'My sergeant was told by a local resident,' İkmen said. 'A man called Rauf Karadeniz.'

Yiannis shrugged. 'I don't know him.'

İkmen sighed. 'So does your wife know about this?'

'No,' he said. 'This is Greek pain. We bear it alone.'

'But surely your wife would want to help you?'

'Ceyda is Jewish,' he said. 'She'll understand. Minorities live

215

in their own bubbles here, you know, Inspector. It's both our strength and our weakness. We wear our secrets like armour.'

'So what about the ayazma?' Süleyman asked. 'Why were you encouraged to go there?'

'Because that's where Sofia is buried,' he said. 'Underneath the flagstones. Why do you think Kemal Rudolfoğlu was smashing the place up all those years ago? That bitch had told him to find her body and burn it. My father told me.'

'And he stopped him.'

'Yes. He beat him senseless too. They'd taken everything from him. His job, his home and his child. I was glad when I heard they'd all been murdered. But I say again, I didn't do it. I had nothing to do with Father Anatoli's death either. We met the day before he killed himself and we prayed at the ayazma. Then we went our separate ways. He appeared to me to be in good spirits.'

'You didn't speak about the Rudolfoğlus?'

'No. We both prayed for Sofia, as we usually do. Then Father Anatoli told me about a meeting he'd had with the mayor of Kadıköy, who had assured him that there was no way the ayazma was going to be closed down, whatever some people of, shall we say, a bullying attitude towards religions that are not their own might think about it. He met me to reassure me.'

'Did you see where Father Anatoli went after you left him?'

'No,' he said. 'I walked inland and got the historic tram back to Kadıköy ferry stage.'

'OK,' İkmen said. 'But you know that we will now have to take you in and get a formal statement from you, don't you?'

'Yes.' Yiannis Apion hung his head. 'This story cannot end well,' he said. 'My father knew that. Which was why he kept it to himself until he was dying.'

216

Chapter 19

Lifting her head was going to be a major military operation. Barçın's father had been an alcoholic, and so she knew how devastating a hangover could be. As soon as she raised her head from the pillow, she knew that this one could be monstrous. And so she lay still, listening to the sound of gentle snoring from the man who slept beside her.

There was no way she didn't know what she'd done the previous night, or why she'd done it. She'd got drunk with a man she found moderately attractive and then she'd had sex with him. She didn't regret it – not exactly. The sex had been urgent, but good. Without taking her head from the pillow, she turned it to look at him. Even sleeping and full of drink he looked good. And he was well endowed. She knew what she'd seen in him even if he wasn't her perfect man. She stroked his chin with her finger and he opened his eyes.

'Hi.'

For a moment his face was static and she began to wonder whether he was regretting what they'd done. Would he roll over, call her a whore and leave? But then he smiled and said, 'Hello, Barçın. Beautiful, beautiful Barçın.'

He kissed her.

When they finally parted, he said, 'That really is almost the best way to wake up.'

'What's the best way?'

He put his hand between her legs.

She laughed. 'Oh, but what's the time?'

He looked at his watch. 'Six. I'm on shift at eight.' He brushed some strands of hair away from her face. 'We have time . . .'

She too started work at eight.

'Ah, but we have to leave before the kapıcı gets up,' she said. 'If he sees us he'll be disgusted!'

He pushed himself up and then leaned over to caress her breasts. Amazingly, he didn't scream with pain as his head left the pillow. No hangover? That was impressive.

He just smiled. 'Let him be disgusted.'

'Ömer!'

'Oh come on, motorbike girl,' he said. 'You're bolder than that.'

But she pushed him away. 'No, Ömer,' she said. 'Maybe we can get away with that story about working together last night, but if he actually sees us walking out of here together this morning, he will make my life a misery.'

Ömer hung his head. He knew that what she was saying was true. Not so many years ago, it had seemed as if men and women could live together without being married, but that was becoming harder all the time. Religious and social conservatism was growing even in parts of the city that had exuded a more liberal atmosphere.

He got out of bed. 'OK.'

'If he doesn't see us leave, then he can fool himself that nothing immoral happened in his building,' she said. 'Even if he had his ear pressed to the door and heard our every gasp and scream.'

'Did he try and stop the process?' İkmen asked Kerim Gürsel when he sat down at his desk.

'No,' he said. 'Just opened his mouth for the swab like a good boy.'

218

'It will take a while to compare it to our unidentified DNA samples,' İkmen said. 'But you know I don't think it will be positive.'

Süleyman looked up from his newspaper. He and İkmen had been up all night interrogating Yiannis Apion. Both of them were exhausted, but the younger man was tetchy too.

'You swallowed Apion's . . . Kaiserli's . . . whatever his name is, his story,' he said.

'You didn't?'

'No.' He put his newspaper down. 'How many times do we hear the story about how they were in the right place at the right time but it wasn't them? Then we find out that it was. What makes you think he's different?'

İkmen had seen his colleague like this before. When he was tired or under pressure he became angry and sometimes unreasonable. Occasionally he could explode into violence.

İkmen asked Kerim to go and get them all coffee. As he handed over money, he said, 'I need to go home and get some sleep, but I need to do some work first. Coffee, very strong, is the only way forward.'

When the sergeant had gone, he said, 'What are you supposed to be doing today, Mehmet Bey?'

Süleyman lit a cigarette. 'Oh, you'll love this!' he said. 'Encouraging silent Ali Erbil to speak.'

'Why? Elif Büyük has identified the Teufel Ev as the place where they stayed.'

'She's mad,' he said.

'So? She's not stupid, she knows where she's been. She didn't see any of the Rudolfoğlus. I can accept that. The cellar is partially blocked.'

'She claims she didn't see them. She could have killed them, or Ali Erbil could, or both of them together.'

'Forensics are not in on Ali and Elif yet, are they?' İkmen said.

'No.'

'So we must reserve judgement. Just as we have to reserve judgement about Mr Apion.'

'Yes, but . . .' Süleyman ground his teeth in frustration. 'Do we?'

'Yes we do,' İkmen said. 'If only so that you keep that temper of yours in check.'

'You know I won't—'

'No, I don't,' İkmen said. 'Remember, I've seen you beat up a suspect.'

'Years ago!'

'Indeed. You were young and going through some sort of romantic torment at the time, as I recall. But Mehmet, look . . .'

He walked around his desk and sat down next to his friend. 'I am completely aware of the fact that you and I are very different men. Without the stability provided by my wife and family, I couldn't cope—'

'I love Gonca,' Süleyman cut in.

'I'm sure you do,' İkmen said. 'But I do sense a . . . shall we say a dissatisfaction . . . a need for your wilder side to express itself . . .'

'If I were unfaithful to her, her family would kill me. It's taken them years to accept that I even exist!'

'I know. I know,' İkmen said. 'And don't worry, I'm not going to drive you to fury going on about how you knew all along that a gypsy family would not be easy to negotiate. But you must, *must* leave your frustrations at home. God forgive me, Mehmet, but if that means having the occasional adventure far away from the Şekeroğlu family and their associates . . .'

'Oh, so I just pick up a girl and fuck her?'

İkmen, mildly irritated, lit a cigarette. 'No,' he said. 'And yes.'

'Oh for God's—'

'Far be it from me to advise you in matters of sex,' İkmen said. 'I know how close you are about these matters. But if you're not getting what you need, then either you put up with it or you go elsewhere from time to time. Gonca is my friend and I would hate you to do anything that might cause her pain. But you cannot be like this when you are at work. You cannot be angry and insensitive and boorish. I know there are some officers who prize such attributes, but not me and not Teker. I'm sorry to have to speak to you like this, Mehmet.'

'No, no.' He put a hand up to his head and rubbed his temples. 'It is I who should apologise. There is nothing wrong with Gonca, it's me. I don't know why, but every so often I have to . . .'

'You've always turned to extracurricular sex when you're unhappy,' İkmen said. 'You know that's your pattern. What . . .'

'Zelfa is making things difficult for me,' he said.

Zelfa Halman, his ex-wife and mother of his son Yusuf, had moved back to her native Ireland some years ago. She'd taken Yusuf with her.

'In consultation with her, I booked leave so that I could go to Dublin and spend a couple of weeks with my son. It was all arranged, but now it seems my wife has changed her mind. Apparently it is more important for my son to visit some relatives in Cork at that time. The weeks she has suggested as alternatives are not suitable for me.'

'Why not?'

'I'm on a training course and it is also Gonca's birthday. You know what a song and dance gypsies make of birthdays.'

İkmen smiled.

'Gonca would understand if I had to go to Ireland, but she'd hold it against me.'

'So let her,' İkmen said. 'And to hell with the training course. I know I shouldn't say that, but if the mother of your child

221

says "jump", then to my mind, the only logical response is "how high?".'

'Not very dignified.'

'Dignity is something your Ottoman ancestors did, Mehmet,' İkmen said. 'You don't have that luxury. Welcome to my world.'

Süleyman grunted. Then he said, 'Apion's sister was murdered by the Rudolfoğlus. If someone killed my brother, I would want him dead.'

'Of course,' İkmen said. 'I'm sure that Yiannis Apion did want the Rudolfoğlus dead. But wanting and doing are two different things. And Mr Apion is not you. He is not an Ottoman; he is a member of a dwindling minority. He is vulnerable and very aware of the fact that his behaviour might reflect negatively on his fellow Greeks. I'm not saying that I believe he didn't kill that family. But I am happy for him to be released pending forensic results. He has not confessed. All he has done is tell us an old story about our victims. Now I would suggest that you allow me to interview Ali Erbil while you go home and rest, or whatever it is that will make you feel better.'

'Ali Erbil is not your prisoner.'

'No, but the time the couple spent in the Teufel Ev concerns me,' İkmen said. 'Have you any further insight into why they killed those people on the street?'

'Why Elif killed them, you mean. Yes. On the face of it, they appear to be random acts of homicide. A spree for kicks. She certainly found the whole process exciting. But then I think that the loss of the stability she found at the Teufel Ev is significant. I think that for a short time she imagined she might have found peace. Just her and Ali shooting up in safety. She's been on the streets all her life. She's been used by men all her life. When she lost that stability, her anger exploded. Incarcerated in a hospital, provided she is treated kindly, I doubt she will ever harm anyone again. She will have achieved the stability she craves. I don't believe that she killed the Rudolfoğlus. I'm of the opinion that when she says she didn't know they were there, she was telling the truth. It was Ali Erbil who apparently saw someone in the cellar, not her.'

'Mmm.'

Kerim returned with coffee.

İkmen drank down half his cup in two long gulps.'What do you make of Ali?' he asked Süleyman.

'Weak, in love, a junkie. Not actually bad.'

'But you think he's trying to play mad to be with Elif.'

'He's besotted,' he said.

'Mmm.'

İkmen opened his office window and lit a cigarette. Then he said to Kerim, 'Can you print off that mug shot of Yiannis Apion for me? Or shove it on an iPad or whatever it is you do with photographs these days.'

He was cold. It was over thirty degrees and Yiannis Apion felt as if he was in a snowstorm. As soon as the police had let him go, he'd got on a ferry and given thanks to St Katherine at the ayazma. Soon, hairy-knuckled officers would arrive to dig up the floor in order to verify his story. Would they find his sister? And if they did, what would they do with her? She had to be there. His father had, in his own words, thrashed the shit out of Kemal Rudolfoğlu in order to prevent him from desecrating her grave.

Now, sitting alone in the corner of the Koço's garden, he drank coffee and smoked. Ceyda had gone to work as usual, but he'd been able to tell that she was shaken. When the police had taken him away, she'd not accompanied him. He hadn't wanted her to. So she was still largely in the dark. He'd have to tell her the

223

whole sorry tale – sometime. One day he'd have to tell her how much he loved her. Because he did.

He looked around at the usual mid-morning habitués of the Koço. Mainly old men reading newspapers, and discreet homosexuals conversing in low tones about politics. They'd all been coming to the Koço for years – just as he had; just as Father Anatoli used to. Of course the priest had frequently come here after performing his devotions in the ayazma. But he also knew all the regulars and sometimes even had a glass or two of rakı after his prayers.

The clergy were good at keeping secrets. They were supposed to be. When Yiannis had told Father Anatoli what Konstantinos had told him, he'd freely admitted that he'd known about Sofia for years. Like Father Kostas before him, he'd seen it as his duty to protect her remains.

So why had he killed himself? As far as Yiannis knew, he hadn't been ill or in trouble. Maybe his suicide had nothing to do with Sofia.

'I've been told that the main problem with methadone as a substitute for heroin is that you don't get the initial rush,' Çetin İkmen said as he smoked in front of a completely unresponsive Ali Erbil. 'That's got to be disappointing. But I don't think it can make you go mad. Not according to my sources.'

The guards had managed to get Erbil to sit at a table so that İkmen could talk to him. But that was all he was doing.

'Addicts are often conflated with people who are mentally ill,' İkmen continued. 'And sometimes, of course, people with problems may self-medicate using street drugs. I know this. I imagine you do too. Very complicated thing, the mind. Can't say that I can even begin to understand it. I'm not an expert. I don't know, for instance, how a psychiatrist can tell whether or not someone is faking. By that I mean pretending to be insane so they get a reduced sentence. Or so they think. In reality that doesn't happen, of course, because if a person is judged to have committed a crime while he was insane, then his detention within hospital may be permanent. Not that I think that's your reason.'

Ali Erbil didn't so much as blink.

'You want to be with Elif, which I can understand,' İkmen said. 'When you love someone, you want to be with them. But if you do indeed love that person, then you must think about what is best for them. To a large extent this means putting your own needs to one side. Elif needs treatment over and above her addiction. This is inevitable and will be prescribed by psychiatrists. That may include contact with other patients, but it may not.

'Now I know that you come from a wealthy family, and so I imagine you think that money will give you some leverage with staff in a psychiatric hospital. It may or it may not. But what I can absolutely guarantee is that you'll have to endure a lot of being taken up the arse first. You won't offer yourself for this pleasure, but it will happen as surely as you will almost inevitably have to go down on whoever shares your cell in prison. Good-looking man like you. Admittedly, you may get a fix or two in return, but that's the up side. What I'm saying is that whether you go to hospital or prison is irrelevant. You won't get to see Elif. Not to put too fine a point on it, I will actually recommend that you don't see her.'

Ali looked up.

'Got your attention? Good.' He smiled. 'Because while all that sinks in, I'd like to show you a photograph. It's got nothing to do with any of the murders committed by Elif Büyük. I'd just like to know whether you've ever seen this man, and if so, where. Specifically, I'd like to know whether this photograph I am going to show you is of the man you saw in the Teufel Ev in Moda. And yes, I know you denied ever having been inside the Teufel Ev, but we know you've been there.' There was a pause as İkmen

225

looked into Ali's eyes. 'If you want to know how we know this, then you will have to ask me. I'm not just going to tell you.'

He put the photograph Kerim Gürsel had printed out on the table between them.

Ali Erbil looked at it. Then he looked away. For a long moment İkmen thought he'd say nothing. He'd not appeared to be visibly shocked by any of the institutional horror stories İkmen had told him. If that were the case, why would he even look? But he had.

He cleared his throat. 'I've seen him.'

'At the Teufel Ev? The house in Moda?'

'No,' he said. 'I saw him at that café Inspector Süleyman took me to when we went to Moda. He was with a priest.'

Father Anatoli.

'What were they doing?' İkmen asked.

'Talking.'

'How? Intensely? Happily?'

'Normally. Only for a few seconds.' He paused. 'How do you know we were in that house?'

'Because Elif said so and now you have confirmed it,' İkmen said. He smiled again. 'So not this man in the house. That's excellent.' He stood. 'Anything—'

'I'm done talking,' Ali Erbil said.

'As you wish.'

İkmen told the guard to unlock Erbil's cell. Just before he left, he said, 'Think about what I said, about the benefits and drawbacks of being insane. If I were you I'd give some serious thought to what you can do to help the police. After all, you have killed nobody.'

They'd travelled to work separately. Barçın had got a taxi while Ömer had taken the tram. Now, in the office İkmen had given her, Barçın was finding it difficult to concentrate on the many spidery-scripted Ottoman letters that she still had to transliterate.

226

She didn't think that Serkan Bey, the kapıcı of her building, had seen Ömer leave. He'd run out of the door a good half an hour before she passed the old man on the stairs. Had he seen that she'd been flushed? Probably, but that didn't mean he could prove anything. Not unless he went sniffing around her apartment. Which he could . . . Barçın tried not to think about that.

She looked at the dusty pile of Ottoman letters. Her eyes moved sideways to the much smaller number of modern Turkish notes. Of course anyone could read those, but because they were on her desk, İkmen probaby intended her to at least look at them.

A lot of them were banal notes from utility companies. A letter from her bank asking Miss Fatima Rudolfoğlu whether she might consider having one of their credit cards. And then there were some letters from her lawyer, Erdal Bey at Kenter and Kenter. Unlike the other communications, these were carefully written on thick, good-quality legal paper. The first one she came to, dated 2014, detailed the limits of Miss Fatima's property, giving the exact location of the border between land belonging to the Teufel Ev (called here the Tulip Kiosk) and that owned by Moda Municipality. She had obviously been anxious about what belonged to her and what didn't. Very old people did that a lot. Fearing they would die soon, they wanted to get their affairs in order.

The second letter, also from Erdal Bey, contained a summary of Miss Fatima's will. What they already knew was detailed – that the Teufel Ev plus any monies and investments owned by Miss Rudolfoğlu would revert to her three brothers, Yücel, Kanat and Kemal, after her death. In the event of the brothers' deaths, everything was to go to the Oriental Club of Moda. But there was also a personal warning from the lawyer to Miss Rudolfoğlu. It was this that made Barçın jump out of her chair.

*　　*　　*

İkmen read the passage again.

I have to urge you in the strongest terms to reconsider your son. Issues such as this have a way of re-emerging, even if, as you claim, this gentleman has no knowledge of his true origins. I refer you to the enclosed document regarding the current status of DNA technology, which I would encourage you to read with some attention. If this person should make a claim on your property on the death of either yourself or whichever siblings survive you, it may prove injurious to your stated heirs, the Oriental Club, or your own posthumous reputation. A small bequest to your son, on condition that he makes no public statement regarding his parentage, would, I believe, save you and your benefi-ciaries a lot of potential anxiety and heartache in the future.

The letter was dated 15 June 2014. İkmen looked up. Barçın Demirtaş, who was sitting on the other side of his desk, said, 'It was there all along. I was so caught up with the correspondence between the siblings . . .'

'I employed you to transliterate the Ottoman letters,' İkmen said. 'I could have read this myself. Don't beat yourself up. We've found it now.'

'A son,' she said. 'Her baby survived.'

'So it would seem. I will have to call Erdal Bey. I doubt he knows the identity of this man, but maybe he knows about the circumstances surrounding his birth.'

'There was a girl in my mother's village who, so people said, was the result of a father-and-daughter coupling,' Barçın said. 'She had a strange, lopsided face. I've no idea why. The family married her off when she was thirteen. She died in childbirth.'

They both sat in silence. Child marriages were still a big

228

problem in some parts of the country. Everyone had a story. But Fatima Rudolfoğlu had been, it was said, so very young.

'Go back to the Ottoman letters and leave this to me,' İkmen said.

'Sir.' She rose.

'Oh, and just to bring you up to speed, Inspector Süleyman and I interviewed the son of the Rudolfoğlus' gardener, Konstantinos Apion, last night. Yiannis Apion claims that Perihan Rudolfoğlu gave birth to his father's child in 1931.'

'We knew she was pregnant . . .'

'Yes, and she gave birth to a live child,' İkmen said. 'Which Fatima Rudolfoğlu and her brothers killed.'

'They killed a baby?'

'They stabbed her through the heart,' İkmen said. 'Familiar modus operandi, eh?'

Barçın sat down again. 'God,' she said, 'that is monstrous!'

'Apion claims that he didn't kill the Rudolfoğlus in spite of the fact that he has known about this since his late father told him four years ago. So far there is no forensic evidence that links him with the Teufel Ev, and so currently his statement is just a story. But his priest, Father Anatoli, knew, and he was seen talking to Apion the day before his suicide.'

'So Apion could have done it?'

'It's possible. But he volunteered the information. And in spite of the fact that priests are supposed to respect the sanctity of confessions made to them, I wonder whether Father Anatoli told someone else about the Rudolfoğlus and their crimes. His wife is of the opinion that his responsibilities had begun to weigh heavily upon him in recent years.'

'He did kill himself?' she said.

'Oh yes, no foul play there,' İkmen said. 'But why? What, if anything, did he know over and above what was told to Yiannis Apion?'

229

'Does Apion think he knew more?'

'Yes,' İkmen said. 'He's no idea what, so he says. And I don't think he is trying to point the finger at the priest for the murders. Although that said, I really don't know.'

Mehmet Süleyman had gone to his apartment in Cihangir and fallen asleep on his bed immediately. Had he returned to Gonca's house in Balat, the noise from all her many relatives would have kept him awake. And Gonca herself would have wanted attention. The older she got, the worse it was becoming. His mother said that the gypsy had bewitched him, and although he was an otherwise rational man, he could believe it. She was beautiful, strong and very, very good in bed, but he'd had a great many beautiful women over the years, and none of them had affected him like Gonca. None of his women had ever made him afraid.

When he finally woke up, just as the heat of the day was diminishing, he remembered what İkmen had said about his trip to Ireland. He'd have to tell Gonca that he'd miss her birthday. She wouldn't kill him. In fact she wouldn't do anything to him. He had always had the upper hand in their relationship, and she knew it. Not only was he over fifteen years her junior, he was a police officer from a good family. She, for her part, was a respected artist, but she had no power beyond that bestowed by her enormous extended family. And even they weren't everywhere.

Before he'd left his office to accompany İkmen to Beşiktaş the previous evening, he thought he'd seen Ömer Mungun leave with Constable Demirtaş. He hoped they'd just gone for a drink and nothing more. Not that he was jealous. Barçın Demirtaş was a good-looking woman with more than a touch of wildness in her soul – the motorbike was testament to that – but Süleyman told himself that his concern was purely paternal. Ömer was a young man who was shy with women and he didn't want him to get hurt. But was that the truth?

He pictured her young, firm-breasted body and it made him feel horny. If Barçın Demirtaş offered herself to him, he would take her, and he knew it.

Chapter 20

It was late by the time Erdal Bey of Kenter and Kenter returned Çetin İkmen's call. He had been in a meeting. Also, by his own admission, he'd had to spend a little time collecting relevant pieces of information before he called the policeman.

'I inherited the Rudolfoğlu business from my father,' he told İkmen. 'I went to see Miss Fatima once, when I took over the practice in 1979. She was old then, and far from the world's most gracious hostess. I remember that her housekeeper, or whatever she was, made the worst tea I can recall outside of my old school, which is saying something.'

İkmen wondered whether, like Süleyman, Erdal Bey had been to the prestigious Galatasaray Lisesi.

'Did you know about her son when you went to visit her, Erdal Bey?'

'My father had mentioned him,' he said. 'Not that he had any more idea about who he might be than I did. In fact, over the years, I must say I have wondered whether he was some figment of her imagination. My wife had a spinster aunt who constantly fantasised about non-existent lovers and chimerical children. But, as you saw in my letter to Miss Fatima, I felt compelled to advise caution with regard to her will.'

'Would a child have a claim on the property?' İkmen asked.

'Provided he could prove his identity, yes. Miss Fatima gave no instructions for her body to be buried complete and intact, and so samples could be taken for DNA comparison. But as no one has yet come forward, I am at the moment inclined to believe that it was possibly a fantasy. That said, at the time, I had to take what she told me seriously.'

'Do you have any idea about who may have fathered this child?'

'Not really, no. My father did tell me there were rumours that Rudolf Paşa had had relations with his daughter, but Fatima would have been a child at the time and so the production of issue would have been a remote possibility. I think it much more likely that she became pregnant after the death of her mother.'

'Yes, but by whom? I have been led to believe that once the family locked themselves away, they had few visitors.'

'Few, but not none,' Erdal Bey said. 'Or maybe it was one of the brothers . . .'

Maybe it was. Maybe that was what all the spite had been about all along. One of the boys had crept into her bed . . . or perhaps been invited. However . . .

'If it was one of the brothers, then surely they would have kept the child?' İkmen said.

Erdal Bey sighed. 'Sadly, Çetin Bey, that would not necessarily follow. The Rudolfoğlus were Ottomans, remember.'

Too proud to acknowledge such things as illegitimacy or incest even if it was their own fault. Even if it caused them pain.

'I know,' İkmen said. 'What about these occasional visitors? Any ideas?'

'Apart from my father, no,' he said. 'And let me reassure you right now, it wasn't him.'

'I didn't—'

'I know you weren't implying anything,' Erdal Bey said. 'But just to clear this up, my father was a lot younger than Fatima Hanım, he was wealthy, and he had a vast stable of young, pretty mistresses. I've no idea who else may have visited that house. But if you can track down the servant who attended the old woman when I visited in 1979, she might know. Inappropriately, to my mind, she was at her mistress's side the whole time I was there. Even when I was discussing matters of personal finance. Even, as I recall, when I first brought up the subject of Miss Fatima's son.'

Sinem was ill again, and the Gürsel household revolved around her pain. Pembe Hanım was an uncomplaining carer, but she'd enlisted the help of some woman from an LGBT pressure group who didn't approve of the police. So Kerim was not welcome while she was around.

Kerim and his wife Sinem had grown up together. When they were kids, everyone had assumed that they'd marry. But then Sinem had developed arthritis and Kerim's family had discouraged their friendship. What they hadn't known, and still didn't, was that Kerim and Sinem had both been aware from an early age that they were gay. No one could understand why clever, handsome Kerim had insisted upon marrying a cripple. But not only had it been the perfect cover for both of them, it also meant that as best friends they would never be alone. And even when Kerim had fallen in love with the transsexual Pembe Hanım, nothing had changed between him and Sinem. In fact Pembe was a lifesaver for Sinem, whose condition was deteriorating. Only this woman, who meant well but whose name Kerim didn't even know, had altered the dynamics of the Gürsel apartment.

So Kerim kept out of the way. He'd spent almost all day at the Teufel Ev, after which he had taken himself off to the Koço via the ayazma of St Katherine. He'd spent a long time looking at the floor, which was covered in what looked like ancient stone flags. He wondered how whoever had buried Perihan Hanım's child had got them up. He had to have been strong. A manual labourer, maybe? A gardener, like the baby's father, Konstantinos

Apion? Soon, İkmen had told him, on Teker's orders, the stones would be lifted.

After the ayazma, he'd gone up into the Koço and ordered a vodka and tonic. A nice long alcoholic drink after yet another grim day's work.

The Koço was much livelier in the evenings. Some of the largely elderly daytime crowd were in evidence, including Rauf Bey, who smiled at him before returning to his newspaper. Fortunately he didn't seem to want to talk, which suited Kerim. The old man had been very useful at the beginning of the Teufel Ev investigation. But the feeling Kerim had got from him, that maybe he had a personal interest in him too, made the policeman want to avoid the elderly lawyer. The last thing he needed was an admirer, especially one who lived with a fish. His life was already way more complicated than it should be. But then at least he wasn't like Ömer Mungun, who, he suspected, had started seeing Constable Demirtaş.

Kerim had only spent a very short time at headquarters that morning before heading out to Moda, but he'd seen Ömer, starry-eyed and slightly dishevelled, sneaking sly peeks at the Ottoman script transcriber and then smiling. He wished the younger man well. But he feared for him too. Süleyman, Kerim had observed over the years, rarely took kindly to other men courting attractive women of his acquaintance. There could only be one peacock in his yard, and it had to be him.

He finished his drink and ordered another. It had just arrived when İkmen called him.

There was Moda, and there was Moda. The İnce family lived in what was a fast-disappearing part of the district, i.e., affordable Moda. Not for them the Ottoman villas, venerable mid-twentieth-century housing, or steel-and-glass apartment towers with views of the sea.

Çetin İkmen had visited the tatty, garlic-scented apartment before, when he'd managed to get Bilal İnce to admit his theft of an expensive boncuk from the Teufel Ev. This time it was his wife he wanted to see.

'My husband is out with the children at some political meeting,' Selin said as she showed İkmen and Kerim Gürsel into her sitting room. 'I can't tell you how furious I was with him over that boncuk. How stupid can you get?'

The two men sat down.

İkmen said, 'Well actually it is you we've come to see, Selin Hanım.'

'Me?' She too sat. 'About Fatima Hanım again? I've told you everything I know.'

'Possibly,' İkmen said. 'Mrs İnce, may I ask whether your mother is still alive?'

'No. She died five years ago. Why?'

'Your mother worked at the Teufel Ev before you.'

'Yes, I told you that,' she said. 'And my grandmother.'

'Information has come to us about a child born to Fatima Hanım . . .'

'Well that's a lie!' she said. 'She never had any children; she was a spinster.'

'Spinster she may have been,' İkmen said. 'But virgin she was not, I'm afraid, Selin Hanım. During the course of his examination of Fatima Hanım's body, our pathologist discovered that she had given birth to a child by Caesarean section. Now the Rudolfoğlu family lawyer has informed me that this child may have survived. He also told me that back in 1979, when he visited Miss Fatima, a female servant was present. I assume that was your mother.'

'Probably.'

'Well, do you know whether Fatima Hanım ever had any other servants?'

236

'Not that I know of.'

'Then it seems it had to be your mother, doesn't it?'

She shrugged. Her manner was studiedly offhand. Both İkmen and Gürsel had seen suspects in interview use that method of attempted concealment hundreds of times.

'And assuming it was your mother, then according to Erdal Bey of Kenter and Kenter, she was present when he and Fatima Hanım were discussing this child, a boy. Or rather a man . . .'

'Don't know anything about it,' she said. 'Before my time.'

She'd become very pale, and when she went to take a cigarette out of a packet, İkmen noticed that her hand shook.

'Yes, but I doubt your mother would have let you take over her job blind,' Kerim said. 'She must have told you things . . .'

'Yes.'

'Some of them intimate,' İkmen said.

She said nothing.

'Hanım,' İkmen said. 'I know you know something. Believe me, everything about your demeanour at the moment screams that you know something. Also, why would Erdal Bey lie?'

'I don't know!'

'He wouldn't, and I'm struggling to understand why you are. Selin Hanım, your husband has already admitted stealing from Fatima Hanım's apartment. How do we know that you didn't kill her and her brothers in order to silence them about that theft?'

Knowing that the kapıcı was almost certainly listening out for her, Barçın Demirtaş tiptoed up the stairs to her apartment in bare feet. She'd taken her shoes off at the front door of the building, even though she hadn't been able to see or hear him. When she was halfway up the stairs, he'd loomed out of a broom cupboard. She'd said 'Good evening, Serkan Bey,' and he had returned the greeting but his eyes had betrayed his disgust.

She'd heard other tenants talk about how he listened at doors. He must have heard Ömer making love to her, especially when he'd done it against her apartment door. They'd never be able to do that again. But then would they anyway?

Fortunately Barçın had been busy all day. In spite of her tiredness, she'd made a considerable breakthrough with the legal documents she'd found. İkmen had been pleased and had let her leave early. Then she'd gone shopping. However, while she was at work, she had noticed that Ömer kept coming into her office and looking at her from the corridor. It had been unnerving, and although she'd had fun with him the previous night, she was beginning to wonder whether seeing him again was a good idea.

The sex had been enthusiastic and sensual. Unlike a tragically large cohort of men, he knew his way around a woman's body. But could she continue seeing him just for sex if he was going to turn creepy and obsessive on her? She'd been there before. And anyway, he wasn't strictly her type . . .

'My grandmother Muazzaz was an evil bitch,' Selin said.

It wasn't every day that İkmen heard a woman speak with such lack of respect about her own grandmother.

'When Fatima Hanım and her brothers killed their mother's baby, she said she wasn't there. But I've always wondered. She was a racist, a bigot; she thought that women who didn't cover were whores, and she treated my mother like dirt. All she cared about were her ladies, Perihan and Fatima Hanım. But she was also scared of Fatima. She once told my mother that Fatima wasn't even Perihan Hanım's child. Rudolf Paşa, she said, had mated with a female devil. She blamed him for all of it, probably because he was a foreigner. But she didn't like it when Perihan had an affair with the Greek gardener. It was my grandmother who gave Konstantinos Apion the child's body to dispose of. She was vile and frightening. But as I say, she was scared of Fatima Hanım.'

'And so was your mother?' İkmen asked. 'And you?'

'Oh yes,' she said. Then she laughed nervously. 'She was the Devil.'

'Really? So why are you protecting her? You seem to me to be a rational woman. Fatima Hanım is dead.'

Selin shook her head. 'Is she?'

'You know she is; you found her.'

'Can the Devil die?' she said. She shook her head again. 'Yes, of course I know about her pregnancy. My mother told me. But I can't tell you anything about it.'

'Can't, or won't?' İkmen said.

'I can't,' she said.

'Because you're still frightened of her?'

'What do you think?'

İkmen sighed. 'So if I were to ask you whether you know who the father of the child was . . .'

'I don't know,' she said. 'And that's the truth.'

'You knew the child survived?'

She said nothing.

'I see. What about when it was born? Do you know that?'

Again she said nothing.

'You do know that I can very easily connect you to your husband's theft charge,' İkmen said. 'In fact I'm not sure that I actually believe you didn't know what he'd done.'

She looked at him and held his gaze.

'What did Miss Fatima do to you, Selin?' he said. 'Did she say she'd reach out from beyond the grave and harm your family if you told the truth? You know that's not possible, don't you? Your husband may buy into all that, but I can't believe that you really do.'

'How do you know?' she asked. 'It's said you don't believe in anything.'

'Ah, but that isn't strictly true. Not that I'm material to this

239

conversation,' he added. 'We are working on the theory that the child Miss Fatima gave birth to was born sometime around 1928. We have arrived at this date purely on the assumption that Rudolf was the father. That was the year he died. Fatima was nine. This would make her son almost ninety, were he still alive. Now if you can confirm or deny this date, it would be very useful to us.'

She shifted in her chair. Her mobile phone rang; she ignored it.

'As you say,' she said, 'I'm not a foolish woman, but I am superstitious. I admit that. Also I know what she was like, the awful things she said, the way she used to pinch me underneath my arms when I tried to bathe her. She'd hang on until I bled sometimes. She used to beat my mother.'

'So why did your mother allow you to work at the Teufel Ev?'

'That goes back to Granny Muazzaz,' she said. 'Perihan Hanım died because of complications after the birth of her little girl. But Fatima told Granny that if she ever left her, she'd tell the police that she'd killed her mother. She said our families were tied to each other forever. That if one of us told what had happened in that house, we'd all hang.'

'But that can't happen now,' İkmen said.

'Provided you believe me.'

'Well convince me,' he said. 'Whatever happens, you won't hang, will you?'

'No.'

'So . . .'

She took a breath. 'Mum told me that the baby was born in 1939. She didn't know who took it – or she didn't tell me, and that is the truth.'

'And it was a boy?'

'Yes.'

'Did your mother know whether it was given a name?'

She bit her lip.

İkmen leaned forward. 'Come on, Selin, you've got this far.'

She began to cry. 'I said I'd never tell! I said . . .'

'Come on,' İkmen said. 'Fatima Rudolfoğlu wasn't kind to you; you owe her nothing.'

'Yes, but she'll—'

'No she won't!' He took one of her hands. 'Fatima is dead. And unpleasant though she was, she wasn't the Devil and she can't hurt you. I promise you that on the lives of my precious grandchildren.'

She breathed in deeply to control her tears, then she said, 'The child was called Rouvin. It's Greek. Mum told me that it means "behold, a son".'

Chapter 21

Elif Büyük had tried to kill herself. According to the custody officers, she'd become agitated when no one would answer her questions about whether her name had appeared in the press. Met with a wall of silence, she had smashed her head against her cell wall until she became unconscious. That no one had stopped her made Süleyman mad. The lazy bastards had probably been looking at ridiculous websites of cats wearing hats. Now Elif was in a rather different hospital to the one that had been expecting her.

On the up side, forensic results on the Yeniköy murder scene had arrived showing that the site was covered in DNA from both Elif and Ali Erbil. The British victim's family had been due to come in and see whether they could identify the pair. Now they'd be taken to see just Ali. It was disappointing. Elif was by far the more recognisable of the two.

Walking down the corridor towards his office, Süleyman saw that Constable Demirtaş was already at her desk. Although her door was open, he knocked.

She looked up. 'Oh.'

'Good morning, Constable,' he said. 'You're very early.'

'Yes,' she said. She smiled. 'I don't know if you've spoken to Inspector İkmen yet, but we had a breakthrough yesterday. We think there might actually be something to this idea that Fatima Rudolfoğlu had a son.'

'Really? So the Oriental Club could have a rival for all that money?'

He walked in and sat on the edge of her desk.

'Potentially,' she said.

'Interesting.'

He was making her uncomfortable, he could see it in her nervous smile. Did it mean anything? He knew she was attracted to him; it was so very obvious.

'Ah, Mehmet Bey . . .'

He turned around and saw İkmen at the door.

'Çetin Bey.'

'Good morning, Constable Demirtaş,' İkmen said. 'Excellent work yesterday. I went to see Selin İnce last night and we have a name for this son. I want you to look for any references to a boy or a man called Rouvin.'

'Strange name,' she said.

'Greek,' Süleyman said.

'Indeed. If you have time, Mehmet Bey, I can tell you all about it,' İkmen said. 'But I understand you've had some problems this morning.'

'Yes.' He jumped off the desk and walked towards the older man. 'Aslan Gerontas is still awaiting transfer and Elif Büyük tried to kill herself last night. She's in hospital.'

İkmen shook his head. 'Weren't you supposed to be trying to get an ID on Elif and Ali from the British victim's family?'

'Richard and Paul Oates, the victim's sons, are due here in half an hour. They'll have to make do with Ali for the time being. They've seen photographs, which neither of them was sure about. I was hoping that seeing the couple in the flesh would help.'

'It often does,' İkmen said. 'Well, come and see me when you've finished, Mehmet Bey. I think you may find my latest discoveries interesting.'

He carried on towards his office.

Süleyman looked round to see what Constable Demirtaş was

doing, and found that she was completely absorbed in transliterating a document.

'The cause of Father Anatoli's suicide could be completely uncon-
nected to the Rudolfoğlus,' İkmen said. 'Maybe their secrets
were just some amongst many that he had to carry around with
him. His wife told me as much.'

'Yes, but why now?' Kerim Gürsel said.

'Oh, I agree,' İkmen said. 'That we must discover. And indeed
the same may be said for the deaths of the Rudolfoğlus. Why
now? We may consider different scenarios, including maybe one
in which whoever killed them has only recently found out about
what they did in 1931.'

'How?'

'From Father Anatoli? Perhaps, tired of being alone with that
awful secret, he shared it with someone who thought they might
exact revenge on behalf of the murdered baby.'

'Apion.'

'Indeed, although Apion says he learned the story from his
father four years ago. He subsequently told Father Anatoli what
he knew.'

'Anatoli wasn't alone with that secret, then.'

'No.'

'So something else happened,' Kerim said.

İkmen sighed. 'OK, back to the beginning. The day before his
suicide, Father Anatoli met Yiannis Apion at the ayazma of St
Katherine. They talked about the future of the spring, they prayed
and then they parted. Apion went to get the ferry back to Beşiktaş
from Kadıköy, and Father Anatoli either went somewhere to do
something or met someone.' He shrugged. 'Yiannis said that the
priest was in good spirits when he saw him. So something changed
that. Something that happened after Yiannis had gone and before
Father Anatoli arrived back home later on that evening.'

'Accepting that Apion isn't lying,' Kerim said.

'I accept he could be.'

İkmen opened his office window and lit a cigarette.

'Kerim,' he said. 'When I called you last night, you were at the Koço in Moda.'

'I'd been at the Teufel Ev all day. The Koço is a nice place, which is just up the road.'

'It's also where you met that old man, the one who first told us about the ayazma and its connection to the Rudolfoğlu family. Have you seen him again?'

'Not to speak to.'

'But he's a regular at the Koço?'

'I don't know about regular . . .'

İkmen wondered whether it was his imagination that made him think Kerim was holding something back.

'He's local and so he knows a few local stories,' Kerim said.

'Like what?'

'Apart from what he said about the ayazma?'

'Yes.'

'Just stuff about local characters: artists, drag queens . . .'

İkmen let it go.

'What we need is a connection,' he said. 'We have a lot of information from many different sources, but it won't hang together. Not yet. Not in any sort of definitive way that means we can make an arrest. We know that the murderer had to know about the Rudolfoğlus' past misdemeanours. For someone to kill them in the way they did, mirroring what happened to the child, is too much of a coincidence.' He paused for a moment. 'I'm aware we've not really explored Perihan Hanım's family. I'm not thinking direct family, but brothers and sisters, nieces and nephews. All these old offshoots of the royal family are coming out into the daylight now our Ottoman past is glorious again. I wonder if one of them was righting old wrongs?'

'More likely to be an attempt to get at the property,' Kerim said. 'The baby Fatima and her brothers killed was the daughter of a Greek servant.'

'True.' He put his cigarette out and crossed his arms. 'According to Selin İnce, the only people who knew about the murder, apart from later on the local Greek priest, was Konstantinos Apion, the servant Muazzaz and the doctor Kevork Sarkissian. Now Kevork, we know, had worked at Yıldız Palace, which is probably where Perihan Hanım lived at some point. As you know, I asked our Dr Sarkissian if he would search through his grandfather's effects to try and find his old medical records. But apparently his grandfather's papers are jumbled up, they're written in Ottoman script and there are, according to the doctor, millions of them. We can't take that on. But what we – or rather you – can do is contact the Yıldız Palace archive and find out if they can trace Perihan.'

'OK. Hopefully some of that will be online,' Kerim said. 'What about Rudolf Paşa?'

'What about him?' İkmen said. 'He was dead. Anyway, he was German.'

'Yes, but sir, aren't there shares in Mercedes Benz involved in this legacy?'

İkmen smacked his forehead. 'Of course!' he said. 'Thank you, Kerim. God, I must be losing my mind! Stupid old man! I'll get back in touch with Erdal Bey and find out if he knows anything. Rudolf Paşa must have had a surname. If we have that, we may have access to his family in Germany. Might not help us, but it's worth a try. You know, I sometimes forget how much money is at stake here.'

Although only half constructed, the new building next door to the Peacock Yalı was already restricting the light. When Maryam returned from Chicago, she'd go crazy.

Unknown to Çetin İkmen, Arto Sarkissian had been trying to find anything he could about his grandfather Kevork's later career as a doctor in post-Ottoman İstanbul. He'd had a few brief conversations with İkmen in the past few days, including one very late the previous evening, and what seemed to be coming to light about the Rudolfoğlu case was far more sinister than either of them had imagined. What disturbed the Armenian personally was his grandfather's involvement. Had he really helped to cover up a horrific crime by declaring that Perihan's baby was stillborn? Arto's uncle, Mesrob, had been convinced that the source of his father's sorrow had been the fact that he'd been unable to save the baby, followed by the death of its mother. But what if his misery had stemmed from guilt? If what İkmen was saying was true, Kevork had helped to cover up a murder. But how could Arto reconcile that with the gentle old man he had known when he was a child?

He'd found no documents to help him. Amid ever-increasing noise from the site next door, he'd looked at page after page of notes, letters and records, most of them in a script he couldn't understand, and had found nothing. Intellectually he knew precisely why Atatürk had Latinised the Turkish alphabet in 1929. The Latin characters reflected Turkish letters far more precisely. But the abandonment of the Ottoman script had also cut most people off from their past.

He'd spoken to Mesrob again at three o'clock that morning – which was why he was so very tired this morning – and told him everything he knew. Oddly, Mesrob had not been as disturbed by the fact that his father might have colluded in covering up a murder as Arto had thought he would be.

'What else was he supposed to do?' he'd said. 'At that time, as an Armenian he was part of the enemy within.'

'Yes, but who would have threatened him? The child's father was Greek. It wouldn't have been him. The Turkish servant?'

Mesrob had responded emphatically. 'No! Perihan Hanım.'

'Perihan Hanım never wanted her children near her again!'

'No, but she equally didn't want them to go to jail,' Mesrob had said. 'However fucking twisted they were, she was still their mom.'

However fucking twisted . . . Arto and Maryam Sarkissian had never been able to have children. In a way, Çetin İkmen's brood were substitutes. Arto's brother Krikor was also childless. Sometimes the pathologist wondered whether his family was actually meant to die out. Natural selection in action. He couldn't see how Perihan Hanım, ill and alone, had threatened his grandfather into silence. But then he wasn't a parent, and so how could he understand? All he knew was that whenever he had done bad things as a child, his father had always forgiven him in the end.

'The family name was Bauer,' Erdal Bey said.

Kenter and Kenter provided excellent coffee for its guests. Çetin İkmen was no exception. Drinking what he had been told was a superior Colombian blend while Erdal Bey consulted a sheaf of yellowing papers, he actually felt a certain sense of well-being, misplaced though it might be.

'From Munich,' the lawyer continued. 'My father put me through the agony of German classes when I was a child, which means I can read documents in that language. Rudolf Paşa's birth certificate gives his name as Rudolf Ignatius Maria Bauer, son of Maximilian Tomas Maria Bauer and his wife Zelinda. The family lived on Leopoldstrasse. Unfortunately for anyone wishing to trace descendants of Rudolf Paşa, Bauer is a common German name, although if the family lived on Leopoldstrasse then they had money, which is always helpful.'

'The poor leave fewer footprints,' İkmen said.

'Sadly. But what I can also tell you, Çetin Bey, is that we

haven't received any enquires from anyone in Germany about the Rudolfoğlu estate. I will willingly give you this address in Munich, as well as that of a property I believe Rudolf Paşa still owned when he came to Turkey. But that is all I have.'

'Thank you,' İkmen said. He drank his coffee. Then a thought came to him. 'Erdal Bey,' he said, 'do you know whether there is any reference to someone called Dimitri Paşa in your documents?'

'It doesn't sound familiar,' he said. 'But if you give me some time, I'll see what I can find. Of course, you must understand that all the older documents pertaining to Rudolf Paşa and his family are in the Ottoman script, so unless we employ a transcriber, they are closed to us.'

'Well, I have a transcriber working for me at the moment,' İkmen said.

'On the letters?'

'Yes.'

'Then I can arrange for him—'

'Her.'

'Her,' he smiled, 'to examine the documents if you wish.'

'Thank you.'

'My pleasure.'

İkmen finished his coffee. 'I'll contact the German consulate and run the name Bauer by them. They must have records of their nationals who came here to "help us out" at the beginning of the twentieth century.'

Erdal Bey sighed. 'If only they'd stayed at home.'

'Oh I expect we would have been drawn into the First World War anyway, without the Germans' help,' İkmen said. 'It was a time of empires, and we were an empire.'

'The world was run by madmen,' Erdal Bey said. 'As usual.'

* * *

The Oates brothers couldn't definitively identify Ali Erbil. According to their statements, neither of them had really seen him.

When the Englishmen had gone, Süleyman and Ömer Mungun followed Erbil back to his cell. Süleyman had taken the decision to keep Elif Büyük's attempted suicide from him. Such acts in a prison situation could, in his experience, spread. And Ali and Elif were lovers . . .

'I'm going to ask Dr Aksu, the psychiatrist, to come back and reassess that young man,' Süleyman said as the two men walked away from Ali Erbil's cell. 'He knows precisely what he's doing. I don't want him to go to hospital when he should be in prison.'

'No.'

Ömer Mungun was subdued. It was uncharacteristic but not unknown. Maybe his father back in Mardin was ill again.

'And I still believe he knows more than he's saying,' Süleyman said.

'About what?'

'I don't know. But it wasn't easy getting what he knew about Father Anatoli and his meeting with Mr Apion out of him. What else is in that clever brain, I wonder?'

'If he's a junkie, he's not clever,' Ömer said.

He was distinctly moody. In fact he was on the verge of hostility. Süleyman frowned. 'Everything all right, Sergeant?'

'Yes.'

'You seem a little tense.'

Ömer shrugged. 'I'm sorry sir. I didn't sleep well.'

'Oh. Well . . . it's very hot at the moment. Not conducive to restful sleep . . .'

But the way Ömer looked at him made the inspector absolutely certain that he was lying. It irked him. And what was the resentment in his voice about?

'Call Dr Aksu, will you?' Süleyman said. 'Ask him to come and see Ali Erbil.'

'Yes, sir.'

Maybe it was the way he said 'sir' that made Süleyman think it was personal. Or maybe it was the memory of Ömer and Barçın Demirtaş leaving together . . .

We are siblings, and siblings stay together . . .

It was just a fragment, written in what Barçın recognised as Kemal Rudolfoğlu's handwriting. It had come from one of the boxes on Miss Fatima's dressing table. She put it down. She couldn't concentrate on it. She couldn't concentrate on anything.

The problem with Şeymus had always been the sex. Had Barçın remained a good girl, a virgin, she would never have discovered this obsession. And it was an obsession. Under control after she finally managed to get rid of Şeymus, her desires had been reawakened by Ömer Mungun. The sex had been frantic, just the way she liked it. But Ömer himself wouldn't do. He was already beginning to exhibit more than just a tendency to cling, and she feared where a relationship with him might lead.

And so that morning, when they were alone, she'd told him it was over. He'd taken it badly; he'd actually asked her whether she'd thrown him over for his boss. Barçın had scoffed at this even though she knew that she'd give herself to Mehmet Süleyman in a heartbeat. But that wasn't happening. He had the formidable Gonca Hanım, who probably did everything he wanted and more in terms of sex. Even if she was old.

Ömer had sloped off after that and no mirra had been forthcoming that morning. She heard him return to Süleyman's office and felt a sudden rush of panic that manifested as heat. She opened her window, fanned her face and unbuttoned her shirt down to her cleavage. She looked at the fragment again and tried to concentrate. But then her door opened and she cringed.

* * *

He was getting used to the methadone. He knew this because his head felt clearer than it had done for a while. Neither of those English boys had identified him. Even if he hadn't been able to speak their language, he would have known by the expressions on their faces. Blank.

The police had his DNA from the shop in Yeniköy, but they couldn't prove he'd killed those men, because he hadn't. Elif had moved so quickly and so violently, the gangster and his henchman had been taken completely by surprise. She'd attacked them in the same way he'd seen big cats attack their prey in TV documentaries about Africa.

Even through the junk haze, why hadn't he moved to stop her? Had he been so desensitised by what she'd already done? The simple answer was that he loved her. But was that even true? Wasn't it much more to do with the fact that she'd had sex with him? Not ordinary sex; dirty sex, sex he'd seen on the Internet. But even that was a long time ago now. He'd not been able to do it for months.

Why did he want to bury himself alive with a madwoman? Even before they'd found that place in Moda and she'd set up her little fantasy home in the basement, she'd done crazy shit. One day, when they'd been sleeping in the street, she'd punched the tiny child of a woman who had tried to share their pitch in a shop doorway.

But if he went to prison, there'd be no one.

Later, she couldn't remember what he'd come to see her about. İkmen had just called to say that he was going out to the German consulate with Sergeant Gürsel. Then Süleyman had walked into her office.

They had spoken, but about what had gone completely from her mind. Her shirt had still been unbuttoned because of the heat, and someone had locked her office door, but Barçın didn't

252

know who. She assumed it was him. What she did know was that as soon as they were locked in, he put his hands on her breasts and then squeezed her nipples. Immediately aroused, she pulled off her underwear so that he could fuck her. She climaxed almost as soon as he was inside her. He too didn't take long.

Afterwards, he whispered, 'You're beautiful.' Then he kissed her. A long, dirty, sensual kiss. She'd not been expecting that. She kissed him back, and as time went on, he became aroused once more. Faintly she could hear the sound of Ömer Mungun on the phone, and more loudly, voices from outside the open window in the car park. But over and above all that, she wanted sex again. With him. Her father would have called her a shameless whore. She bent over her desk, scattering old Ottoman documents on the floor. Again, it was just sex, but that was all she wanted.

As they rearranged their clothing, he bent down to kiss her breasts.

After he had left, Barçın wondered whether any of that had actually happened. How had he known she wanted him? She'd never said so. And what was wrong with her that her need for sex, once awakened, wouldn't go away? Was it some kind of mental illness, or was she just the filthy slag Şeymus had called her when they'd split up?

But then she smelt Süleyman on her and she had a violent urge to call him and ask him to come back. She knew what she'd say. She'd say she wanted his cock inside her again, that she wanted to feel his tongue licking out her mouth. That she wanted to fellate him. But she didn't. He was in his office talking to Ömer Mungun, who she had also pleasured within the last week.

When she'd first met him, Çetin İkmen had told her she was wasted in Traffic. But at least there, interacting almost exclusively with CCTV screens, she wouldn't feel like this. Her mother, she'd always thought, had never had a sexual feeling in her life.

Barçın was clearly making up for that. And it didn't make her happy. Süleyman had used her because he was handsome and because he could, but if she got the chance, she'd let him do it all over again.

The German consul had been polite. İkmen had never been to the vast Prussian-style consulate on İnönü Caddesi before, and he found it an interesting place. In terms of his investigation, too, the visit was enlightening. The Bauer family of Munich were unknown to the consul, but he said he would make enquiries about them. His secretary, however, a man in his sixties, was well aware of Rudolf Paşa.

'He was an opportunist,' Herr Steinmeier said. 'He was in the military in Germany. The Kaiser surrounded himself with a lot of nationalistic people, many of whom were extremely unreliable. Here in Turkey he was offered much and took much. He is buried in the German cemetery in Tarabya.'

'A Christian cemetery?' İkmen asked.

'Largely, yes,' Herr Steinmeier said. 'Why?'

'Rudolf Paşa had a strong interest in the occult,' İkmen said.

The German smiled. 'Ah, that story. Rudolf Paşa liked to frighten people. Particularly his Ottoman troops.'

'I've heard from a most reliable source that he—'

'Trust me, Inspector, it's nonsense,' the German said. 'He had an adjutant, a Greek, a kindred spirit. They controlled their troops, who looked upon Rudolf as an infidel, through fear. Also, in the desert it is said that they sexually abused their men. I don't know if that is true. But the Greek, Dimitri Kazantzoğolu, he was the really bad one. He had many vices.'

It was the first time İkmen had heard Dimitri Bey's surname.

'Could that not just be a German story?' he asked. 'Made up to take the blame away from a fellow countryman?'

The German, who was almost as thin as İkmen, smiled a swift, grey smile. 'You will see a crucifix on Rudolf Paşa's grave,' he said. 'He was no saint, but . . .' He shrugged. 'Dimitri Kazantzoğolu was a known abuser of boys.'

'How do you know that?'

He smiled again. 'Inspector, the German imperial government employed a lot of spies in the lands of their ally the Ottoman Empire. Dimitri Bey had his own file. And no, I will not show it to you without a warrant. But believe me, it exists.'

'So do you know what happened to Kazantzoğolu after the First World War?'

'No,' he said. 'We were defeated; why would we have any further interest in an Ottoman Greek with a penchant for buggery? Maybe he left for Greece? All I know for sure is that Rudolf Paşa is buried in Tarabya, and that from time to time, someone asks permission to visit his grave.'

İkmen frowned. 'The cemetery is closed?'

'Yes.'

'German relatives, maybe?'

'Oh no. As the consul himself told you, we know nothing of the paşa's family. These are Turks.'

'Who?'

'I'm afraid I don't know.'

'Can you look it up?' İkmen asked.

'I can,' the German said. 'Which years do you want me to look at?'

Chapter 22

The psychiatrist was a fucking nuisance. Droning on, not letting him think. Eventually he said, 'Where's Elif? I want to see Elif.'

She was in another cell. He'd even been able to hear her once or twice. But not lately.

The psychiatrist said, 'Did Elif begin an act and then you joined in?'

'Where is she?' Ali reiterated. 'I want to see her!'

'You—'

'I'm not even going to listen to your fucking questions until you take me to Elif!'

A look that Ali didn't like passed between the psychiatrist and the police constable who was guarding him.

'What's happened to her?' he said.

Neither of them spoke, and so he yelled, 'What have you done to her!'

İkmen read: *We are siblings, and siblings stay together* . . .

'I can't find a reply,' Barçın said.

'But you believe this is from Kemal to Fatima?'

'Yes, sir,' she said.

'Trouble is, it can be interpreted in so many different ways,' İkmen said. 'Maybe an exhortation for all four of them to tell the same story about what happened to baby Sofia? Possibly some sort of threat . . .'

'Reminding Fatima that as a sibling she owes her brothers something?' Kerim said.

'Like what?'

'Loyalty? Love?'

İkmen sighed. 'Fatima had a child. It had or has a Greek name. Does that mean its father was Greek? Maybe her mother's lover? Her father's adjutant?'

'I can't see Konstantinos Apion wanting anything to do with Fatima Rudolfoğlu,' Kerim said. 'She killed his child.'

'Maybe it was rape.'

They both looked at Barçın Demirtaş.

'Sex as punishment,' she said.

İkmen shook his head. 'She was an adult by then. She would have aborted. Besides, I think Yiannis Apion would have told us if that were the case.'

'If he knew.'

'True.' İkmen lit a cigarette. 'What about Dimitri Kazantzoğolu?'

'He liked boys,' Kerim said.

'And maybe sometimes he liked girls,' İkmen said. 'You heard what Herr Steinmeier said: he was a bad man.'

'Yes, but that's a very German perspective . . .'

'Possibly. Possibly.'

Barçın hadn't contributed as much to the conversation as she could. Still in a daze from the activities of that morning, she wondered what Mehmet Süleyman was doing and whether he felt guilty. She tried to concentrate. 'Maybe Kemal wanted Fatima to do something for him? Or perhaps for him and his brothers?'

'Like what?'

'I don't know. Some sort of sacrifice? That's how it comes across to me, at least. As a sibling, you have to do what the rest of us do. I don't know.' She shrugged. 'I'm just putting it out there.'

They sat in silence. Barçın pictured Gonca Şekeroğlu and

thought about how much it was said she loved Süleyman. But what she'd done with the gypsy's man had just been sex. Though it had been good sex . . .

'Siblings can and do work in gangs,' İkmen said. 'I know my own children, even now, will line up against in-laws at times. I don't approve, but I can see how it happens. My sons are still ruled by their sisters. However, I don't think, or rather I hope, that wouldn't extend to breaking the law.'

'She, Miss Fatima, is being asked to fall into line,' Barçın said.

'So maybe they were planning something,' Kerim said. 'Barçın Hanım, do you know when that note was written?'

'No, but it's recent,' she said.

She'd only just managed to rescue it from the floor. Süleyman had almost stepped on it when he left.

'But if they were planning something, then what?' İkmen said. 'They were all older than time. What do you plan to do when you're about to die, for God's sake?'

Guilt must have been a feature of his thinking, because he showered thoroughly before he even touched Gonca. Then he made love to her, slowly and with so much passion she was left breathless.

But when he took her from behind, he was reminded of Barçın Demirtaş. Gonca was softer, and so he was more gentle; it was loving, but it wasn't as sexy. It didn't make him come in seconds, and Gonca, though his one and only true love, didn't writhe beneath him like a bitch on heat. He'd never known a woman quite that sexual before. He hoped she only wanted sex from him.

He buried his face in Gonca's hair. 'I love you.' He meant it. But he was replaying the sex with Barçın in his head. Hard and dirty and urgent. He knew that if he'd stayed she would have

258

given him more. But he'd had to leave, because why had he even been there in her office, fucking her on her desk?

She'd had sex with Ömer Mungun as a substitute for him, and then dumped him. Süleyman had seen her desire the first day he'd set eyes on her. He'd also seen Ömer's interest in her. Had he superseded his deputy as a way of establishing his superiority? Or had he just needed to have what he couldn't?

He knew he shouldn't have anything to do with Barçın Demirtaş again, but he also knew that he would. Apart from the fact that her body was firm and tight, she wanted him so much it was irresistible. Women had wanted him all his adult life, but few of them had been like her. Later, as he lay in Gonca's arms, he tried to forget about Barçın but found that he couldn't.

The ayazma was closed. There was no one inside, but there would be. He knew that the police wanted to excavate. Yiannis Apion wondered when they'd start and whether he would ever get to see what they found. His blood was underneath that floor. It should stay there.

It had been a strange day. Ever since he'd woken up, he'd been followed around by a memory he couldn't place. His father had taken him to the shrine – how old he was, he had no idea – and they'd met someone. A woman. She'd been Greek, or rather he assumed she was Greek, because that was the language she had spoken. But he had no idea who she was because he hadn't been able to see her face. He didn't know why.

The woman and his father had touched, but not in a sexual way. Rather in a manner to give each other comfort. He remembered looking at the floor with them but he couldn't recall whether Sofia's name had been spoken or not.

Up in Koço, he could hear voices. Regulars and tourists enjoying cool drinks on a hot evening. But this memory had taken place in the winter. Why was he thinking of it now? He wiped sweat out of his eyes. Had the woman been Fatima Rudolfoğlu? How would he know when he'd never even seen her?

He was about to go home when he heard footsteps on the stairs leading down from Koço. At first he thought it might be a policeman, come to guard the shuttered shrine or even start work on unearthing its secrets. But then he recognised one of the regulars from the café.

'It's shut,' he said.

The man, an old Turk, smiled. 'You must be disappointed.'

'Disappointed? What do you mean?'

'I mean I've seen you come to pray sometimes,' he said. 'At least I assume that's what you're doing.'

The old man turned and went back up the steps. Yiannis breathed in deeply and went as if to follow him, but then stopped. The woman in his daydream had been veiled; that was why he hadn't been able to remember her face. In black, but not in purdah like a Muslim woman; in mourning.

The psychiatrist had phoned Mehmet Süleyman, who was on his way.

'Your job is gone,' Dr Aksu told the quivering constable, who had begged to be forgiven.

'Bey effendi . . .'

'Shut up!'

He wanted to hit the ignorant, thick-fingered fool. But he didn't. From inside the cell the sound of Ali Erbil's weeping was punctuated only by the voices of those who were restraining him. Aksu heard one of them say, 'She's in hospital, but she'll be OK. It was just a joke . . .'

Just a joke! Aksu had left Ali Erbil's cell for no more than five minutes, but when he'd returned, the prisoner had been like a wild man. Constable Stupid had thought it was almost unbelievably hilarious to tell him that Elif Büyük had killed herself. Then he had compounded it by telling him she was going to go to hell. The doctor looked at the constable with disgust. Sometimes he wondered where they got some of these officers from. He tried not to imagine sun-baked villages full of illiterates, but found that his mind wouldn't go anywhere else.

When Süleyman eventually arrived, the psychiatrist told him everything. At first he thought the inspector might actually hit the idiot officer, who by this time was cowering on the floor. Instead he glared at him and said he'd deal with him later.

Süleyman was well known to have a violent temper, but Dr Aksu couldn't be bothered to expend any sympathy on the constable.

'I've no idea why he thought telling Ali that Elif had committed suicide was a good idea,' he said as he and Süleyman walked towards Erbil's cell. 'But then who knows what goes through the minds of such people?'

Süleyman knew what he meant. Conservative men who had been raised in rural Anatolia. Barely educated and almost wilfully ignorant, according to people like the doctor. On occasion Süleyman would agree. But he'd been dragged away from his sleep and didn't have time for city-versus-countryside debates.

'Did he ask for me?'

'Yes,' the doctor said. 'He wants to see Elif, naturally. Do you know how she is?'

'She has brain damage,' Süleyman said. 'Am I supposed to show her to him as she drools?'

God, he was angry. Dr Aksu almost felt sorry for Constable Stupid now.

'He says that if you show him Elif, he'll tell you something,' the psychiatrist said.

Süleyman stopped. 'Tell me what?'

261

'I've no idea.'

Süleyman knocked on Erbil's cell door. 'Open up!'

Now that all the police tape had been taken down and the house was boarded up, Selin could lay flowers. No one cared about the garden, and so she placed her bunch of tulips and roses in the space Kemal Bey had asked her to clear all those months ago. Then she sang. Whether her pronunciation was correct or not, she didn't know. But someone who did know recognised it.

'A hymn for the dead.'

She turned and found herself looking at a ghost in modern clothing. She only just managed to stifle a scream.

'Who are you?' she said. 'Oh God!'

The man crouched down beside her. 'I'm Konstantinos's son, Selin Hanım,' Yiannis Apion said. 'I remember watching you when you were a small child, running around in this garden. My father used to tell me that when he worked here, your grandmother made his life hell. As a child I was afraid of this place. But I only knew why when my father was dying. Why do you sing a hymn that means nothing to you?'

'You . . .'

'My name is Yiannis, I am Konstantinos's son. I am also Sofia's brother.'

She turned her head away. 'Oh God!'

'What?'

'He came here once,' she said. 'Maybe five years ago. He was sick. He wanted to kill her. I sent him away.'

He sat down on the cool night earth. 'If you're wondering, I don't know what I'm doing here,' he said. 'I went to the ayazma but it was shut, so I came here. You know the police think I killed them.'

'They think I killed them too,' she said. Suddenly chilled, she pulled her cardigan around her shoulders and sat beside him. 'I didn't.'

'Me neither. But then I would say that, wouldn't I?'

She shivered. 'I don't know you,' she said. 'And I've nothing to say.'

'Except you sing a Trisagion hymn for the dead that I can only think has to be for my sister. Although why you do it here . . .'

'If you know the story, then you know that she died here,' Selin said. 'My grandmother was a wicked woman, but my mother was kind. She sang what she called the baby's hymn whenever she could.'

'And yet you lay flowers as if you're visiting a grave.'

'That's because this should have been her grave.' She touched the bunch of flowers and smiled. 'The old gentlemen wanted her to come home. I even cleared a space. But she wouldn't have it.'

'Fatima Hanım?'

'The Devil's child,' she said.

'Sofia is better off where she is.'

'Is she?' Selin shook her head. 'The old men feared for her. They believed the city to be full of madmen. They were right.'

'No.' He looked down. 'Did you kill them, hanım?'

'No,' she said. 'Before God, did you?'

'No, but I should have.'

They looked into each other's eyes.

'Did it cause trouble between them?' he asked. 'That the old men wanted Sofia to come home?'

'Letters flew between them like snow,' she said.

'They never spoke?'

'No.'

'My father told me that Kemal went to the ayazma to dig Sofia up and destroy her body because it was an abomination

263

and a stain on the honour of his family. Why the change of heart? Was it just the sentimentality of an old man?'

Selin didn't speak for a while, but when she did, she held his arm. Had anyone seen them, they would have thought that maybe they were a middle-aged married couple trying to recapture some of their youthful romance.

'Had your father listened to Kemal rather than just beaten him, he would have known that his intention was never to desecrate the shrine or destroy your sister's body,' she said. She looked into his eyes again. 'He wanted to bring her home. Even then, all he ever wanted to do was bring her home.'

'You want the truth? I'll tell you the truth.'

'Take me to her,' Ali said.

He was bruised and his lip was split. Süleyman looked at the custody officers with naked contempt.

'Dr Aksu says you have something to tell me,' he said. 'Tell me and I'll take you to her.'

Ali Erbil laughed. 'What's this?' he said. 'A who's got the biggest prick competition? I'm a junkie and you're wearing a Rolex watch. I haven't had an erection this month. You win. Happy? Take me to her.'

'And have you change your mind once you've got what you want? As you said, you're a junkie. I know how you operate.'

'Well then you'll get nothing.' He wiped a hand across his bloodied mouth.

Süleyman sat down. 'All right then. You get the truth. But I won't take you to her until you tell me what you have been concealing from us.'

Ali Erbil said nothing.

'Elif tried to kill herself by smashing her head against the wall of her cell,' Süleyman said. 'It should never have happened and I will be investigating why she was not monitored more closely. She is alive, but there has been a measure of brain damage.'

Ali looked up.

'Whether that is permanent or not, we won't know for some weeks.'

Tears gathered at the corners of the young man's eyes. 'You let her hurt herself.'

'I did not, but it happened,' Süleyman said. 'I am telling you the truth.'

'Why didn't you tell me sooner?'

'Because we didn't know whether she would live,' Süleyman said. 'I feared for your life and so I took the decision to conceal her actions from you until we knew more about her condition.'

'You didn't want me to kill myself.'

'No.'

'How very thoughtful of you.'

'No. You're an intelligent man. It was pragmatism.'

'Yeah, and it's pragmatism that makes me stick to my guns,' Ali said. 'I know something you don't. I can recognise who I saw in the house where all those old people died. You want to know who that is . . .'

Süleyman leaned forward.'A name.'

'Oh you're not getting that,' Ali said. 'You can beat me until I turn purple. You can stick a baton up my arse. I don't care. Take me to her.' He leaned forward in his chair. 'You see, your prick may work properly, but ultimately, mine is bigger.'

Chapter 23

'Begin.'

They'd had to wait for a representative from the Greek Orthodox patriarchate to attend before they could even start to lift the floor of the ayazma.

Commissioner Teker stood beside Father Manuel Phokas outside the shrine as they both watched her officers enter the premises.

'We will try to cause as little damage as possible, Father,' she assured him.

'Thank you,' he said.

But he looked tense.

Teker felt compelled to add, 'We have to try and verify this story we have been told. If there is a body under the ayazma . . .'

'It will be given a Christian burial,' the priest said.

'If our intelligence is correct, then the child's mother was Turkish.'

'I don't care.'

They lapsed into silence.

Inside, men grunted as they attempted to lift stones last removed by Konstantinos Apion almost a century before.

He should have known. People with head injuries could die suddenly even if they were being treated in hospital. Elif Büyük had died. Just over an hour after Süleyman had left Ali Erbil in his cell to think about his options, the love of

Ali's life had suffered a cardiac arrest from which she had not recovered.

He'd told himself he'd left his office to go and get some rest. But that was a lie. He'd looked up Barçın Demirtaş's mobile number on the computer system and called her. They'd met in the street behind her building. Apparently the kapıcı of her block was ever vigilant, and she didn't want him to see a man go into her apartment.

He drove her to his small apartment in Cihangir in silence. As soon as they were through the door, she kissed him, hard, and grabbed his penis. He told himself it was just sex, but there was addiction too. Hers or his or both – it didn't matter. It wasn't right and he knew it. But he fucked her anyway. Losing himself in the hard, almost masculine demands of her body, he only just managed to answer his phone on time. And that was when he heard about Elif.

He was a gentleman and so he took Barçın back to her apartment. As she got out of the car she said, 'Call me.' He didn't answer, even though he knew that he'd phone her as soon as he was free.

Teker had been just about to go out to Moda when he knocked on her office door.

'Ah, they found you,' she said.

'Madam.'

'Well, go down and break the news. While I don't blame you for going home and trying to get some more sleep, I'd rather you'd stayed given the circumstances.'

'I was giving Erbil time to think.'

'You didn't need to go home to do that,' she said. 'You could have caught up on your sleep later. Why am I telling you this? You know I'm right.' She shrugged. 'And anyway, your sleep has done you no good at all. You look like shit.'

Did she know? She probably thought she did. She probably

267

thought he'd been home making love to Gonca. The memory of where he had been and what he'd really done made him feel temporarily dizzy. Or maybe it was the blood loss. She'd stuck her nails so hard into the flesh on his back and buttocks, she'd drawn blood. And she'd bitten him.

Çetin İkmen didn't often go in for fancy coffees. Traditional Turkish, very sweet, was his tried and tested favourite. But on this bright and already hot morning, he tried a cappuccino and was pleasantly surprised. To the chagrin of the owners, Koço had been taken over by the police for the duration of the excavation work on the floor of the ayazma. And while Commissioner Teker had taken charge of the operation, Çetin İkmen and Kerim Gürsel had set up a temporary incident room in the garden of the restaurant.

In spite of the gravity of the task, İkmen couldn't help but feel elated. Here he was, working, while drinking coffee and smoking – and all without fear of being discovered by those he called the 'morality squad'.

Kerim brought him back down to earth. 'I've heard there are plans to ban smoking in public gardens,' he said.

'Fucking hell!'

'Sorry, sir.'

İkmen refreshed his laptop screen. 'I honestly don't understand why sinners aren't being allowed to destroy themselves in whatever way they please. "Nice" people don't like us; we're a fucking nuisance to them. They should be paying me to smoke and then thanking me for being so public-spirited.'

Kerim smiled.

'I suppose I'd better make the most of it, then,' İkmen said as he lit one cigarette from the butt of another.

'That's what I thought.' Kerim frowned. 'Sir, what if we don't find anything in the ayazma?'

İkmen sat back in his chair. 'Doesn't mean that what we've been told didn't happen.'

'We won't be able to prove it, though.'

'No. But we still have four dead bodies and no murderer. This dead child will remain where it is at the moment, a motive in the abstract.'

'We seem to have a lot of those.'

'One always does,' İkmen said. 'Unless one has actually seen the murder take place before one's eyes.'

His computer buzzed as a gaggle of emails came in. He ignored it.

'Logic tells me that because the method used to kill the child was also employed to murder the offending adults, there has to be a connection.'

'Yes. Unless someone did that deliberately to implicate another.'

'Of course,' İkmen said. 'But whichever way we go with this, that person knew at least some of the Rudolfoğlus' secrets. I fear, Kerim, that we may only be at the beginning of our journey into the monstrous history of this family.'

'You really think so?'

'There's so much sexual transgression here. And you and I both know what chaos that can cause. What do you think?'

Kerim shrugged.

'When sex becomes something dirty as opposed to something natural, bad things happen,' İkmen said. 'That's when men make devils out of the frailest human flesh.' He looked at his computer screen. 'Ah, something from the German consulate . . .'

Ali Erbil didn't cry.

'Everyone used and abused her,' he said when Süleyman told him of Elif's death. 'Me too.'

'How?'

'When I still could, I screwed her. The first time we met, I paid her for sex. Then I fell in love with her.'

'And let her kill,' Süleyman said.

'It made a light come into her eyes. When we left Moda, it was as if she died. Then she took control . . .'

'By killing.'

'When you kill, you're God, aren't you?' Ali said. 'Power of life and death . . . the ultimate celebrity. She'd grown up with all that shit on the TV she watched in that terrible place I found her. Full of men in filthy vests smelling of spunk. That psychiatrist spoke about *folie à deux*. But it wasn't that. I didn't join in with Elif. I just didn't stop her. I didn't dare. I couldn't lose her love.'

'But now you have, and you are still holding something back,' Süleyman said. 'There is no need any more. You must understand that. Help us now and you can make things easier for yourself. We know you stayed in the Devil's House, we know you saw a man . . .'

'I saw him again,' Ali said.

'When? Where?'

This time he did cry.

'Ali . . .'

'When you took me to Moda,' he said. 'In that restaurant. He was speaking to a priest . . .'

İkmen said, 'Tell me about him.'

Kerim leaned back in his chair. 'Old, smartly dressed, walks with a stick.' He lowered his voice. 'I think he came on to me,' he said. 'I felt he knew, you know, about me. I avoided him.'

İkmen looked at his screen again.

'Rauf Karadeniz of Moda has visited the German graveyard at Tarabya three times in the last year. His stated reason for these visits was to place flowers on the grave of Rudolf Bauer.'

'Why?'

'We don't know.'

'How did he know him?'

'The Germans don't interrogate those who visit their grave-yards, Kerim. We don't know. But we do know that when you spoke to him, Rauf Karadeniz knew a lot about the Rudolfoğlus.'

'He did. He was our starting point.' Kerim frowned. 'But if Rauf Bey is involved, why reveal himself to me? I didn't start our conversation about the family.'

'We need to see him,' İkmen said. 'You have his number?'

'Yes, sir.'

'Call him. Say you need to speak to him. If you're right about his proclivities, he will agree. This may all be a coincidence, but he's too close to this investigation for us to just discount him.'

Kerim looked around the empty restaurant. 'Normally he'd be here,' he said.

'Mmm.'

They both listened to the sound of stones scraping against each other as they were moved in the cave down below.

İkmen said, 'I wonder what St Katherine makes of all this . . .'

'Koço is closed today,' Süleyman said.

'Why?'

'Inspector İkmen has evidence to suggest that a body is buried underneath the shrine. We're lifting the floor.'

'Whose body?' Ali asked.

Now calmed by his latest dose of methadone, he had stopped crying and was slowly putting on his jacket.

'Not your concern,' Süleyman said. 'But if we can get you out there, maybe the staff will be able to recognise this man from your description.'

'When I saw him in the house, he seemed to be looking for something,' Ali said. 'I thought it was only a question of time before he found us.'

'Why? Could he not also have been a homeless person passing through? Maybe a burglar?'

'He wore good clothes.'

'Sometimes burglars wear good clothes.'

He shook his head. 'I know. But he was old. What was he doing burgling a house at his age?'

'You'll be cuffed to me,' Süleyman said.

'I know. I don't care. When she was alive, I had a goal. I wanted to protect her. Even in the madhouse, I knew I could do that. I'm a junkie, I'll die and that's OK. Do you know what it's like to be so much in love, Inspector?'

Süleyman said nothing. But he did know. If only, unlike Ali Erbil, he was able to completely immerse himself in that other person! Maybe it was true that Gonca had bewitched him into loving her. But what she'd never managed to do was tame him. He knew he would give anything to go back in time and not respond to the very obvious advances Barçın Demirtaş had made towards him in her office that first time they had sex. A moment's desire on his part had caused him to put a hand on a breast that was almost naked. The rest was history.

Rauf Bey was out. Or so he said. Wherever he was sounded very quiet.

'I'm at my doctor's office,' he said. 'May I know what you want to see me about?'

Kerim looked at İkmen, who shook his head.

'About the Rudolfoğlus,' Kerim said.

'I told you all I know,' the old man said.

'Just a couple more questions if you don't mind, sir. You probably don't know any more, but we have to check.'

272

'If you must.'

'So when . . .'

'I'll be home in an hour,' he said. 'But I will need to eat. On top of the arthritis, I am also diabetic and so I must eat regularly. Another cross I have to bear.'

'I'll see you in an hour then,' Kerim said.

When he finished the call, he said to İkmen, 'How many Muslims do you know who talk about having a cross to bear?'

Barçın looked different. If he'd been asked to say how, Ömer would have been unable to do so. All he could describe it as was 'looser'. The way she walked, the way she wore her clothes was more confident somehow. She wore more make-up. And when he saw her talking in the corridor with Süleyman, he knew.

The boss had stolen a woman from his predecessor, İzzet Melik, who had then been transferred back to his native İzmir. The woman, Sergeant Farsakoğlu, whom Ömer had known briefly before she died in an incident in Arnavautköy, had then been rejected in favour of Gonca Hanım. What was it about Süleyman? Yes, he was good-looking and confident, but he was no longer young. He had to be spectacular in bed in some way. But how?

Ömer wanted to ask her, but he didn't. He wasn't in love with her, but they'd had a good time. Or so he'd thought.

Süleyman came out of the cell accompanied by the prisoner, who was cuffed to his wrist, and two constables.

'Inspector İkmen is with Commissioner Teker at the Koço,' he said to Ömer. 'Call him and tell him I will want to speak to the staff.'

'Am I not coming too?'

'No. I'd like you to get an update for me from Bakırköy on the condition of Aslan Gerontas. I want to know whether he's still being pursued by the Devil. And whether he has settled.'

'Seriously?'

273

Gerontas had only been transferred that morning. He had clearly been insane. What did Süleyman hope to achieve by checking up on him? Now he was finally in hospital, surely his part in İstanbul's recent dramas was over.

'You wouldn't question my request if it had come from Inspector İkmen,' Süleyman said.

Was it Ömer's imagination, or was Süleyman being uncharacteristically harsh? People said he'd turned on İzzet Melik when he'd taken Ayşe Farsakoğlu away from him. But was that true? Or was it just gossip?

'The boy in Tarlabaşı saw the Devil everywhere,' Ali Erbil said. 'Everywhere.'

Süleyman and the two constables began walking towards the door that led out to the car park.

Without turning, he said to Ömer, 'Oh, and please phone the Forensic Institute. They owe us some results.'

Ömer didn't answer. Arrogant prick! A woman they both fancied arrived and Süleyman pulled rank. Of course any sane woman would choose a higher-status man over a nobody from Mardin. But it hurt, and also Süleyman already had a woman. Did Gonca Hanım know he was messing around with Barçın? Ömer doubted it.

He wondered whether he should tell her.

By the time he'd climbed the stairs back to Süleyman's office, however, he'd decided that he wouldn't. He had no actual proof, and if he was wrong, it would only hurt Gonca Hanım, who had always been kind to him. He meant her no harm. Her man, however, was another matter.

Four enormous stone slabs had been lifted before they found anything. Under the fifth was a fragment of cloth, finely woven and delicately hemmed. Commissioner Teker called for all activity to cease while Father Phokas investigated.

The patriarchate had no record of any burials under or near the ayazma of St Katherine. But the priest admitted that during times of conflict between his people and the Turkish majority, sometimes bodies had been buried in unusual locations and in a hurry. Also, Teker knew that some branches of the Orthodox faith, namely the Armenians, still practised animal sacrifice. She'd seen it once up at the Church of the Holy Archangels in Balat. So even if bones were found, they might not be human.

The priest gently pulled the cloth out of the ground. Teker could see that the fragment was blue. The fact that the pigment had survived could indicate that the cloth wasn't very old. But what did she know?

Father Phokas looked for a moment and then tipped his chin upwards.

'No?'

'No,' he said. 'Just empty cloth. Who knows? If the child had anything like a proper burial, there would have been a shroud.'

'And a coffin?'

'One would hope so,' he said.

Teker told her officers to take a break for drinks and cigarettes.

İkmen gave Süleyman Rauf Karadeniz's address.

'I would hold off and wait for you and your witness,' the older man said. 'But I'm keen to at least meet this man.'

'Fucking traffic!' Süleyman said. 'Fucking Turkish drivers! On their fucking phones again!'

There had been an accident on the Bosphorus Bridge, and although Süleyman had initially screamed at the traffic officers to clear the obstructive vehicles out of his way, he'd soon realised that wouldn't be possible because there were fatalities.

'Without Ali's ID – if he makes an ID on this man – you've just got some visits to a German graveyard,' he continued.

'We know that his stated reason for those visits was to lay

flowers on Rudolf Paşa's grave, and we can take DNA. And I can talk to him. Given what you've just told me, maybe I can make a connection . . .'

'Yes, I know, but . . . Oh God, another ambulance has arrived. I'll have to go.'

He ended the call and İkmen put his phone in his pocket.

'OK, Kerim,' he said, 'let's go and see your Rauf Bey.'

Kerim Gürsel, who had been observing activity down in the ayazma, said, 'Still nothing, sir.'

İkmen shrugged.

Chapter 24

The Sea of Marmara was one shade of blue, while the sky was another. Where they met, there was a faint line of lilac that very gently oscillated in the heat.

'You have a fine view, Rauf Bey,' Kerim said as he consciously concentrated on the old man's vast living room window.

'Yes, isn't it?'

The old man was in the kitchen. He'd been clearly disgruntled when he'd seen that Kerim was not alone. He'd shown Kerim and İkmen into what he obviously considered to be a normal room; either that or he'd asked them to sit there as a form of punishment. Kerim had never been exposed to so much taxidermy in his life. The exhibits ranged in size from small scorpions right up to an adult wolf.

'This is not normal,' he whispered.

İkmen put a hand on his shoulder. 'You're an İstanbullu, Kerim,' he said. 'You can take it.'

But İkmen wasn't sure he actually believed that. In spite of the fact that he was desperate not to pre-judge the old man, he did find his apartment unsettling. And it wasn't just the faintly musty smell from the taxidermy that was making him feel queasy. It wasn't just the eyes of the stuffed creatures watching İkmen and Kerim Gürsel perch uneasily on Rauf Bey's sofa. Ikons hung on every piece of wall that wasn't covered with photographs of a handsome woman in Victorian clothes. She was very dark and very tall, and sometimes she stood beside an even taller, thinner,

277

luxuriantly moustached man in a long black coat. There was a look around his eyes that reminded İkmen of Rauf Bey.

The old man walked in from the kitchen. 'I do apologise,' he said. 'This diabetes is a nuisance. Do you mind if I eat while we talk? In fact, why don't you join me? It's lunchtime.'

'Thank you, but I rarely eat lunch,' İkmen said. He looked at Kerim. 'But Kerim Bey, if you would like to . . .'

'Oh, I would be thrilled if you would,' the old man said. 'I've prepared halibut. Very light. I eschewed meat many years ago because of my cholesterol. But fish I can eat, in moderation.'

'I'd be delighted to join you,' Kerim said.

'Excellent.'

He turned.

'Ah, Rauf Bey,' İkmen said.

He turned back and smiled. 'Yes?'

'You have a lot of taxidermy. Is it a hobby?'

'No,' he said. 'I prefer animals to be alive. But my father fancied himself as something of a hunter. These are some of his kills. He enjoyed a challenge. He believed it was honourable to track and kill dangerous species. I'd rather conserve them.'

'And the rather handsome couple in these photographs,' İkmen said. 'Are they perhaps your parents?'

'Indeed,' said the old man. 'And do you know something, Inspector, you know exactly who they are.'

'What's going on?'

Süleyman had cuffed Ali Erbil to one of his constables and was out on the bridge talking to a traffic officer.

'Shut up,' the constable said.

'I was only asking,' Ali said.

'Shut the fuck up.'

Süleyman ran back to the car.

'They're going to let us through,' he said.

'What's happening, sir?'

'The moron who was on his phone is dead, but his wife is trapped. They're going to have to cut her out.'

'What about the other driver?'

'I don't think there's enough diamorphine in the city to help him,' he said.

The fish had been prepared in what İkmen could only describe as an oriental fashion. There were thin raw slices fanned out on a vast white plate. Fried pieces in a bowl were accompanied by a green salad and an eggcup full of thin brown liquid. There was pide bread, and in the middle of the table, a dark gelatinous item sat in solitary state on a blue tile. The delicate spread, probably Japanese-influenced, looked out of place in an apartment apparently given over to dusty dead animals, photographs of the departed and forbidding renditions of saints.

'I'm afraid you have the better of me,' İkmen said as he sat down at the table. 'Your parents, Rauf Bey, are unknown to me.'

The old man blinked. 'Of course,' he said. He put a jug of water on the table and then some glasses. 'Please help yourselves to water.'

'Thank you.'

Rauf Bey sat, and then Kerim.

The old man commented upon it. 'My goodness, it's so refreshing to see a young man with such fine manners!'

İkmen looked at his sergeant. Rauf Bey's proclivities hadn't just been in Kerim's imagination.

'Rauf Bey, to get to the point—'

'Oh how very un-Turkish of you,' the old man said. 'I should have imagined that a man of your vintage would have been rather more traditional in his approach.'

'Ah, but we all have our crosses to bear, don't we?' İkmen said. 'Or rather you do.'

Rauf Bey said nothing.

İkmen continued. 'I'm simply repeating what you said to Kerim Bey when he called you on the telephone. And if I put that expression together with the marvellous collection of ikons in this apartment, I could, I believe, sir, be forgiven for thinking that you have Greek connections.'

The old man smiled. 'Please do help yourselves to food,' he said.

Kerim took a small fried nugget from the bowl, and some salad.

'The sauce is soy,' Rauf Bey said. 'One should really use chopsticks to dip the meat, but I find that Turkish people don't do well with those.'

'Rauf Bey,' İkmen said, 'can you please tell me why you visited the German cemetery in Tarabya three times in the course of the last year? I'd also like to know, beyond your assertion to my sergeant that the tale about Konstantinos Apion and Kemal Rudolfoğlu is a commonly known story, how you heard about it.'

Şeymus had pursued her because she was the most beautiful girl in the quarter. He'd fallen so hard for her because she was also the only girl who would willingly do what he wanted. He hadn't had to teach her to suck him off. She'd just done it – and enjoyed it. Later, when she broke up with him, he'd accused her of fucking every man in the area. That was when she'd left. Only Turgut, who was already in İstanbul, had supported her. Only poor, emotionless Turgut had possessed the balls to stand up to Şeymus. But then, bully though he was, Şeymus was no fool. It had taken time, but eventually he'd stopped hassling her, because Turgut had threatened to kill him. And Şeymus knew that Turgut Zana never made idle threats.

Did she love Turgut so much because she'd never slept with

him? He was a good-looking man, but there was no desire in him and he was like a brother to her. Even if he had sexual feelings, would he be able to express them, given how he was? It wasn't just Mehmet Süleyman's good looks and exquisite manners that made him so irresistible. It wasn't even that he was a skilled lover. It was his appreciation that Barçın adored. The way he touched her body with such desire, and how he let himself melt into every sexual adventure she offered him. And he had a big cock. She laughed at her own crude thoughts before a dark notion entered her mind. What if she went to see Gonca Hanım and told her what her lover had been doing? What if she ran it by Turgut and asked his advice?

'She'll kill you,' he said when she phoned him. 'Be content with what you have, Barçın abla. Don't try to threaten Süleyman or any of his people. He has a poor track record with women. If you must carry on with him, then be his other woman. You will never be anything else.'

When she put the phone down, she wondered why she'd ever spoken to Turgut. She'd known he'd say that. She read the first line of a letter dated February 2015 yet again. In modern Turkish, it had not come from any of Fatima Hanım's brothers.

Dear Fatima Hanım, dear mother . . .

'My father knew Konstantinos Apion, and everyone in Moda knows that story,' the old man said.

'I beg to differ,' İkmen said. 'The Rudolfoğlus had been largely forgotten. Certainly Konstantinos's son, Yiannis, knows about it . . . oh, and Father Anatoli, the local Orthodox priest, he knew.'

'So if the local priest knew, the net widens . . .'

'Not really, no,' İkmen said. 'Priests are not supposed to gossip about things told to them in confidence. And I know Father Anatoli took that aspect of his role very seriously. I think you know that too.'

'I heard the priest had died.'

'The day after you were seen speaking to him, yes,' İkmen said.

'I haven't spoken to Father Anatoli for years.' The old man handed Kerim a pair of tongs. 'Have some of the sushi, it's wonderful.'

'Thank you.'

'He committed suicide,' İkmen said. 'A disturbing course of action for a priest.'

'Inspector, why do I get the impression you are accusing me of something?'

'Tell me how, when most people in Moda seem to have forgotten the Rudolfoğlus, you appear to know so much about them. I understand you are not a young man, and the Rudolfoğlus' tales are not young men's stories. But I'm curious. I'm also curious, I repeat, to know why you have visited the German cemetery in Tarabya so frequently in the last year.'

'Mm. Now under normal circumstances I would say at this point that I need to consult my lawyer.' He looked at Kerim and smiled. 'There are two different types of sushi,' he said. 'The slices on the left are delicately flavoured with sesame.'

'You are entirely at liberty to consult your lawyer,' İkmen said.

'Thank you.' He carried on looking at Kerim. 'May I help you?'

But Kerim didn't move. He was looking at something. İkmen followed his gaze to an empty fish tank on the floor beside the kitchen sink.

'This is halibut?' the sergeant said.

'Yes. Fresh today. I bought it after I left the doctor's office.'

'You have an empty fish tank . . .'

'Ah yes,' he said. 'I'm changing Zenobia's water.'

'So where is she?'

'In the bath. She's perfectly fine, I can assure you. Zenobia has been my companion for many years, I take her care very seriously.'

İkmen's phone rang. He looked at the screen and saw that the caller was Barçın Demirtaş. If it had been Süleyman, he would have answered, but the traffic constable could wait.

'Aren't you going to answer that?'

'No,' İkmen said. There was a small picture of a fish on the side of the tank. 'Is that Zenobia?'

'Yes,' the old man said.

Kerim Gürsel took a piece of sushi and put it on his plate. But he didn't eat it. Then his phone rang too.

'Is Çetin Bey at the ayazma?' Barçın asked.

Ömer Mungun looked up. He'd been put on hold by a nurse on Aslan Gerontas's ward at Bakırköy. Apparently finding out how the young man was responding to treatment was no easy task. But then the boy had only just arrived at the hospital. Ömer suspected Süleyman had given him this job to keep him out of the way. Now that he was fucking Barçın, he wanted to see as little of her ex-lover as possible. Or was he being paranoid?

'Yes,' he said. He knew that his face had assembled itself into a sneer.

'He's not answering his phone,' she said.

'He doesn't. I've told you before. Call Kerim Bey.'

'I have,' she said. 'He's not answering either.'

'I can't help you,' Ömer said.

'Where's Inspector Süleyman?' she asked.

'On his way to Moda,' he said. 'I'm surprised you have to ask.'

Barçın felt her face burn. 'What's that supposed to mean?' she said.

'What do you think?'

283

She heard someone say something to him on his phone. He said, 'Yes, I'll hold.'

She moved towards him. 'Just because I didn't want to carry on after that night,' she said. 'We were drunk . . .'

'I felt something,' he said.

'Yes. We had sex. It was great. But you're too intense, Ömer. I've been through a relationship that was too intense before.'

'Oh, so now you sidestep that by taking someone else's lover!'

For a moment she was speechless. He knew? Of course he did.

'If Gonca Hanım ever finds out about the two of you, she'll tear you to pieces,' he said. 'As for him . . . You know it's a dominance thing, don't you? He has to stick his big, privileged cock inside you just to prove he's better than I am. He doesn't want you!'

She shook her head. 'I'm not talking about this. I've got to get in touch with Inspector İkmen – urgently.'

'Oh?'

'Yes,' she said. 'So for God's sake forget your bitterness for one moment and help me. I know the identity of Fatima Hanım's son. I've just found it in her correspondence. Çetin Bey needs to know, right now. Because if this man behaves the same way that he writes, then he could be dangerous.'

Ömer said nothing for a moment, then he said, 'I'll call the boss.'

'I don't know why you boys don't answer your phones,' the old man said. 'Why have them if you ignore them?'

'Why prepare lunch when you don't eat it?' İkmen countered.

'I am diabetic.'

'Then you'd better eat,' İkmen said.

The old man smiled.

Kerim said, 'Sir, may I please use your bathroom?'

'Of course,' Rauf Bey said. 'At the end of the corridor, turn right.'

Kerim stood up and left.

'Why don't you eat, Rauf Bey?' İkmen asked. 'In fact, why don't you eat whatever that is in the middle of the table? Is it the liver?'

Rauf Bey said, 'Let us wait for Kerim Bey to return, shall we?'

İkmen's phone beeped, letting him know he had a text. He looked at it and frowned.

'A problem?' Rauf Bey asked.

İkmen smiled. 'No,' he said.

Kerim returned from the bathroom.

'Rauf Bey,' he said as he sat down, 'there was no fish in your bath.'

Mehmet Süleyman liked to drive himself. That way he was in control. But this time he had no option. With Ali Erbil handcuffed to his arm, all he could do was shout at the constable who was driving.

'You've lights up, and sirens!' he yelled. 'Put your foot down!'

'Sir, there's a—'

'I don't care if it's a bus full of grandmothers! Push the fucking thing if you must!'

The constable added the sound of his horn to the siren and shouted at the driver of the minibus in front to 'Fuck off out of the way!'

But the bus driver just shrugged. Like the Mercedes beside him and the Mini in front, he had nowhere to go. İstanbul was at maximum gridlock and it was hot enough to grill meat out on the tarmac.

Barçın Demirtaş had read out the salient paragraphs of the letter Fatima Hanım's son had sent her only four months ago.

It's not the money, it's the recognition. It's about names. I need one. I need yours because yours is mine and mine is yours and you know it. I will have my name before I die! Deny me and I will prove to you in the most graphic way that I can, that I am your son. Recall, Mother, if you can ever forget, that you are the daughter of the Devil, and think about what that makes me.

In spite of the heat, his recollection of his conversation with Barçın made him shudder.

The letter was signed 'Rouvin', which was the name Fatima Rudolfoğlu's baby had been given at birth. So far, so familiar. But what worried Süleyman was Rouvin's address and his surname.

'Come on!' He pounded on the back of the driver's seat. 'We need to get to Moda now!'

'Ah, but of course I put her in a bowl in my bedroom,' Rauf Bey said. 'Silly old fool! I am so forgetful these days!'

İkmen peered closely at the picture of the fish on the empty tank.'Is that why you have a photograph of Zenobia?' he said. 'To remind you what she is?'

The old man smiled and said nothing. He did that a lot.

'You know, if you have a lot of children, as I do, you get to know some very strange things,' İkmen said. 'You follow their interests and their passions. For instance, two of my sons trained as doctors. One is a surgeon. Theoretically, as opposed to practically, Orhan taught me how to amputate a leg. Not a skill I will use every day, or even at all. But I can talk about amputation with some degree of authority. Then take one of my younger boys, Bülent—'

'Does this have a point?' the old man said.

Kerim reached across the table to take another sliver of sushi. İkmen held up a hand. 'Not yet, Kerim Bey.'

'Sir.'

Rauf Bey said, 'Oh but—'

'When he was twelve, Bülent wanted a tank of piranha fish,' İkmen said. 'My wife almost fainted when he put this to her. She imagined fish floating about in a tank beside her chair with human fingers in their mouths. So my son compromised. He told his mother he wanted a puffer fish. He showed her a picture of a nice, friendly-looking beast and she said yes. Puffer fish don't bite off fingers, do they? I checked them out and they are perfectly harmless. Unless you eat them.

'Young boys often want a dangerous animal or two. It makes them feel powerful. Zenobia is a puffer fish, isn't she, Rauf Bey? I recognise the picture. And although you didn't know whether either Kerim Bey or myself would be able to recognise a puffer fish, that didn't really matter did it? That was just a potentially amusing detail?'

The old man laughed.

İkmen looked at Kerim. His face was white.

'Do your lips feel numb?' the inspector asked.

'No, why . . .'

'You're OK. The flesh is usually harmless; it's the liver that is particularly toxic.' He pointed to the dark mass in the middle of the table. 'Rauf Bey, why did you kill Zenobia when you couldn't have known we were coming to see you?'

'But I did know,' he said.

There were fragments of cloth twisted around a few of the ribs and across the head. The tiny corpse had probably been shrouded. But it hadn't been put in a coffin.

The priest muttered words that Teker didn't understand over the baby's dark resting place. She took her telephone out of her pocket and made a call. When it was answered, she said, 'Dr Sarkissian? Good afternoon. Or rather, it would be . . .'

Chapter 25

They all turned towards the direction of the front door at the same time.

'Who else has a key to your apartment?' İkmen asked.

'Only the kapıcı.'

İkmen stood. 'What's his name?'

'Mustafa Bey.'

'Mustafa Bey,' İkmen called out, 'is that you?'

'Çetin Bey!'

It was Süleyman's voice.

'We're in the kitchen.'

Kerim Gürsel, the old man and İkmen around a table covered with food was not what Süleyman had been expecting.

'You get my text?' he asked İkmen.

'Yes. Enlightening. This is Rauf Karadeniz,' İkmen said. 'Rauf Bey, this is Inspector Süleyman.'

The old man said, 'Delighted.'

Süleyman stared. Once he had recovered his breath he said, 'Also known as Rouvin?'

'We were, I believe, coming to that,' Rauf Bey said.

Süleyman called back into the hall. 'Constable!'

A slightly world-weary constable came in cuffed to Ali Erbil.

'Look at this gentleman here, Ali,' Süleyman said. 'Think carefully and then tell me whether you recognise him as the man you saw talking to a priest when I took you to the Koço restaurant.'

It clearly wasn't easy for Ali. He'd been crying in the car as tendrils of grief for Elif broke through the methadone. These had been sprinkled with fury as he accused Süleyman of lying. An entire scenario about police officers raping and then killing Elif had spilled out of him. Could anything he said be relied upon?

Then the old man spoke. 'You must tell the truth, you know. Don't be frightened.'

There was a long silence as Ali appeared to look deeply into Rauf Bey's face.

'Ali . . .'

'I think so,' he said. 'The man I saw at Koço was definitely the man I saw in that house we squatted in.'

'Yes, but was it this man?'

'I feel dizzy.'

Kerim Gürsel stood up and gave him his seat.

'I only caught a glimpse of him,' Ali said. 'That he was there, in that context, shocked me. The priest was upset. That's all I know.'

İkmen looked at Süleyman, who shook his head.

'Well,' İkmen said, 'what do we do, gentlemen?'

The old man said, 'I—'

'What we do, Rauf Bey,' İkmen answered his own question, 'is take you into our custody and hopefully get some sense out of you. I have what I believe is a reasonable suspicion that you have been involved in some way with the illegal activities that have taken place at the Teufel Ev. I may also charge you with the attempted murder of my sergeant.'

Süleyman said, 'What?'

'I'll explain later. In the meantime, Sergeant Gürsel, would you please inform headquarters that they need to send a forensic team down here to analyse this fish.'

* * *

'To be honest with you, Sergeant Mungun, he is not, as yet, responding to treatment. We've only had him a few hours. If anything, his condition is still deteriorating.'

Aslan Gerontas's psychiatrist sounded young, and so Ömer Mungun felt rather more inclined to trust her than most psychiatrists he came across. So often they were disillusioned men in their fifties or sixties, waiting to retire. At least this woman, Dr Berkan, seemed interested.

'He remains convinced he sees the Devil. He still believes it is in some way his fate to confront this entity. The Devil and his agents are everywhere. It's apocalyptic stuff. Looking at his history, there is a clear case for a diagnosis of religious mania. But this has all been exacerbated, in my opinion, by recent developments in domestic and international politics.'

'You mean like the situation in Syria?'

'That would be a big part of it,' she said. 'Aslan is an Orthodox Christian. These people, unlike groups such as American Evangelicals, are not known for dwelling particularly on, well, end-of-the-world myths. But in the Christian Bible there is a book called Revelation, where what they call "the last days" are described. Given that we know from his mother that Aslan as a child was influenced by a priest who dwelt on such subjects, I'm fairly sure I know where all of this has come from. Doing something about it, however, is something else. When terrible things that only serve to confirm such beliefs happen in your region every day, it's difficult to refute any sort of theory about cause and effect, and that includes the supernatural. He will be denied TV access and shows no inclination, at present, to read. But I can't control what he hears on the ward or what happens in his head.'

'Can he, in your opinion, be charged under criminal justice?'

'No,' she said. 'Not as he is now. What are you going to charge him with? Possession of a firearm? My understanding is that he was given the gun, which he then fired at a rat. Aslan is a very agitated young man, Sergeant. He's already had to be restrained twice.'

'Has he tried to kill himself?'

'He believes that the Devil has been unleashed into this world to engage in a final battle with God,' she said. 'He sees him everywhere. But he also claims that, at the same time, he is hiding in the body of a particular human being. I don't know how that works for him. Logically it doesn't, but then delusions are not always internally consistent.'

'Has he given you any idea about whose body the Devil might be hiding in?'

'No,' she said. 'Though according to the notes that Dr Aksu passed on to me, it's none of the usual suspects – politicians, terrorists, the Pope. According to Aslan, the Devil has a comfortable home in the body of a very ordinary person. That, he says, demonstrates his truly tricksy nature. A sort of cosmic illusionist. For me, it's fascinating. But for Aslan it must be torture.'

'Might I have something to eat, do you think?'

İkmen looked at the old man sitting next to him. 'I'm afraid, Rauf Bey, that your fish is off the menu.'

'I didn't mean that. You will discover that it was indeed halibut, as I told you. But I am feeling a little queasy now. My diabetes . . .'

İkmen shook his head. He addressed his colleagues in the car with them. 'Anyone got anything to eat?'

No one had.

'Sorry,' he said. 'We'll get you something when we arrive at headquarters.'

'I can't wait that long.'

They'd just managed to cross the Bosphorus Bridge. Still accident-bound, it had taken them half an hour.

'I sometimes go to the wonderful hotel they made from the ruins of the old Çırağan Palace,' Rauf Bey said. 'The Gazebo Lounge serves excellent coffee.'

'Does it.'

'Yes, and one can sit outside. Perfect for smokers.'

'Really.'

'And I would pay,' he said. 'For all of us.'

İkmen swivelled in his seat to face the old man. 'Rauf Bey, I am not going to take a detour so that you can have some overpriced coffee in an Ottoman palace.' His phone rang. 'İkmen.'

'Where on earth are you?'

It was Teker.

'And what is this I hear about poisoned fish?'

'I'm taking a man called Rauf Karadeniz in for questioning, madam,' he said. 'I have reason to believe he is the son of Fatima Rudolfoğlu.'

'Do you.'

'According to information I've been given by the Ottoman transcriber, yes,' he said. 'I also believe he tried to poison Sergeant Gürsel and myself when we went to his apartment to confront him about an alleged conversation he had with the Greek priest who later killed himself, Father Anatoli.'

'Well, we've found a body under the ayazma,' she said. 'An infant. I'm hoping that Dr Sarkissian will be able to tell us more when he gets here. I'm told that the Bosphorus Bridge is hell on earth.'

'We've just crossed, but it wasn't what you'd call easy,' İkmen said.

As they exited the bridge, İkmen felt something jolt against his shoulder. It was Rauf Karadeniz's head.

Ali Erbil had fallen asleep. Mehmet Süleyman let him. He was strapped in to his seat and attached to Süleyman's wrist by handcuffs. He wasn't going anywhere. Anyway, the policeman understood. When his brother Murad had been told that his wife had died in the 1999 earthquake, he hadn't cried or screamed; he'd just curled up on his old bed in their parents' house and slept.

For Ali, the death of Elif had robbed his life of purpose. Committed to following her into whatever treatment regime she was going to be given, now he was just a prisoner. A heroin addict, temporarily maintained on methadone. He had a rich father who would attempt to redeem him, but what did that matter? For some reason he had exchanged his comfortable life as the son of a doctor for junk and the street and a woman who killed people to get famous. Something had to have been wrong in the Erbil household. But what? And was it even Süleyman's concern?

What was clear was that Ali, now that he had nothing more to lose, had no reason not to tell the truth about the identity of the man he'd seen in the Teufel Ev and, later, talking to the priest at Koço. Every motive for concealing information had dropped away. So the fact that he'd been unable to positively identify Rauf Karadeniz meant that either he really had forgotten what that man looked like, or he was so afraid of making a mistake it was clouding his judgement. Behind the junk, he wasn't a bad man. Süleyman suspected that Elif had not been a bad woman. Desperation had made her a killer; desperation and the promise of a quick fix for a life that was never going to get any better. She had thought that notoriety was the answer, while her only real way out had been the much quieter but more painful option of giving up drugs.

He was about to close his eyes for a few moments too when suddenly the car stopped.

* * *

293

'I've spoken to Inspector İkmen about this already,' Erdal Bey said. 'I don't know the identity of Fatima Rudolfoğlu's son.'

'I know, sir,' Barçın said. 'But we think we may have found that out now.'

'Oh, so the horrific scenario I warned Fatima Hanım about comes to pass,' he said.

'With the . . .'

'The Oriental Club is the sole beneficiary at the moment, but this could change things.'

'Erdal Bey, it has occurred to me that you may know this man,' Barçın said. 'You're both lawyers.'

'We don't all know each other, you know,' he said tetchily.

She'd caught him just as he'd come back from lunch, which, from the faint slurring of his words, she suspected had been partially liquid.

'His name is Rauf Karadeniz,' she said.

Nothing happened for so long she thought that maybe the line had gone dead.

'Sir?'

'Are you sure?' he said.

'He wrote a letter to her,' she said. 'In itself, not a lot, I know. But there are details in it that lead me to believe he is genuine. Inspector İkmen is bringing him in for questioning. Do you know him, Erdal Bey?'

Again he didn't answer immediately. Then he said, 'I thought he'd died.'

'Do you know him, sir?'

'Yes,' he said. 'He's a business acquaintance. Not a close friend, but . . . I met him professionally many years ago, when he was still in practice. We share an interest in property law. He retired a few years ago.'

'Why did you think he'd died?' Barçın said.

She heard his breathing labour. 'He had cancer,' he said.

'Did he tell you that himself?'

'I had cancer myself some years ago. I'm still required to have regular check-ups. I saw him at my clinic last year. He told me he only had months.'

'I can't eat that.'

The old man pushed the simit roll away.

'What *do* you want?' İkmen asked.

'Chocolate. Or coffee.' He looked out of the car window. 'We are near Çırağan now. Let's go there.'

İkmen left the car. They'd pulled up by the side of the road beside the Dolmabahçe Palace so that food could be obtained for the hypoglycaemic old man. The first thing that had come to hand had been a ring of sesame-sprinkled simit bread.

He walked over to Kerim Gürsel. 'He won't eat the fucking bread,' he said. 'Is there anywhere to get a bar of chocolate round here?'

'No.'

İkmen sighed. 'Then he'll have to eat it or die. Oh, and Kerim, could you please tell Inspector Süleyman what's going on. Tell him to go ahead without us.'

Kerim ran over to the car that had stopped behind İkmen's, while the older man went back to speak to Rauf Bey.

'It's the simit or nothing,' he said. 'You almost passed out on the bridge, so I would suggest that you at least take a few mouthfuls. I'll get you coffee and chocolate when we arrive at headquarters.'

'No,' he said.

'What do you mean, no?'

'I mean that I can't eat something like that.' He pointed to the thick bread ring. 'It'll kill me.'

'It'll kill you if you don't,' İkmen said.

Süleyman's car pulled out into the traffic and overtook them.

'You don't understand, Inspector. If I eat that, I will suffer from the most horrific stomach pains. I can't take bulk any more, not now. Take me to Çırağan and I'll tell you everything.'

'You'll tell me everything anyway,' İkmen said.

The old man looked up at him and suddenly İkmen felt very cold. 'Not if I end up in hospital I won't,' he said. 'If I go there, I will never answer your questions because I will never come out.'

'Çetin Bey is on his way back,' Ömer said.

'Yes, I know,' Barçın replied. 'I've spoken to him. Several times.'

She was expecting him to go, but he didn't. He stood in the doorway.

'What?' she said.

He shrugged. 'I'm sorry.'

'What for?'

'For being childish about what is clearly your choice. You love who you love, just as everyone does. That I did not appeal to you . . .'

She put her pen down and raised her hands in the air. 'What can I say?'

'Nothing.'

'We had a good time, Ömer,' she said. 'I think you're great. I really do. What happened . . . Look, I've had some bad experiences with Kurdish men, or rather a man. He was too controlling and I know that you're probably not . . .'

'And, like I say, you're in love with the boss.' He shook his head. 'It's OK, you can tell me. I won't tell him. I won't tell anyone.'

She said nothing.

'Women fall for him,' he said.

'Women will fall for you, Ömer.'

'Not the right ones, though, eh, Barçın Hanım?'

He left just before Barçın began to cry. It was the word 'love'
that had brought tears to her eyes.

Chapter 26

They sat out on the terrace. Kerim Gürsel watched from inside.

The old man drank his coffee black and full of sugar.

'My name at birth we will come to,' he said. 'The name I was given was Rouvin Kazantzoğolu. My father was Dimitri Kazantzoğolu, a Greek from a good family from Trabzon. My mother was Zenobia, also an Anatolian Greek. When I was born, neither of them was in the first flush of youth. My mother told me that they had been trying for a child for fifteen years when God finally gave me to them. I loved my mother very much. She didn't deserve the life her God inflicted upon her. She didn't deserve my father.'

'Rudolf Paşa's adjutant,' İkmen said.

'In the First World War, yes,' he said. 'He called the paşa his devil. He said he used to stake men out in the desert to burn to death if they questioned him. Every day the Arabs harried them. They blew up troop trains and cut lines of communication. If they caught an Ottoman soldier, they tortured him to death. Rudolf Paşa did the same to them. My father resisted it at first. But in return for his compliance, the paşa turned a blind eye to my father's many lovers, both male and female. In the city of Jeddah he had a harem of Arab girls, while on the field he took the handsomest and youngest men into his tent. All he had to do in return was allow Rudolf Paşa to bathe in the blood of his enemies, and sometimes his own men.'

'I've been told that Rudolf Paşa and your father performed ceremonies invoking the Devil.'

He smiled. 'There are many stories. Who knows if any of them are true? My father was a soldier and a hunter. Rudolf Paşa practised the occult – oh my God, did he – but that didn't include my father as far as I know. I'm not trying to excuse my father, you understand. He was a cruel man, and I'm sure he saw people he considered inferior to him as little more than animals, but he was a man of his time.'

'Like Rudolf Paşa.'

'Ah no, I do believe he was more than that,' the old man said. 'Call it an enchantment, but when the war ended, my father found that he couldn't break ties with the paşa, in spite of the fact that by that time the city was occupied by the enemies of the empire. There was no Ottoman army. But still they met, they talked, and even after Rudolf Paşa died, my father continued to visit the family. When the paşa's wife then also died, my father turned his attentions towards Fatima Hanım. You know for a long time my mother thought he was having an affair with Perihan Hanım, but she despised him. Maybe she knew how thoroughly brutalised war had made him. Or perhaps she'd seen him looking at her daughter. When he eventually told me the truth, I was twelve. He said, "Your real mother was just a girl, but she seduced me. She was the very Devil for a man's body."'

He drank some more coffee. İkmen lit a cigarette.

'I don't just have diabetes, you know.'

'Arthritis too, I believe,' İkmen said.

The old man tilted his head to one side. 'A little,' he said. 'But I do have cancer.'

'Where?'

'Everywhere.'

'Hence the . . .'

'I can't take heavy food like bread any more. Will you put a dying man in prison?'

'That depends upon what you tell me, Rauf Bey,' İkmen said.

'So far, in your story, you have only been guilty of being born to Fatima Rudolfoğlu.'

'That's true. So I was born Rouvin Rudolfoğlu. Apparently as soon as I appeared, Fatima Hanım gave me to my father and told him to take me out of her sight. Dear Zenobia, my mother, was waiting with a wet nurse to receive me, and I never saw Fatima Rudolfoğlu again until my mother took me to see her when I was twelve. By which time my father had told me who she was. I disliked her intensely and the feeling was mutual. But I liked her big house. I also liked the fact that she was the daughter of a paşa. I enjoyed that association and that name. Because you know, Çetin Bey, names are important. Names have power.'

Arto Sarkissian rarely went to church. The last time had been for his mother's funeral. But in the tiny shrine of St Katherine, he felt something. What it was, he didn't know. A presence? A sense of peace? Or maybe it was just the sight of such a tiny skeleton. He touched it with one gloved hand.

Behind him, Commissioner Teker said, 'Can you estimate the age at death?'

'Not exactly without further examination,' he said. 'But an educated guess would be newborn.'

'That would fit.'

Teker was apparently entirely disengaged. Arto felt like crying, while her voice was as dry and detached as dust. But then maybe she was just cutting off in order to protect herself. Hürrem Teker hadn't had children. Now, without intervention, it was probably impossible. Arto had sometimes wondered whether she regretted that. He wished he'd been able to have a family. But Maryam's health had always been so fragile, they'd never even seriously tried.

He touched the tiny skull bones. What possibilities had been snuffed out when this child died? Why did people have to kill?

With no gravestone or even a coffin, this little one was nameless, and that was very, very cruel. To be without a name was never to have put a footprint on the world.

'Did you kill Fatima Rudolfoğlu and her brothers?'

'You are getting far too ahead in the story,' he said. 'But just so that you know you're not wasting your time, yes.'

'Why now? Because you're dying?' İkmen wasn't always blunt; in fact with elderly people he was usually gentle. But Rauf Karadeniz was . . . What was he?

'I didn't actually ever meet Yücel, Kanat and Kemal, you know. My mother – Zenobia – took me to the house, probably because we were summoned by the old witch, and introduced her to me as Fatima teyze, even though we all knew she wasn't my aunt but my mother. But no one said that. You can imagine my confusion as a child, can't you?'

'Yes.'

'I remember thinking that if that awful, grim woman was my mother, then what did that make me? My father was drinking heavily by then. He'd Turkified all our names, except my mother's. He wanted to forget the past and blend in with the new order that was Turkey. He chose the name Karadeniz because his family came from Trabzon, which is on the Black Sea. He was, in many ways, a simple man. I became Rauf and my father was Deniz.'

'Deniz Karadeniz? Seriously?'

'He said he couldn't think of anything else. Mother, however, remained Zenobia. She said that it was important to her to die with the name she was given at birth. I was not allowed that luxury.

'When my father died in 1950, he was buried as a Muslim. Mother and I lived in a terrible leaky house near the French Church of the Assumption. I wanted to become a biologist when I was young. My entire existence revolved around my fascination with animals. Perhaps it was a rebellion against my father and his obsession with killing things. But we had no money and so I became a lawyer. I joined the partnership of Unal and Yilmaz on İstiklal Caddesi and I became a go-to guy in property law. I even, although I didn't realise this until much later, had regular contact with Kenter and Kenter, Fatima Rudolfoğlu's lawyers.'

'Yes, we know.'

He smiled. 'And so you are ahead of me, Çetin Bey.'

'Only just,' İkmen said. 'I feel that to be too far ahead of you would be almost impossible, Rauf Bey.'

The old man appeared to ignore him. 'So life continued. As I am sure your sergeant has told you – I feel he is a very observant young man – I was unable to love women, so I didn't marry. Unlike my father, I couldn't just change my sexuality at will. And in this society, where such things are frowned upon, I became very distressed. I didn't want to become one of those sad men one sometimes saw cruising the back streets of Beyoğlu in the fifties and sixties, looking for like-minded males and getting beaten up by religious lunatics or, worse, arrested. That was when I started going to church with my mother. I even made confession to a priest. I also came into contact with Konstantinos Apion.'

'Did he tell you about his connection with Perihan Rudolfoğlu?'

'My mother introduced him as the Rudolfoğlus' gardener,' he said. 'I thought little of it at the time. In those days I actively rejected that part of myself. But then I discovered that my mother was spending time with this man outside church. I wasn't angry with her for this. My father was dead, and anyway, I'd never really loved him. Who could love a person who killed with impunity? Who even as an old man went to prostitutes and paid boys to come to the house so that he could bugger them in my mother's bed? Then, one day, I was taking coffee in Koço and I saw them. My mother was veiled but I knew her by her tiny waist and her voice. Konstantinos Bey kissed her hand outside the ayazma and then they parted. They didn't see me. Later that day I asked her what she had been doing, and she told me. Those bastards killed that man's child.'

'The child Sofia's death was the key that unlocked the notion that the Rudolfoğlus' murderer had to have some connection with their past,' İkmen said. 'You killed them in the way that you did in order to reflect—'

'Ah, but you're getting ahead of yourself again, Çetin Bey. Before that, we must consider Fatima Rudolfoğlu's will.'

He'd never seen a personality fragment in front of him before. He'd heard about the phenomenon that some called a nervous breakdown from his ex-wife Zelfa. But it still came as a shock.

Ali Erbil walked into his cell and sat down. For a moment he seemed quiet but untroubled. Then it was as if his body rebelled. He began shaking and his face turned white.

Süleyman said, 'What's going on?'

He could see that Ali was trying to speak but couldn't. He fell off the chair.

'Call a doctor!' Süleyman yelled into the corridor.

He crouched down beside the man and checked to see whether one side of his face was drooping. It wasn't, but now he was grinding his teeth and his eyes were rolling back in his head. Then he screamed. He carried on screaming even after the doctor came.

'I don't know when it was – years ago,' the old man said. 'Erdal Bey ran a problem by me as he sometimes did. It concerned a woman who wished to leave her property to her three brothers after her death. So far, so straightforward. But then in the event of the brothers predeceasing her, or after their deaths should they survive her, she wanted to bequeath her estate to her late father's

303

club. In addition, if one or more of the brothers survived her, they could live in the house they all shared for as long as they wished, provided the property and any monies remaining went to the club on their deaths. Relatively straightforward, I thought, until he told me that the woman also had an illegitimate son. This person was unacknowledged by the woman, who wished to have nothing to do with him. Erdal Bey had counselled that the son, if he knew of her, could mount a challenge to the will upon her death. But she stuck to her guns. You can imagine how I felt.'

'Yes.'

İkmen noticed that Rauf Bey's cup was empty. 'Would you like more coffee?'

'That would be nice.'

İkmen called a waiter to the table and ordered.

'I advised Erdal Bey to keep on trying to make the woman see sense, which I believe he did for a while. But in the end Fatima Rudolfoğlu got her way. As she always did.' He paused. 'Don't get me wrong, Çetin Bey, I never wanted her money or her property. In fact I put all of that out of my mind for decades. Other things took my attention. My mother died, and I finally managed to fill my home with beautiful living creatures. I also had the odd liaison. Then I got old. First arthritis, which was manageable, then diabetes, and then, finally, cancer. My own fault: I ignored symptoms for, well, years probably. I was told I was terminal in March. I saw Erdal Bey at the clinic. He had just been given the all-clear. I was happy for him. But seeing him like that brought Fatima Rudolfoğlu to mind once again. I stood outside that house for the first time in decades and I wondered whether any of them were still alive.'

'How did you find out that they were?'

'I went to the house again, and this time I saw a man coming out. I asked him if anyone lived there, and he said that it was occupied by three men and a woman. It's difficult to express

304

how that made me feel. The woman who had given birth to me and then taken away my identity was still alive. This woman for whom I was nothing – less than nothing. Who had only ever seen me once, out of curiosity rather than love. She was going to outlive me. I was furious. Had I not been furious, I couldn't have done what I did to them.'

'How did you get in?' İkmen asked.

His phone rang and he switched it off.

The old man laughed. 'What do you think happens when a group of deaf, half-blind old fools all live in the same building?' he said. 'No one hears or sees anything. They had squatters. In the basement.'

'What about Fatima's cleaner? And the man you saw. I assume that was Yücel's carer?'

'I don't know. I only saw him the once. The squatters – a couple of junkies by the look of them – rarely turned up in the daytime. The Rudolfoğlus were alone. I killed them on a Sunday afternoon, when I knew that house would be effectively mine.'

'So how did you do it?'

'Sergeant Gürsel tells me that Çetin Bey and this Rauf Karadeniz are taking coffee in the Gazebo Lounge of the Çırağan Palace Hotel,' Teker said. 'Is this true?'

Süleyman wiped sweat from his forehead. Ali Erbil's physical symptoms had been bad enough, but when he'd started speaking what had sounded like utter nonsense, it had really unnerved him. What he needed was a lie-down. What he was getting was a dressing-down from the commissioner.

'I don't know,' he said. 'I left Çetin Bey parked up outside the Dolmabahçe Palace. Rauf Karadeniz is being brought here in connection with the Rudolfoğlu—'

'I know,' she said. 'So why isn't he here?'

'I don't know,' he repeated. 'Have you asked Sergeant Gürsel?'

'Yes, of course! He says that Çetin Bey is questioning the man over coffee!'

'Then that is what he's doing. Mr Karadeniz is diabetic, and my understanding is that he needed to eat.'

'He could have eaten here, or from an ordinary büfe! Why the Çırağan Palace hotel? What's he doing?'

'I don't know.'

She dismissed him. Back in his own office, he listened while Ömer Mungun updated him on the condition of Aslan Gerontas, which wasn't good.

When he'd finished, Süleyman said, 'You know we're going to get more of this, don't you, Ömer?'

'More crazy people?'

'When I was born, this city had a population of two million. Now we are near enough sixteen million and counting. A vast number of them are poor, and those who aren't are paranoid about becoming poor. We all press up against each other like rats in a sewer. We fight for survival, we steal each other's food and we go mad. Even the slightest tendency towards weakness or insanity will be exacerbated in this environment. Had he lived in a small town on the Aegean, maybe Aslan Gerontas would not have disappeared into his religious mania. Perhaps the beauty of the coast and the fresh air would have allowed him to think more rationally. Who knows?'

He closed his eyes. He was exhausted. Every day in this city exhausted him. But he only acknowledged it very infrequently.

'Sir, would you like me to get you a drink?' he heard Ömer say. 'Shall I shut the door and open the window so you can have a cigarette?'

He didn't sound hostile any more. Maybe he'd worked through the demons Süleyman acknowledged he had aroused in him.

He opened his eyes. 'Thank you, Ömer,' he said. 'Tea would be good. And don't take too much notice of me, I'm just tired.'

Ömer left. But before he closed the office door, Süleyman caught a glimpse of Barçın Demirtaş across the corridor.

'For a couple of weeks I had been walking around the house whenever the junkies were out. On that particular afternoon, I knocked on Fatima Hanım's door.'

'And she let you in? Who did she think you were?' İkmen said.

'I told her who I was. And yes, she let me in. I even took my shoes off like a good boy.'

'Yes, but . . .'

'I wanted to explain my situation to her,' Rauf Bey said. 'I was under no illusion that she'd do as I asked. But I had to give her one more chance. Of course, before she opened the door, she told me to go away, but then her curiosity overcame her.'

'What did you actually want from her?' İkmen asked.

'My name,' he said. 'I wanted her to name me in her will as her son. I didn't want money, I didn't want that house. I told her that I knew she and her brothers were murderers, and she admitted it. She was proud of it. She asked me why I wanted the name of a murderer. I said because it was mine. Because I'd lived a lie all my life and she owed me. She laughed at me.'

'And then you killed her?'

'No, then she told me about my father and how she'd seduced him. It hadn't been difficult. What was more difficult, for me, was hearing about her incestuous sex with her own father. She said, "We're devils, all of us, and so are you." If I fought what I was, I'd only become like my uncles, who she described as weak and sentimental.'

'Why?'

'Because they experienced guilt. Apparently Kemal had wanted to bring the baby's body to the house to be buried in the garden. He'd been trying for years to, as he put it, "bring her back to

307

life", using the supposed occult magic that his father had studied. But he needed her body. What he'd done must have driven him insane. It had driven them all insane. Kanat's apartment was like a sewer, full of filth and rats and cockroaches. Fatima refused to have the child's body anywhere near her. She described her own mother as a filthy whore and her child as a Greek abomination. That was why they didn't talk. Because she controlled all their lives and they hated her. They also hated each other, I believe. I think that every time they saw one another, they remembered what they'd done.' His eyes filled with tears. 'She made me feel as if poison ran in my veins, and I hated her so much for it, I picked her up and laid her on her bed and told her I was going to kill her. I was going to smother her with a pillow.'

'Why didn't you?'

'Because she tried to kiss me,' he said. 'Not as a son, but . . . You know, Çetin Bey, she *was* a devil. I know that sounds mad, but it's true. She lay on that bed like a whore, daring me to kill her, telling me I couldn't do it because I didn't have my real name. And she wasn't going to give it to me. I walked away. She thought I'd given up and she laughed. But I went into the kitchen and took one of the knives out of the drawer, and I pushed it through her brittle, evil breast. Had she closed her eyes, had she given me the luxury of not having to look into her black soul, I would not have killed the others. But she was still laughing when I killed her, and my hatred for all of them was so great at that moment that I knew they all had to die too.' He was sweating now and he wiped his brow. 'She had all their keys on a chain around her neck. I think she must have wanted to feel she had them by the balls every minute of every day.'

'All the men were also found dead on their beds.'

'Yes. I closed her eyes and then I went to Yücel's apartment. He was asleep, so I killed him as he slept. Kanat was dying, in my opinion. I could hear the death rattle in his throat. But I stabbed him anyway. I can't say I consciously did it for that baby; I did it for myself. But I did have a picture of my dear mother Zenobia and poor Konstantinos Apion in my mind. Only Kemal was awake. I told him who I was and what I knew, and he cried. I let him show me all that shit he had gathered to try and raise the dead, and I told him that it meant nothing. I said that if he was truly sorry for what he'd done, he'd lie down on his bed and let me kill him. And he did.'

'So if you are dying and you meant no harm or distress to the son of Konstantinos Apion . . .'

'I don't know him.'

'Then why didn't you just give yourself up?' İkmen said.

The coffee arrived.

When the waiter had gone, Rauf Bey said, 'I've asked myself that on many occasions. I led you, or rather Sergeant Gürsel, in the right direction. But I'd had no plans to do that. I did it because he was a nice young man and I rather fancied him.'

İkmen wondered whether the old man had sensed that Kerim was gay. But he didn't ask.

'Had you arrested anyone else for those murders, would I have given myself up? I don't know. All of this – my diagnosis, my realisation about what I wanted, the murders – it's all come about almost in spite of me. Maybe that's what happens to people whose lives have been lies. Or perhaps it's all part of being a child of the Devil. Yes.' He smiled. 'Now that was devilish and knowing of me.'

'What was?'

'Ever since my mother died, I've had animals. One of them has always been called Zenobia in her honour. Until last week, when she sadly died, I had a puffer fish with that name. My last pet. I buried her in the window box. But that picture you saw on the side of her tank was not of her. I cut it out of a book I have about puffer fish.' He laughed. 'When Sergeant Gürsel said that he was coming to see me, I knew you must have found something out. I thought it would be fun to see how bright he was. I already had the halibut, which I butchered as you saw. Putting the picture of the fish on Zenobia's tank just amused me. I'd told the sergeant I lived with a fish, but I hadn't told him what *kind* of fish. I wondered how observant he was, and how clever. But you beat him to it.'

'You shouldn't have told us she was in the bath,' İkmen said.

'I was thinking on my feet.' He drank his coffee. 'Because that is what little devils do, isn't it? Oh, and I'm not sorry I killed my mother and my uncles. They deserved to die. They were a waste of skin. Now look, if you're going to put me in prison, I'd like it very much if you'd register me, or whatever it is you do, as Rouvin Rudolfoğlu.' His face dropped. 'Even Rudolf Paşa has his correct name on his headstone. As you know, I've seen it. And he was a really evil man.'

Chapter 27

'Whenever we transfer anyone to Bakırköy, it makes me feel cold,' Ömer Mungun said.

'We can't help Mr Erbil,' Süleyman said. 'What can prison do for him? Nothing. The hospital is where he wanted to be when Elif was alive.'

'But she's dead.'

'Did they tell you whether he had settled?'

'Yes. He hasn't.'

Süleyman sat down. 'All that carnage just because Elif wanted to be somebody,' he said. 'What does that even mean?'

'My sister says it's a magic trick,' Ömer said.

'What?'

Peri Mungun was a very forthright and unusual woman, but this was left field even for her.

'The fame thing,' Ömer said. 'Get everyone chasing impossible fame dreams, keep them watching television and buying the products that support the delusion – Botox, make-up. It's how capitalism makes sure we all behave ourselves . . .' Then, realising that might sound a bit too radical, he added, 'According to Peri.'

'And Elif was an addict with, if Ali is to be believed, a horrific past. Those who know about these things claim that one never really gets over suffering sexual abuse as a child. That rage has to be expressed sometime.'

'She tried to anaesthetise herself with drugs . . .'

'With impossible dreams . . .'

'And then the one place she felt safe she had to leave because the only man she'd ever been safe with was afraid,' Ömer said. 'It is incredibly sad.'

'Sad for the people she killed and their families too,' Süleyman said.

'Of course. But it is also a lesson in how, if you brutalise a person, you potentially create a monster. No one ever gets away with a free pass, do they, sir? Not really.'

Hürrem Teker closed her office door and locked it. Then she opened her window.

'I would probably have paid to see your faces when you realised that Zenobia the puffer fish wasn't in the bath,' she said.

'It was no laughing matter at the time, madam, I can assure you,' Çetin İkmen said as he lit up a cigarette.

'Well now we know the fish was halibut, we can relax,' she said.

'Have scene-of-crime officers found Zenobia?'

Teker lit a cigarette of her own. 'They've found a desiccated puffer fish, yes,' she said. 'What an extraordinary old gentleman your Mr Karadeniz is.'

'Rudolfoğlu,' İkmen corrected. 'Grandson of a paşa, remember?'

'Albeit the Devil.'

'Maybe we shouldn't joke about that,' he said. 'He's been around a lot in this city lately. We shouldn't invoke him.'

'You're an extremely strange man, you know, Çetin Bey,' she said. 'You're not religious and yet you acknowledge all sorts of supernatural myths and entities as if they were real.'

'I like to keep my options open.'

She laughed. Then she asked, 'Have you spoken to that other Greek man?'

'Yiannis Apion. Yes,' he said. 'Poor, sad man. I believe he feels that his sister's body has been dug up for no reason.'

'Such crimes have to see the light.'

'Crimes against children so often go undetected,' he said. 'Even now we dismiss them. We ignore them or we justify them by reference to convenient beliefs. I don't know whether Rudolf and Dimitri were evil, but they both certainly created it.'

'The terrible Fatima Hanım.'

'And all her victims, in which I include her brothers,' he said. He shook his head. 'Poor Rauf Bey. A kind, gentle man with a great love of the most despised of animals, and yet there is a small devil in him. I can see it.'

Teker said nothing. Sometimes his flights of occult fantasy irritated her.

'But you know puffer fish can be quite attractive,' İkmen said. 'If Zenobia was anything like that picture on her tank, she was a looker.'

'Ah, and talking of lookers, I assume you don't need the services of Constable Demirtaş any longer?' she said.

'No. Not until the case comes to court.'

'Well then I'd better contact her superiors,' she said. 'In view of that carnage on the bridge, they'll need all the help they can get.'

'Yes, madam.'

'Ask her to tell you how long it will take her to finalise her reports.'

'Yes.'

'Oh, and İkmen, I assume you have been satisfied with her work?'

'Absolutely. It's been fascinating. Like looking through a scrying glass into the past.'

She glanced down at her paperwork. 'I won't mention her misdemeanours, then?'

'Misdemeanours?'

'With Inspector Süleyman,' she said. 'Don't you two talk any more?'

'I don't . . .'

'Don't even try to dissemble, İkmen,' she said. 'I have eyes and ears everywhere. I can't prove that you knew about their romantic trysts, but . . . I will discipline him myself, then that will be an end to it.'

İkmen walked slowly back to his office. He'd known that Demirtaş had possessed feelings for Süleyman, but he hadn't realised that anything had happened. When he drew level with his colleague's office, he saw that he was alone. He went inside.

Süleyman looked up at him. 'Çetin?'

'You know I always say that you're the younger brother I never had?' İkmen said.

'Yes.'

'Well if you really were, I would thrash you.'

'What?'

İkmen pointed to the office that was being used by Barçın Demirtaş. 'You messed with that woman,' he said. 'A woman not your own. You have your own. What is wrong with you?'

'Çetin, how . . .'

'I just know, OK,' he said. 'Don't ask. I know women throw themselves at you, I've seen them. I've even encouraged you to make the most of it! But not at work. That is screwing on your own doorstep. It's risky and it's wrong. I don't blame the girl. I don't blame girls! You are entirely culpable, and let me tell you, it's making carrying on loving you as a brother really hard.'

Barçın went home to her apartment. Going back to looking at driver machismo on screens all day long was going to be tough. But she still had to finish her reports for Inspector İkmen, and she was glad that she had been part of a successful investigation.

It would look good on her record. It was also making her think that maybe she should think about utilising her language skills more in the future.

The old man who had killed the Rudolfoğlu siblings had looked so small and weak. He must have been in the grip of such terrible rage. And what a background to come from! Hideous secrets and lies, and on top of that, an ethnicity that he couldn't express. But then was that so odd? Things hadn't changed much over the years. Turgut said they should both go home to their own communities, their own people. She had never and would never believe in a separate homeland for the Kurds, but she knew that he did. He couldn't see how that could lead to war, because as he never tired of saying, 'war is not rational'.

She couldn't leave the city. Here she rode her bike when she liked, and she could drink and smoke and wear what she wanted without her relatives threatening to lock her in the house. And then there was Süleyman. What was going to happen with him? Ömer had been right, she was in love, but the most she could expect would be sex. But that was OK. Wasn't it?

She could be the other woman. Couldn't she?

'Baby, you have blood on your shirt.'

Süleyman felt a sudden dart of anxiety.

'On the back,' Gonca said. 'Take it off and I'll wash it for you.'

'Not now,' he said. 'There's no need.'

His shirt was unbuttoned. She put her hands on his chest and began to push it from his shoulders.

'Oh, come on,' she said. 'Give me the shirt and I'll suck your cock. Fair exchange.'

He felt his entire body solidify. If she saw his back, she'd know. But then she was going to see it sometime. Barçın had bitten deep.

Gonca took his shirt off and then, briefly, licked one of his nipples. She held the garment up to the light.

'Mehmet!' she said. 'What happened?'

Çetin İkmen had told him that this time he wouldn't get away with it. Teker knew – somehow. And now Gonca was going to know. He turned around.

The breath when it came out of her body made a grunting sound. When he turned back, she was sitting on a chair.

What he'd expected to happen next, he didn't know. But it wasn't calmness.

Eventually she spoke.

'Who is she?'

'Just a—'

'Just a girl, just for a fuck?'

'Well . . .'

'Young?'

He was sounding pathetic! He had to be a man about this even if it meant she killed him.

'Yes,' he said.

Gonca looked as if she was about to speak again, but he cut her off. 'And it was just sex,' he said. 'She was there, I was there . . .'

'And so you just had to stick your cock inside her.'

'That's what men do, isn't it?' he said. 'We fuck. Occasionally we make love. When we're in love, we make love. I make love to you each and every time we have sex.'

'Well that makes the old woman feel a whole lot better,' she said.

'It should do.'

He reached down to touch her, but she pulled away.

'Whoever that bitch was, she tried to take lumps out of you!' she said. 'Passion, was it? What did you do? Go down on her? Make her come like she'd never come before?'

'No. Yes. I . . . Gonca, you knew this about me. You knew about my poor track record.'

'And you knew that if you were unfaithful to me I'd fucking kill you,' she said. 'Because I told you. I said that if you screwed around I would be unable to take the wound to my honour and . . .'

She broke down. She raised her hands to her face and wept.

'Gonca . . .'

He wanted to go to her and comfort her, but he couldn't. When she'd finished crying, she screamed. Alarmed by the fierceness of her misery, he took her in his arms, fighting with her as he attempted to placate her.

'How can I love you when you do this?' she wailed.

'I don't know,' he said. 'All I know is that I do love you! And if I could go back and undo what I've done, I would. Gonca, it was a moment of stupidity!'

It had been more than a moment, but he couldn't tell her that. He couldn't tell her that just the thought of Barçın's hard breasts aroused him.

Gonca slapped his face. 'Cunt!' she screamed. 'You filthy fucking cunt!'

His face stung so badly he thought she'd probably drawn blood. But he kissed her. He placed his mouth over hers, even as she struggled to hit him again, and then he pulled her towards him.

Barçın Demirtaş was nothing on Gonca Şekeroğlu. This was not violent sex but furious sex. It was sex with a heart that was broken. By the time she'd had enough of him, he was bleeding not just from his back. And she was still angry.

As she gathered her fallen clothes to her naked body she said, 'I knew this day would come, Mehmet. So now that it has, you can take your things and go!'

He said nothing. What had the sex been? A bloody goodbye?

317

'You don't live here any more. If you try to stay, I will tell my father and my brothers what you did and they will kill you.'

'I understand.'

'No you don't,' she said. 'I will have to keep it from them. That will not be easy. Nobody walks away from one of my family, and that includes you.'

She picked up his bloodied shirt from the floor and threw it at him.

'When I want you for "just sex", you will come,' she said. 'But you'll fuck me and then you'll go. I will not be humiliated by you! My family will never know how you preferred another woman over me. Do you understand? Never! Now get out and go and fuck whoever you want. But come here when I want you or I will have my brothers cut off your balls and feed them to the dogs!'

Chapter 28

The day that Rouvin Rudolfoğlu died, Aslan Gerontas became suddenly calm. He didn't make some sort of miracle recovery, but he did appear to settle. The staff at Bakırköy said that it was as if a weight had been lifted from him.

Çetin İkmen was taking Mehmet Süleyman to the theatre. Although he'd not asked, he understood that his colleague had moved back into his apartment in Cihangir on a permanent basis. He was sad that Gonca Şekeroğlu was no longer in Süleyman's life. He liked her and she'd been good for him. But he'd always known that it couldn't last forever. Gonca was hardly policeman's wife material, and Süleyman was not a gypsy. His friend had sadness stamped all over him. But İkmen just continued as usual.

'This isn't so much a theatre as a house where people perform,' he said as they walked down a tiny alleyway near the Kamondo Stairs in Karaköy.

'I wasn't expecting La Scala,' Süleyman said.

He looked gaunt, and was smoking heavily.

İkmen stepped into a shabby doorway and disappeared down a long, dark corridor.

'Follow me,' he said to Süleyman. 'Professor Vanek awaits.'

Süleyman sauntered into the darkness. 'Why are all your friends so odd, Çetin?' he asked.

'Because I'm easily bored,' İkmen said.

The auditorium, which had once been a ballroom, was

packed with people. A lot of them were young, and there were many tattoos on display. The two officers sat between a couple of men in flat caps and greasy suits and a group of excited teenagers.

As the lights went down, İkmen said, 'Prepare yourself for magic.'

The ayazma of St Katherine was open again. The flagstones were back in place and a new priest, Father Aristotle, had been installed to replace Father Anatoli.

Yiannis Apion prayed that he could soon rebury his sister Sofia in a proper grave with a stone that recorded her existence. That way she would take her name and her place in the world. She would have lived.

He looked around the shrine, which was illuminated by the many candles well-wishers had lit when it had reopened. Yiannis had lit his not for Sofia, but for the soul of Father Anatoli.

The man who had killed the Rudolfoğlus, Rauf Karadeniz, had told the priest what he'd done just after Father Anatoli had spoken to Yiannis at the ayazma. Yiannis didn't know the man, but when Inspector İkmen had described him, he'd recognised him as a local resident. He'd even seen him in church from time to time. But they'd had no connection. Except the priest. Father Anatoli knew everyone and everything. He knew this Rauf Karadeniz. He knew too much.

Had the old man's confession been the last straw for Anatoli? What he'd known about Yiannis's family was enough to drive a person mad. But he must have reasoned that, although the Rudolfoğlus had literally got away with murder, there was no point in pursuing them. When Rauf Karadeniz had told him that he'd killed the siblings, it must have seemed as if the past was coming back to bite him.

Had he feared that perhaps the police would discover that

he'd kept his knowledge of these old crimes to himself and blame him in some way? Had he felt that Muslim Turks would not understand the sanctity of the confessional? Or had the responsibility Yiannis knew the priest felt for his tiny, often stifling community finally become too much? Christians were fleeing Muslim lands to the south in their thousands. Maybe it was time for them all to go? The war in Syria was finally at Turkey's eastern back door, with ISIS terrorists actually at the border. ISIS terrorists who enslaved Christians like him.

Now Yiannis lit a candle for his sister too. His family had been in İstanbul for a thousand years. Just like Father Anatoli's people. And yet the priest had lost faith. He must have done. Either that or he had surrendered to fear. But Yiannis couldn't surrender. Not because anyone was threatening him or urging him to stay, but because this was his home. Soon it would be where his sister was buried in a grave with a headstone that finally gave her dignity.

'That was . . . amazing!'

Professor Vanek, aka Sami Nasi, took Süleyman's hand and smiled.

'Of course,' he said. 'My great-grandfather's signature illusion is the best in the world!'

The young woman taking off her stage make-up in front of a scarred full-length mirror said, 'You have to forgive Sami, Mehmet Bey, he has no genes for modesty. It's the Hungarian in him.'

They laughed.

After the show, in which, to Süleyman's horror, Professor Vanek had beheaded his assistant and then passed her severed head around the audience on a platter, İkmen had taken him to the filthy room that passed for backstage. Up close, Süleyman discovered that the professor was a lot older than he looked on stage. But he was still a handsome, vigorous presence who he could easily see fulfilled every need that even İkmen had for the unusual.

'One day we will find out how he does it,' İkmen said.

'No you won't.'

İkmen put a hand on his arm. 'I was joking.' He turned to Süleyman. 'You know, Mehmet Bey, Sami's great-grandfather performed for Sultan Abdülmecid.'

'Really?'

'Yes. And Sami, you should know that Mehmet Bey is related to our imperial family.'

The magician gave a deep bow. 'Honoured.'

'Oh, it's nothing, believe me,' Süleyman said.

The professor took him at his word and changed the subject. 'Well, my news is that I am finally going to marry,' he said.

İkmen almost dropped his cigarette. 'You? You've run away from commitment all your life!'

The assistant came and stood beside the magician.

'Rüya has done me the honour of accepting my proposal of marriage,' he said.

'A man who cuts my head off, how crazy am I?' she said. But she was laughing.

'Oh, that's wonderful!' İkmen said. He shook his friend's hand. 'I don't know how you've managed to bewitch this beautiful woman, Sami, but I am truly, truly happy for both of you.'

Süleyman said, 'Congratulations.'

'Thank you,' said Sami Nasi. Then, oddly, he frowned. 'Are you married, Mehmet Bey?' he asked.

Rüya hit him on the arm. 'Sami! That's personal stuff! You don't ask those questions.'

'Oh don't be so Turkish!'

'I am Turkish!' she said. 'Stop being so Hungarian!'

He looked at Süleyman. 'Well, Mehmet Bey?'

'No,' he said. 'No, I'm not.' Then he added, 'I believe that particular boat may have sailed for me.'

The magician widened his eyes. 'A young, good-looking man like you? Nonsense.'

Süleyman smiled but looked away.

Later, they all walked up to İstiklal Caddesi to go to a bar. İkmen, arm in arm with Rüya, led the way. Süleyman walked behind them with Sami Nasi, who suddenly turned to him and said, 'You know, you should send roses to her, Mehmet Bey. Seven. No more, no less.'

For a moment, he felt angry. Had İkmen told this man about his split with Gonca? Though he hadn't even told İkmen himself!

'Imbue each one with your love.'

'My love? What are you talking about?' Süleyman said. 'You don't know anything about me!'

'Oh, I think I do,' Professor Vanek said. 'And if you take my advice, you will win her heart. But only seven roses, mind. Five won't work at all, eight will be a disaster, and six, well six is just a joke.'

They arrived in the middle of the night. Her father was entertaining his friends with stories about his dancing bears. Gonca had heard them all before, and so she went out into her garden.

She'd just lit a cigarette when she saw them. A bunch of flowers on the table half hidden by the mulberry bushes. As she got closer, she saw that they were red roses. Neatly arranged in a vase, they were fresh, dewy and beautiful.

Hard as she looked, she couldn't see any sort of card attached to the arrangement. But she knew who they'd come from, and for a moment, the realisation winded her. She sat down. There were seven blooms. How did he know about the power of seven? Someone like him? Had İkmen told him?

Seven was special. If a child was born on the seventh day of the week, he or she was blessed. That was what her mother and her aunts always said. She had no idea why. Gonca herself had been born on the seventh day of the week. Her mother, all her life, had believed that her daughter had been given special magic because of this.

But what was she to do with these roses? And why did she suddenly feel so exposed and lonely without her terrible, unfaithful, beautiful lover? If she had been asked to describe how his absence made her feel, she would have said that it was as if someone had stolen her life away. Was this maybe his way of saying he wanted to give it back?

If you enjoyed THE HOUSE OF FOUR, try the previous novels
in the Inspector İkmen series . . .

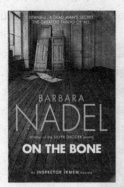  

For more information about Barbara Nadel's novels visit
www.headline.co.uk or follow Barbara on Twitter @BarbaraNadel

DEADLINE

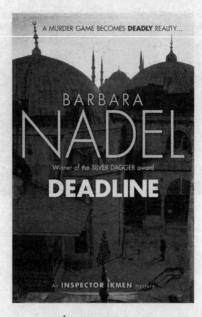

When Inspector Çetin İkmen is invited to a murder mystery
evening at Istanbul's famous Pera Palas Hotel he finds himself
embroiled in a deadly game of life imitating art.

Halfway through the evening, one of the actors is found actually
dead in the room where Agatha Christie used to stay when she was
in Istanbul. Walking in the steps of the great, İkmen experiences
fear and hatred which have echoes deep in his own and his
country's past.

www.headline.co.uk

DEAD OF NIGHT

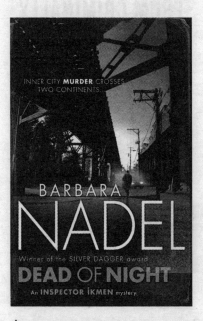

Inspectors Çetin İkmen and Mehmet Süleyman from Istanbul are sent to a policing conference in Detroit, but little can prepare them for the corruption that lies at its heart.

When Ezekial Goins, an elderly man of Turkish descent, approaches them to crack the long-unsolved murder of his son, a quiet trip takes a far more sinister turn. As they delve deeper into the case, the pair find themselves immersed in a terrifying world of inter-gang drug war and racial prejudice that puts them in mortal danger, and forces İkmen to confront some demons of his own . . .

HEADLINE

www.headline.co.uk

THRILLINGLY GOOD BOOKS FROM CRIMINALLY GOOD WRITERS

CRIME FILES BRINGS YOU THE LATEST RELEASES FROM TOP CRIME AND THRILLER AUTHORS.

SIGN UP ONLINE FOR OUR MONTHLY NEWSLETTER AND BE THE FIRS TO KNOW ABOUT OUR COMPETITIONS, NEW BOOKS AND MORE.